The Sleeping Partner

The Sleeping Partner

A Sarah Tolerance Mystery

Madeleine E. Robins

Plus One Press
San Francisco

Plus One Press

THE SLEEPING PARTNER. Copyright © 2011 by Madeleine E. Robins. All rights reserved. Printed in the United States of America. For information, address Plus One Press, 2885 Golden Gate Avenue, San Francisco, California, 94118.

www.plusonepress.com

Book Design by Plus One Press

Cover portrait photo © 2011 by Annaliese Moyer, used under license from Stage Right Photo: www.stagerightphoto.com.

Publisher's Cataloging-in-Publication Data

Robins, Madeleine.
   The sleeping partner: a sarah tolerance mystery / Madeleine Robins.—1st. Plus One Press ed.
       p. cm.
   ISBN: 978-0-9844362-5-5
   1. Women private investigators—England—London—Fiction.
2. London (England)—Fiction. 3. Murder—Fiction. I. Title.
II. Title: Graceland
   PS3568.O2774 S64 2011
   813'.54—dc22
                                                    2011936050

First Edition: October, 2011

10 9 8 7 6 5 4 3 2 1

For Penny and Emil, with love and history

The Sleeping Partner

Another London, April 1811

Chapter One

No one who had seen Miss Sarah Brereton as a child would have taken her for a heroine. She was a well-behaved girl, affectionate and active, given to rolling hoops and running races with the gardener's children. Her upbringing was neither intellectual nor revolutionary, being designed to make her what she was destined to be: the well-bred wife of a gentleman of means. That she had failed to achieve this goal was not the fault of her family but derived from some flaw in her character: at sixteen, Miss Brereton had fallen in love with her brother's fencing master and eloped, ruining forever her chances at respectability and marriage. Seeking to contain the damage, Sir William Brereton disowned his daughter and forbade to have her name mentioned. With the girl as good as dead, the honor of the Breretons was restored to a near-unsullied state. The family went on much as before.

In this, Sir William was particularly prudent. Society is harsh to those contaminated by the breath of female indiscretion. Should he have suffered his neighbors to whisper after him in ballrooms, or permitted his daughter's misjudgment to spoil her brother's chance at an advantageous marriage? Sir William saw no reason to waste further resources upon a child who had so lightly and ungratefully disposed of her virtue. He washed his hands of the girl; his heir did the same.

For society exists to suffer revelry in men, reward virtue in women, and to promote and protect the sanctity of marriage as the best instrument to secure property. Even in the Royal family these distinctions are observed. The Princes carouse as they please; only the Prince of Wales married young, and that marriage, to a Catholic widow, drove his Royal father to the madhouse and removed the prince from succession. There was no doubt that marriage and family had tamed the Prince's most exuberant impulses; one had only to look at the excesses of his brothers. And the Queen Regent took care to arrange marriages for her six daughters as early as she might, in the belief that an unmarried woman, even a Royal one, was always in danger of corruption.

By such examples is a nation led. Women learn early that unblemished virtue is the brightest jewel in their adornments. Young men learn that any girl with a question about her may be ripe for the plucking. And families know the dire consequences which any breach of feminine virtue may bring to them. Once her reputation is lost, a woman might as well adopt a *nom d'amour* and resign herself to a life of whoredom. Reputation, more than virtue itself, must be protected.

This laudable goal is sometimes achieved with pistol or sword in a private meeting at dawn. Sometimes it is achieved through the power of a bit of information brought to light, or a secret well hidden. Miss Sarah Tolerance, who had begun her life as Sarah Brereton, was of the opinion that a woman who makes her living by the acquisition and protection of information had best keep her pistols primed and her sword edged and ready.

Miss Tolerance had been set down by a hackney coach in Fleet Street at Whitefriars, not far from Bridewell Prison. Even at six in the morning the streets around the prison were thronged, both with victualers who were fetching in provisions, and with the hangers-on of prisoners. The street was clamorous: vendors and visitors yelled to each other; the prisoners screamed out at the windows. The stench of too many persons packed tight together—few of them given to bathing—vied with odors from the prison sewer. In the crowd whores and pickpockets moved freely; every brief stir or outcry meant busy fingers at work.

Miss Tolerance followed Whitefriars toward Salisbury Square, happy that she had no business at the prison today. The morning fog was burning off, leaving thin, coal-hazed sunlight and a damp breeze in its wake. She turned left and through the arched entrance to Hanging Sword Alley, where many of London's *salles des armes* were to be found. Half-way down the street she entered a building much papered over with bills advertising cures for pox and fever, and climbed to the second floor. She had barely raised her hand to knock when the door was opened by a scrawny, spry man quite old enough to be Miss Tolerance's grandfather. His face was narrow, his eyes small and bright blue, and his lopsided jaw gave him a comical look. His white hair was worn in an old-fashioned queue bound with black ribbon. He wore breeches, shirt, and waistcoat, and was stocking-footed. He looked in turn and without surprise at Miss Tolerance's unusual attire: men's breeches, boots, and coat, and a sword hanging at her left hip.

"Come ready, have you?" The old man grinned. "Come in, then, Miss T., and let's to work."

"Thank you, Mr. Blaine." Miss Tolerance shed her coat and removed her boots.

Mr. Richard Blaine's fencing *salle* was not the most celebrated in London; Mr. Blaine himself was not an extraordinary fencer. He was, however, an excellent teacher and, quite as much to the point, he was willing to have Miss Tolerance bout with him when she had the time. That she

5

paid for her lessons was, he assured her, beside the point. It was a pleasure to him to fence with a pretty girl, particularly one who could teach him a trick or two.

"If that is so, perhaps you ought to be paying me?" Miss Tolerance stretched and lunged, feeling her chilled muscles begin to warm.

"Ah, but there's the rent on this magnificent space," Mr. Blaine said quickly.

"And the upkeep of the magnificent Mrs. Blaine and your grandchildren," Miss Tolerance agreed. "I don't begrudge the shilling, Mr. Blaine. Now, sir, are you ready?"

The two fencers saluted each other briskly and went to it. Mr. Blaine was, by his nature, a quick and dramatic fencer given to sudden inspiration. After a flurry of attacks in the high line, he lunged for Miss Tolerance's left hip; Miss Tolerance parried in *sept* with enough force to knock Mr. Blaine's sword from his hand, and had her point at his throat before he could move. Blaine laughed; Miss Tolerance dropped her point and permitted him to retrieve his blade.

"A neat touch, Miss T!"

They returned to work.

Within a quarter hour Miss Tolerance's shirt clung damply to her back and her face was flushed with exertion. Mr. Blaine had ceased his regular stream of quips and comments and saved his breath for his work. Both fencers were grinning with the pleasure of hard work well done, and so involved that neither one heeded the first, or even the second knock on the door. At the third, Miss Tolerance dropped her point and stepped back. "Someone is here, sir."

Blaine dropped his own point and looked to the door.

"Sit and rest you, Miss T. I'll return in just a moment." Mr. Blaine put down his foil, wiped his face and hands with a spotted kerchief, and went to the door. Miss Tolerance dropped onto a bench and wiped her own face and hands, paying no attention to Mr. Blaine's conversation until the visitor in the doorway shoved the old man into the room and advanced upon him threateningly.

"You'll give me what I come for, you mick sharper! You and them false tats! You ain't comin' over me—" The man was square-jawed, square-built, and grubby. His color was high, and in his maroon coat he resembled a bad-tempered brick.

Mr. Blaine held out a placating hand. "Mr. Wigg, I tell you true, I keep no money here. I could not return your money even were I of a mind to do so. And as the dice I used were honest as the dawn—" Mr. Blaine spoke quietly, the only sign of distress a Killarney lilt to his speech that Miss Tolerance had never detected before.

"Is there a problem, sir?" Miss Tolerance rose to her feet and spoke clearly, as calm as her fencing partner.

If Mr. Wigg was startled to find a witness in the *salle*, he did not permit it to distract him from his quarry. "You took seventeen shillin' off me," he said to Blaine. "Ain't no one could do that but they was cheatin'."

Miss Tolerance stepped closer. "Is it the sum that troubles you, sir? I have known thousands of guineas to change hands at dicing, with quite honest dice. What makes you believe that Mr. Blaine's dice were fixed?"

This time Mr. Wigg turned his head. "You'll keep out of it," he snarled.

Then he stopped, dumbstruck, taking in the sight of Miss Tolerance. Her dark hair was pulled back from her face and braided; her waistcoat covered the most obvious evidence of her gender. Still, it was clear to anyone with an eye to see it that Miss Tolerance was a female in the costume and occupation of a man. Mr. Wigg looked as appalled as a man who has found half a worm in his apple.

"You keepin' a nuggery, now?" he snarled at Blaine.

"Merely a fencing school, Mr.—Wigg?" Miss Tolerance said "It is very nervy of you indeed, insulting a man with a sword—and his student. But I suppose you think we will not offer much resistance to your bullying."

Mr. Blaine looked at Miss Tolerance warily, as if he was not certain her interference was wise. Miss Tolerance was not to be intimidated; she had taken Mr. Wigg in dislike.

7

Mr. Wigg appeared to return the feeling.

"Have you evidence that Mr. Blaine's dice were fixed?"

Wigg faltered, then turned back to Blaine. "Seventeen shillin' you took off me, and I want it back. *Wiv* interest!"

"I haven't got it, I told you," Blaine said. "I would be happy to permit you to win the money back, or even to have you come at another time to discuss—"

"So you can 'ave a bunch of bully-boys ready to crush me skull for me? The 'ell with that. You'll give me my money or I'll take it out your skinny 'ide." Wigg stepped forward again, towering over Mr. Blaine.

"Do you prefer to handle this yourself, sir, or may I assist?" Miss Tolerance asked politely.

This appeared to be more than Mr. Wigg could stand. "You? 'Elp? I'll soon teach you to mind your place, you whore!"

"There have been a good number of gentlemen who have tried to do so, sir. Curiously, none has yet managed it." Miss Tolerance took a relaxed stance in the center of the room, her sword point down.

"Don't think that cheese-toaster'll 'elp you," Wigg warned. "What you need's the sense beat into you." He glanced around him nonetheless and made for a rack of weapons near the window. He swung back to Miss Tolerance with a rapier in his hand. He had chosen badly, she noted; while none of Mr. Blaine's swords were untended, this was an old blade, the grip too small for Wigg's beefy hand. Mr. Blaine made a noise of professional dismay at the mismatch of man and blade.

"Forgive me, Mr. Blaine. Do I interrupt? Would you prefer that I step back?"

Blaine shook his head. "He appears to wish for death, this fellow. Do what you must, Miss T." He sat down on a bench and wiped his face again.

Wigg hefted the sword in his hand and charged at Miss Tolerance. He had, perhaps, hoped to frighten her. He misjudged his opponent; she stepped away from his charge, spun and brought the flat of her sword up against his backside with a sold *thwack*. Wigg stumbled forward, caught himself on the wall, and turned back to her.

"I'll have that damned thing off you!" he roared. This time he advanced upon her deliberately, swinging his sword from side to side, his other hand outstretched.

"If you grasp my blade, sir, please be careful. I keep it very sharp."

Wigg was not cautioned. He continued forward until Miss Tolerance cut in *sixte* to stop his blade moving, stepped in and delivered a sharp blow to his sword hand which knocked the blade to the floor.

Wigg jumped backward, looking wildly from side to side, apparently for another case of swords, but Miss Tolerance stood between him and any other weapons. Behind him was only the door to the *salle*. This seemed to enrage Mr. Wigg enough to defeat all common sense; he began to advance, swordless, upon his opponent. Miss Tolerance, who had no real desire to skewer the man, stood her ground until he was a little less than five feet away, then brought her point up to his throat. In so doing, she slit the flying tail of his neckerchief.

"Please stop." Her tone was mild.

Wigg stood, looking cross-eyed at her swordpoint, then followed the blade back to Miss Tolerance. She stood, strong-armed but relaxed, looking at him with an expression of polite interest.

"Hell," he said. He turned his head a little to look to Mr. Blaine. "'ide behind the whore's skirts, do you?"

Miss Tolerance pushed her point very gently forward. "I cannot tell you how much I dislike being called whore, Mr. Wigg."

"Beg your pardon," Wigg muttered, eying her point again.

"Spoken like a gentleman. Now, you are done with your business here. You have lodged your complaint with Mr. Blaine, he has given you his answer, and I think you ought to go off and break your fast somewhere. Everything will look better after you have eaten, I'm sure. Perhaps you will drink my health?" She paused to put a hand in her breeches' pocket and drew out a coin. "Coffee, I would suggest. In the future you will know to avoid dice games."

Wigg stepped forward to accept the copper and was briefly brought up short by the point of Miss Tolerance's blade. She withdrew the point and dropped the coin into his hand.

"The door is there, sir." She nodded her head in that direction. Wigg backed toward the door, looking malignly first at Blaine and then at Miss Tolerance. When he reached the door he put Miss Tolerance's coin into his own pocket. Then, looking very sour, he turned and thundered down the stairs.

"Well." Mr. Blaine exhaled. "That was exciting, sure."

"I generally prefer my excitement after breakfast," Miss Tolerance said. "Do you often have men coming to accuse you of cheating?"

Blaine grinned. "'Tis the first time," he allowed. "I'd have thought him too far gone in the drink to have noticed anything. I'll have to be rid of them tats, indeed."

Miss Tolerance could not decide whether to chide or laugh. "Mr. Blaine, I am very disappointed in you. A man of your years, and a grandfather."

"Miss T., I shall try to do better."

"Will you throw away your crooked dice, sir, or only endeavor not to be caught out again?"

Blaine chuckled. "You're a caution, Miss T., you are that."

Miss Tolerance agreed that perhaps she was. She was not likely to reform a man old enough to be her grandfather. "Well, sir, if you have had sufficient rest, are you ready to resume?"

Another half an hour with Mr. Blaine and Miss Tolerance departed, streaming with sweat and pleasantly tired. She made her way through the crowds in Salisbury Square and returned to Manchester Square, where she lodged in a cottage behind her aunt's establishment. Mrs. Dorothea

Brereton was the proprietor of one of the most refined and celebrated brothels in the city, and mornings were a busy time there, with patrons to be sent upon their way, staff to be fed, and mountains of linens to be gathered for the laundress. Not wishing to add to the servants' burden, Miss Tolerance sent a request for hot water for bathing "when quite convenient." Miss Tolerance broke her fast with bread and cheese and a mug of coffee, bathed, and dressed again, this time in clothing appropriate to her sex. A little past eleven she left her cottage, wearing a steel-blue walking dress and a neat straw bonnet, and headed toward Henry Street and the handsome Palladian structure which housed Tarsio's Club.

Tarsio's was remarkable in that it was the only establishment of its sort whose membership included both men and women. Nor did the membership committee make respectability its first concern; so long as a member was able to pay the commons fees and charges and conform to the establishment's rules, anyone—courtesan, MP, actress, lawyer, even a poet—might belong. For Miss Tolerance, who preferred to keep business away from her cottage and from her aunt's establishment, membership in Tarsio's provided a neutral place to meet with clients. As she had lately been unemployed, she made it a point to spend a part of her day there, available for consultation.

She moved through the busy streets, dodging between a flower girl and a dairyman who, backs to each other, were crying their wares as they approached collision. The chill of the morning had warmed away with the increasing sunshine. Mingled with the smells of ordure, human sweat, and fish from the barrow just now being pushed past, Miss Tolerance detected a green scent. Spring was coming to London. She stepped across a gutterful of muck and turned onto Henry Street.

At Tarsio's she was greeted by the hall-porter, Corton, a large, older man whose respectable demeanor put the lie to Tarsio's raffish reputation.

"I hope I see you well today, miss."

"You do, Corton. Very well, as I hope you are. Any messages?"

Corton shook his head with genuine regret. Miss Tolerance, when in funds, tipped well. "Nothing yet today, Miss. Was you expecting something?"

Miss Tolerance shook her head. "Expecting? No. Hoping, perhaps."

"Hope's the great thing, miss. Will you require anything today?"

Miss Tolerance bespoke a pot of coffee and made her way upstairs to the first floor and the Ladies' Salon. In one corner of this spacious chamber she observed a game of whist played with quiet ferocity by a quartet of lady-essayists. In another, two very expensive females sat with their heads close together, likely exchanging trade secrets. Miss Tolerance took a chair by a window, turned it to face the door, and opened the *Times* before her.

She finished her coffee and read both the *Times* and the *Post* over the next two hours. There was nothing left to read within reach, and Miss Tolerance was thinking that if she must rise to seek some other reading material she might as well return home, when Cordon appeared beside her and murmured that a lady was inquiring for her.

"What sort of lady?" She would see her visitor regardless, but often found the porter's impressions useful.

"A *real* lady, miss. A bit anxious about the eyes."

A real lady in a state of anxiety bode well for business and thus for Miss Tolerance's pocket-book. She directed Corton to bring the visitor up.

She was a pretty woman, several years younger than Miss Tolerance and several inches shorter, dressed with elegance in a walking suit of snuff-colored twill. The curls visible under her deep-poked bonnet were a soft golden-brown, and her eyes were large, brown and, as Corton had said, anxious. Miss Tolerance had the impression of a gentlewoman with money, taste, and a problem.

She rose and curtsied. Her visitor curtsied likewise, and looked around the room.

"This is very pleasant," she said, as though she had not expected to find it so.

"It is, ma'am. Now, no one here pays the least attention to anyone else, but if you would prefer to take your business to a more private place—"

"Is that what is done?" The woman looked around again. The nearest persons were seated a dozen paces away and appeared absorbed in their own conversation. "You will know best, of course, but if you are comfortable I beg we will not move for my sake."

Miss Tolerance rarely encountered such a degree of consideration from prospective clients; the woman was very anxious indeed.

"Let us sit here, then. May I offer you some wine? Tea, then?" Miss Tolerance took her chair again and gestured to her visitor to sit. She took a moment to order tea, then turned back to her visitor.

"Now, how am I to help you, ma'am? Perhaps we may begin with what you would like me to call you." Miss Tolerance placed a mental wager that the lady would not give her real name.

"I am Mrs. Brown." The name did not roll from her tongue.

A point to me, Miss Tolerance thought. "How may I help you, Mrs. Brown?"

"I was told by—by a mutual acquaintance—that you are able to find things. People."

Miss Tolerance nodded. "Is this acquaintance a former client of mine, ma'am?" Mrs. Brown nodded. "I hope you will convey to her—or him—my gratitude for this confidence. And you have lost...someone?"

Mrs. Brown nodded. A fuller reply was delayed by the arrival of the tea tray and the pleasant ritual by which the drink was dispensed. When Miss Tolerance had poured her own tea and moved the plate of biscuits closer to her guest, Mrs. Brown began again.

"Can you find a lost girl?"

Miss Tolerance had been expecting to hear of a husband

lost to the fleshpots or a brother on the run from the bail-iffs. Little girls of good family were not allowed to stray.

"How old is the child? Where was she lost?"

Mrs. Brown blushed. "I misspoke. She is not a child but a young lady. She is sixteen."

Miss Tolerance was briefly relieved. A child lost for more than a few hours suggested kidnapping, ransom, death. A missing young lady of sixteen was a wholly different matter, and generally a problem more sordid than sinister.

"She has eloped?" Miss Tolerance was gentle.

Mrs. Brown nodded.

"Can you tell me the circumstances? Are you acquainted with the man?"

"I don't believe so." The woman looked down at her hands. "I have not been so much in my sister's confidence since I married. But I should never have thought—"

No one does. "Of course not. Perhaps you will tell me how you learned of the elopement?"

"She left a note. It was—" Mrs. Brown flushed. "She had quarreled with our father that morning, and the note was very...severe."

"May I see it?"

"The note? Oh." The woman looked distressed. "Oh, dear. I do not *have* it."

Miss Tolerance suppressed a sigh. "Do you recall what the note said, Mrs. Brown?"

"Oh, yes." She pursed her lips and frowned. "It said that she could not longer remain in the house under my father's *harsh rule*—that was the phrase she used—and that she knew her own best happiness would be secured with someone who loves her. She apologized to my brothers and to me for any pain her elopement would cause. I believe that was the whole of it."

"Your memory is excellent. Can you tell me if her writing appeared hurried or forced?"

"Oh, no. I didn't *see* the note." Mrs.Brown's brows drew together. "My father was in a great rage; he read the letter aloud to us, then crumpled it up, shoved it into his pocket, and locked himself in the office."

Father is given to melodrama. Miss Tolerance felt a stir of anger on behalf of Mrs. Brown's vanished sister. "Perhaps, ma'am, if you can tell me the exact sequence of events which led to that moment? Start with the beginning of the day."

"Sir—my husband and I are visiting in my father's house. He—my husband—went out very early. I did not leave my room until about ten that morning; my sister had taken her breakfast downstairs with my father, as was usual. By the time I came downstairs Father was closeted in his office. I had to go to my hat maker's, and called to Evie—my sister's name is Evadne—to see if she wished to come with me; she came out from the schoolroom to say no, and that is the last I saw of her. I went out, and when I came back Evie was gone."

"You knew that at once?"

"At once? No." Mrs. Brown tilted her head. "I had a little headache and went upstairs to rest. Later I went up to the schoolroom to show Evie the hat I had bought. She was not there, but I was not much concerned; her governess and I thought she must be in the garden, or in the kitchen teasing ginger knots from the cook."

"I take it she was in neither place?" Miss Tolerance tried to imagine a girl who begged sweets in the kitchen one moment and eloped in the next.

"No, but we didn't learn that until—but I am ahead of my story. I had some letters to write, and went down to the little parlor I use when I visit. I had been there perhaps a half hour when my father came from his office in a great state, calling us to him and waving the letter."

"Your father read the letter to you," Miss Tolerance suggested.

Mrs. Brown nodded. "When we had gathered to hear him, yes."

"The letter said nothing about marriage?"

"Not specifically, but it is my hope—" Mrs. Brown looked very troubled. "Miss Tolerance, I am sure you hear

15

such stories every day, and I know I have said I have not been much in my sister's confidence in the five years since I married. But Evie is *not* a light-minded girl, and I should have said that her principles were strong."

"Even the strongest-minded girl may find the combination of fancied love and an argument with a parent powerful enough to outweigh her principles—for a time." Miss Tolerance was brisk. "A few questions, if you please. You say your father called out. To whom?"

"To me, of course. And my older brother, and Miss—the governess. Father waited until we had gathered around him in the hall outside his office and then he read the letter."

"That seems a peculiarly public place to read so delicate a letter."

"My father was beside himself, Miss Tolerance. I am sure he had no thought for where he was or—"

"Perhaps so," Miss Tolerance said. "Well, then. Is there any man for whom your sister might have fancied affection? A dancing master or art teacher? A childhood beau or the brother of a friend?" To each of these Mrs. Brown shook her head. "The governess knows of none?"

Again Mrs. Brown looked stricken. "My father turned Miss Nottingale off—"

"—in a rage," Miss Tolerance finished. "He was very thorough, your father. Mrs. Brown, I mean no criticism, but are you certain that your father wants your sister returned to you?"

"I am certain he does not," Mrs. Brown said sadly. "He has refused to have her returned. When he heard of what happened my brother John wished to go after her and bring her back—"

"Your brother John is not the brother who was there to hear the reading of the letter?"

Mrs. Brown was momentarily confused by the question. "No, that was—I am sorry, Miss Tolerance. I am not used to thinking out a story to tell it straight. It was my older brother Henry who was there; my brother John does not live in my father's house. As I say, John wanted to go after Evie, but my father forbade it in the strongest possible terms. He threatened to cut my brother off if he did so! Miss Tolerance, this does not paint my father in an amiable light, I know, but—"

"It is an attitude more common than flattering," Miss Tolerance said. "And one quite familiar to me. *You* take a risk, then, in seeking your sister."

Mrs. Brown looked at Miss Tolerance without confusion or fluttering. "I am married. My father no longer controls what I do. What sort of sister would I be if I allowed Evie to go into the world unprotected, liable to insult and danger?"

Miss Tolerance smiled. "You are clearly of a better sort than that, ma'am. I honor you for your concern, and will do my best to help you."

"You can find her?"

"I can try. Now, Mrs. Brown, I understand that you do not wish to give your real name—" Miss Tolerance waved away the other woman's protest. "'Tis quite a common thing. For now, I will not require you to divulge it, but you should know that secrecy hampers my ability to interview persons who might be of use to us—the servants in your father's house, for example. This will likely result in a higher cost to you."

"The cost is not important," Mrs. Brown said at once. "But I have risked as much as I dare in coming to you."

"I understand, ma'am. Can you at least tell me the neighborhood in which your father's house is located? There are dozens of coaching inns in London, and I must have some way to narrow their number. And I shall need a description of your sister. I do wish you knew the name of her lover—" Mrs. Brown flinched at the word—"but we will do what we may with what we have."

"My father's house is in Duke of York Street. As for a description—" Mrs. Brown reached into her reticule and brought out a small package wrapped in linen which she offered to Miss Tolerance. "Will this help? It was done a

17

year ago, as a present from my father; the likeness is thought to be rather good."

The package contained a small painting in a porcelain frame, the sort suited for display on a table or shelf. Miss Tolerance examined the portrait. It showed two young women, both fair-haired and rosy, one blue-eyed, the other brown. They were dressed alike in white muslin gowns, and each wore a gold locket on a chain. Mrs. Brown was the shorter and more delicate of feature; she looked directly at the artist with a demure smile. Her sister was considerably younger, and apparently several inches taller; her hair was more golden, and she was rounder of chin and more ebullient of nature. The artist had depicted her laughing, one hand upon her sister's shoulder in a graceful expression of affection.

"Who painted this, ma'am?"

"Mr. Hoppner. T'was painted only a sixmonth before he died. Evie would hardly sit still, but you see he caught her very nicely."

"It is a lovely portrait. May I borrow it for a few days? I will undertake to return it to you as soon as I may, but it will be useful to be able to show it when I am inquiring for your sister."

Mrs. Brown nodded. "That is why I brought it."

Miss Tolerance looked again at the pretty, laughing girl in the portrait. "She is charming looking." She reflected that it might take very little time for the girl's looks and high spirits to be ruined along with her name. "How long has she been gone?"

"Ten days." Mrs. Brown looked down. "Miss Tolerance, you said you honored me for my concern, but I must tell you it took me several days to summon the resolve to come to you. I am not proud of it, but I love my father, and the habit of obedience is strong."

Miss Tolerance, dismayed that so long a time had been permitted to elapse, sighed. "I understand those habits, ma'am. You need not reproach yourself, but from now on I hope you will tell me anything you learn more timely.

Now, the day is half gone, and I should probably be out upon your business while I may. A few things first." When she outlined her fees her opinion of Mrs. Brown's station was confirmed. The woman agreed without hesitation to three guineas a day, plus expenses.

"And how shall I contact you, when I have news to report?"

Mrs. Brown's face fell. She had clearly not considered this consequence of anonymity. Miss Tolerance was moved to contrive a solution.

"If you wish to call here, or to have a servant do so every day or so, I will leave any messages addressed for you with the porter."

Mrs. Brown nodded. The expression of anxiety which she had worn at the beginning of their meeting had been replaced with one of confidence. Miss Tolerance would have found that touching had she been more certain of her ability to find, in a city of more than a million, one gently-reared girl of sixteen years.

Chapter Two

Miss Tolerance was by nature inclined to occupation. It was only a few hours past noon, and while she had an engagement that evening, she was thriftily aware of how much of Mrs. Brown's business might be accomplished before that time. It was regrettable that Mrs. Brown knew so little and had been unwilling to reveal all of what she knew; the girl's family name would likely have been a help, and information from the household staff might have resolved the matter instantly. Dismissing the governess was a fine way to encourage the servants to silence; perhaps that had been the aim of the girl's choleric father. Finding a dismissed governess was likely to be as protracted a task as finding the girl herself.

Lacking recourse to the servants, Miss Tolerance's first chore, and it was like to be a lengthy one, was to inquire at coaching inns. For the purpose she invented a pretty story of a country cousin alit at the wrong inn, with herself in the role of anxious relative. She walked briskly toward

Picadilly, where she inquired first at the White Bear and the White Horse. They were closest to Duke of York Street, and while she felt that it was a chancy thing to elope from an inn so close to the bride's home, she did not know that Miss Evadne and her seducer would have felt the same caution. She showed the portrait round at each inn but had no satisfaction, and asked an ostler to hire a chair to take her to the more distant precincts of Aldgate (the Saracen's Head) and Fleet Street (the Bolt and Tun), where eastbound carriers were found. Again she showed the portrait in the stables and taproom, asking for word of "my poor sweet cousin Evie." She did not specify why she was seeking the girl in the picture; a liberal application of silver generally served to divert attention from any holes in her story. The tapsters and stableboys in both houses disclaimed any knowledge of the girl, nor did inquiry yield any suggestion more than that she should ask any of the old women who who sat in the taproom with the attitude of habitués. Miss Tolerance reminded each of the persons she spoke to that she could be reached through Tarsio's Club on Henry Street, and hinted broadly at a significant reward

Then she took herself to Ludgate Hill and the Bell Savage, where she had an acquaintance with the owner. Mrs. Wallace ran a small empire from her office above the coffee room. The inn was an enormous structure built around a courtyard where coaches arrived and departed on the quarter-hour. The stables took up one full wall of the courtyard, with a hurly-burly of ostlers, drivers and passengers milling about the yard. Miss Tolerance made her way through the throng and into the coffee room, where several dozen persons—travelers just off the stage, or waiting for the next departure—took their meals with one eye upon the door, waiting for the announcement that the coach was leaving. As she had expected, neither the barman nor the maid would tell her a thing until they had Mrs. Wallace's leave to do so.

Miss Tolerance was pointed to the narrow staircase just behind the bar, and found herself in the hall outside Mrs.

Wallace's office, in time to see the lady scolding one of her maids.

"...and if I iver catch you doing such a thing again, Sukey Pitt, it's oot on the road you'll be, sa fast t'will make your arse burn. It makes me nae mind what your uncle did in his taproom—this is the Bell Savage, and we doon't water the whisky. Na, fetch up a bottle of wine for me and my guest and be smart aboot it!" Casually, Mrs. Wallace boxed the girl's ear before she sent her off down the hallway.

Mrs. Wallace waved Miss Tolerance into the room. "Ye'll have some wine, I hope? Na that idiot child has gone off to fetch it for us?"

"Thank you, ma'am. I shall." Miss Tolerance took the seat she was offered. The office was a narrow rectangle, its windows facing into the busy courtyard. Two tables were both stacked high with papers, ledgers, and strong-boxes. The smell of coffee and ale mingled, not unpleasantly, with the earthy smells of the stables below, and with Mrs. Wallace's lingering scent of lavender. The hosteliere was a short, bony woman of advancing years with a ruddy complexion. She had a fondness for turbans which hid her thin, graying hair, and wore today's turban with a dress of purple bombazine.

"Na, to what d'I ooe the honor?"

"Why, I have come to beg some information from your staff, ma'am, which they quite rightly will not give me until you have said they may." Miss Tolerance took the glass which Mrs. Wallace passed her and sipped at the wine, a light, sour claret.

"What sart of information?" Mrs. Wallace drank her own wine down in a gulp and put her glass down on the table with a force which seemed intended to shatter it.

"Only if anyone in your coffee room saw a young woman waiting for a coach sometime in the last fortnight?"

"Runaway?"

"It is possible. She is not suspected of anything criminal."

"Ah, weel. I don't suppose there's any harm to it."

"Rather a considerable good." Miss Tolerance took up her reticule. "Indeed, Mrs. Wallace, I would be grateful to the tune of—"

Mrs. Wallace waved her hand. "Keep your sil'er for them as need it, Miss Tolerance. That lad at the bar doonstairs will be grateful, I'm sure, although I've little faith he'll have noticed anything. Not the observing sart. You're going to all the coaching inns? That'll give ye a good several days' work. You'll do better asking the auld bawds that wait to collect stray girls, rather than the ostlers and tapmen. Or seek her in places like that Rillington woman's reformatory. I'll give ye that advice for gratis. You and me air wimmen o' business, and must stick together when it don't discommode us to do so."

Miss Tolerance understood this to mean that Mrs. Wallace hoped to beg a favor at some future time. "Indeed we must, ma'am. I shall always be honored to render assistance to you in turn," she said dryly. It was worth some extra effort to stay upon Mrs. Wallace's good side.

Mrs. Wallace nodded her satisfaction. "Well, you tell Seth and the rest doon stairs that they may tell you what e'er they may. More wine? Ah, weel, then. I shall hope to see you another day, Miss Tolerance."

"Thank you for your kindness, Mrs. Wallace."

They exchanged curtseys and Miss Tolerance went down the narrow stairs again to speak, first to one bar maid, then the other, and finally to the tapster. She showed each of them the portrait of Miss Evadne without much expectation of satisfaction.

The barman said at first that he had not seen the girl or any like her. When Miss Tolerance insisted that he actually look at the picture rather than giving all his attention to polishing his tankards between customers, he took the miniature in his hand and examined it.

"No," he said flatly. "Ain't seen either on 'em. Ain't to say she mightn't 'a been 'ere when I was off me time. Talk to Jase, he'd might know. Or ask the grannies." He gestured with his chin in the direction of three comfortable-looking women who sat near the fire, positioned to face the doorway. "They's always on the lookout for pretty girls at loose ends, so to speak."

Miss Tolerance nodded. "Thank you." She slid a six-penny piece across the satiny surface of the bar. "If you should happen to see the young woman, you will let me know?" She gave him a card with Tarsio's direction and asked him to pass on her question to the other tapmen.

The tapster slid the coin into his pocket, his mind apparently on the next pint of bitter to be drawn off. Miss Tolerance turned to the table where the women sat, to find that all three had disappeared as if they had been absorbed into the wall behind them. They might like to approach unescorted females, but clearly she did not constitute the sort of woman that tempted them.

The afternoon was now coming to a close, and Miss Tolerance had an engagement to prepare for. She requested one of the Bell Savage's ostlers to find her a hackney carriage, and directed it to Spanish Place, where a gate in the ivied wall permitted her direct access to her cottage. She left her bonnet and gloves there, then entered her aunt's house through the perpetually busy kitchen. Cook, up to her elbows in dough, offered the information that Mrs. Brereton was in her little salon, taking tea and writing letters.

"Do you go up and join her, Miss Sarah. There's cakes, fresh made. You look as if you could do with some feedin' up." Cook, ample herself, believed everyone to be on the verge of inanition.

Miss Tolerance was not hungry, but thanked Cook cordially and passed through the green baize door which marked the division between the servants' area and the public rooms. In one of the large salons an elegant tea was spread out for the delectation of the patrons and whores. Miss Tolerance turned away from the room, in which half a dozen men were drinking tea or wine, piling cakes onto their plates and ogling the girls in their neat muslin gowns. Miss Tolerance preferred not to socialize with Mrs. Brereton's clientele; they reminded her of her own equivocal position in the house and in society. She proceeded up the stairs to the little salon, a pleasant, neatly furnished room with a couch, desk, small table, and a window that looked onto the rear garden. Mrs. Brereton sat at the desk, frowning at something before her.

"Who has offended you, aunt?"

"My dear Sarah!" Mrs. Brereton at once put the letter aside and rose to greet her niece. She was a tall woman with a commanding presence; she regarded her niece with a slow smile, as if each passing moment served to recall her affection for the younger woman. Mrs. Brereton, owning some fifty years, looked a good decade younger. Her figure was slender and her complexion well-tended, as befit a woman who had been, for many years, the crown jewel in her own establishment. These days Mrs. Brereton had only a few patrons of her own, but considered the maintenance of her appearance to be part of the effort she owed her business, and spared neither time nor money. Today she wore a gray silk gown with a half-jacket of cherry-striped silk; her short, silvering dark hair was pomaded into artful curls that looked less girlish than sensual.

"Come sit with me, my dear. How is it I have not seen you in a week?" Mrs. Brereton softened the reproach by tilting her head to receive her niece's kiss.

"A week, aunt? Surely no more than half that."

"Well, it has seemed like a week." Mrs. Brereton said. "How do you do?"

"I do well. Cook sent me to eat some of your cakes."

"I wish you will. I cannot think why she gives me so many; I cannot eat them all, and it is wasteful." Waste was Mrs. Brereton's particular abhorrence.

"I am sure I can help you with one or two of them, aunt." Miss Tolerance seated herself and took up the cup Mrs. Brereton had poured for her. "Thank you. You seemed very vexed with what you were reading."

Mrs. Brereton maintained a flat ban upon gossip regard-

25

ing her clientele among her employees. Her scruples on her own account were, however, a little more elastic.

"It is a letter of complaint regarding the new boy. Or perhaps merely a complaint that he is too popular to be constantly available to *this* gentleman." She flicked the sheet in her hand with a finger. Mrs. Brereton, unlike most London brothel keepers, was liberal enough to keep a male whore in her employ, reasoning that she was not in the business of judging her clients' needs, but supplying to them.

"Who is complaining?"

"Lord Holyfield. Which surprises me. He was so passionately fond of Matt that I did not expect him to warm to young Harry, let alone demand his undivided attention." Mrs. Brereton sighed. The late Matt Etan had been liked by everyone in her establishment, and by a number of gentlemen of particular tastes. His death—upon an errand for Miss Tolerance—had caused a rift between her and Mrs. Brereton which had only slowly healed.

"Matt used to complain of Lord Holyfield's particularity. Perhaps it is not Harry, but his lordship, who is the problem? Young Harry seems an agreeable enough fellow."

"My rules are very clear, and particularity or favoritism is a great offense. Harry is too anxious to please. He hasn't Matt's spine."

"If Harry had been pimped out at dockside as a boy, as Matt was, I don't doubt he would have more spine, aunt. And even Matt worried from time to time that you would banish him to die as a bum-boy in the Cheapside stews."

Mrs. Brereton clicked her tongue. "Don't use slang, Sarah. 'Tis common. Harry grew up in Lambeth; he has had no experience of the harsher side of our business. At least he is not given to temperament or complaint. That," Mrs. Brereton said flatly, "would get him only a trip to Mother Poke's molly house."

Miss Tolerance sipped her tea and considered Harry's spine. At last she spoke on a different subject altogether. "I have a new task today."

"Task?" Mrs. Brereton raised an eyebrow. "An assignment? Is it something you may speak about?"

"As always, ma'am, in the most general terms only. And yet, I would be glad to hear your opinion. I am seeking a runaway girl."

"Ah. Of good family?"

"Good enough."

"Is she pretty? If she should require employment—"

"*Aunt!*" Miss Tolerance found she was shocked. "Is that your only thought?"

"The first one," Mrs. Brereton agreed, unconcerned. "I am in the business of—well, not selling young women, but renting some part of their flesh in the short term. What else should my first thought be? You imagine I want this girl, whoever she is, to be miserable. My idea is that, as it is likely she is ruined, she might as well find herself in the employ of a liberal and thoughtful madam." She indicated herself. "It is a kindness on my part."

Miss Tolerance was horrified and amused. "I can see that, ma'am. But in fact, her family wishes to find her and, if possible, regularize her situation."

"Well, then, she's a lucky girl," Mrs. Brereton drawled. "If you find her, and if her family defaults of their kindness or she decides that *regularizing* does not suit her, do let me know."

Miss Tolerance put her cup down. "*If* I find her. The Devil is in it that the family don't seem to know who her seducer is. There is no evidence that they left for Gretna— other than her family's belief that her principles were too strong to intend anything other than marriage."

"Show me a mother who truly understands what is in her daughter's heart—"

"Yes, aunt, indeed, I know: all families are humbug, all marriages are unhappy. Your views may have some foundation, but they are not helpful to me in this instance. So far I can find no trace of the girl at the coaching inns. Where would you look, ma'am?"

"In my own parlor."

"It is rather too soon for that," Miss Tolerance said. "How long did it take you to go from—" she searched for a tactful way to say the thing.

"From schoolgirl to *fille de joie?* A matter of months. You know my first was an army man. And a gentleman." The memory appeared to amuse her. "He was prodigiously elegant in his red coat, I may tell you, and we looked very fine when we danced together. He never told me that he had an affianced bride at home, or that all his expectations were tied up in marrying her."

"And when you discovered that he did not mean marriage, what did you do with yourself?"

"Ah, well." Mrs. Brereton smiled. "By the time it was clear to me that our aim was not Gretna Green and marriage over the anvil, but Brighthelmstone and the faro tables, another gentleman had indicated his interest in me—a far richer one. I decided that if I was committed to a life of sin I would just as soon sleep on silk sheets, and—"

"You took charge of your fate." Miss Tolerance regarded her aunt with admiration.

"I did. As have you, my dear."

Miss Tolerance refused to be distracted to her own story. "But what does a gently-reared young lady do who has not your resolve?"

"If she fancies herself in love with the fellow? Stay until he tires of her, cry when he leaves her, and then? If she doesn't have the sense to find a protector among his friends as I did, she might decide to starve. Most do not, though. When she is hungry enough to overcome her scruples she'll find herself in a brothel somewhere. In the city, most likely. Your country brothels are generally not refined enough for a well-bred girl."

Miss Tolerance had hoped that Mrs. Brereton would disclose a name or place likely to attract a Fallen Woman only starting out in her career. "It must be a rude awakening for a gently bred girl. Mrs. Wallace at the Bell Savage suggested that I try Mrs. Rillington's reformatory in Chelsea."

"You might. Although I'd wager that most of the females

to be found there have been at the life long enough to despair of doing better. What girl of spirit would subject herself to sackcloth-and-ashes and gruel for dinner, else?"

One who did not care to be handed from man to man, Miss Tolerance thought. "So I should not expect to find her at a reformatory until she has had more opportunity to be miserable?"

"Use some sense, Sarah," Mrs. Brereton was brisk. "If the girl has not run off with some mawkish boy and been married over the anvil, and not too much time has passed since the elopement, 'tis likely she's still with her protector and they are lying abed, trying to avoid just such a search as you are making."

Miss Tolerance did not care for the image her aunt's words evoked. Still, "'Tis what I fear myself, aunt. But I must find her and offer her the chance to be helped."

"If that is what you have been hired for—" What Mrs. Brereton might have said next was lost when Cole appeared at the door.

"Mr. Tickenor to see you, ma'am."

Mrs. Brereton rose with an uncharacteristic flutter. "My dear Gerard! What a pleasant surprise."

Miss Tolerance rose to be introduced to the man who had entered upon Cole's heels. He was a little taller than Mrs. Brereton, and perhaps a few years older than she; his hair was silver, but his back was straight, his step was firm, and his eyes clear. In all, a very handsome gentleman of mature years. Miss Tolerance curtsied, but Tickenor was too busy kissing Mrs. Brereton's hand to acknowledge her. Mrs. Brereton, for her part, blushed and bridled like a girl. Miss Tolerance, who rarely saw her aunt playing the part of the courtesan she still was, was discomforted.

At last Mrs. Brereton looked up. "Gerard, this is my niece, Miss Tolerance. Mr. Gerard Tickenor, Sarah. You may have heard me speak of him."

Miss Tolerance curtsied again. "Indeed, ma'am." After a moment she recalled that Mr. Tickenor had been one of Mrs. Brereton's early lovers, and had advanced her a deal of money, since repaid, when she was establishing her business. "How do you do, sir?"

"Oh, the better for seeing your aunt, young lady." The man returned her bow, then returned his attention to Mrs. Brereton. Miss Tolerance had the sense that she was very much *de trop*. She looked at the clock with some relief.

"I am delighted to have met you, sir. Will you pardon me, aunt? I have an engagement of my own." Miss Tolerance kissed her aunt's scented cheek and fled. She still had to dress for the theatre.

Sir Walter Mandif, a magistrate from the Bow Street Offices and, more significantly, her friend, had lately made it his business to educate Miss Tolerance in the dramatic arts, particularly in the works of Shakespeare. Tonight she was bespoke for a performance of *Twelfth Night* at the New Covent Garden Theatre. A little before eight Miss Tolerance left her house and took a chair southeast to the theatre.

The streets around Covent Garden were thick with carriages and wagons, tradesmen and farmers departing the market, society in evening dress arriving for the theatre, and the usual crowd of flower-sellers, streetwalkers and petty criminals come to work among the swells. Might her missing girl already be known to someone in the crowd?

Miss Tolerance met Sir Walter just outside the theatre.

"I wish you would let me call for you," he chided, after they had exchanged greetings. Sir Walter, slight and sandy-haired, and dressed in neat evening clothes, gave no impression of the formidable pillar of the law.

"What, you would call at my aunt's brothel and advertise your presence to the clientele and whores? Or perhaps rap upon the gate to my garden and hope that I should hear you?" Miss Tolerance shook her head. "My life is not set up to accommodate callers on anything other than business. This truly is the simplest way."

Sir Walter inclined his head. "Perhaps so. But it leaves me feeling distinctly un-gallant."

Miss Tolerance laughed and tucked her hand into his

arm. "Alas, Sir Walter, if you insist upon consorting with Fallen Women your sensibilities will be constantly put to the test."

Sir Walter put his own hand on top of hers on his arm, as if to hold her there. "As there is only one Fallen Woman with whom I regularly consort, I think my sensibilities are elastic enough to see me through. And if it is a choice between my sensibilities and your company, the pleasure of the latter must always delight the former."

Miss Tolerance, always rendered uncomfortable by compliments, made light.

"La, Sir Walter. You will have me blush."

His eyebrow rose, and Sir Walter's foxy, intelligent face was lit by a smile. "I should like to see that," he said, and led Miss Tolerance up the stairs to their seats. The actress Mrs. Jordan was in form that night: despite her years and girth her Viola was very fine, even if no one in the audience was deceived for a moment by her appearance in boy's clothes. When the play was over there was the usual press to find a hackney carriage—like Miss Tolerance Sir Walter kept no carriage—and they hung back for a time, waiting until the crowd should lessen before they started back to Manchester Square. They spoke of the play and then, comfortably, of crime and criminals, and of politics. With the King long mad and the Queen Regent incapacitated by apoplectic stroke, there had been a long process of declaring her regency at an end and selecting a new regent. The Prince of Wales, widowed and the father of two in whose upbringing he was much involved, now seemed on the verge of attaining the Regency himself. However, each of the other Royal Dukes (and there were a good number, even despite the usual depletions of infant death, disease and warfare) had his adherents; the political jockeying was still fierce, and nearly as good as a play itself. They acquired a carriage, still talking. Sir Walter was in the process of delivering a blunt appraisal of his Highness the Duke of Cambridge's chances, to Miss Tolerance's appreciative laughter, when the carriage drew up in Spanish

Place. Still laughing, they alit at the gate to her garden, and Sir Walter insisted that he would see her in.

"Since I wound your chivalrous instincts by arriving at the theatre on my own, I suppose I cannot ask you to sustain another blow by leaving me here."

"Indeed, no. Who knows what might happen to you between the gate and your doorstep?"

"In my aunt's garden, with her staff ready to come the moment I call?"

Sir Walter smiled. "I will take no chances with you."

Miss Tolerance unlocked the gate. The garden was silvered by the moon; on the right hand Mrs. Brereton's house glowed with candlelight, and Miss Tolerance heard music: one of the girls playing upon the pianoforte. She paused for a moment just inside the walls; there was a dark green smell of new spring leaves and, less appealingly, the faint foul odor of Mrs. Brereton's well-tended necessary house in the far corner of the garden. Sir Walter stopped, a shadow at her elbow. He was much of her height, and close enough that his breath stirred the hair above her ear. Miss Tolerance found herself suddenly self-conscious.

"'Tis very peaceful here," Sir Walter said quietly.

She nodded. "One would hardly know the city is just outside the gate." The breeze was soft and cool against her warm face. "Well, Sir Walter, I suppose—"

"I shall see you to your door." He offered her his arm again. "My upbringing requires it, I am afraid."

"There is nothing to be regretted in gentlemanly behavior," Miss Tolerance said. She took his arm, her gloved hand a white blur upon the dark fold of his sleeve. In ten steps they were at her door; the cottage was ivy-covered and dark, but here and there the whitewashed walls were stippled by moonlight. Sir Walter's arm under her hand was solid, and she was aware of his warmth at her side. She was relieved to relinquish his support and step away.

"There, you have done your duty. Thank you, Sir Walter. For the play and the company." She curtsied.

"The pleasure was all mine." Sir Walter took her hand and bowed over it. Then, slowly, he raised it to her lips. The kiss was light, but the impression of it she felt even through the kidskin of her glove. "Good night."

"Good night," Miss Tolerance echoed, and was inside her cottage with the door closed before her words died on the night air. She locked the door and prepared for bed, thinking.

For a Fallen Woman, Miss Tolerance was peculiarly chaste. Her liaison with Charles Connell had lacked nothing but the ceremony itself to make it a marriage; they had been faithful to each other, maturing from the first surprises of passion to a companionable domesticity. Connell's death had left her much in the same case as a young widow. She had not intended to become involved with another man—she had devised her profession to ensure that she would not need to become someone's mistress in order to avoid starvation.

Then, almost a twelvemonth ago she had formed an attachment to the earl of Versellion—against her better judgment but not, certainly, against her will. Their liaison had been a matter of attraction both sexual and emotional, and while Miss Tolerance had not been able to imagine how a relationship between a Fallen Woman and a politically ambitious peer could prosper, she had not had the will to quit it. Not, at least, until she had discovered that the earl had murdered a woman, and she had turned him in to Bow Street—to Sir Walter Mandif, in point of fact. In the difficult time after, when Miss Tolerance had gained brief notoriety by testifying against Versellion, Sir Walter had been a friend as well as a colleague. She relied upon that friendship, and made every effort to ignore the possibility of any shift in their association. Love, she believed, was a danger and a liability to a Fallen Woman with no interest in whoredom.

Her dress brushed and hung away, Miss Tolerance put on her nightshft and brushed her teeth. The kissing of hands was an old-fashioned gesture, but it was not entirely out of style. And Sir Walter had likely been much swayed by the romance of the play; he was a greater fancier of Shakespeare's work than she. The kiss had meant nothing more than friendship. A courteous gesture.

She still felt the pressure of his lips on her hand.

Miss Tolerance brushed her long, dark hair, braided it, and climbed into her bed to listen to the whispering of ivy at her window.

Chapter Three

Miss Tolerance dreamed.

It was dark, night, roiling with thunder. Each burst of blue-white lightning illumined her father's face like a pantomime mask, a caricature of glaring eyes and hawk nose. She stood in her father's hall, Connell's hand clenched in her own. Sir William's voice echoed, calling her whore and threatening to kill her and her lover. They fled the house, riding through the storm with certain knowledge that they were pursued. Rain drummed upon her back—in the dream she wore the linen shirt and breeches in which she had fenced—and could smell the wet wool of Connell's coat under her cheek. She felt her heart pounding, knew that death was following them even to Dover and the hurriedly bought passage to the Continent. It was not until they reached foreign soil that she felt safe. She and Connell, still handfast, arrived at a tiny pension in Oostende. They were lighted along a narrow passage by a woman so elderly and wizened she might have been carved of wood, who cackled about young love and the honor they did her inn. She opened the door with a winking smile and they stepped in. Connell shut the door. When he turned back her father was there, pistol drawn, to shoot her lover through the heart.

Miss Tolerance woke with her own heart pounding.

She lay in the dark listening to the tap of ivy on her window, waiting until she was calm again. She had not had that dream in a very long time. With Connell dead she had thought never to have it again. It was all lies, after all.

It had been daylight when her father learned about her and Connell, and she had been alone. Her father had not been cold and pale but so red-faced she had feared he would have an apoplectic fit. He had called her whore, and promised to send her to a convent (no small threat from a man so opposed to Popish influence as Sir William Brereton). But first, he said, he would find Charles Connell and run his sword through the bastard's heart. He had dragged his ruined daughter to her room in a grip so tight it had left bruises upon her arm for a week, and locked her in, unaware she had long ago learned to climb down from her window. Miss Tolerance had been very young—sixteen, just as Mrs. Brown's sister was—and had believed that her father would challenge Connell and would be killed. She was not so lost to filial affection that she wanted her father dead; much less did she want her lover hung for his murder. Rather than see that happen she had raced to find Connell and persuaded him to fly with her—not on horseback but prosaically in the stage coach. She had never seen her father again.

Her mother, Miss Tolerance recalled now, had sat in the parlor, bent over her needlework, during the whole brutal scene. She had said nothing, either in comfort or defense. Her brother Adam had been at away at school, but Miss Tolerance had later reason to believe that his view of the matter was in accord with their father's. Those servants who caught her eye during the tirade had shaken their heads in silent apology for their inability to do anything to help.

Altogether an unpleasant memory.

When her heart had resumed its normal rhythm Miss Tolerance lit a candle and took out her inevitable recourse on sleepless nights, Mainley's *Art of the Small Sword*. When that soporific text lulled her back to sleep she did not dream again.

Parliament was near to its vote upon the Regency, Miss Tolerance read in the *Times* the next morning. That part of the paper that was not taken up with the question of Regency was devoted to news of the war in Spain, and with the progress of the Commission of Inquiry convened to examine the failures of the War Office in the Walcheren invasion. There were few notes from Court, as neither King nor Queen was capable of presiding.

Miss Tolerance finished her tea, washed the plate which had lately held a slice of bread and butter, and dressed herself for the day. She intended to visit more inns, this time focusing upon the women who waited in hope of luring country girls into brothels. She dressed again in her blue walking dress and asked Keefe to find her a hackney coach to take her to Snow Hill Street. There, and in the vicinity, were coaching inns that served the southern and western routes. Miss Tolerance privily hoped the girl had not been seen there; anything but departure for the north suggested that Miss Evadne was not headed for Scotland, where she could be wed with no questions asked. Still, Miss Tolerance had visited many of the most prominent inns serving the northern routes the day before with no success. She must be thorough.

She arrived at her destination with her bones no more than usually wracked by the carriage's poor springs, the street's bad paving, and the driver's ineptitude. She began at once with her interviews, but as on the afternoon before, Miss Tolerance had little success. No barmen remembered having seen the girl, and in those taprooms where women waited for easily-cozened girls to descend from the stage and into their talons, these same women seemed to disappear upon sight of Miss Tolerance. Finally, at the Saracen's Head in Friday Street, she approached a pair of middle-aged women sitting near the window, both pleasantly stout, neatly dressed, and of maternal demeanor, both apparently taken up with knitting and gossip but much engaged in looking out at the courtyard to watch for the next coach.

"I beg your pardon?" she began.

"Yes, my dear?" The woman who answered was the plumper of the two, with a comfortable bosom and a merry eye. She had the countenance of a beloved nursery maid or doting grandmother. "Are you lost?"

"No, ma'am. I was wondering if I might—" Miss Tolerance considered. "If I might buy you a glass of wine."

The second woman, taller of the two and not quite so delightful in demeanor, smiled broadly enough to show that her lower front teeth were missing. "That's very sweet of you, my dear, but you must let *us*—"

"I am not looking for employment, ma'am. Nor am I newly arrived in the city. I merely have a question or two to ask you ladies, and thought I might purchase answers with a glass of wine."

The two women, markedly cooler, looked at each other. The plump one's eyebrows went up; the tall one's eyebrows went down. They appeared to achieve consensus of sorts.

"I'd be delighted to take some wine with you, dearie," the plump one said. "If indeed you're buying."

"I am," Miss Tolerance said. "And you, ma'am?"

All pretense gone, the taller bawd shook her head. "I'll go wait for the Lincoln Flyer to arrive," she said. "Do you go ahead, Rosie." She stood, gathered her skirts, and left the coffee-room.

Madame Rose waved Miss Tolerance to the vacated seat and called for gin-and-water. Miss Tolerance ordered coffee. They waited until refreshments arrived.

"Now, dear," Madame Rose leaned forward confidingly. "What is it you was wantin' to ask?"

"I'm seeking a girl," Miss Tolerance. "I am under no illusion as to your purpose at the Saracen's Head, ma'am; it is obviously your job to note what females come and go here. This young lady might have been waiting to board the stagecoach. She might have been accompanied by a gentleman. I am sure you and your friend would have remarked her had she been here."

"And when would this ha' been?"

"Any time in the last fortnight," Miss Tolerance tasted her coffee; it was drinkable. "Her family would very much like to find the girl."

Madame Rose puffed out her cheeks and pursed her lips. "Fortnight? That's a long time in a business like mine, dearie. People come and go, you know, and an old woman like me's got not such a good memory at the best of times."

Miss Tolerance sighed inwardly and took out a half-crown piece from her reticule. "Perhaps this will be an aid to memory."

The bawd pocketed the coin, her motherly smile breaking out again. "What would the girl 'ave looked like?"

Miss Tolerance produced the portrait. Madame Rose examined it closely, tssking and running her fingers over the painted surface as if to memorize the image that way.

"That's a pretty one," she said at last, with some regret. "Both on 'em. She didn't come to me." Then, as if she sensed that Miss Tolerance would depart at once she added, "That ain't to say I han't seen 'er." She looked at the table as if she expected to see something materialize there.

"Have I not already encouraged your memory, Mrs.—"

"Mrs. Codfinger, dearie. Rosie Codfinger." The bawd grinned, delighted by her own *nom d'amour*. "I thought the encouragement was just for the setting down together," she added.

"The gin-and-water was for our conference. The half-crown was for information. Ma'am."

The bawd sighed. "As it 'appens, I think I did see the girl."

"Did you?" Miss Tolerance's tone did not betray her excitement, but the bawd paused to examine the table again. This time Miss Tolerance pushed another shilling across the table.

"P'raps a week ago, talking with a female as sometimes comes to cut into my business 'ere. A Mrs. 'arris, a very *respectable* woman she is."

Respectable enough not to have taken a false name, Miss Tolerance thought. "Where was this?" she asked.

Mrs. Codfinger shrugged. "Don't recall. Well, you know—" she added in the face of Miss Tolerance's evident disbelief. "You remember a face, but don't know when or where you seen it, like. Not here, that I know."

This was irritatingly plausible. "Do you know where I might find this Mrs. Harris, Mrs. Codfinger?"

"I do." The bawd looked at the table one more time, coyly drawing a circle with one finger on the greasy surface. Miss Tolerance, all out of patience, brought her own finger down on Mrs. Codfinger's.

"I think I've paid for the answer, ma'am. If you don't have it, I'm sure someone else will." She looked in the direction of the courtyard and Mrs. Codfinger's confederate.

The bawd frowned at Miss Tolerance, then, seeing there would be no change in her attitude, mimed deep thought. "Ah, well, let me see. Yes, yes. She lodges in Marigold Street, Bermondsey."

Miss Tolerance rose. "Thank you, ma'am. You have been most helpful."

Mrs. Codfinger nodded. "So I 'ave." She smiled again.

"If you hear more of the girl, Mrs. Codfinger, send word to me at Tarsio's Club in Henry Street at once, please. You will be rewarded if your information allows me to return the child to her family." She added that last lest Mrs. Codfinger be tempted to invent further information.

Mrs. Codfinger tssked. "Henry Street? Ain't we fine!" She gulped down the remains of her gin-and-water. "Tarsio's Club? Well I 'ope this reward of yours is *substantial,* for it's money out me own pocket if I see that one and 'and her back to you, and that's the truth. A very pretty girl."

Miss Tolerance thanked the bawd for her restraint, reiterated that the reward would indeed be substantial and, after a mutual exchange of courtesies, the two parted company. As she went through the stableyard Miss Tolerance saw Mrs. Codfinger's companion watching the passengers descend from the Lincoln Flyer.

The trip to Bermondsey took some time, as the carriage had to thread its way through streets clogged with vehicles, animals, and pedestrians of all description, and to cross the Thames at the London Bridge. The jarvey, perhaps concerned for the sensibilities of his passenger, tried when the carriage reached the south side of the Thames, to avoid the sordid streets around the docks by driving a considerable distance south—until Miss Tolerance rapped sharply on the roof and announced that she would not pay the fare for a trip to Lisbon, and expected to be taken to her destination the most direct way possible. The jarvey protested a little, then turned his horses east, through neighborhoods both ramshackle and depressing. Miss Tolerance, who had seen these streets before and on foot, felt no obligation to gaze out at the misery on view there. She closed her eyes.

After a quarter hour the smells and sounds suggested that the carriage was moving into a better quarter of the city. Miss Tolerance looked out to find that they were in a neat neighborhood, well built-up, with a handsome church and a crowded churchyard to her right, and a street full of shops to her left. The jarvey pulled up before a well-kept building with a prosperous-looking bootmaker's shop on the ground floor. Miss Tolerance alit and looked about her. Three little boys of no more than six years sat at the foot of the door into the building, poking at the remains of a sparrow with a pocketknife.

"Do any of you gentlemen know Mrs. Harris?"

The boys guiltily pulled away from the corpse. Two of them stared at the third; he looked at Miss Tolerance, frowning.

41

"She's my granny," he said. "What you want with 'er?" He had a sharp, pointed nose, dark eyes, and a fall of dark, dirty hair, and stared at Miss Tolerance impertinently.

"Just a few minutes of talk. Will you take me to her, please?" Normally Miss Tolerance would have purchased the boy's assistance with a penny, but she did not like to encourage his sly manner.

"I s'pose. Come along." With the aplomb of a boy twice his age the child led her across the street, into a wooden-framed house, and down the dark hall to the stairway. "You alone?"

"And if I am?" Miss Tolerance followed him up the stairs, aware that the other two boys had vanished as completely as a sugarloaf dropped in boiling water.

"Usually they comes with friends," the boy said. "Makes me no mind."

Who were *they*? "I'm delighted to hear it." Miss Tolerance could not remember when she had last taken such a dislike to a child. "I'm sure Mrs. Harris is here somewhere."

"Yehr. Righ' 'ere." The boy shoved hard on a door at the end of the corridor—like most such the hallway was unlit and visitors were expected to find their ways by guess and luck—and the door yielded. "Gran! 'Ere's a lady for you."

He nudged Miss Tolerance forward. She found herself blinking after the dark of the hall. An uncurtained window faced out over the street and filled the room with white sunlight. The room was furnished with a heavy, old-fashioned sofa and two chairs, a table, two lamps, and a rug which, although shabby, had once been of good quality. Miss Tolerance caught a faint whiff of some astringent scent, just under the homelier smells of beeswax and blacking. There was no one in sight, but a creak to the left announced that someone was coming. A moment later a tall, stocky woman of advanced years appeared in the doorway. She wore a gown of blue muslin with a spotless white work-apron, and an old-fashioned muslin cap on her iron-gray hair. Her eyes were a pale, faded blue, and her smile attempted the maternal. She had the steely pleasantness of a senior nursery maid.

"Thank you, Martin. That'll do." The boy, who had stood behind Miss Tolerance with his arms crossed as if he thought she might steal the plate, bolted from the room. The woman stepped forward to close the door. "Now, my dear. How can I help you?" Kent-born, Miss Tolerance fancied, but many years in London.

"Are you Mrs. Harris?"

"I am, my dear. Please, come in, come in." The woman waved a hand at the chairs. "Now, who sent you to me?"

That was a forceful way to begin a conversation with a stranger. "A Mrs. Codfinger, ma'am, says—"

"Mrs.—Did she, then? I'm surprised, I confess it. Rosie Codfinger fancies herself in my line of work, and I'd not 'ave expected 'er to turn away a bit of business. Well, 'tis obliging of her, to be sure." Mrs. Harris took a seat on the sofa opposite to Miss Tolerance and leaned forward. "Well, my dear—how do you find yourself here?"

Another curious question. "I took a hackney carriage."

Mrs. Harris shook her head. "Now, sweetheart, all will go better if you are frank with me," she chided. "How far along."

"Ma'am?"

Mrs. Harris reached for Miss Tolerance's hand and patted it between her own two square, callused ones. She leaned forward, lowering her voice. "How far along? When did you miss your courses?"

Miss Tolerance sat back. All was suddenly clear to her; how had she not realized it before? "I am not with child, ma'am."

Mrs. Harris appeared unsurprised by this answer, but an edge came into her voice. "What, do you think it is some sort of illness you have, my dear? Come, come, even ladies will have their fun, and when they find that they must pay the piper the come to me to—"

"You mistake me, ma'am. I am not here to avail myself of your services." She took a breath. "Perhaps we should

43

start anew. Permit me to introduce myself. My name is Tolerance, and I was sent by Mrs. Codfinger, who said that she had seen you in conversation with a young woman I am seeking to find."

Mrs. Harris frowned. "I don't talk about the ladies that come to me, Mrs. Tolerance—"

"*Miss* Tolerance."

"*Miss* Tolerance?" The woman shrugged. "Well, *Miss* Tolerance, do you think, if word got out that I gabbed, I'd ever see another penny for my services?"

As discretion was one of the most important aspects of Miss Tolerance's own services, she was sympathetic. "I do understand, ma'am. But I do not believe this young woman came to you to avail herself of your—your services. She has run away from her family, and I am attempting to return her to them." Miss Tolerance extracted the portrait from her reticule and handed it to the other woman.

Mrs. Harris held the picture out, almost at arm's length, and squinted at it. Just for a moment Miss Tolerance thought she saw recognition in the older woman's expression. Then she shook her head. "I'm sorry you've come for nothing, miss. They're both pretty girls, but I've never seen either one of 'em. The shorter one looks a bit like Daisy Quiller, from three streets over, but she'd never have the brass to pay for a picture like that."

She returned the portrait to Miss Tolerance.

"Why would Mrs. Codfinger have told me she had seen you with the girl, ma'am?"

"What would I be doing chatting up girls? I'm not in *that* business." Mrs. Harris's disdain was complete. "Rosie Codfinger's souse enough to imagine any number of things. She's also the sort would enjoy sending another person off chasing cat-phantoms. I'm that sorry for your time and trouble but I can't help you. I'm sorry for the girl,' she added more feelingly. "Gentle-bred thing like that probably don't know the first thing about what she's got herself into."

"My fear is that she is learning, ma'am." Miss Tolerance rose. "You are quite certain you have never seen her?"

Mrs. Harris stood also. "What, are you calling me a liar? I said I han't seen her, and that's God's truth." She raised one square hand as if taking her oath. "Now, you'll oblige me by leaving. I have business to attend to." She crossed her arms as if to present the sturdiest obstacle possible to continued conversation. Miss Tolerance curtsied and departed.

It appeared that Mrs. Harris had been a waste of her morning. Miss Tolerance went out past Martin and his friends, who had returned to examining the carrion on the front step, and reluctantly moved aside to let her pass. Miss Tolerance sought out her hackney coach where it waited for her.

As she returned to Tarsio's late that afternoon, Miss Tolerance calculated that she had visited seventeen coaching inns that day, with nothing to show for it except her own growing conviction that Miss Evadne had not left London, with or without a companion, by stage. Unless the girl's seducer was wealthy enough to hire a private chaise—and Miss Tolerance had not the resources to send inquiries to every posting house on the northern roads—it appeared likely that her quarry was still in London. It was a pleasant thing to have ruled out the rest of England, she thought, but not much comfort when she considered all the places in London where a runaway couple might hide.

No messages awaited her at Tarsio's. Miss Tolerance bespoke dinner in one of the small withdrawing rooms and went up at once to write a report to Mrs. Brown. She wished, as she did so, that the lady had been more forthcoming. As things were situated it would be nearly impossible to speak with servants in the Brown household (or whatever their name was). It would be difficult to speak to the girl's friends without alerting them to the possibility of scandal, and that was a real loss. What sixteen year old girl ever nourished a secret passion without confessing it to a friend? There was the governess, turned off before she could be of any help. She wrote a line to ask for the governess's direction. It was clear to her that her lover's identity was the key to finding the girl. She finished her note and consigned it to the care of Steen, another of Tarsio's porters, then fell to her beef and pudding with a sharp appetite.

When she finished her dinner she remained at Tarsio's for a while, thinking that perhaps someone she had spoken to earlier in the day might seek her out in this more private setting. Miss Tolerance disliked waiting; she ventured from the withdrawing room to the book room to find something to read. An hour spent in the company of *A Letter to the Women of England, on the Injustices of Mental Subjugation*, convinced her (had she required convincing) that the life and concerns of a bluestocking would not have suited her. The hour was drawing on for ten o'clock and she was tired. She left the club, hired a chair, and was returned to Manchester Square.

Miss Tolerance did not intend to enter her aunt's establishment that evening. When possible she avoided those hours when trade was most brisk, as she had on more than one occasion been mistaken for one of her aunt's employees. She directed the chair to leave her in Spanish Place, went in through the gate there, and made for her cottage. There she found a note from her aunt requesting her to call. She was reluctant—the hour, the rigors of the day, and her lack of success had left her tired and irritable—but affection and duty won out. Miss Tolerance took off her bonnet and crossed the garden to Mrs. Brereton's house.

She found her aunt at her desk, two branches of candles melting down as she pored over the pages of a ledger. Mrs. Brereton must have sensed a presence behind her; her back stiffened and she slammed the ledger closed as if to prevent its secrets leaping out to take refuge with her enemies. When she saw who her visitor was Mrs. Brereton unbent a little.

"You ought not sneak about in that fashion."

"I am sorry, Aunt Thea. Habits of stealth are a hazard of my occupation."

Mrs. Brereton sniffed. "Where are you off to now?"

"My bed, ma'am. I am just returned home, but you left word you wished to see me."

"I wanted you to sup with me, but I see you have been jaunting bout town with your tame magistrate again."

Miss Tolerance blinked. "I rarely jaunt, Aunt. And I wish you would not call Sir Walter such a name. He is neither tame nor mine, and would dislike it very much."

"Were you not out with him last night?"

"We went to the theatre, yes. I have also gone to the theatre with you, and with Marianne. Do you have a sudden objection to Covent Garden, ma'am?"

Mrs. Brereton pursed her lips. "It seems to me that you are hardly at home."

"Another hazard of my occupation, aunt, but not Sir Walter's fault."

"You were not with him tonight?"

"No, ma'am, I was not. I was at Tarsio's, waiting for an informant who never arrived. I should have been far better entertained had I been supping with you. As to Sir Walter, do you so dislike my friendship with him?"

"You might be making money from it," Mrs. Brereton suggested.

"Not in the way you mean, ma'am. Sir Walter and I are colleagues. We discuss our work and politics, just as you and I do."

Mrs. Brereton opened her ledger and stared fixedly at it. "Don't be stupid, Sarah. There is no such thing as friendship between men and women. You may not mean to attach Sir Walter, but I do not doubt that he means to attach you. Now, if all you mean to do is talk nonsense you might as well leave me to my accounts."

Miss Tolerance did not like to leave on such a note. Since her illness a sixmonth before, Mrs. Brereton had been more volatile of temper and more likely to take offense where none was meant. She kept her temper with her clients;

Miss Tolerance heard enough from Mrs. Brereton's lieu-tenant, Marianne Touchwell, to know that she was equally evenhanded in dealing with the staff. Her odd moods were reserved for Frost, her dresser, for Marianne, and for Miss Tolerance, the three persons in the household to whom her ties were closest. That this was a mark of trust made it no less disturbing.

Miss Tolerance bit her lip, gained a firm hand upon her own temper, and smiled. "Will you dismiss me so out-of-hand, aunt? I am here, now."

"I do not want you now!" Mrs. Brereton snapped. "You are never here when I want you."

"But you know what my life is like, aunt. And I did visit with you yesterday before I went out." Miss Tolerance saw that her aunt was not mollified. "May we not make an ap-pointment to dine tomorrow? I will promise to be there."

"Had I not better invite you to dine, you mean." Mrs. Brereton was grudging.

"No, indeed. If you wish to come to my cottage for din-ner, I will lay on the best possible meal—"

"Don't be stupid, Sarah." But Mrs. Brereton appeared more diverted than affronted by the notion of dining in the cottage. "What would you serve me? Gruel and tea? Bread and butter?"

"Connell used to say I made a very tasty stew."

"God preserve me. I don't doubt your fencing master ate anything placed in front of him, like most men. No, I'll thank you to come dine with me—if you can undertake to cease jaunting about the city for an evening."

"I rarely jaunt," Miss Tolerance said again. "I would be delighted to dine with you. We dress, of course?"

"My dear child, just because we are Fallen is no reason to neglect the habits of civilized society." The unevenness of Mrs. Brereton's smile made her look rather melancholy, but Miss Tolerance knew this was one of the remaining physical signs of the stroke from which her aunt had oth-erwise recovered. "Wear that pretty green gown, and I will—"

What Mrs. Brereton intended was not to be known; one of her girls appeared in the doorway at that moment. "Excuse me, ma'am."

"What is it, Clara?"

The whore, a slender girl with bright eyes and a tumble of dark curls, was apologetic. "There's a problem in the yellow saloon. Two gents is—are—asking for Lisette and neither one will give way. She says Mr. Creevey was her appointed for the evening, but Mr. Sainsbury says she promised him, and they're a bit in their cups and—"

"A schoolroom quarrel!" Mrs. Brereton frowned. "Cannot Marianne sort this out? It seems to me I gave her authority to do just that."

The girl flushed. "Marianne's with a gent, ma'am. Keefe might—"

But Mrs. Brereton had risen to her feet. "One does not ask a servant to mediate between gentlemen, Clara. Keefe is only to be involved when a client requires a show of force." She turned to her niece. "I don't suppose you would deal with this, Sarah?"

Miss Tolerance shook her head. "Like Keefe, ma'am, I am only to be involved when the client requires a show of force."

"How do you know this is not such a time?"

"Given that Clara entered the room at a decorous walk, and the only clash she mentions is one of dates rather than steel, I deduce that no threat presently exists. You do not need me to interfere, aunt."

"Well, I wish you would. You might save me the exertion of going down stairs. "

"Untangling a quarrel like this will be best done by you, aunt. I have no standing in this house. Nor do I want any," she continued before Mrs. Brereton could make her inevitable comments about the desirability of Miss Tolerance interesting herself in the business. "I will leave you to your business, aunt, and promise faithfully to dine with you tomorrow evening."

Mrs. Brereton sniffed. "Go away, then." She offered her

cheek for a kiss, then followed Clara out the door to deal with Messers Creevey and Sainsbury.

Chapter Four

Miss Tolerance woke early, broke her fast, dressed, set her cottage in order, and left Manchester Square on foot. An idea had come to her as she waited to sleep the night before. Mrs. Brown would not give Miss Evadne's real name, but there was no doubt that possession of it would make finding the girl easier, and she had not forbidden Miss Tolerance to seek that name out. It was a quarter-hour's walk to Duke of York Street; the morning was fine and the streets full of tradesmen and vendors bent upon provisioning the well-to-do. She enjoyed the walk.

Duke of York Street runs from Jermyn Street to St. James's Square. Miss Tolerance went past tobacconists and haberdashers on Jermyn Street who at this hour were engaged in taking down the shutters and making ready for the start of business. When she turned the corner onto Duke of York Street she could see, at street's end, the pleasant greenery of the square beyond. The street itself was lined with substantial houses, a few set back a little from the street but most modern enough to front directly on the flagged sidewalk. If Miss Tolerance had had any doubt that her quarry came from a family of substance, her first stroll down the street put paid to it. The occupants of these houses might not all be wealthy as the rich themselves define the term, but compared to the vast majority of London and the nation they were wealthy enough. The houses were all well kept, of stone or old pink brick, broad enough to admit of parlors on either side of the entry, and climbing three or four stories above the street. In front of two of them footmen had emerged to sweep the sidewalk, causing no little consternation to the crossing-sweeps stationed at the corners, underfed boys too young to be put to better use, who eked out pennies sweeping the ordure and muck from the path of the better fed.

Miss Tolerance strolled leisurely to the corner, made a circuit of St. James's Square, and walked back up Duke of York again, wondering to which of these houses Miss Evadne belonged. What the Devil was the girl's surname? Thinking of her as Miss Evadne made the girl sound like a child; it made Miss Tolerance feel like a cross nursemaid to call her so. As she neared the corner her attention was drawn by an altercation between a porter and several of the boys in grimy togs, regarding possession of the sidewalk. Miss Tolerance was seized by inspiration, and paused to admire a wrought iron fence while she waited for the dispute to be resolved.

When at last the porter withdrew from the fray, Miss Tolerance approached the knot of crossing-sweeps who stood gloating in victory. As she neared them the three largest boys broke off celebrating and elbowed each other out of the way, begging to sweep for her. Miss Tolerance shook her head, but before the boys could slink away muttering their hopes that the stingy mort would tread straightaway in a fresh clod of horseshit, she informed them that she might have silver to spend upon a clever boy who kept his eyes open.

In an instant the half-dozen boys assumed expressions

of such angelic, open-eyed character that Miss Tolerance was hard put not to laugh. "Do you gentlemen regularly sweep this street?"

There was some snickering at her use of the word *gentlemen*, but all of the heads bobbed in agreement.

"And do you consider that you are familiar with the people who live here?"

This caused some confusion: none of the boys was rightly certain what they were to make of the word familiar, and several of them feared they were being accused of something. Miss Tolerance cleared up the matter by asking if any of them thought that, if they were shown a picture, they might recognize from which house the person had come.

The largest of the boys, apparently the leader, looked round at his small troop, then nodded to her. "Yes, miss. I think so."

"Well, then. Kindly look at this and tell me if either of these two ladies is familiar to you." She took the portrait from her reticule and, holding on to it firmly lest the temptation to make away with the frame prove too strong, showed it to them. The boys studied the picture with grave attention; this was a new game to them and they seemed determined to play fair at it.

Finally the largest boy raised his head, looked around to his mates and, on some signal of group agreement, pointed to a good sized house of gray stone across the street and half-way to St. James's Square.

"You are sure?"

The heads bobbed in ragged agreement. Miss Tolerance dispensed a penny to each of the boys, which caused a second ripple of bobbed heads, and mumbled *thankees*. Miss Tolerance took a tuppenny piece and held it up between gloved fingers.

"Can any of you tell me the name of the people who live there?"

The leader turned to his mates, eyebrows lifted as if to encourage an outpouring of information which did not come. "Noffin'?" he prodded. The boys looked back and forth between the coin and the house; she watched each one consider and abandon the idea of a lie.

"Never mind it," Miss Tolerance said bracingly. "What can you tell me about the people who live in that house? How many are there?"

"Fambly or servints?" the leader asked.

"For now, just the family."

"There's your young ladies," one of the smallest boys piped up. "Only the sittin' one in the picher, she ain't always 'ere no more."

"Catch-fart! She's married! 'Er 'usban' come to visit wiv'er."

Miss Tolerance was required to head off a quarrel by reminding the boys of the question under discussion.

"The one that was standin' in the picher, she live here," the small boy reported.

"Yeah, and 'er da, too," said another boy, in the tone of one who is telling a tremendous joke. Miss Tolerance looked down her nose at him and his merriment subsided. There was some subsequent discussion of the nip–farthing ways of the men of the house, who never paid for a sweeping.

"Nah, the young gent pays," a sandy-haired boy offered. "'E's aright. Ast me once 'ow many we 'ad at 'ome, and 'f we got enough to eat."

"Whot 'e want to know that for?" the leader objected.

The sandy-haired boy shrugged. "Dunno. Maybe 'e wanted to invite us all over for Sunday dinner." This was met with a roar of merriment.

"When is the last time any of you saw the younger lady?"

This question caused a good deal of head-scratching and twisting up of faces. In the end the consensus was that it had been more than a week. "The young 'un, miss? Spec' she's gone to the country," one of the boys said. "A-huntin' of foxes or summat, 'ey, miss? They cuts the tails off," he added with relish. The other boys were much impressed with this bit of trivia. Miss Tolerance wrenched the topic back to the family in the stone house.

"I have a task for as many likely boys as I can find. I need to have that house carefully observed, and I will pay each boy who works for me..." she paused thoughtfully. "Thruppence a day upon my errand."

"What we observin' for, miss?" the tall boy asked.

"To see who comes in or goes out, over the next few days. But you must be careful that no one in the house knows what you are doing—including the servants. I will need a report each day of the visitors that come to the house. Can any of you write?"

After a moment of silence one of the smaller, grubbier boys raised his hand. This occasioned a chorus of ooohs, half-taunting and half-admiring, from his fellows.

"I can't spell so good, missus, but I know me letters. Me mum taught me 'fore she died." The boy, who gave his name as Ted, eyed his mates with some anxiety, but being orphaned apparently legitimized his literacy.

"Excellent. Then each morning you and—what is your name?" she indicated the ringleader.

"Bart, miss."

"Ted and Bart shall gather up all the information and make up a report and leave it for me with the porter at Mrs. Brereton's house." She gave the direction. "He will give you your money. If you do not distribute the coins to all your mates, I shall hear about it."

Bart nodded. "But what about sweepin', miss?"

"Sweeping?" It was necessary for Miss Tolerance to re-assure the boys that she did not wish them to stop sweep-ing, and more particularly that she did not require a cut of whatever money they took in. She had no interest in de-veloping a syndicate of street-sweeps. She had the boys recite their instructions again, and left them to their watch. Not one of the boys had expressed any curiosity as to why she wanted the house watched. Clearly the motives of a madwoman with money to spend were less important than each boy getting his share.

Having put spies in place in the vicinity of Miss Evadne's home, Miss Tolerance took another turn up the street and around the green in St. James's Square. Upon her return she observed her agents at the corner of Jermyn Street sweeping the crossing and keeping covert watch upon the gray stone house. Pleased by the sight of youth at work, Miss Tolerance continued to the next part of her chore: discovering Miss Evadne's family name.

Miss Tolerance extracted a slip of paper from her reticule and clutched it in her hand, peering at it with a good counterfeit of myopic anxiety. As she progressed along the street she squinted at the doors of the houses, looked to count their number, peered again at the paper. When a stout man in a leather apron backed his way from the tradesman's entry of the house next door to that of her quarry, Miss Tolerance bustled up to him and asked, in the most agitated tones, whether this was number 11.

"Nah," the man said shortly. He was carrying an empty cage; from the skirl of white feathers that eddied in the bottom of the cage it was evident he had been delivering poultry.

"Are you certain?" Miss Tolerance was insistent. "I am positive they said—Oh, dear. Are you certain that isn't number 11? Where the Pontroys live?" She permitted her voice to tremble a little.

The poulterer regarded her with an expression of exasperation and dismay. "H'aint no Pontroys live there, miss. Naow, you'll escuse me?" He hefted the cage and started up the stairs.

"Well, who does live here?"

"Family name of Hampton," the man said.

"Hampton? No, that's not right. Well, what of this one?" She pointed to the gray stone house. "Is that where the Pontroys live?"

"That's Lord Lyne's 'ouse, miss. No Pontroys there, neither."

"But I don't want Lord Lyne. I was told specifically—" Miss Tolerance's pitch climbed. "They told me number 11,

Mrs. Pontr—and that's not even number 11, you stupid man! Whatever shall I do?" Miss Tolerance turned her back on the poulterer and stalked off toward St. James's Square, muttering unhappily.

When she turned the corner she tucked the scrap of paper into her reticule, called a chair, and gave the direction of Tarsio's.

The Library at Tarsio's Club was a small room generally reserved for the use of the club's male subscribers. Women were permitted in the library only if a porter was sent beforehand to ascertain that feminine presence would not perturb the men dozing there over the newspapers.

Miss Tolerance, mindful of these rules, arrived at the club and at once enlisted Corton as her advance guard.

"I only need to look at a book for a few minutes, then I shall take myself back to the Ladies' Salon," she promised.

After this anxious preparation it was a disappointment that there were no men in the Library whom Miss Tolerance could inconvenience with her female self. She went at once to the Peerage, a thick, important looking tome bound in gilded calf, which rested on its own stand but, by the evidence of a slight rime of dust, was not much consulted by Tarsio's members. Miss Tolerance paged through until she found the entry she sought.

Lyne of Wandfield

Charles Loudon Thorpe, Third Baron, b. June 12, 1758, Wandfield, Warwickshire, m. September 12, 1781 Henrietta Mallon, daughter Sir Peter Mallon (d) and Anne Crossways of Warwick. Issue: Henry Mallon Thorpe, b. 1782; John David Thorpe, b. 1784; Clarissa Adele, b. 1787; and Evadne Henrietta, b. 1795. Principal residence Whiston Hall, Wandfield, Warwickshire.

There was more regarding the family's history; the book was also a decade old, and did not mention the husband to which "Mrs. Brown" had referred, but it was quite sufficient for Miss Tolerance's purposes. Blessing the fondness of her countrymen for setting down such information usefully where a working woman could find it, Miss Tolerance copied the entry, made her way downstairs, and desired Steen to call her a hackney carriage to Savoy Court. She intended to call upon an expert of her acquaintance, to see what she could learn about the family of Evadne Henrietta Thorpe.

The Liberty of Savoy has been since the days of Henry III a harbor from arrest for debtors and Sunday-men of all sorts. Here can be seen gentlemen whose silver buttons, pocket watches and handkerchiefs have lately been pawned to pay for dinner, drink, or another round of play; businessmen hoping to stay ruin by borrowing at calamitous interest; ladies picking their way through the muck to find a sympathetic cents-per-cent with an open purse; and, always, poor men on the lookout for the Bailiff's staff. The air in the Liberty of Savoy might smell of ordure, sweat, mold, and coal dust, like many other London neighborhoods, but the underlying reek was of desperation.

Mr. Boddick, the tapster at the Wheat Sheaf, was drawing off a pint. On observing Miss Tolerance he nodded cordially, delivered the ale to its purchaser, and inquired what her pleasure might be.

"Good afternoon, Mr. Boddick. How do you do? And Mrs. Boddick? Is Mr. Glebb very busy?" She looked toward the corner nearest the fire, where an elderly man wearing blue broadcloth and a clean, highly starched shirt was in close conversation with an anxious fellow in smock and gartered sleeves.

"There's two or three already waiting for 'im, miss. Will you take something?"

Miss Tolerance slid a coin across the bar, ordered coffee for herself and, as was her custom, urged Boddick to draw a pint of something for himself. The tapster nodded his thanks, served Miss Tolerance, then drew off a pint of bitter and drank a long gulp with every evidence of pleasure.

"The weather is turning warm," Miss Tolerance observed.

"'Tis that, miss. What brings you 'ere today?"

"The search for understanding, Mr. Boddick. A consultation with Mr. Glebb seemed the place to start." Miss Tolerance drank a little of her coffee and looked around the room. In one corner near the fireplace Mr. Joshua Glebb held court over a crowd of five or six people. The rest of the room was near empty; she did observe a man sitting on a stool at the far end of the bar by the hearth, in an attitude which suggested that he was not a patron but a member of the establishment. The man's singular aspect of misery drew Miss Tolerance's eye; he was pale, unshaven and, despite the fire burning nearby, shivering.

Mr. Boddick's gaze followed Miss Tolerance's. "My brother Bob. Used to be an Army man 'til his lot got sent to Walcheren with Chatham's force that took the fever."

Miss Tolerance regarded the unhappy Bob with sympathy. The British assault upon Napoleon's naval forces in the low-lands of Holland in 1809 had been turned back, not by force but by a virulent malaria which had killed more than four thousand men outright, and invalided twice that number.

"Bob was sent 'ome to us; sixpence-a-day pension, and 'e's a good worker when 'e's well. But when the fever's on 'im, ain't much 'e can do but sit as you see 'im."

"I am sorry to hear it. Is there no help for him?"

"Quinina—that's what the Spaniards call it—stops the shakin' and the fever. Peruvian bark, that is. But it's 'ard to get and dear when you find it. Damned Frenchies run up the price by attacking merchant ships. Now if the Crown was doing what they ought—"

For the next quarter hour Mr. Boddick maintained a monologue highly critical of the Government's pursuit of the Peninsular War. Boddick was a whole-hearted Tory, while Miss Tolerance's sympathies partook more of the Opposition line, but both maintained a keen interest in the progress of the war. Mr. Boddick, like his brother a veteran, was vehemently anti-Bonaparte; it was one issue upon which he and Miss Tolerance, who had lived under the Corsican's rule, were wholly in sympathy. Poor Brother Bob, withdrawn and shuddering at the end of the bar, offered no opinions.

When they had disposed of the war, Walcheren, and the politics of the commission investigating that debacle, they returned again to the weather, thence to the price of corn, which looked to return them to the subject of politics again. But Boddick looked back to Mr. Glebb's table. "Ah, seems 'e's free now, miss. A pleasure talkin' with you, as always."

Miss Tolerance wished him a good day and carried her coffee off to Mr. Glebb's table.

Joshua Glebb's head, bald, with a long fringe of yellowed hair circling the back, shone in the dusty light from the far window. His entire being appeared to be in the process of succumbing slowly to gravity; his mouth turned down, and his chin, shoulders and gut all looked to be making a slow progress downward until they would puddle around his boot-soles. Until that should happen, Mr. Glebb resembled a fussy and dyspeptic head clerk, respectably dressed and sour of expression. His mouth attained—not a smile, but an absence of frown—when he looked up at Miss Tolerance, and his shrewd eyes lit.

"You'll forgive me if I don't rise, miss. My bones is giving me some trouble today."

"You must not stand upon ceremony with me, Mr. Glebb." Miss Tolerance took a seat opposite him. "I have come, as usual, to ask questions."

"Well, asking's free. It's answers cost the ready." Glebb looked into his coffee pot, found it empty, and gestured to Boddick. "Answers is what I have."

Mr. Glebb did a brisk trade in information of a specific sort: he had ties to virtually every money lender in the city, from respectable banks to the meanest sharks, and to the pawnshops and fences as well. Mr. Glebb was a sort of financial matchmaker, putting those in need of money together with those of a lending disposition—for a fee. He loaned no money, but he knew everyone who did. Miss Tolerance had always found him to be reliable, if somewhat tainted by cynicism. She opened her pocket book and withdrew several coins.

"I shall get straight to the matter. What can you tell me of Lord Lyne?"

Mr. Glebb pursed his lips together in a soundless whistle. "Flying high, are we?"

"Oh, I mix in the best society."

"Well, they ain't the best if they ain't beforehand with the world," Mr. Glebb advised.

"Do I understand that to mean that my lord is deep in debt?"

Glebb shook his head. "Just speaking in a general way, miss. Lyne—" Mr. Glebb put his finger to the side of his nose as if that constituted an aid to memory. A drop of clear fluid hanging there trembled but did not drop. "Banks with Coutts and with Hammersely. Man of property and business, as I recall it."

"And what sort of business would that be?" Miss Tolerance asked.

Glebb shrugged. "New World trade, I think. And the usual sorts of property here at home as well. I can find out more particulars if you're desirous of it. There's something else, something in the last few years, but I can't call it to mind. Tomorrow I can get you a full accounting."

"'Tis why I come to you, sir."

"A full dow-see-hay for you on the morrow." Glebb mangled the French with relish. "This a new customer? No, no, I know you won't tell me so." Boddick arrived at that moment with a fresh pot of coffee. "Thankee, Boddick." Glebb nodded but did not look up at the tapster. "D'you come back, miss. I'll have something for you."

Miss Tolerance rose. "Thank you, Mr. Glebb. May I ask one more favor of you? Would you ask about to learn if this young woman—" she took the portrait from her reticule and showed it to him—"pawned anything here in

London in the last fortnight?"

"*Anything?*" Glebb blew his nose. "That's a mighty broad question. You don't know what she'd be a-pawnin' of?"

"Something of the sort that a young woman of good family might have to hand."

"I take your meaning, miss. Gee-gaws and prinkery. I'll ask about. Might I know the lady's name?"

Miss Tolerance shook her head. "That I cannot tell you, Mr. Glebb."

Again Glebb shrugged. "Half of them that gives a name gives a lie anyway."

"You have seen what the girl looks like and you may imagine what might be available to her to pawn. If the lack of her name makes the task more difficult, console yourself with the sum you can command of me when the job is done." She slid a half-crown across the table. "Shall I leave this on account, to be going on with?"

Glebb nodded. "That'll do for a start." He regarded the coin with fondness before he deposited it in his waistcoat pocket. "Good afternoon, Miss Tolerance."

"Good afternoon, sir." Miss Tolerance curtseyed and departed, nodding farewell to Boddick as she went.

She walked back to Henry Street, enjoying the fine day and the sight of her fellow citizens about their business. On her return to Tarsio's she ordered tea and went up to the Ladies' Salon; she had promised her client a report and meant to write it now.

It proved a more difficult note than she had anticipated. Miss Tolerance had not been idle, but she had not been particularly successful, either, and she was certain that a long list of the inns at which Evadne Thorpe had *not* been seen would not allay Mrs. Brown's anxieties. At last Miss Tolerance began to write, framing her note in terms of what the lack of news told her about Miss Thorpe's whereabouts.

Unless Miss E and her companion have been more than usually sly, I believe that they must still be in London. No one at any of the coaching inns I have approached has seen any sight of her; and whilst they might have traveled from the city by post, such travel is expensive. As I have not been able to determine any information about the gentleman, I do not know what his finances are and thus how likely post travel might be. It would be very helpful if you could tell me

Here Miss Tolerance paused and sipped at her tea. She had been about to ask if any of the sister's jewelry was missing, but would that mean the girl had taken it with her, or that it had been pawned over a period of time to finance the elopement? The latter argued a degree of fixed purpose (or moral laxity) which seemed at odds with Mrs. Brown's description of her sister.

"Beg your pardon, Miss Tolerance."

Miss Tolerance looked up. Corton, the hall porter, was offering an envelope on a tray.

"This just come for you, and I was sure you'd be wishing to have it."

In fact she was grateful for the distraction from her own writing. Miss Tolerance thanked Corton, took the letter, and tore it open. It was written in a clear, bold hand.

Dear Miss Tolerance:

It is imperative that I speak to you. Please call this afternoon at Number 7, Duke of York Street. I shall await your visit eagerly.

CB

Miss Tolerance read the letter twice, folded it, put it in her reticule, and finished her tea. This was curious: by summoning her to her father's house Mrs. Brown was giving up that anonymity which had been so crucial a few days before. Miss Tolerance could only conjecture what this meant. Had more information had turned up regarding Miss Thorpe's seducer? Perhaps Lord Lyne had thought better of his harsh stance regarding his daughter. She looked again at the note; it was rather more abrupt in tone than she would have expected from Mrs. Brown, such suggested some excitement of mind. Might the girl have returned on her own? Had there been some new development? Miss Tolerance put on her gloves; the only way to know was to call upon Mrs. Brown.

At the corner of Duke of York Street Miss Tolerance saw Bart and his fellows still at the corner; several of the boys were tussling, but one of them stood with an air of abstraction, ignoring his fellows and ostentatiously not staring at the Lyne house. Pleased, she put her hand to the brass knocker.

The door was opened at once. Miss Tolerance was ushered in by a servant in black broadcloth; sensitive to the ways in which upper servants assess a household's visitors, she was pleased that, after observing her walking dress, hat, and boots, the footman appeared to find them and their wearer acceptable. The man took Miss Tolerance's name and left her to wait, briefly, by the door. The house was pleasantly warm and smelled of beeswax and verbena. Miss Tolerance was admiring a cluster of nautical prints when the footman returned.

Whatever had transpired in his few moments away, the man now looked unsure of himself, or perhaps of his visitor. Even his voice, as he bid her follow him, was uncertain. Miss Tolerance put herself on guard and followed the man up the stairs. On the first floor he guided her along the hall, opened a door, and departed with speed. Miss Tolerance, as much forearmed as she could be, entered.

The room was gloomy. Miss Tolerance made out green walls, brown sofa and chairs, a case of books bound in brown and green leather, and more of the nautical prints she had seen downstairs. Spread out upon a large table was a map of the continent, held at the corners with books. There was a good fire in the grate and a branch of candles on a well-ordered desk, but no natural light. A man stood facing the fire. Despite the warmth of the day his hands were stretched out as if to warm them.

"Come in." He spoke to the fire. "Do not stand there all day."

"I beg your pardon," Miss Tolerance advanced a little further into the room. "I was looking for Mrs. Brown."

"Hah. Is that what she called herself? Yes, I know who you're looking for." The speaker turned. He was an older man of middle height, his sparse light hair combed forward over a high forehead, his eyebrows thick. He wore gold-rimmed spectacles pushed well up on his nose; the eyes behind them were cold. "I know all about it."

"I am happy to hear it, sir." Miss Tolerance curtsied. "Perhaps you will have the goodness to explain to me. Have I the honor to address Lord Lyne?"

The man gave a bark of laughter. "You know that, d'you? My daughter thinks she has been very clever, but I see you know all about her."

"Hardly that, sir. But you cannot expect me to enter a house unknown to me without a little inquiry into its owner." Miss Tolerance kept her tone mild. "My lord, if I was summoned here by your daughter—"

"You were not," the man snapped. "I wrote that letter, bid you come so I could tell you to your face to cease your interference in my household."

"Ah, I see." Miss Tolerance kept her tone neutral. "Does Mrs. Brown know that you have done so?"

"Why should I tell her? I am telling you. Hi, there!" Lyne craned his neck to look past Miss Tolerance. "You, sir. Come tell this—woman—that your wife don't require her services."

Miss Tolerance heard footfall behind her and turned to see in the doorway a prosperous looking gentleman of perhaps thirty years. He was dressed well but without pretension to high fashion; his hair was cropped, but not too close, his neckcloth and shirt points were of moderate height, and the buttons on his coat were no more than an inch in diameter. He was a little taller than average, of unremarkable build—in fact, there was nothing particularly remarkable about the man at all. He might have been a prosperous squire from any county in the nation.

Miss Tolerance took a sharp breath. The unremarkable man was known to her; his name was Adam Brereton, and he was her brother.

Chapter Five

Miss Tolerance was so surprised that she neither spoke nor heard what her host was saying. As she watched him, Sir Adam entered, closed the door behind him, and stood before it with arms crossed, as if to bar the way. He did not regard her with any surprise or recognition; either he had known before she arrived that Sarah Tolerance was Sarah Brereton, or he did not recognize her at all. Should she reveal herself? Not here and now, certainly—she doubted that Sir Adam would want his ruined sister to declare their relation before Lord Lyne, who was—his father-at-law?

Lyne, turned back to the fire, was speaking.

"I beg your pardon?" She turned back to him. "I am afraid—I did not hear what you said."

"What part did you not hear?"

"I apologize, my lord, but I must ask you to repeat the whole of what you said. I beg you will forgive a moment's inattention; it is rather close in this room." There, let him think the heat had her close to swooning.

"I said that you were to cease insinuating yourself into my household affairs," Lyne said.

"Yes, sir. So you did." Miss Tolerance could feel her brother watching. Resolutely she put the thought of him from her mind and concentrated on Lord Lyne. "What I do not understand is the reason for it. Has Miss Thorpe been found? Is there dissatisfaction with my work? I have not had much time to complete the task I—"

"If I say you are to stop, you baggage—" Lyne looked at her over his shoulder; his thick brows were drawn down in a scowl and his lips were pressed thin. Light glancing off his spectacles hid his eyes.

"My name is Tolerance, Lord Lyne."

"I know that!" the man barked. "D'you think I do not know that?" He turned away from the fire and, without inviting her to sit, took a chair himself. Miss Tolerance knew well that no great courtesy was due to her as a Fallen Woman, but she believed the baron's rudeness licensed some brusqueness on her part.

"That you are angry, sir, does not authorize you to speak to me as if I were a fishmonger's drab."

Lyne's eyebrows raised a fraction. His mouth moved, as if it were seeking something devastating to say.

"You have taken it upon yourself to go hunting for the girl," he said at last.

"Taken it upon myself, sir? No. I am a businesswoman, I cannot afford to go seeking runaway girls unless I am hired to do so." She turned to include Sir Adam Brereton and recognized his expression from their childhood: he believed that there was trouble, that he might be in for his share of it, and that he might be able to lay the whole of it off upon her. As for the source of the trouble, his eyes kept returning to Lyne. He had not recognized her. "Surely your—wife? Lady Brereton must have told you as much."

"Lady Brereton has no authority in this matter," Lyne said flatly.

Miss Tolerance gave no sign of her anger; half a dozen years in business had taught her to maintain the illusion of composure. But she took a seat, all uninvited, and smiled pleasantly.

"My dear sir, if you have washed your hands of your younger daughter's fate, it becomes a matter for any other person who has the kindness to concern himself. Or herself. I take it as a mark of good principles that Lady Brereton intends her sister not be left to the mercies of the city."

"The girl has cut herself off from her family and from respectable society."

"Your daughter might have been too young or innocent to understand what that means, sir, but you and I are not. Should that innocence and youth be rewarded with heartbreak, poverty, disease, starvation, the lowest kind of whoredom?"

"All she need to have done, to avoid those things, was to stay in my house," Lyne snapped.

Sir Adam intervened. "Come, Miss Tolerance." These were the first words he had spoken in her presence, and she was shocked at how familiar his voice, and the scoffing tone meant to make light of what she said, were to her. "We have no reason to believe that Ev—that the girl will meet any of those things. Her father's wishes must be paramount."

Miss Tolerance was so furious that she was, briefly, unable to speak. That her brother could say such a thing suggested that her own elopement had taught him nothing. Blood first flushed her face, then departed, leaving her pale and cold.

"Have you *any* experience of the matter, sir? Do you have any idea what happens to a gently reared young woman once the stews get hold of her? Would you suffer a young woman of your own family to be so abandoned? If you knew it might mean her death?"

Sir Adam was red-faced, looking from her to Lyne and back again. "Keep a civil tongue! Remember to whom you speak!"

"I know well to whom I speak, Sir Adam. *You* might remember *of* whom I speak," Miss Tolerance said coldly.

"Your wife's sister."

"What would you have my father-at-law do? Bring the girl home and attempt to pass her off at Almack's as whole goods?"

"That is not the only alternative. See that the fellow marries her, and save her reputation and your own. If you fail of that, bring her home and make arrangements for her. Give her some occupation! Let her be of use, if only by handing out liniment and calf's foot jelly in the village. Do not force her away from all the persons who meant safety and home for her." Miss Tolerance's voice shook. This was dangerous ground; far better to return her attention to Lord Lyne, who was watching her with peculiar detachment.

"Perhaps Sir Adam is right, Lord Lyne. Perhaps I paint the matter too black. If your daughter is lucky, she and her lover will live in some kind of domestic situation for a time before he passes her along to another man of similar fortune. She will make a life as a demi-rep until she has no looks to recommend her and then, if she has been thrifty with the presents and jewels that her keepers have bestowed upon her, she will set herself up with her money invested in the Navy Funds and live a quiet, retired life, almost respectably. If she is less lucky her seducer will pass her along to someone who cares nothing but a pretty face, or who may enjoy defiling a woman better born than he—"

"Enough! I hear enough of this from my son. The girl has made her bed—"

"And you require her to occupy it," Miss Tolerance finished. "Does the girl truly stand so low in your regard that you would abandon her to the London stews?"

Sir Adam made a noise of revulsion. Miss Tolerance ignored him and kept her gaze upon Lord Lyne. He stood with his back to the fire, hands in his pockets, warming his backside. He appeared unmoved; Miss Tolerance changed her tack.

"Is it not most likely that what your daughter did was

done upon impulse, with the impetuousness of youth and under powerful persuasion from a man she believed loves her? My lord, she is your child. Surely you do not wish such dire harm to come to her. Let me ascertain that she is alive and well. After that your family may decide—"

Lyne's voice was cold. "The girl dishonored us, without a care to how it would affect her family. She deserves no further attention."

Miss Tolerance felt her own spine stiffen. "So you say, sir. But you are not my client and cannot, therefore, dismiss me. Your elder daughter has hired me, and I will take my direction from her."

"By God, Miss Tolerance, I'll give you your direction!" Sir Adam stepped further into the room. "It is as Lord Lyne says. You are—"

"Sir Adam, you did not hire me either. As I often am employed by wives seeking information about husbands' indiscretions, I have made it my policy that who hires me must dismiss me as well. Else there would be any number of men in London eager to pay me to forget all I have learned of their amours. When Lady Brereton tells me—"

"Lady Brereton has no standing—" Lyne began again.

"I cannot concern myself over-much with matters of standing, my lord."

Lyne left his position by the fire—he favored one leg, Miss Tolerance noted. "Then I shall summon my daughter to attend you," he said. "Wait here."

"As you wish, sir." Miss Tolerance rose and curtsied.

When the older man had left the room, Miss Tolerance sat again and regarded her brother. Better to tell him, she thought. Were he to learn in some other way who she was, would he not likely resent it? It did not seem fair, or safe, to keep him unaware.

"You should not have drawn my wife into this," Sir Adam said into the silence.

Miss Tolerance stared at him. "I beg your pardon?"

"I said—"

"I heard your words. And to the contrary, it was your

wife who drew me in. How fortunate that you married a woman who sees so clearly what her duty to family is."

"Yes, she—" Sir Adam stopped. "What do you mean?"

Miss Tolerance had lost all sympathy for her brother. "Really, Adam," she drawled. "Can you scruple to leave Miss Thorpe to her father's mercies?"

Sir Adam pulled back as if from a snake. "What did you say?"

"I asked if it was necessary to abet Lord Lyne in treating his daughter as our father treated me."

Sir Adam stepped closer, circled her, staring. As recognition came he leaned away from Miss Tolerance, his eyes large. "Good God!"

"So you might say."

Sir Adam went to the door, closed it, returned and sat heavily in one of the brown chairs, regarding his sister as if she might explode.

"How do you come to be here?" he asked at last.

"I was summoned by your father-at-law."

"That wasn't what I meant. How it is you are—I thought you were in Europe, or dead!"

"The two being very like each other?" Miss Tolerance sat. "I was in Europe for eight years, Adam. When Connell died, I returned to London."

"He died? Did he marry you?"

"Would that somehow make his death more acceptable? No, Connell and I could never settle how to wed—he wanted a Roman ceremony, I a Protestant one. And we were first in France and then in Belgium, which complicated matters even more."

"You're mighty casual about it, Sally!"

"Not in the least. But I have had many years to devise an answer to those who have no business asking in the first place."

"No business?" Sir Adam appeared to think better of debating that point. He looked at his sister with amazement. "But why are you here?"

"Your father-at-law wrote a note," she said again. "And

as I believe I hear him returning to continue his rebuke, perhaps you will wish to continue this discussion at another time?"

Indeed, the sound of Lord Lyne's voice, audible but indecipherable, came from the hall. Sir Adam rose and signed Miss Tolerance to hush. Lyne returned to the room.

"My daughter is coming."

"Thank you, sir. Before she arrives, I wonder if I might make one more point with you?"

"You will not change my mind," Lyne said.

"I did not think I would. But I will set my own mind at ease that I have done my best. You feel that your daughter's elopement has left you vulnerable to disgrace. Would not it be in your own best interest to know her situation? As matters stand you can have no idea how Miss Thorpe's disgrace might come back to haunt you or your family. If you provided for the girl and were thus able to know where she was, there would be less likelihood, when your sons come to be married, that this old scandal would surface again."

She heard a muffled sound from Sir Adam but kept her eyes trained upon Lyne.

The baron pursed his lips. "I am prepared to take that chance, Miss Tolerance."

"Would not your wife prefer to know if the girl lives?"

"My wife, I am thankful to say, did not live to see her daughter disgrace the family. I would ask why you are so hot upon the subject, but of course, if we let you continue your inquiries, you get your fee whether we take the girl back or no."

Miss Tolerance rose to her feet. "My lord, it is no secret that I am Fallen. If I am hot upon the subject it is because I know as well as any person living what your daughter has lost by her actions. I will point out again that you are not my client." She turned to Sir Adam. "Nor are you, sir. Lady Brereton has engaged me, and I will answer to her. She strikes me as a woman of common sense and feeling. If she wishes to abandon her sister I shall listen to her."

"So you shall. Here is my daughter."

Lady Brereton had appeared at the door, followed by the footman in black who had admitted Miss Tolerance to the house. The man was not holding Lady Brereton's arm, but his manner suggested that he would block an attempt to escape, and he kept his eyes upon Lord Lyne as if hoping for instruction. Behind the servant another man came who seemed by his languid movement to be strolling in at the end of a parade. He was a little more than medium height, rumpled and unshaved, a few years Lady Brereton's senior; given his remarkable resemblance to Lord Lyne, Miss Tolerance took him to be one of Lady Brereton's brothers. From his air of curious unconcern, it did not appear that he was there to support his father.

Lord Lyne dismissed the servant. As the door shut behind the man, "Well, Papa, what's to do?" Mr. Thorpe flicked an imaginary mote from his cuff.

"You may stay, but keep quiet," Lyne snapped. He had not expected this addition to the party, Miss Tolerance thought.

"Please, Henry," Lady Brereton echoed. She extended a hand to her brother as if to warn him away. Instead the man raised it to his lips; Miss Tolerance thought she had rarely seen the gesture made so satirically.

Lady Brereton took her hand back and stepped further into the room. She wore pale pink muslin with embroidered roses, and looked demure and fragile until one noted the expression in her eyes. At their first meeting Miss Tolerance had been impressed by the sweetness of Lady Brereton's countenance. Today what was remarkable was the mixture of apprehension and anger. She looked at her father, then back to Mr. Thorpe, and finally to Sir Adam, as if waiting for support to come from some quarter. At last she turned to Miss Tolerance.

"Good afternoon, Miss Tolerance. You know me as Mrs. Brown, but my real name, as these gentlemen will have informed you, is Brereton."

Miss Tolerance curtsied. "They have, Lady Brereton.

Good afternoon. Would you prefer to have this conversation in private?"

"She does not require privacy for what she is to do," Lord Lyne said.

"Is that not for her to say, my lord? Your daughter is of age and a married woman, and I believe she can answer for herself. Lady Brereton?"

Sir Adam made a strangled sound and looked from his father-at-law to his wife. Lady Brereton forestalled his attempt to speak.

"My father is correct, Miss Tolerance." She took a few more steps into the room and nodded at her father. Miss Tolerance thought, from the anger in her eyes, that she was about to receive another scolding. "I do not need to be private to say what I must say."

Lyne gave a satisfied snort.

"I am very sorry to have drawn you into our misfortunes, Miss Tolerance." Lady Brereton took a breath that squared her shoulders and removed any suggestion of fragility in her bearing. "I should not have done so, but that the persons most responsible for my sister's welfare have defaulted of that charge."

Lord Lyne took a step from the fireplace. Sir Adam's mouth gaped.

"As to your employment, I regret that my father wishes me to dismiss you from your search. For myself," Lady Brereton stuck her chin out. "For myself, I am more determined than ever that you should locate my sister so that I may help her out of any distress in which she finds herself."

Bedlam ensued.

Lord Lyne spun on his heel and retreated to the fire, shouting "Damn you, sir, control your wife!"

Sir Adam, to whom this was addressed, stood between wife and father-at-law, turning first one way then the other with an expression of panic Miss Tolerance recalled from her childhood. And Henry Thorpe observed the chaos with as much satisfaction as if he had created it himself, first laughing, then clutching his head, as if merriment was painful.

At the center of this riot Lady Brereton stood, her back straight and her lips set. Despite this show of resolution,she appeared stunned by the effect of her rebellion.

"You will continue?" The lady said, low, to Miss Tolerance..

"It will be my greatest pleasure, ma'am. I congratulate you on your firmness of mind."

Sir Adam joined his wife, interposing himself between her and his sister. He turned to glare at Miss Tolerance as if she was responsible for the ado, but when Lord Lyne again told him to control his wife or *he* would, Sir Adam reminded him that Lady Brereton was no longer under his rule.

"Well, she's damned well under my roof, and I tell you again, sir, to get control of her or—"

"We shall go to Claridges, then," Sir Adam snapped. "If you wish to lose both your daughters."

Lyne turned without replying and left the room.

Well done, Adam, Miss Tolerance thought. Aloud she asked Lady Brereton, "Will you be all right?"

Lady Brereton nodded and looked at her husband, in whose arms she sheltered from her father's wrath.

Mr. Thorpe had recovered from his mirth and joined Lady Brereton. He had the red eyes and pinched brow of a man who had drunk deep the night before. Miss Tolerance wondered if he had only just returned home. "The old man will make you pay for that, Clary," he said. He turned his attention to Miss Tolerance. "And who is this? Your hatmaker come to dun you?"

Lady Brereton frowned at her brother. "What a fright you are, Henry. You have not been home since dinner, have you?" She fussed with his collar. "And you're talking of things you don't understand. Miss Tolerance? Please permit me to introduce you to my brother, Henry Thorpe. Henry, this is Miss Tolerance, whom I have hired to find Evie."

Miss Tolerance curtsied. Thorpe did not return the courtesy, but looked her up and down as if she had been a horse on display at Tattersall's auctions. His decision about what civility was due her was evident in his expression. He turned to Lady Brereton.

"Is that your notion, Clary? Set a whore to catch a whore?"

Lady Brereton brought her hand up and boxed her brother's ear with force.

Miss Tolerance decided it was time to step in. "Do you know something about your sister's whereabouts, Mr. Thorpe, that you would give her such a character?"

Sir Adam, who had been shocked into silence when his wife slapped Thorpe, cleared his throat. His face was red. "This is Evie, man. As m-m-Miss Tolerance says—"

Thorpe ran a thumb along his jaw where his sister's blow had landed. "How do you intend to find my sister?"

"By asking questions, Mr. Thorpe. 'Tis a job to which I am far better suited than whoring. I do not suppose you have any idea of the identity of her seducer?"

"No, how should I? The girl did not confide in me."

"You have no friends who admired her?"

A look of revulsion passed across Thorpe's face. "My crowd? God forefend. I thought the chit had run off to Gretna—"

"There is no sign of it," Miss Tolerance told him. "She has not been seen in any of the inns that handle northern coaching routes. Is it so unlikely that Miss Thorpe might have met one of your crowd when he was visiting—"

Thorpe snorted. "I play with the Corinthian set, gamblers and drunkards and whore-masters. Precisely the sort my father would welcome into his house."

"Then your sister could never have met any of these upright persons?"

"*Never?* London society is a small world, Miss…Acceptance. Evie might have met anyone. But I don't think it likely; respectable girls are hedged round with maids and governesses. Who'd make such effort?" He turned to Lady

77

Brereton. "Spend your silver as you like, Clary, but I don't see how anyone will be able to turn the girl up until she wants to be found." He nodded at Sir Adam and, without further acknowledgement of the women, strode to the door. There he turned to give a warning. "My sister will not tell you so, Miss *Lenience*, but hiding in her skirts won't keep you harmless if you cross my father."

Too late to worry about that.

Mr. Thorpe left. Lady Brereton hastened to apologize for her brother again. "He has had no sleep, I think. He would never speak so otherwise."

Miss Tolerance wondered if the idea that one of his friends could be involved in Evadne Thorpe's disappearance had struck Henry Thorpe too close. That was not something she could discuss with Lady Brereton until she had learned more. "Lady Brereton, shall I continue to leave my reports to you at Tarsio's, or here, or somewhere else?"

"Oh. I had not—Tarsio's is still best, I think. I cannot be certain that anything you leave for me here will reach me."

"Given your father's opinion of the matter," Miss Tolerance agreed. "Now, before I take my leave of you, I have several questions to ask to speed our inquiry."

Lady Brereton took a seat on the sofa and invited Miss Tolerance to sit as well. Sir Adam went round to stand behind his wife, his arms crossed and his expression closed.

"First, ma'am, is there any way I might interview the servants of this house? Not here, of course—I can imagine your father's reaction. But elsewhere? You need not answer now, but consider, please. Next: can you—or you, Sir Adam—think of any man who might have fixed his interest with Miss Thorpe? I was quite serious in asking Mr. Thorpe the same question. What about you, Sir Adam?"

"Me? Good God, no, I barely saw the girl."

"I will think harder," Lady Brereton promised.

"Thank you: a list of men who were regular callers here would be helpful. And can you tell me if Miss Thorpe took anything with her? In particular, jewelry she might have sold? To finance an elopement?"

"I will find out."

"Had your sister any particular friends in whom she might have confided?"

"Not in London, no. In Warwickshire there was—" Lady Brereton frowned thoughtfully. "She was friends with Anne Harlow, I know. And the Ball sisters. Perhaps some of the Lutonage girls?"

Miss Tolerance, sensing that the discussion could devolve into a catalogue of all the young women in Warwickshire, suggested that Lady Brereton might send her a note at Tarsio's. "Lastly, do you have the direction of your sister's governess?"

"Father dismissed her almost at once. I don't know where Miss Nottingale would have gone—I should have asked, I know, but we were all so upset."

Sir Adam surprised his wife and sister. "She has a brother who's a parson somewhere in the east of London." He ducked his head, looking abashed. "John'd likely know. I came looking for the paper one day and found John asking Miss Nottingale about poor relief at her brother's church."

Lady Brereton regarded her husband with delight. Miss Tolerance found herself a little shocked that her brother could be the target of such uncomplicated affection. "How clever of you to remember, Adam! Miss Tolerance, my brother John is studying to take orders; most days you will find him working in Pitfield Street at the almshouse there. I know he will tell you how to reach Miss Nottingale; he feels just as I do that Evie must be found. Now, shall I ask my husband to escort you home, Miss Tolerance? I know you are quite independent, but it is a very pleasant thing to have a masculine arm to lean upon."

Miss Tolerance expected that her brother would revolt against the suggestion. Instead he agreed at once, and, when Miss Tolerance attempted to demur, told her he quite insisted.

Feeling as though she had stumbled from farce into

comic nightmare, Miss Tolerance curtsied, took her leave, and left Lord Lyne's house on her brother's arm.

"This is all very well, but you don't think you can find the girl, do you?" Sir Adam asked as he hurried Miss Tolerance up the street.

"Adam, if you do not wish to walk with me you have my permission to return home. Otherwise please do not push me through the streets as if I were a wheelbarrow. I do not know if I can find Miss Thorpe, but I shall certainly try."

"What you were doing before—talking to us, asking questions. Is that what you do?"

"In the main, yes. I ask questions and consider the answers. I have been an agent of inquiry for several years. It suits my talents."

"Talents." He was dubious.

"Talents." Miss Tolerance was firm. "I always liked to puzzle things out. Did I not know when you had been rusticated from Cambridge before you told Father?"

"You never said anything to him, did you, Sally?"

It had been years since Miss Tolerance had been called so. Hearing it twice in an hour recalled to her how much she disliked it. "Discretion is another of my talents."

"But how did you come to *this?*" Sir Adam spread his hands as if to indicate London and investigation in equal measure.

"Connell and I taught fence in Holland, but when he died I could not continue to do so. I had to find some way to keep myself. Despite our father's predictions, I have no taste for whoredom. So I came up with a different employment for myself."

"But why here, in England? How could you?"

Miss Tolerance deliberately misunderstood. "I took passage on a corvette from Le Havre, and the mail coach thence. I would doubtless have been more comfortable on a private yacht and in a chaise and six, but as I spent most of my money burying Connell and bribing the dock officials, I made shift as best I could. Our aunt took me in—"

"What aunt?"

"Papa's sister Dorothea. The mistress of the house of joy in Manchester Square? Surely Father warned you about her, the Black Ewe of her generation! From what Aunt Thea says, Father studied to cast me off by watching how Grandfather behaved on the occasion of her fall. Whatever her sins, Aunt Thea acted more familial to me than you or my father ever did. You will be happy to know, Adam, that she disapproves of my career as much as you do." Miss Tolerance smiled. "Aunt Thea believes I would be better off as a whore, with the promise of inheriting the business from her some day."

The look of horror on Sir Adam's face was very rewarding, but it was too easy to tease him. She steered him around a knot of people trying to extract a very fat woman from a carriage and resolved to be more conciliatory.

"When did you marry?" she asked.

"Trafalgar year. You would have been—wherever you were—"

"In 1805? In Amsterdam."

"I was in London for the season, met Lady Brereton—Miss Thorpe, she was—at Almack's."

"My father must have been beside himself with joy. How did you marry so well?"

"How did I—what do you mean? Why should I not marry well?"

"One of the last things Father said to me was that I had ruined your chance of marriage with a respectable woman. Obviously he was pessimistic."

"It made the matter more difficult—I wanted to tell Lyne that you were dead—I was afraid to lose Clarissa. But Father insisted we reveal it all, and Lyne—it was not what he liked, how could he? But in the end, when Father assured him that you were as good as dead—"

"He was comforted?"

Sir Adam was impervious to irony. "Reassured. And he could see that our attachment was very strong."

"Well, I congratulate you, Adam. I like her."

Sir Adam's expression softened. "She is the dearest girl—"

For a moment Miss Tolerance felt only pleasure in her brother's happiness. "I am very glad for you, Adam." She patted his arm.

This moment of genuine family feeling seemed to be all Sir Adam could tolerate. He hurried them across the street.

"Why *aren't* you dead?" he asked. "And Connell, how did he die? In the war?"

"Nothing so romantic. He had a feverish cold that went to his chest. It killed him. And I lived." Miss Tolerance had no intention of edifying her brother with the grief and difficulty that had surrounded her return to England.

"And you are here."

"I am. And I had as well tell you, Adam, that I intend to help your sister-at-law if I can."

"Yes, I see that," Sir Adam agreed. "Lyne is not a cruel man, Sally."

"Nor was our father a cruel man. But men who are not cruel can yet do cruel things. And stupid things. Look, we are nearly to Manchester Square and my aunt's house. I shall not trouble you to walk me further."

"Sally—" Sir Adam put his hand on Miss Tolerance's and would not let her leave him. "You must promise me. You cannot tell. My wife is not like you. She has been sheltered, she is—what's the word?"

"Fastidious?" Miss Tolerance did not think that Lady Brereton was so easily shocked as her husband believed, but he was very anxious. She took pity on him.

"Did I not say that discretion is one of my talents, Adam? What possible purpose would it serve for me to tell anyone of our relation?"

"You must promise," Sir Adam urged.

"I will say nothing to your wife or her family. No one who does not now know we are related will have any word of it from me."

Sir Adam released his sister's arm. "Thank you. And you think Evie must be in London?"

A little startled by the shift in topic, Miss Tolerance nodded. "Well, as what I have so far learnt suggests that she is in the city, I choose to focus my investigation here."

"You choose?"

"In my profession, Sir Adam, one frequently has recourse to instinct, and my instinct is that Miss Thorpe is still in London."

"Oh, well, then." Sir Adam bowed over Miss Tolerance's hand. She was left with the impression that he had no particular faith in her instinct, but that as he would find his life very much easier if she should fail to find Miss Thorpe at all, it did not trouble him.

Chapter Six

It is not to be supposed that an unexpected reunion with her brother left Miss Tolerance unmoved. However, she had work to do. She turned south to Wigmore Street, hailed a hackney coach, and gave orders for Pitfield Street, where she hoped to find Mr. John Thorpe. As the carriage moved through the congested streets, she considered if her interview at Lord Lyne's house had added to her investigation. She had already satisfied herself as to Evadne Thorpe's identity. She had met Lord Lyne and Mr. Henry Thorpe; Lyne she discounted, as he would do nothing to assist in her investigation. But Henry Thorpe interested her: a dissolute brother with unsavory friends was worth at least a second glance.

Miss Tolerance thought it unlikely that Lady Brereton could arrange for her to interview the servants in Lord Lyne's house, and yet that was her chiefest desire. Butlers and housemaids have useful opinions of their employers' families, and the most reliable intelligence regarding their movements. The governess Miss Nottingale might have an idea of Evadne Thorpe's admirer, but the man who opened the door and delivered a note upon a tray, or the maid who laced the girl into her gown and listened to her chatter, was likely to be more broadly informed. She must hope that Mr. John Thorpe would have something useful to add beyond the governess's direction.

When the carriage arrived in Pitfield Street Miss Tolerance stepped down, ready to take her inquiry where she could. It was a sullen, dreary neighborhood; to her left a crowd of grimy, tired men waited on the step of a gin-shop; there was not enough room for them all inside. Before her she saw a second-hand clothes shop and a pie cook and a cobbler. Most of the other buildings were blank-faced tenements. A ruddy, elderly woman in several layers of ragged clothing scurried by. From the corner of her eye Miss Tolerance saw a movement; almost without thought she seized the gnarled paw which had fastened itself around her reticule.

"Let go," Miss Tolerance said firmly.

The old woman's eyes rolled, showing a dramatic amount of white. Her face was weathered, the nose heavily veined. "What, miss? Don' 'urt me, miss, leggo, do!"

"Certainly, as soon as you let go of my bag." Miss Tolerance tightened her grip on the crone's wrist.

"I dunno whotcher talkin' about," the old woman whined. "You come up and grab me on the street, an—" she tugged again on Miss Tolerance's reticule. Her brazenness was impressive. "Leggo! I wan't doing noffin!"

A small crowd was gathering. Miss Tolerance took a step away from the old woman, holding her wrist at arm's length so that the woman's grasp on the small reticule, hanging from its sash at Miss Tolerance's waist, was revealed to the crowd.

"Giver up, 'Ettie," a man in a butcher's apron said. "The mort ain't stupid." He turned back toward the gin shop. The crowd dispersed, until only a pair of crossing-sweeps were left. With an expression of disgust the old woman released the reticule and pulled her hand out of Miss Tolerance's grasp. She stood for a moment, rubbing her wrist and glaring.

"If you would like to earn some money honestly, tell me where the alms house is." Miss Tolerance was mild.

"'Ow much money?"

"As much as the question is worth. Or I could ask one of these gentlemen—" Miss Tolerance waved her hand at the sweeps who were watching impassively.

"Dahn the street, cross at corner, that big red 'ouse." The old woman pointed one impossibly crooked finger at the alms house; her other hand, palm up, she extended under Miss Tolerance's nose. Her odor was not pleasant. Miss Tolerance put two coppers in the hand; the old woman scuttled off with her prize while the sweeps looked on.

"Good as a pantomime, 'Ettie is," one boy said to his mate.

"Or a 'anging," his friend agreed. The boys walked away, and Miss Tolerance followed Hettie's direction to the brick house on the far corner of the street. It was a cheerless structure, one meant to have a shop on the ground floor and rooms above. A window intended to display the shop's wares had been papered over to provide some privacy within; the only other sign of the place's mission was a small wooden plaque on which was written: *Squale House for the Relief of the Poor.* Who was Squale? Miss Tolerance wondered. She knocked upon the door and waited.

When after several minutes no one had answered, Miss Tolerance tried the door, which opened to her touch. She stepped into a hallway with a series of doors on either side. Candles burned in sconces along the length; generations-worth of greasy soot stained the walls above them. A little girl of perhaps ten years skipped up to Miss Tolerance and examined her frankly.

"You ain't come for bread, 'ave you? You don't look like you come for bread."

Miss Tolerance agreed that she had not.

"You come for work?" The girl looked doubtful.

Miss Tolerance smiled. "Is this your job? To interview visitors?"

"I 'elp Mr. Thorpe and Mr. Parkin," the child said proudly. Her dress, while old and twice turned, was clean and neatly mended, and her face had been washed within recent memory. "I'm their 'ssistant, Mr. Thorpe says so." Mr. Thorpe was clearly a favorite.

"And you are surely a good one. I have come to speak to Mr. Thorpe, in fact."

The child looked distressed. "Oh, no, miss. You can't. 'E ain't available."

"Gone home, has he?"

"No, miss. 'E's up t'stairs 'elpin' Matron pick nits."

"Oh." Miss Tolerance tried to imagine a son of Lord Lyne delousing the poor. "Do you think when he is done you might ask if he will speak to me? I am Miss Tolerance."

The child giggled. "I'll tell 'im." She dashed up the hall; the soles of her boots, displayed as she ran, were more hole than leather.

A few minutes later the girl appeared at the top of the stairs, pointed at Miss Tolerance, and skipped away again. A young man started down the stairs toward Miss Tolerance. He wore a leather apron over waistcoat and shirt-sleeves, and carried a toddler in a grubby shift. His likeness to Evadne Thorpe was in his rounded chin and eyes, although his hair was not golden but a sober brown, and his complexion was pale rather than rosy. As they reached the ground floor the toddler in his arms reached up to grab his nose, so that his words were much compressed.

"How may I help you?"

"Mr. John Thorpe?" He nodded. "May I have a few minutes of speech with you, sir? 'Tis regarding Miss Nottingale."

Thorpe absently pulled the child's hand from his nose. "Miss Nottingale? My sister's governess?"

"Yes, sir. I need to find her. Lady Brereton suggested you would know where she would be."

"Would I? Excuse my manners, Miss Tolerance; please come." Thorpe turned, shifted the child to his other arm, and led the way down the hall. There was a murmur of voices from rooms on either side of the hallway; from one Miss Tolerance heard a woman's voice reciting the alphabet and a man's voice offering correction. Mr. Thorpe entered a large, whitewashed room that held several tables flanked by benches. He put the child on a table and casually kept a hand upon her to keep her from escaping. "May I ask what need you and my sister have of Miss Nottingale? Stay here, Lucy, your mother will be down in a moment," he added to the toddler.

"Mam! Wan Mam!" The child began to whimper. Unflustered, Thorpe took out his pocket watch and held it before her until she left off crying with a hiccup and reached for the watch.

"You have much to do. I shall not keep you long, sir. Lady Brereton has retained me to find your sister—"

"To find Evadne? Do you think there is a chance of it?"

Miss Tolerance did not intend to explain herself to yet another member of this family. "'I hope there is, sir. Lady Brereton thought you might know Miss Nottingale's family—a brother in eastern London?"

"He is the vicar of Saint Hester's in Bethnal Green." Thorpe said. "But Miss Nottingale had nothing to do with—"

"Of course not. But she might know, without being aware of it, some clue which will help me find Miss Thorpe. Did you ever hear your sister speak of a young man, sir?"

The child Lucy stood on the table and grabbed a handful of Mr. Thorpe's neckcloth, crushing the plain-tied knot and leaving a smudge on the cambric. Frowning, Thorpe pushed the child's hand away.

"Stop, Lucy. I beg your pardon, Miss Tolerance." He turned away and called out the open door. "Matron? Is Mrs. Petty done yet?"

Another man appeared in the door. He was considerably

older than Thorpe, but had a youthful aspect with a high, intelligent brow, a sparse combing of brown hair, a long nose and a small, well-shaped mouth. "Matron sent me to tell you she is finished combing out Mrs. Petty's hair and is rinsing it. And to fetch this lady away—" the man reached for the toddler. "Come along, Lucy. You will like to see your mother, eh?"

"Thank you, Godwin. Tell Matron to give them something to eat, will you?" Thorpe turned back to his visitor. "I beg your pardon. May I ask a question? Does my father know of this?" He scratched his head, then dropped his hand as if he had been burnt. "Dear me. Lucy's mother—drunk *and* lousy. It has been an exciting afternoon."

Miss Tolerance was not certain whether to laugh or commiserate. "Your father knows that I am working for Lady Brereton. I cannot tell you that he approves."

Mr. Thorpe looked unhappy. "He and my sister had quarreled; I hope he has regretted his temper. You asked if Evie had an attachment to any young man? None that she ever told me of. My sister was—*is*—not lightminded. I do not mean she is above fun, but I should have said she was...virtuous. That sounds priggish, I suppose. I sound like a prelate when I should sound like a brother. But to run away, even if our father had been unkind to her, does not seem at all her sort of behavior. What will our father do if you find her?"

"He has not offered to do anything. Depending upon her circumstances and the circumstance of the man who— Lady Brereton and her husband have promised to make provision for her." It felt curious to Miss Tolerance to speak of her brother so, to imagine him giving aid to some other Fallen girl.

Thorpe nodded as if to himself. "That is for the best. I wish I could give you more help, Miss Tolerance. My sister never spoke of any man to me."

"And you never saw any callers?"

Mr. Thorpe shook his head. "Since I left the Navy I am barely suffered to visit in my father's house; he hoped I would be another Nelson and I disappointed him. Bad enough that I wished to take orders, but I made matters worse by joining a Dissenting church." He smiled sadly. "I was not in a position to see if anyone was dangling after Evie. But that is not what you came to learn."

"I think you have told me what I needed, Mr. Thorpe. Saint Hester's in Bethnal Green."

"Yes. Nottingale is a good fellow, and kindly does not disapprove of me too much. If Miss Nottingale is not with him he will certainly know—" Thorpe was interrupted by a sudden scream of Cockney outrage from the floor above them.

"You are busy, sir," Miss Tolerance said. "I shall let you return to your work."

"And I you, Miss Tolerance." Thorpe bowed. "I shall pray for your success. And if you find my sister, tell her she may always come to me."

Miss Tolerance curtsied. "I will, Mr. Thorpe. Good bye."

The street outside Squale House was odorous and cold; the sun had dropped below the houses, dusk was drawing in, and the men outside the gin shop were beginning to be merry and racketing. Miss Tolerance had to walk a good way along Old Street, conscious all the time of her vulnerability, alone, unarmed, in women's dress. At last she found a hackney carriage and directed it to Manchester Square. When the carriage arrived there she descended, paid the driver, and unlocked the ivied gate into Mrs. Brereton's garden. A bowl of soup, she thought, and some bread. And then the chance to make some notes.

Marianne Touchwell was standing at her door.

"To what do I owe the honor? Have you no assignations this evening?" Miss Tolerance asked.

"I have, and so have you, if you've forgotten." Mrs. Touchwell wore the preferred working dress of Mrs. Brereton's whores, a simple gown of pale muslin. She had come out without a shawl, and had her arms crossed against the chill. "You are supposed to dine with your aunt tonight. I do not suppose you will ever hear the end of it unless you do so."

"Good lord, you're right. But my dear Marianne, how long have you been waiting here?"

"Only a moment or so; Keefe said he'd heard a carriage stop in the lane, and I hurried over, hoping it was you."

Miss Tolerance had a sense of crisis narrowly averted. "If you will tell my aunt I expect to be with her in a quarter hour? I must change, and—"

"You are not late yet. Let me come do your hair while you dress. I wanted a word."

Miss Tolerance unlocked the door to her cottage and the two women went inside. What followed was a sort of contained whirlwind: Marianne stirred up the fire and put the kettle on for wash water while Miss Tolerance shed her walking dress and took out her dress and slippers for the evening. She washed quickly, grateful for the comfort of warm water, dressed, then sat as Marianne brushed her heavy dark hair.

"What did you wish to talk with me about?"

Marianne parted the hair over Miss Tolerance's ear and brushed the front down over her eyes. "Your aunt, of course."

Miss Tolerance, hidden behind a veil of hair, felt uneasy. "Is something amiss?"

"You know nothing been quite right with her since she was ill last winter."

"She has been more irritable—"

"And mistrustful. Perhaps that's because she's not used to sharing authority in the house; perhaps 'tis my fault in some way." Marianne teased a knot from a lock of hair. "There's none but you and I—and Frost—that would notice the change. At least until this last month or so, and Mr. Gerard Tickenor."

"Mr. Tickenor?" Miss Tolerance recalled. "She introduced me to him the other evening. Are you saying he has become close enough to my aunt to notice a change in her?"

"No, no, you misunderstand. I mean that in the last

month he's suddenly had the run of the house. It's not like Mrs. B. to have favorites."

Miss Tolerance considered. "He was one of her earliest protectors. He loaned her a good deal of money to start this house—"

"So he did. And she repaid it. He's come now and then over the years, at least as long as I've been with your aunt. But in the last month he has been here more nights than not. Your aunt don't generally receive that often—"

"And only among a chosen few, I know. Clearly Mr. Tickenor is one of those."

"Yes, but—Sarah, there's something odd afoot. I heard her telling him—you know how close she holds information, it took her falling sick for her to trust me to order the candles and vinegar—"

"What was my aunt telling Mr. Tickenor?"

Marianne gathered Miss Tolerance's back hair high on her crown, twisted it into a long coil, and secured it with pins. "She was telling him what the house makes on a fair night, against the costs of the business. She said he could look at her ledgers if he did not believe her."

"*Look in her ledgers?*" Miss Tolerance parted the hair over her face to regard her friend. Mrs. Brereton kept her ledgers as close as another woman might have kept her virgin daughters. Only in the last year, and after considerable urging by Miss Tolerance, had Marianne been permitted to view them—"and you'd have thought she was admitting me to the Queen's jewelry cupboard!" she had observed at the time.

"Could it be that she and Mr. Tickenor propose to do some sort of business together?"

"It could." Marianne parted the front hair into half a dozen locks and began to twist them away from Miss Tolerance's face. She secured each with a pin. "But what would that business be? And there is the matter of how she behaves with the man—have you seen her with him?"

"She seemed fond of him. I assumed it was because they were old friends."

"They are. But you know Mrs. B's never been the sort to drape herself about a man, even in the way of business. Even with history between them. This is more, Sarah. I don't know what to make of it. Now—" she twisted the last lock of hair and fixed it in place, then stepped around to view the effect from the front. "This is Mrs. B's s house. She's never made no representations to me that I'd have any part of it—at any time. I don't say any of this to protect a stake of my own, for I haven't one. But if I, or the other whores here, must be on the lookout for new employ—"

Miss Tolerance stared at her friend. "You think my aunt means to close the house?"

"Or sell it to Tickenor." Marianne nodded. She leaned forward, adjusted the placement of a pin and nodded in satisfaction. "Or *give* it to him. I don't know, Sarah. And it is not for me to ask."

"No." Miss Tolerance sighed. "It appears it is for me to ask. Aunt Thea has always wanted me to succeed her here, despite my dislike of the idea. I had as well tell you I expect her to laugh at the notion of her giving up the house."

"We just need to know what's what. Thank you, Sarah."

Miss Tolerance looked in the mirror. "At least you have rendered me presentable. 'Tis always easier to speak to my aunt when she approves of my dress." She locked her cottage and followed Marianne back to the brothel. Mrs. Touchwell left her for the salon, where she expected to find a patron waiting. Miss Tolerance went upstairs.

"Aunt Thea?"

Mrs. Brereton was seated at her writing table with stationery spread before her. She looked up and smiled at her niece. "You look very handsome tonight. Have I seen that dress before?"

"Many times, Aunt. Perhaps it is the shawl that is new to you?" Miss Tolerance extended an arm draped with fine merino dyed a warm, dark green. Mrs. Brereton examined the fabric closely.

"Very handsome. You should wear green more often, Sarah. And it is not even eight yet! I have lost my wager."

"Wager, ma'am?"

"I thought you would forget our engagement for dinner."

Miss Tolerance decided not to gratify her aunt with the intelligence that she had had to be reminded of the appointment. She took a seat by her aunt's table. "Am I so unreliable?"

"Oh, I suppose not, child. Now, let me put my letters away." Mrs. Brereton gathered the papers into a neat stack, but not before her niece caught sight of one which opened with the salutation *My dearest Gerard*. Mr. Tickenor's name. Marianne's fears seemed suddenly more reasonable.

Mrs. Brereton sent to tell Cook that she was ready to dine.

"Sit down and tell me what you are working at now, Sarah."

Miss Tolerance smiled. "You know I cannot do that, aunt."

"I do not mean tell me details. Tell me in the vaguest possible way. Entertain me. Are you still seeking your runaway?"

"I am. The matter would be rendered much easier if anyone could tell me the name of the man she eloped with. In my experience it is far easier to find a man than a woman in this city; men rarely scruple to hide their tracks, nor do they change their habits. A man who bought his snuff at Freybourg and Treyer is likely to continue to do so, and may be seen there and followed. A young lady has fewer habits—"

"Find out where she buys her hats!"

"Can you imagine a young, wellborn girl, recently Fallen and well aware of the censure she must encounter, exposing herself to contempt for the sake of a hat? And it is likely Miss—this girl and her suitor have very little money. Would not the sort of man who would seduce a young woman from her family be the sort of man who will save his money for snuff and riding boots for himself?"

"You're very harsh toward men, Sarah. Do you, of all

people, imagine that a Fallen Woman has no part in her own ruin?"

Before Miss Tolerance could frame an answer their dinner arrived, borne in on trays by Frost and Keefe. The table was laid, Miss Tolerance exclaimed over the array of food sent up for them, and she and her aunt started their meal with a dish of hake. Keefe poured wine and withdrew; Frost, whose jealousy of Miss Tolerance was an open secret, left them with a sour look. As they finished the fish and started upon beef *en croute,* the conversation went to politics.

"You have met the Prince of Wales, Sarah. Will he make a creditable Regent?"

"From the little I have seen of him, I think he is likely to do better than his brothers might. Given how hard he has worked on the establishment of military schools, I hope he will at least have some concern for the men fighting on land and sea."

Mrs. Brereton took leave to doubt. "Why should he?"

"If he does not, we will run out of men to do the fighting!"

"Then we had all best practice our French," Mrs. Brereton said. "What sort of care do these fighting men require? Feather pillows and beef filet?" She served herself from a dish of pigeons.

"At least to have their pensions paid, and medicine when it is needful," Miss Tolerance said. "I met a Walcheren man today who could only sit in the corner by the fire, weak as a cat and shivering for lack of Peruvian bark. It is scandalous."

"I suppose so." Mrs. Brereton appeared unmoved. "I do hope the Prince will not forget his friends among the Whig party. Will you have a squab, my dear?"

Miss Tolerance took a little from the proffered dish. A new subject occurred to her. "You can not imagine who I met today, Aunt Thea."

"You credit me with very little imagination. Was it the Emperor of Russia strolling along Bond Street on the lookout for a new pair of gloves?"

"Not so exalted, but no less surprising. I met my brother Adam."

"Ah." Mrs. Brereton seemed unimpressed. "Is he in town?"

"It may make very little difference to you, but recall that I have not seen him in a dozen years.

"Is he much changed?"

Miss Tolerance considered. "In some ways, not at all." She remembered Sir Adam's willingness to lay off as much of Lyne's anger upon her as he might. "In other ways, considerably." He had, after all, taken his wife's part and sworn to protect Evadne Thorpe, should she be recovered. "I think he is more likely than my father to forgive my sins."

"You mean he actually spoke to you?"

"Yes, aunt. We talked for a little time. He was…startled to find me alive and in London. Did you know he is married?"

"Of course. Six or seven years ago, before your father died. Just because the family cast me out is no reason for me to be ignorant of what became of them. Did you *not* know?"

"I had no idea of it. I met his wife as well."

"Did you?" Now Mrs. Brereton was impressed. She pushed away her dish. "You must tell me everything, my dear. What is the girl like? How did it come about? Did your brother introduce you to her?"

Miss Tolerance realized that she was upon uncertain ground. What could she tell her aunt without breaking confidence?

"Your brother let you speak to her? What is she like?" Mrs. Brereton repeated.

"She is pretty—"

"Dark or fair?"

"Fair, with light hair and brown eyes, a few inches shorter than I, and a little plumper."

"And her clothes?"

Miss Tolerance laughed. "I promise you, aunt, I was so surprised to learn of our relation that I noticed little about her dress except that it was ladylike and well made. If we meet again, shall I make a closer note of what she wears?"

Mrs. Brereton nodded. "I hope you will. But you say— does the girl know who you are?"

Miss Tolerance shook her head. "No. We met by coincidence, not design." That was close enough to the truth.

"Will you tell her?"

"No, aunt. I have promised my brother that she shall not know of it."

"As easy as that? You might have lorded it over him a little before you gave way, Sarah!" Mrs. Brereton's eyes lit with amused malice.

"I've no doubt Adam was thoroughly overset, and I will not deny that the idea occurred to me. But no." She shook her head again. "'Tis not fair to punish my sister-at-law for the sins of my own family."

Mrs. Brereton took a seat and regarded her niece with disappointment. "You are far too ready to sacrifice my amusement to this girl's comfort."

"Would you force a gently-reared female to acknowledge her brother's Fallen sister?"

Mrs. Brereton shook her head in disgust. "Does your brother know what you do to keep yourself?"

"I told him. I think he was surprised. He had been imagining me dead or working in a brothel on the Continent all these years."

"And his wife? Shall she hire you to find out about your brother's mistresses?"

"I do not think he has any, Aunt Thea." Miss Tolerance regarded her aunt with surprise; Mrs. Brereton was rarely coarse. "He dotes upon his wife. In any case, if Lady Brereton wished to hire me for such a task I should not know what to do. I did not tell tales on Adam when we were children; I should not like to begin now."

If Mrs. Brereton received this as a rebuke she gave no indication of it. "Then you are the only younger sister in the history of man who did not. Business is business, Sarah. Yes, Keefe?"

The porter had announced his appearance in the doorway with a low cough.

"Mr. Tickenor has called, ma'am. Shall I show him up?"

"Oh, at once, please!" Mrs. Brereton's voice was eager. She rose a little stiffly from the table and put her hand to her hair. "Frost! Where are you? I hate to dismiss you so sudden, Sarah, but we had finished our dinner, and I wish particularly to see Mr. Tickenor. Ah, Frost, do I look a fright?" Mrs. Brereton was as immaculately dressed and coiffed as ever, but Frost fluttered forward to smooth her employer's hair. Miss Tolerance, dismissed, curtsied unseen to her aunt. At the door she met Mr. Tickenor and curtsied to him before she left the room. When she looked back she saw her aunt, all smiles, extending a hand to her caller. Frost scowled, unnoticed by anyone but Miss Tolerance, who was surprised to realize she had been supplanted in the maid's bad graces by Mr. Tickenor.

That made two visits by Tickenor in less than a week. Marianne was right. Something was afoot there. Miss Tolerance moved through the brothel with her eyes downcast, not wishing to notice or be noticed. Evening was when custom was most brisk, and there was a good deal of genial noise from below. A thought occurred to her and made her stop on the first floor in her aunt's book room, a small, square room lined with shelves of books which to Miss Tolerance's knowledge were rarely opened by anyone but herself and Marianne Touchwell. As usual the room was unoccupied. Miss Tolerance took down the Baronetage. This volume was more current than the one at Tarsio's, as Mrs. Brereton occasionally referred to it. Miss Tolerance turned quickly to the entry she sought.

Brereton of Briary Park
Adam James Brereton, Fourth Baronet, b. November 30, 1779, Briarton, Herefordshire, m. May 8, 1805 Clarissa Thorpe, daughter Charles, Baron Lyne. Principal residence Briary Park, Briarton, Herefordshire.

Miss Tolerance took up the Peerage then, turning to the passage she had read earlier that day.

Lyne of Wandfield
Charles Loudon Thorpe, Third Baron, b. June 12, 1758, Wandfield, Warwickshire, m. September 12, 1781 Henrietta Mallon, daughter Sir Peter Mallon (d) and Anne Crossways of Warwick. Issue: Henry Mallon Thorpe, b. 1782; John David Thorpe, b. 1784; Clarissa Adele, b. 1787; and Evadne Henrietta, b. 1795. Principal residence Whiston Hall, Wandfield, Warwickshire.

So much information and so little. Evadne Thorpe was not only a hapless girl, a sister in ruin. She was her brother's sister-at-law and therefore her own. In Miss Tolerance's mind she was as much responsible for the future of this new-found relation as Lord Lyne, or his sons, or Lady Brereton herself.

Chapter Seven

Having arranged to hire a hack for the ride to Bethnal Green, Miss Tolerance dressed in boots, breeches, and a man's coat the next morning. She crossed to her aunt's house to give Keefe some money to pay her street-sweep spies when they came, but as she was leaving the house the boys themselves appeared at the front door. Keefe, standing just behind Miss Tolerance in the doorway, so clearly disapproved of this ragtag invasion that the boys seemed like to turn tail and run. Instead Miss Tolerance gathered them to her, explained to Keefe—and to Ted and Bart—that in future they would use the tradesmen's door, and led the boys through the house and into her garden. Both boys were a little dazed by the elegance through which they passed; it took several minutes in the fresh air for them to regain the power of speech.

"I am delighted with your promptness," she told them. Keefe, who had followed the party into the garden, stood by the kitchen door lest the boys make an attempt upon the house. Miss Tolerance was certain she would hear from her aunt about this visit. "This is Mr. Keefe. In future, if I am not here, you may leave your report with him, or with Mr. Cole, and they will have your money for you."

Ted, the literate one, held out a grubby scrap of paper on which he had written his report.

"We get the money first, then, miss?" Bart reached out his hand to snatch the paper back.

"Yes indeed." She counted out penny pieces. Bart grinned and Ted offered the paper again.

"Thank you very much. I shall look for another report tomorrow. Mr. Keefe, may I ask you to see if Cook can spare them a bite?"

"Yes, miss. So long's these gentlemen behave themselves." Keefe gathered the boys to him with a look and started back for the kitchen. As they went Miss Tolerance heard Ted ask respectfully, "Was you a prizefighter then, mister?" She did not hear the affirmative reply, but did hear an awed "Oooo" as the door closed.

Miss Tolerance examined the report, which was highly original in its spelling. There had been only four visitors to the Lyne house the day before: two tradesmen (fishmonger and green-grocer), herself, and "a gennelman come just ater you, miss, what we seen before, wiv a red head and a green coat." A red-haired man in a green coat?. She made a note to inquire into the identity of the visitor, and went to fetch her hired mount.

St. Hester's Church, Bethnal Green, was a pretty building of gray stone, not very distinguished as to architecture, but well kept, with vines trailing up the southern wall and a tiny cemetery on the eastern side. Miss Tolerance walked around the church, taking its measure, before she went inside. There she found a man of middle years standing on a ladder, poking with a long pole at the eaves. He wore a leather apron; his coat was folded over the back of a pew, and he appeared to be trying to knock down a wasp nest from the roof.

"I beg your pardon, sir. Are you the sexton?"

The man smiled pleasantly. "I'm afraid not. Mr. Wantros is almost seventy years old, and I do not like to ask him to climb much these days. May I help you?" He climbed down the ladder, dusted off his hands, and stepped forward. "I am Mr. Nottingale; I am the vicar of St. Hester's." He bowed.

Miss Tolerance returned the bow; she suspected the vicar had not looked closely enough at his guest to discern her sex. "Indeed, sir, you may help me. I am hoping to find your sister, who was lately employed by Lord Lyne."

The vicar's cordial expression dimmed. "May I ask upon what errand? My sister did not part...comfortably...with that household."

"Lord Lyne is not a comfortable man, sir." Miss Tolerance smiled sympathetically. "His older daughter, Lady Brereton, has asked me to make certain inquiries, and suggested that I talk to Miss Nottingale—about whom she has made only the kindest report." This last was an exaggeration, but Miss Tolerance was fairly certain Lady Brereton would not disclaim the sentiment. "Has Miss Nottingale confided in you the circumstances of her dismissal?" Nottingale nodded. "I have been hired to find and return Miss Thorpe to her home."

Mr. Nottingale had stepped further into the light, and when he looked again at Miss Tolerance his frown deepened. She thought he had discerned her sex and thus, from her peculiar dress, her status as well.

"How do you come to be so employed?"

To spare the vicar the need for tactful circumlocution, she was blunt. "I am Fallen, Mr. Nottingale, as you have doubtless surmised. To keep myself from further error, I hire myself to assist in inquiries requiring delicacy, such as this one. It is my earnest hope that I can keep Miss Thorpe from a fate such as my own." It was a trifle melodramatic, but Miss Tolerance suspected that melodrama might make her troubling presence more acceptable.

The vicar still frowned. "Would not your task be more

readily accomplished in more modest attire?"

"It might, sir. But my work sometimes takes me to dangerous neighborhoods, and this imposture, which seems odd to you here in this pleasant place, keeps me safe there."

The vicar appeared to weigh this information. "Lady Brereton sent you?" Miss Tolerance nodded. "It is not what I like, although you speak like a lady, however you are clothed. My sister would wish to help her charge, I know. She is staying at my house; you may try if she will speak to you. If you will leave the church and go along the path by the south wall, you will reach the vicarage in a minute or so. I hope that you will not dredge up unpleasant feelings for her. She was sincerely attached to Miss Thorpe, and the girl's elopement surprised and hurt her."

"I will do my best, sir. Oh, and Mr. Nottingale? You will want to smoke the wasp's nest before you knock it down—less chance of a sting so."

The vicar was struck by this homely piece of advice. "As one does for bees. I should have thought of it. Thank you."

Miss Tolerance left hoping he did not find himself covered with welts at day's end, and turned down the path to the vicarage. This was a square brick structure, more modern than the church. Like the church it was a tidy building, the path freshly swept and the brass bright with polish and effort. She knocked.

After a moment a slender woman of about Miss Tolerance's own age appeared. She was raw-boned and high-complected, with an air of distraction accounted for by the clamor of children at the back of the house.

"Yes, sir? May I help you?"

"How do you do? I am looking for Miss Nottingale. The vicar said I might find her here?"

"Well, then, you must come in." The woman stood aside to permit her visitor's entry. "If you'll sit in the parlor I'll fetch her at once. Did you see my husband at the church?"

"I did, ma'am. He was attempting to take down a wasp's nest."

"Oh, dear!" The woman's distracted manner increased. She gestured to a chair in the parlor, a room of brown furniture and little light. "Please wait. I will send May to you." She left, calling "Thomas! Run to church and tell your father he's not to hit that nest with a stick!"

There was a little activity at the end of the hall, a door slamming, and the sound of a boy's feet pounding toward the church. Then another woman, older and heavier than the first, appeared in the doorway.

"Yes, sir? Mrs. Nottingale says you wished to speak with me?"

Miss May Nottingale was clearly her brother's senior; her hair had once been red, but gray had softened it to a soft, rosy hue. She had a fair, freckled complexion, dark eyes, and an expression of puzzled concern which, from the deep lines between her brows, Miss Tolerance thought was habitual. When she realized that her visitor was not a man but a woman the frown deepened and she took a step backward into the hall.

Miss Tolerance rose and bowed.

"Mrs. Nottingale, I apologize for my unconventional dress. I hope you will not permit it to prejudice you against my inquiry. Lady Brereton has employed me to find Miss Thorpe—"

"Oh, thank heaven!" Miss Nottingale's frown vanished. She stepped into the parlor and closed the door. When she moved her dress gave off a scent of lavender which mingled pleasantly with the household smells of beeswax and linseed oil.

"I realize this may be a painful topic, ma'am, and I—"

Miss Nottingale appeared to have so far forgiven Miss Tolerance's equivocal status that she sat beside her on the settle. "I am so *pleased* she has done so! I warrant it never occurred to Lord Lyne that Lady Brereton would go against his wishes. Have you any notion where Miss Thorpe has gone?"

Miss Tolerance had expected some bitterness, not only toward her employer but perhaps toward Miss Thorpe as well. "I have not yet, ma'am. I am still trying to understand what happened. You knew Miss Thorpe very well, I think? Was there any sign that she was contemplating elopement?"

"None." Miss Nottingale was decisive. "It was what was most distressing to me. No sign, nothing even now I can reproach myself for missing, and I beg you will believe that I have thought it over most carefully. Was she more than usually affectionate on the day before she left? Did she show a guilty conscience or appear to be much distracted? None of those things." The governess shook her head sadly. "I should not have thought her capable of such deception, or of such thoughtless behavior toward her family."

"Not toward her father?"

"No. Not even with their quarrels. Although his reaction to Evadne's elopement—" Miss Nottingale shook her head. "Lord Lyne could be stern with his children; it is only natural for a father with a growing daughter to be wary of independence of mind. But I swear to you that nothing in her education or attitude suggested lightmindedness. You must not think she was addicted to novels or romantic poetry. That morning, in fact, she was reading a political essay Mr. John Thorpe had given her." She paused. "Lord Lyne did not like it."

"What was the essay?"

"*A Vindication of the Rights of Women,* by Mrs. Godwin."

"And she was reading this at breakfast?" That seemed to Miss Tolerance enough to put anyone off their meal. "Her father disapproved of young ladies forming political opinions?"

"He disapproved of young ladies forming opinions contrary to those of their parents." More moderately Miss Nottingale added, "He could be...harsh in expressing his displeasure."

"Was Lord Lyne's disapproval that morning so ferocious it would have moved the girl to run away?"

"Oh, no. His manner that morning was stern, that is all.

105

Nothing like his rage—quite understandable, of course—when he learned what Evie had done. His voice shook when he read her letter to us! Although—" Miss Nottingale was thoughtful. "I was surprised that he showed no softer feeling, sorrow or anxiety. Not that he should not have been angry; what Evie has done is very grave."

Miss Tolerance's own father had been singularly lacking in softer feeling even before her elopement. She had no certain idea what the appropriate reaction of a more affectionate father might be. "Will you tell me the events of the day? In order, please?"

The governess chewed thoughtfully on her lip, as if marshalling her memories to be as exact as possible. "We went for a walk on the green that morning. Evadne stopped to buy a bottle of scent in King Street—she had saved her pin money for the purchase, and was quite delighted with it. We meant to visit the subscription library, but Evie had forgotten the book she meant to return." Her expression was of affectionate amusement. "So we came home. I ordered a bite for the child to eat. Evie went to write some letters and I—" Miss Nottingale's voice sank. "I took a nap. I had a cold; I was tired."

"Of course." Miss Tolerance hoped the woman would not begin to cry.

"I was wakened by Lady Brereton looking for her sister. But we did not know then what had happened, of course, so Lady Brereton showed me the hat she had bought—white straw, with a green silk poke and a cluster of yellow roses, very pretty. And then—" Her mouth pinched as if to contain a sob. "Then Lord Lyne called us all together."

"Before that point had there been any concern about Miss Thorpe's whereabouts?"

"Concern? The worst thought I had was that she was sitting in the kitchen eating bread and jam. I blame myself very much that I did not know when she left the house. Perhaps we might have overtaken her—" Miss Nottingale's mouth pursed again.

"Did someone try to overtake her?"

"Oh, no. I am sorry, I am telling my tale roundabout. No, I was asleep for an hour or a little more before Lady Brereton returned to the house and woke me."

"And Lord Lyne was out that morning?"

"No, I think he was in his office." Miss Nottingale smiled. "But you must not think that he told *me*, Miss Tolerance. I was little better than a servant, and not privy to Lord Lyne's comings and goings. Is this necessary for you to know?"

"I am only trying to fix the whereabouts of all the family. Mr. Henry Thorpe would have been—"

"I am not certain. Mr. Thorpe has his own rooms in Albemarle Street, although he is sometimes at the house."

"He would have had no callers in Duke of York Street?"

"It is very unlikely. Lord Lyne does not like his friends."

Well, Henry Thorpe had said as much. "Was he in the house when Miss Thorpe's absence was discovered?"

"No, I don't believe so. Mr. John Thorpe was; he had come from his work at the alms house in Pitfield Street. *Unitarian*," she added. As the sister of an Anglican clergyman Miss Nottingale was clearly torn between disapproval of Mr. John Thorpe's unorthodoxy and approval of his good works.

"So: Lady Brereton woke you, you spoke, you wondered where Miss Thorpe was. Did anyone go to look for her?"

"I went myself to the schoolroom, but that was empty. She was not in her room or in the little parlor where her pianoforte is. Lady Brereton sent one of the maids to look in the garden and in the kitchen to see if Evadne was there. I think her ladyship was more cross than worried."

"Did the girl often disappear?" This was something Lady Brereton had not suggested.

Miss Nottingale closed her eyes. "Disappear? No. But she was of that age when young people sometimes need a moment alone. That is a far cry from elopement, though!"

"Then no one was very much concerned until Lord Lyne raised the alarm. What happened? Did he find a note from Miss Thorpe?"

"I do not think so. I believe it must have been delivered to the door; Pinney brought it in to Lord Lyne's office. A little time after the bell rang I heard a door slam and Lord Lyne called us all downstairs to hear what Evie had written."

"And when he had read the letter to you?"

Miss Nottingale flushed. "Lord Lyne looked to Lady Brereton—I believe Sir Adam was with her—and swore that the girl was dead to them all from that moment. He looked around the room, and when his eye fell upon me he pointed, saying my laxity was to blame for Evadne's ruin. He ordered me from the house within the hour. Poor Lady Brereton looked her sympathy, but she could not come to my defense. And of course," the governess raised her chin, "if Evadne was gone from the house there was no point in my continuing there. But to be practically accused of conniving at her elopement was a very grave blow."

"I see it must have been. Only a few more questions, Miss Nottingale, and we may stop revisiting these unpleasant memories. Was there *any* man—young or old, in city or country, for whom Miss Thorpe might have had a partiality?"

"I know of none," Miss Nottingale said flatly. "Her drawing teacher was a fat old Italian man with a wife and several children, and snuff upon his waistcoat. He was an excellent teacher, but no figure of romance. The dancing master was younger and more presentable but—" Miss Nottingale leaned forward—"I hope I do not shock you, Miss Tolerance, but he was not the sort of man who marries, or even contrives liaisons with women."

"He preferred the company of men. Well, even such men have arranged elopements for the sake of a fortune." Immediately Miss Tolerance feared that she had shocked Miss Nottingale. The governess's eyes grew wide, but she gave the idea some thought before refuting it.

"Her dowry wasn't enough to tempt anyone; Evadne herself knew that. A matter of a few thousand pounds—surely a fortune hunter would not exert himself for a hundred and fifty pounds per annum! In any case, Mr. Benson's manners were not those calculated to endear him to a young woman."

"No brothers of her friends? No young men met at parties or in the park?"

"Miss Tolerance, I know my duty. Miss Thorpe did not meet young men in the park. She was not yet out, and could have met no one at a party. I had cudgeled my brain and can think of no one—"

"I do not doubt you, Miss Nottingale. Only sometimes we do not know what we know until a questions is asked; thus, I ask. Now: if the girl had wished to sell some of her jewelry would you have known of it?"

Miss Nottingale's eyes widened. "Of a surety! She did not have much, only those articles which are suited to a girl not yet out. And how would she have sold them? She was constantly in my charge."

"Someone else might have done it for her."

"Oh. I suppose Mr. Henry would know all the places to go for that sort of thing, with his debts so great. But—" she realized where the inquiry was tending. "You mean her—the man—he might have done it?"

"I must consider the idea."

"That would argue a hardness of purpose I honestly cannot attribute to her, Miss Tolerance. And nothing was missing but what she wore."

Miss Tolerance's nose twitched. Something was burning in the house. At the same moment Miss Nottingale sniffed the air. "Oh, dear. My niece is learning to make muffins." She rose. "Have you all the information you wished? Forgive me, but—"

"Of course, ma'am. Thank you exceedingly for your assistance. And—"she brought out her pocket-book and extracted a note from it—"I have it in my power to give you thanks that may be more useful to you than mere words."

Miss Nottingale stared at the five pound note Miss Tolerance had extended to her.

"Please take it, ma'am. Whatever your parting with Lord

Lyne, Lady Brereton would not wish you to be in difficult straits, and she would surely appreciate your help."

Miss Nottingale took the note. "Thank you. My brother has a full household, as you see. An extra mouth to feed is hard on him; this will certainly help." She looked as if she might say more, but a wailing rose from the back of the house. Miss Nottingale gathered her skirts and ran.

Miss Tolerance showed herself to the door, stopping at the church long enough to leave a substantial donation in the Works box.

The sun was bright but there was a cool breeze. Miss Tolerance had promised to return to Mr. Glebb and see what he could tell her. She reclaimed her hired horse and rode through the pleasant streets of Bethnal Green and thence back to the river and the Liberty of Savoy, deep in thought. It was curious that no one had any idea of Evadne Thorpe's lover. A girl of sixteen might be as virtuous as she pleased and still pine romantically for the baker's boy or a friend's brother—or her brother's fencing master. But how many sixteen-year-old girls were able to keep such a secret? Miss Tolerance considered her own past: who had known her passion for Charles Connell? Her brother had known she was fencing; her maid had giggled with her over the flirtation, although Miss Tolerance had said nothing when the affair became earnest; it was very likely that other servants had seen the two of them together. *If only I could persuade Lord Lyne to let me speak to his servants.*

When Miss Tolerance reached the Strand she turned the horse onto Ivybridge Lane, looking ahead to the whitewashed walls of the Wheat Sheaf, and urged the horse forward. Instead the horse faltered. Miss Tolerance looked down to see a man's hand on her bridle, and the man himself glaring up at her with every evidence of loathing.

"What is this? Loose my horse at once, sir!"

"Won't," the man said. He was square-headed, a hat mashed down on the back of his head; he wore several days' growth of beard. From the evidence of his bloodshot eyes he had been drinking heavily and for some time. "Not 'til I—you're that fil-fithy bitch—Took my money and I'll 'ave it back!"

Miss Tolerance snapped her crop against her boot in warning. "I do not know you, sir. I have not got your money, and I sincerely urge you to loose my horse and let me pass."

"You and the mick, that sharper," the man continued, quite as if Miss Tolerance had never spoken. "In league agin me. I'll not 'ave it. Unnatural b—"

Miss Tolerance brought her crop sharply down on the man's hand. This caused him to release the bridle. It unfortunately had the simultaneous effect of outraging the horse, so for the next moment or so, while the stranger crumpled to the ground, keening drunkenly over the welt on his hand, Miss Tolerance had to regain command of her startled mount and urge it on toward the Wheat Sheaf. She was alert to any sound of pursuit; hearing none, when she reached the Wheat Sheaf she gave the reins and a ha'penny to the child waiting there to watch the horses and went inside.

"Good afternoon, Mr. Boddick. How are you today?"

Boddick shrugged. "I'm well enough, miss, for the heat. What will you 'ave?"

"Ale, please. And draw one for yourself and—your brother Bob, is it?" She looked over at the man who sat, as he had the day before, near the fire. Today he had something less of the aspect of misery which had characterized him the last time she saw him.

"That's kind of you, Miss. You got time for it. Mr. Glebb's busy as always."

She took her ale and tasted it. "Excellent. Your brother looks better today."

Boddick drew off another tankard of ale. "'E is, miss. Pothecary 'ad some bark for sale; turns the fever 'round quick as Canby."

"So I have heard." Miss Tolerance raised her tankard to her lips for another sip. The ale was warm and nutty.

111

"Whore! You! I want me money!"

Miss Tolerance sloshed ale on her coat sleeve.

The drunkard from the street stood in the doorway, brandishing a cudgel. He was red-faced and unsteady, his attention entirely upon Miss Tolerance. As he staggered two steps into the room Boddick started out from behind the bar. Miss Tolerance gestured to him to wait.

"Sir, you are disturbing everyone here," she said quietly. "Let us take this discussion outside."

"You think I care for them? I want what that mick sharper took from me! I want me seventeen shillin'"

It was the the sum which recalled to Miss Tolerance her would-be assailant.

"Mr. Wigg! From Mr. Blaine's fencing *salle*." Wigg took another step toward Miss Tolerance, blinking as if to focus his eyes. "I do not have your money, sir. Nor am I in any way—"

She did not finish the thought. Wigg charged at her, cudgel raised. Miss Tolerance ducked under his arm, pivoted and seized it, and twisted the arm hard behind his back. The stick dropped with a clatter. She shoved the man belly-first into the bar. Air bellowed out of him in a foul rush, and Wigg sprawled across the bar, wheezing. A few feet away Bob Boddick's face split into a grin.

"Neatly done, mate," he said. "That bruiser ain't going to trouble you no more. Oi, Tom, want me to remove this from the premises?" he asked Boddick.

"Go to, Bob," Boddick said.

"Give me just a moment if you will, sir, and then, thank you." She turned back to Wigg. "How did you know to find me here?" she asked. To encourage his answer she drew his arm a little further up his back.

"Find you 'ere? I din't find you. Look up and there you was, 'igh and mightly on yer giddyap. Cost me a chance to get in a game—a *good* game wi' a batch of gulls, would ha' made me fortune. But no, I hadn' the ready for it on account of that mick—"

"Mr. Wigg, if you wish to be an object of sympathy you

cannot brag that you would have played cards to cheat a group of stupid young men had you not been cheated out of your own funds. It defeats your authority. Now, know this: I do not have your money. I do not play at dice, and you need not apply to me for funds to fleece others as stupid as yourself."

"You wiv' that cheese-toaster—"

"I did not use a sword this time. Please leave me alone, Mr. Wigg. We will both be the happier for it."

Miss Tolerance released Wigg's arm. Bob Boddick, looking as lively as Miss Tolerance had seen him, hustled the man out the door. When he returned a few minutes later he appeared exhausted by the exercise, but also much cheered by it.

"Thank you, sir."

Bob Boddick nodded. "Best bit 'o fun I've had the day." He had a shyer manner than his brother.

"You're looking much more fit today. I am sorry to see so brave a fellow invalided in his nation's service."

"Ain't 'ardly a glorious thing, is it though? A fortnight at Walcheren and I'm ruin't forever. And I was a lucky one! Privateer sailed up a few days after I took ill, carrying a hold full of cinchona bark. Army paid top price for it, I had me doses, 'ere I am to tell the tale, where many of me mates ain't. Still, I won't never be right again."

"I hope you are wrong."

"When I've got the bark I do well enough, but when I don't! Fever and sweats and pukin'—them as 'as the sellin' of that stuff must make a fortune, just on men like myself what was at Walcheren."

Brother Bob returned to the symptoms of his fever, and Miss Tolerance gradually ceased to listen. Unlike his brother, his conversation appeared limited to this one topic. Mr. Boddick, apparently noting the glazing over of Miss Tolerance's eyes, called his brother off on an errand.

"Sorry, miss. 'E's as good a fellow as any in England, but since Walcheren... Now, if the War Office 'ad thought through what they was doin'—" Boddick took up his usual criticism of the government prosecution of the war.

Miss Tolerance had nearly finished her ale, and Boddick had moved from the Peninsular campaign to his own service in Holland with Cornwallis, when Mr. Glebb caught her eye and waved her to his table. Miss Tolerance thanked the tapster and made her way across the room.

Mr. Glebb smacked his lips as if he tasted something bitter, and the habitual drop of fluid at the tip of his nose trembled with his disapproval. "I enjoy our meetings, miss, but if bruisers like that are going to follow you in and offer vi'lence—"

Miss Tolerance was contrite. "A hazard of my work, Mr. Glebb. I am very sorry for the disturbance." She took out her pocketbook and laid it on the table.

"Now, sir, am I wrong in thinking you have information for me?"

Glebb eyed the pocketbook. "Yon Baron Lyne's a busy fellow. Had you asked me two years ago I'd have had a different tale for you."

Miss Tolerance was intrigued. "Different in what way, sir?"

The old man smiled and dabbed at the drop on his nose with a damp, crumpled handkerchief. "I'd have said he was done up, not much hope of recovery. Properties mortgaged—his older son's of the expensive variety, I'll have a word to say about him. Nor marryin' off daughters ain't cheap. And he'd some nasty reversals in business. Twice cargo from Lyne's plantation in South America was taken by the French; there was concern the property'd be seized outright. And there was some sort of revolt on his property in India, and one of his debtors defaulted on a loan and dined upon 'is pistol, which cuts down the likelihood of repayment."

Miss Tolerance blinked away the image this colorful phrase produced.

"So two years ago he was in dire straights. I saw no sign of it when I called at his house. What happened?"

"The ready flowed to him from some place, Miss T.

What's troublous is, I can't tell from where." Glebb scowled. "I'd know about loans, in course. Unless they was private. To my mind there's somethin' havy-cavy about a fortune I can't find a trace of."

To my mind as well. "And how does Lyne's business now?"

Glebb shrugged. "Prospering. No debt to speak of, the Indian property's back in 'is hands. The South American plantation's still his, though I don't know he's seen a penny from it lately, even trading with his contacts there. But how'd he come about? Where'd that money come from? Offends my professional dignity that I can't find it out."

"I understand completely, Mr. Glebb." Miss Tolerance grimaced sympathetically. "And the son?"

"Older son, yes. No love lost there; a regular Squire of Alsatia, can't wait to spend 'is Dad's money. Cards and drink and money, mostly, if I understand right. Deep in debt, he was, only a year ago. Then all 'is trade debts paid—which means the gambling debts must 'a been paid long before. Trade is always paid last. There was talk a few years ago that Lyne meant to ship the boy off to South America to learn some business—and keep 'im from the card sharps—but when things got so unsettled there nothin' came of it."

"I imagine all Mr. Thorpe's associates are similarly dissipated?"

"Oh, proper noblemen, every one of 'em. From what I hear, he ain't the worst of his set by a long chalk—more for cards and wine than—" Glebb paused, as if concerned for his guest's sensibilities.

"The others prefer fornication to faro?" Miss Tolerance suggested. Glebb nodded. "Well, this is very useful. Now, what of my other question?"

"Pawning of items by that pretty girl? I'll assume you don't want me sayin' the name of Lyne's daughter in the same breath—"

"You understand me very well. Has this nameless female pawned anything?"

115

Glebb shook his head. "Nothing's come on the market that was recognized as belonging to that household. Nor anyone recognized a girl of that description pawning trinkets. She might 'ave sent an agent, but that could be anyone: Abigail, friend—"

Lover. "Have you any other counsel, Mr. Glebb?"

"I hear Lyne's a rough man to cross, Miss T. Do you 'ave a care. As for the girl—" he shrugged and dabbed at his nose with the kerchief. "I'd not be happy to have a girl of mine without friends in the city."

Miss Tolerance roles. "Nor would I. For the moment at least, I have appointed myself her friend, Mr. Glebb."

Chapter Eight

Miss Tolerance did not consider Men as a group to be a particularly tidy species, and it piqued her considerably that Evadne Thorpe's lover was so tidy a fellow that he had left no discernible trail. Not a single person she had spoken to could name man or boy who might have been in the girl's confidence, let alone her lover. To further muddy the waters, the girl had disappeared after a quarrel with her father which did not involve the lover (that might have made her elopement more comprehensible). Lord Lyne, with his business reversals and repairs, was an interesting study, as was Mr. Henry Thorpe. Did they bear more scrutiny? And if so, with which should she start?

Miss Nottingale and Mr. Glebb had both mentioned Thorpe's profligacy. Thorpe himself said he ran with a bad crowd. Is it possible, Miss Tolerance wondered, that this is not a simple elopement? That one of Thorpe's creditors might have taken the girl as a means to compel payment?

The note Evadne Thorpe had left behind gave the lie to that theory, but anyone might force a girl to write a note. To think the thing out to its conclusion: if Evadne Thorpe had been taken and Henry Thorpe contacted to pay a ransom, would he be so facetious? Would even a hardened rake let his sister be taken in lieu of payment? And would not the family have produced the cash to redeem the girl by now? Mr. Glebb would have learned of it had Lyne suddenly shown a need for a large sum of cash, but he had said nothing. Miss Tolerance was inclined, in the absence of other intelligence, to dismiss the florid notion of ransom. Still, information was what she needed, and she had a notion of how to acquire it.

She would have to return to Duke of York Street.

Bart and two of his confederates were standing on the corner of Jermyn Street when she approached him. She watched with a little amusement the dawn of apprehension on his face, that the fellow who walked toward him was actually herself. Miss Tolerance had no wish for Lyne or his family to find her talking with sweeps at the end of their street.

"A stroll, miss? A walk, like?" Bart's *sang-froid* was admirable.

"Exactly like a walk." They went up Jermyn Street, pausing to examine a handsome blue coat in a tailor's window, then continuing to thread between pedestrians until they were several streets away. They stopped again, this time in the perfumed doorway of a tobacconist whose wares could be seen in tiers of neat white canisters and jars.

"Your assignment has changed," Miss Tolerance told the boy.

Bart shrugged. "No more money, then, miss?"

"On the contrary, I shall need you boys to work for several days. I hope an extra sixpence a day will not burden you?"

The boy's regret that the assignment was about to end was expressed by his relief at its enlargement. He grinned widely, his ragged teeth bright against a grimy face. Miss Tolerance was warmed by that grin.

"No, miss, 'ardly a burden t'all, that is."

"Well, then. I shall need a boy to follow each of the family members in that house—that is, Lord Lyne, the father—"

"That ol' man's a lord?" Bart was impressed.

"He is. Lord Lyne, the father. His two sons, Lady Brereton—"

"Wait, oo's that?"

"The older of the two ladies in the picture I showed you yesterday. And her husband, Sir Adam—" she gave a brief description of her brother. "That's five boys, and one to stay behind and watch the house. Neither son lives there, but when either visits I should like to know where he goes afterward. And I shall need a report each morning of what you observe. Can you do all that?"

"'A bender apiece, each day?"

"Sixpence, yes."

"And we can still sweep when there's no follerin' to be done?"

"Yes, of course."

The boy puffed out his chest and became very important. "We's your men, miss."

"Excellent." They stepped out of the doorway and continued on along the street. "Now: I am very interested to know to whom Mr. Henry Thorpe—that's the older brother—speaks. But any visits to or from the house, to any member—"

"I understand, miss. Is they—Bart stopped dead and looked up, his eyes bright. "Is they *spies?* 'Ave you told the Watch?"

Miss Tolerance sighed. In the current climate what was the boy to think? There were likely not so many spies in England as the broadsheets liked to suggest, but the threat was real; she herself had clashed with a pair in the last sixmonth. But most of the villainy to be encountered on the streets of London was not authored by Bonaparte but by more local criminals. "No, they are not spies. The Watch

119

does not need to know of my inquiry. I am simply doing a job of work that requires silence from me—and my assistants."

"Gotcher, miss." Bart nodded. "Quiet as mice, we is. And you want us to start today?"

"Now," Miss Tolerance said firmly.

"Right-o, then. I'm off." As good as his word, Bart turned and ran off, showing Miss Tolerance a pair of heels far cleaner than any other easily viewed part of himself. Miss Tolerance followed more leisurely, reclaimed her horse from the boy she had charged with watching it, and returned to Manchester Square.

She had exhausted most of the inns she might reasonably expect a girl and her lover to utilize in flight from the city, promised lavish payment and extracted assurances at nearly all of them that she would be alerted should a girl answering Miss Thorpe's description appear there. She saw little point in visiting more inns; it was a tedious job, and she was glad to think she might quit it. Still, there were hours of daylight left.

She determined to use them to visit as many of the Magdalene houses as she might. It was possible Evadne Thorpe could have taken refuge in one. To approach such an establishment in men's dress would hopelessly prejudice the proprietors against her; she changed once more into her respectable blue walking dress and set out again, this time by chair.

Most reformatories were small, established by some organization or person with a charitable bent, and housing only a handful of women who had come to escape a life they found intolerable. "Beaten into submission with religion," Mrs. Brereton had said of these women. "Trained in hemming and psalms, and sent off to be laundry maids and die early." Miss Tolerance thought a woman was as likely to die early as a whore as by working in a laundry, but she knew better than to argue with her aunt upon the subject. She gave the direction of a Magdalene house of some fame—the proprietor, a Mrs. Rillington, was known to give tours on Tuesday afternoons for the edification of the gentry, in order to raise subscriptions for the support of her good works. Miss Tolerance did not expect to enjoy the visit, and in this expectation she was not disappointed.

Mrs. Rillington's was a tall, narrow house of dark brick. There was something severe in its aspect, as there was in the dress of the girl who answered the door. She was a wan little thing in a cheap brown gown with a muslin apron over all, her light hair scraped back and hidden in a muslin cap. She took Miss Tolerance's name without expression, disappeared for a moment, then returned to lead her down the whitewashed hall. From behind a closed door Miss Tolerance heard a woman's voice reading scripture. There was no other sound in the house. At the end of the hall the girl opened a door, stepped aside to let Miss Tolerance enter, then vanished silently.

Miss Tolerance stepped into a comfortable parlor filled with heavy, old-fashioned furniture. There was a sofa, several chairs paired with small tables, and, at the end of the room near the fireplace, a large table in use as a desk. Seated behind the desk in the attitude of royalty receiving an embassy from afar was a square-faced woman of middle years.

"*I* am Mrs. Rillington," she said, as if there might be dispute about the honor. She rose and inclined her head. She was massively built, her silk gown of the same brown as the maid's. If Mrs. Rillington dressed in imitation of and solidarity with her inmates, it had not that effect. Her dress was clearly worth a dozen of the maid's gown, and her gray hair was covered with a cap of expensive lace.

Miss Tolerance curtsied. "I thank you for seeing me, ma'am."

"I am happy that you have come to us, my dear." Her tone, as much as her words, suggested that she had delivered this homily often. "It is time to turn your back on a life of—"

Miss Tolerance interrupted. "I am not come to be reformed, ma'am, although I do ask for your help."

From the look on Mrs. Rillington's face it was clear that she was not much accustomed to interruption. "If you do not wish to turn away from sin, how may I possibly help you? From your name—"

"My name is my name, but I am not one of those women whom you aim to assist. "Miss Tolerance had no intention of discussing her history with this woman. She hurried on. "I am searching for a girl—"

Mrs. Rillington nodded and smirked. "A lost lamb. A young sister, perhaps, who has gone astray? Who can say what hardships your sister has already faced. If you find her here you will know, at least, that she has received the most tender care and instruction. With God's help—"

Dear heaven, must I hear the entire sermon? Miss Tolerance sought a way to cut the other woman short. She struck upon a politic lie.

"Mrs. Rillington, our mother is very ill. It is her wish to see my sister one more time before—" she paused delicately, her voice suggestive of tears. "And if my sister is not here I must look elsewhere. You will pardon my impatience?"

The melodrama of a dying parent appeared to excuse Miss Tolerance's haste. Mrs. Rillington rose from her desk and proceeded, like a great ship under sail, to lead Miss Tolerance down the hall to the door she had passed earlier.

"Girls!" Mrs. Rillington stood in the doorway blocking Miss Tolerance's view of the room, but from the sudden attentive bustle she understood that all the women in the room had come to attention. "We have a visitor who is seeking her sister. She will pass among you; turn your faces up to God's light, my dears!" She stepped aside to let Miss Tolerance enter.

The room was a little smaller than the parlor they had lately quit, whitewashed and with no ornament but two windows that admitted afternoon sunlight. Wooden benches lined three walls, facing two chairs at the head of the room where two women sat, both with Bibles open in their laps. On the benches sat the rest of the inmates of the house, perhaps a dozen women, each with a workbasket at her side and a piece of sewing in her hands. There were candles—the room reeked of tallow—in tall holders at the ends of each bench, but they had not yet been lit, and the women bent to peer at their work.

Mrs. Rillington urged her visitor forward. "Walk among them, madam. Girls, your prayers!"

At her command all the women in the room raised their faces up and began to murmur the Lord's Prayer. Miss Tolerance walked among them as required, looking at each woman's face. They were of varying ages, all thin and tired looking; several appeared sickly; at least two of them had once been very pretty. None of them was Evadne Thorpe. Miss Tolerance finished her circuit, shook her head, and thanked the women for their time.

Mrs. Rillington frowned. "Back to your work, then!" She turned and left, compelling the visitor to follow. The readers took up their Bibles again. In the hall Mrs. Rillington waited to dismiss Miss Tolerance.

"I am sorry your sister was not here, my dear. If you will give me her name I can tell you if she comes—"

Miss Tolerance had no intention of giving Evadne Thorpe's name to this woman. "By then it is likely to be too late to help my mother, ma'am. I thank you very much indeed for your assistance. I must continue my search, but first," she took a coin from her reticule and pressed it into the other woman's hand. "Let me give you something toward the maintenance of this good house."

Mrs. Rillington nodded as if it were only her due. She did not wish Miss Tolerance luck in her search—apparently no girl not fortunate enough to come to her was anything to her—but did wait until Miss Tolerance was on her way out the door to examine the amount of the coin she had been given.

The rest of Miss Tolerance's afternoon was very much the same. She managed to visit four more reformatory homes, all similar in look and piety to Mrs. Rillington's.

Two were under the aegis of the church, one was a private charity, and the last was run by a pair of beleaguered Roman Sisters, but all of them depressed Miss Tolerance mightily. By the time she had left the last it was near dusk and she was hungry. She had not been to Tarsio's that day; perhaps Lady Brereton had left a message for her. She gave the chairmen orders for Henry Street and sat back. She had now a long list of places Evadne Thorpe had not been seen, and between that and the effect of visiting five Magdalene houses in a single afternoon, she felt in need of restoratives.

Corton, Tarsio's second porter, met her at the door. "I was just about to send round to you, miss. You've a visitor just come."

Miss Tolerance raised her eyebrows interrogatively. "Salon or kitchen, Corton?" If this was a tapster from a coaching inn neither he nor Tarsio's clientele would be comfortable with her interviewing him in the Ladies' Salon. Corton took her meaning at once.

"I'd reckon you might want to go somewhere else, miss. The Spotted Dog, p'raps? He's waiting downstairs."

Miss Tolerance understood from this that her caller was an upper servant whose dignity would not permit him to be visited in the kitchen. "The Spotted Dog is an excellent suggestion." She pressed a coin into his hand. "If you will tell the man that I will meet him there in five minutes?"

Corton, delighted to have provided an appropriate solution to a problem, bowed Miss Tolerance out of the club before going to give her message to the visitor.

The Spotted Dog was one of those public houses which cater to London's serving class. As its habitués were in the main upper serving-men with strong opinions on what constituted proper service, it was as comfortable a meeting place as Tarsio's might have been. Miss Tolerance arrived, causing a little stir by bringing her female self into a surrounding as masculine as any club in London, bespoke a pot of coffee, and sat by a window. There was an observable hierarchy among the clientele, based both upon their own rank and the position of their employers. Miss Tolerance witnessed a passage between a senior servant from a gentleman's household, attempting to maintain his status with a junior man in service to a Marquess. The Marquess's man appeared to be winning. Faint strains of "When *we* were visited by the earl of Liverpool..." could be heard from the footman as she went past.

"Miss Tolerance?"

The man who inquired for her was short, bandy-legged, and wiry. From his build Miss Tolerance would have taken him for a stableman, but he wore a suit of broadcloth appropriate to an indoor servant. He had short-cropped white hair, very blue eyes, and the ruddy complexion of the inebriate. He seemed sober enough now, however. He presented a note to her.

"Lady Brereton's compliments, miss. I believe you were wishful to speak to someone from the house."

"Indeed I was, sir. Pray sit. Will you take coffee, ale, or wine?" Miss Tolerance opened the note from Lady Brereton, which introduced her visitor as the chief footman at Lord Lyne's house, by name John Wheeler. Mr. Wheeler requested ale, which was ordered at once.

"Lady Brereton will have told you why I wished to meet with you?"

"You're going to find Miss Evie."

I hope it shall be as easy as that. "And you have no reluctance to speak to me?"

Wheeler shook his head. "Known Miss Evie all her life, miss. A very sweet little girl she was, and growing into a fine woman. Family didn't ought to let her go without they try to find her."

"I presume that Miss Thorpe's disappearance has been discussed in the servants' hall?" At Wheeler's nod, "What is the sense among you? Was the elopement a great surprise?"

"It was, miss." Wheeler's ale arrived and he tasted it with satisfaction.

"There had never been any sign that she was attached to some young man?"

Wheeler leaned forward confidingly. "None any of us noticed. Not gifts nor letters. When Miss Clarissa—Lady Brereton as is now—was out, there was always flowers and notes and the like. In course, Miss Evie wasn't out yet. When the season started, though, she'd have had beaux. But for now? Naught."

"Nothing came to her from Whiston Hall?" That was Lord Lyne's Warwickshire house.

"No, miss. Not for Miss Evie. Things come back and forth to the master, in course of business, but nothing come for Miss Evadne."

"Well, let us talk of other things. Can you tell me what happened that day—who came and went at the house, if anything caught your attention?"

Wheeler took another draught of his ale, set it down, and closed his eyes as if attempting to recall.

"There was—Lord Lyne and Miss Evie had words about something at breakfast—he found her reading something he didn't like, something about windows? Quite angry he was, red in the face, looking at her over his spectacles with his eyebrows all drawn together. Miss Evie spoke up quite spirited about her book, but milord called it trash and called her a stupid girl. Miss Evie run up to the school-room, and that was the last I saw of her until after noon."

How useful the servants' hall could be, Miss Tolerance reflected. "Lady Brereton was not at breakfast?"

"No, miss. She takes hers in bed."

"And what were the comings and goings that morning?

Wheeler thought long. "Miss Clari—Lady Brereton come down a little later and wrote some letters in the little parlor, then went up to see if Miss Evie wanted to go to Bond Street, shopping. Milord stayed in his office—"

"Was he still angry?"

Again Wheeler appeared to give the question substantial thought. "Not that I could see. Milord may rant, but he don't carry it forward nor hold a grudge, as they say. In any case, he was closeted away all morning. Miss Notting-gale and Miss Evie went out for a walk, what Miss Nottingale calls a good ramble. And round about noon Lady Brereton and her maid left to go to the shops. Miss Evie came home a little time after that, and Miss Nottingale sent down for a collation, which was brought up to the schoolroom. And then—" Miss Tolerance had the distinct sense that Mr. Wheeler was frustrated by his lack of knowledge."—then Lady Brereton returned home, might have been two o'clock, and Miss Evie wa'n't nowhere to be found. No one thought much of it until my lord come out his study, maybe an hour after Lady Brereton come home. He come out calling for Miss Evie, red in the face and roaring mad. You know the rest, miss."

"I do. Thank you, Mr. Wheeler." Miss Tolerance was trying to make a picture for herself of what the family's movements had been that morning. "Were there other comings and goings that morning? Deliveries, mail, messages? Anything for Miss Evadne?"

"Miss Evie? A man did come from the library with a package for Miss Evie. Mail come, and messages for milord. Business, like."

"A package from the library. Was she expecting it?"

Wheeler shook his head. "That I cannot say, miss. I was on my way down to the servants' hall when it come; Pinney went up to fetch her."

"And what time was that? Who was the last to see her?"

"Annie, one of the maids, she saw Miss Evie when she brought the tray to the schoolroom, which'd be about half past one. I asked particularly before I come tonight. Annie, and then Pinney, as I said. That was the last anyone in the servants' hall saw of her."

Miss Tolerance nodded. "There is usually a footman at the door? How could Miss Thorpe have let the house unobserved?"

Wheeler looked faintly embarrassed. "Servants' hall has its dinner at two o'clock, ma'am, although there's a man left upstairs to answer the door. Pinney'd ha' seen her did she leave that way, 'less he was called away. Or she might have slipped out the garden gate to the alley and none the wiser."

"I see." Miss Tolerance bit her lip. "And there was surprise in the servants' hall at Miss Thorpe's elopement?"

"You might have knocked us all down with a feather!"

"Because there was no sign of a lover?"

"Well, that. But, too, Miss Evie ain't that sort of girl even if she did fancy herself in love. Nor if she were mad at her pa; not one of us can imagine her doing such a thing for spite. You'd ought to ask Miss Nottingale, of course."

"Miss Nottingale is of the same opinion." Miss Tolerance paused to think. "Lord Lyne was in his office all day? That room is on the first floor?"

"To the right of the top of the stairs, yes, miss. It's paired with the little withdrawing room in the back of the house, then—"

"How do you think Miss Evie left her letter for her father?" Miss Tolerance interrupted. "If he did not read it until, what? Three o'clock? And milord was in his office all day? Unless she asked someone to deliver it to him, surely her father would have seen her leave the letter."

Wheeler's ruddy face grew redder still. He thought, thought again, and looked at her with surprise. "I don't see how she could. She didn't give it to no one. There's a tray left out for mail to be franked by milord; she could have dropped it there."

"Would the footman have seen her do so?"

Wheeler's face fell. "Pinney'd have been in and around the hallway and likely to see her, but he might not ha' taken note."

Miss Tolerance agreed. "This suggests one of three things: that Pinney was in her confidence—" she cut Mr. Wheeler off as he began to sputter a protest "—that she put the letter on the tray unseen; or that the letter was delivered to the door and thence to Lord Lyne."

"Miss, I'd take my oath that Pinney would 'ave said if 'e'd seen 'er." In his anxiety Mr. Wheeler's aitches were deserting him. "We've all known Miss Evie since she was born, miss. There's not one of us wishes 'er 'arm."

"I am sure that is so, Mr. Wheeler," Miss Tolerance said

128

gravely. "May I ask that you have a word with Mr. Pinney—you will know, I am sure, whether he is telling the truth or no—and leave word of what you learn for me at Tarsio's?"

Mr. Wheeler, who had neglected his ale, refreshed himself with a hearty draught. When he had emptied the pot and licked his lips, he nodded solemnly. "I'll see to it, miss. If I find Pinney's been keeping secrets, do you wish to speak to him?" The ale, and a moment of reflection, appeared to have restored Mr. Wheeler to self-possession.

"If it is possible to do so without creating problems with Lord Lyne, yes, I should very much like to speak to him. One last question, Mr. Wheeler." Miss Tolerance took a sip of her coffee. "You have been with the family for many years?"

"Over twenty-five, miss. Started out in the country at Whiston Hall when I was a boy."

"Would you say you are acquainted with Lord Lyne's ways?"

A half-smile quirked the corner of Wheeler's mouth. "I suppose so, ma'am. Milord is not one of the confiding sort. But a man keeps his eye open and knows the family's ways."

"Precisely my thought." Miss Tolerance took another sip of coffee. "You said Lord Lyne is not a man to hold grudges."

"I'd not say so, miss. No."

"Can you think why he might be so determined against assisting his daughter?" Miss Tolerance thought she recognized in Mr. Wheeler's face a reluctance to indict his master. "Since I cannot see the note Miss Thorpe left, I am trying to understand if there might have been information in it which he did not share with the family, which would explain his attitude."

"I can't tell you, miss. I'd have said his lordship was very fond of Miss Evie. This'd have been a blow to him on top of—"

"Yes?"

Again Wheeler looked uncomfortable. "It's no secret mi-lord wanted Mr. John for the Navy; and it's no secret that Mr. Henry—"

Miss Tolerance took pity on Wheeler's scruples. "You need say no more about Mr. Henry; I think I understand that."

"Lord Lyne's a man sets great store by the family, by the name. Miss Evie running off like that would be a blow. I'd just not ha' thought—"

"—that he would show more concern for his name than his daughter? It does seem harsh. Mr. Wheeler, I thank you for your help." She took out her pocketbook.

"Oh, no, miss." Wheeler put his hand out to stop her. "You put that away. I won't take money from you. We're all worried about Miss Evie. Just you find her." He got to his feet.

Miss Tolerance promised to do her best. "But take this, and drink Miss Thorpe's health in the servants' hall, if you will." She slid a pair of coins across the table. This time Mr. Wheeler did not refuse.

Miss Tolerance emerged from the Spotted Dog to find that night had fallen while she was inside. She looked about for a chair or hackney; seeing neither she deter-mined to walk back to Manchester Square. In this neighborhood most households were scrupulous in ob-serving the ordinance requiring a lantern or torch in the doorway; there was a good deal of foot traffic beside, and carriages in the street. Miss Tolerance crossed Bryanstone Street and turned on to Upper Seymour Street. It was as she approached Portman Square that she first sensed that she was being followed.

The hour was not late. Despite her dress and relative lack of weaponry (after an episode where she had been forced to defend herself with a pocket mirror, she had be-gun to keep a small pistol in her reticule, but considered it a tool of last resort) she did not feel particularly apprehen-sive. Seymour Street was too well traveled at this hour for her to feel much endangered. She could not have said why she was certain she was being followed; she had learned to trust her instincts and the odd crawling sensation between her shoulder blades. She increased her pace and took her reticule in hand, just in case.

Two young men, dressed gentlemanly but foolish with drink, were attempting to scale the iron fence that surrounded the green in the square. Miss Tolerance observed them and wondered, if she had to call for help, whether they would respond. As she left the square the sensation of being followed ceased. She kept her reticule in her hand and walked purposefully along, turned on Duke Street, and very quickly arrived at Mrs. Brereton's house. After a moment's thought she decided to avoid the darkness of Spanish Place, and knocked on the door of the big house.

Cole opened the door. The hall was unoccupied, and Miss Tolerance thought she might pass through the house to her own cottage without notice. She went past the stair toward the back of the house, noting a good deal of cheerful noise from one of the salons. She skirted the room and had very nearly reached the servants' door when she was hailed.

"Sarah!"

Miss Tolerance turned. Marianne Touchwell stood in the door of the blue salon. Her expression was unremarkable, but there was something in her manner which expressed wariness. She advanced and laced her arm through Miss Tolerance's.

"'Tis a good thing you've come," Marianne said. Her tone was serene, but there was warning in her eye. "You must come and join the toast. Parliament has just voted the regency to the Prince of Wales, and your aunt says she's to be married."

Chapter Nine

"Married?" Speaking the word drove every other consideration from Miss Tolerance's mind. Her aunt to wed, who had always spoken with the greatest feeling against the institution of marriage and in favor of her own form of unfettered enterprise? "Aunt Thea?"

Marianne's nod was a warning. "Yes, to Mr. Tickenor. Come and wish them well." She put her hand over Miss Tolerance's own, where it lay on her arm, and led her into the salon. As Mrs. Brereton's whores were required, when in the public rooms and not directly engaged with a customer, to be appropriately dressed, it might have been any scene of respectable celebration: women in *mouseseline de soie* and men in evening dress drank punch and engaged in muted conversation. Yet there was a scent of anxiety in the room at odds with merriment. Not one whore there, Miss Tolerance thought, but must be wondering what this news meant for her. As she entered the room a masculine voice called out, "To the happy couple!"

"The happy couple!" The words repeated around the room.

Mrs. Brereton had the place of honor, seated on a sofa near the fire with her intended Mr. Tickenor by her side. Her color was high, her eyes bright; she looked exalted, Miss Tolerance thought. After all these years, could her aunt be truly in love?

"Sarah, you do not drink to me?" There was an edge to Mrs. Brereton's voice.

"With the greatest joy, the moment I have a glass in my hand, Aunt." Miss Tolerance approached the sofa, bent, and kissed her aunt's cheek. "I wish you every and all happiness, ma'am." She straightened and curtsied to Mr. Tickenor, who was observing her with interest. "And you, sir, have my congratulations."

Tickenor inclined his head in the manner of royalty. He had, she saw, his arm around Mrs. Brereton's waist, and was running one finger along the side of her breast. Miss Tolerance had never seen her aunt permit such a caress in public. She looked behind her for Marianne, but her friend was at the table where punch was being served, being talked to enthusiastically by a young man with poetical hair. Miss Tolerance was sure her friend was as disturbed as she herself.

She turned back to her aunt. "When is the happy day to be?"

"We have not yet decided. Tickenor swears he cannot go on long without my undivided attention!" Mrs. Brereton chuckled and tapped Tickenor's thigh with her fan. "But I must have time to get my bride-clothes ready."

"Oh, certainly, ma'am." Miss Tolerance cast about for something else to say. This had the quality of nightmare: her aunt was many things but she had never before been *vulgar*. "And after, will you have a bridal trip? The war makes the matter difficult, but—"

"We haven't planned that far, have we, my dear?" Tickenor squeezed his intended to him in a rough caress and smiled at Miss Tolerance. The smile did not reach his eyes. "My dear niece, if I may call you so? For now, we plan only to come back and see to the running of matters here."

"I hope you will not let worry for the house keep you from indulging in a trip, aunt. You know that Marianne and your staff could manage without you for a time."

It seemed an inoffensive remark, but Mrs. Brereton was determined to take offense. "What do you mean, Sarah? If Tickenor says we will return here, that is what we shall do. Are you trying to prise the management of the house from my fingers?"

"Not in the least, aunt. You know that I have no aspirations in that direction! I meant only what I said: that you should not deny yourself the pleasure of a honeymoon out of concern for your business."

"Well, it is *my* business," Mrs. Brereton snapped. "That will not change because I am marrying."

"I am sure everyone here is delighted to hear it."

"Everyone?" Mrs. Brereton looked around the room as if she had forgotten the other occupants. "Why?"

"Why, because they care for you and wish you well." Miss Tolerance gestured to the crowd, most of whom had left off their own conversations and were attending to this one with considerable interest. "And because their livelihoods depend upon you."

Mrs. Brereton pushed Tickenor's hand from her breast and stood up. She was nearly as tall as her niece, and looked into Miss Tolerance's eyes with icy displeasure. "What business is that of yours?"

Miss Tolerance did not wish to quarrel with her aunt. She particularly had no wish to quarrel here, in the parlor of London's most elegant brothel, with half the world attending. She kept her tone light and agreeable.

"You are perfectly right, aunt. It is no business of mine. I only—"

Mrs. Brereton slapped her. It was so unexpected that Miss Tolerance had not prepared herself to meet the blow, let alone to defend against it. Tears of pain came to her eyes, and she brought her hand up to cover the spot. Mrs. Brereton sat down beside Tickenor again, quite as though nothing had occurred. The rest of the room was silent for a moment, then talk began at an even louder volume.

Mrs. Brereton sipped her wine and said, quite as if nothing untoward had occurred, "Have you heard, Sarah, that Parliament has at last voted? The Regency Act names the Prince of Wales, and poor Queen Charlotte is relieved of all authority. I'll warrant our friend Sheridan must be in a frenzy tonight."

Miss Tolerance forced herself to speak. "I imagine the entire Whig party are meeting to see how they can turn the Regency to their best ends. But ma'am, I—"

Marianne was beside her and pressed a glass of punch into her hand. "Drink their healths and say good night," she murmured.

"Aunt, Mr. Tickenor, again I wish you the greatest joy." Miss Tolerance raised her glass and drank. "I hope you will excuse me. I am very tired."

"Of course, my dear." Mrs. Brereton was all solicitousness, neither vulgar nor enraged now. "Marianne, tell Cook to send supper to the cottage."

Miss Tolerance murmured her thanks, curtsied, and frankly fled.

In the hall she and Marianne faced each other.

"Has she been bewitched?" Miss Tolerance ran her fingers along her jaw. "What in God's name could have caused such changes in her? Is it Tickenor? I should not have thought—"

"I think yon Tickenor has his eye upon the business. I've seen him prowling about with the same eye a man uses to size up a good horse. But your aunt?" Marianne turned toward the kitchen. She did not continue until they had passed through the green baize door that led to the servants' hall. "She hasn't been right since she was taken ill last winter."

"She has not seemed an invalid—"

"I don't mean sick; she hasn't had so much as a sniffle

since. But you know her manner's changed. I'd put it down to—I don't know what to call it. Knowing that she's none so young as she used to be, nor her looks won't hold out forever."

"But how could vanity account for such a sea-change?" Miss Tolerance considered. "I suppose it would explain Mr. Tickenor, if love does not. But the rest—" Gingerly she put her fingers to her jaw again.

"I don't know, Sarah. But I'll tell you what it reminds me of. There was a woman at my—at my first house—"

Miss Tolerance had never before heard so much as a hint that Marianne had not joined Mrs. Brereton's establishment straight from her ruin. "Last house? Where? When was that?"

"In Westminster. I left there a year before you came to us. T'was not so *congenial* a place as this one." A wealth of sobering information was contained in one word. "The abbess's mam lived in the house. She was an old whore, retired, and we all thought her fit as a horse. She kept household, a merry old thing. Saw to the table, ordered the candles and the laundry done. Then, as winter started to come on she—first she wanted to start whoring again. Kept nosing about the gentlemen who came for us girls, talking coarse and shoving her bubbies at them. Flirting with them! You might imagine how it took the men aback! Then she took the notion that someone was trying to poison her. She flew into tempers over nothing, went for the cook with a knife! Finally Mrs. Deeper—that was the abbess—had to lock her in her room."

"What happened to her?" Miss Tolerance could not forbear to ask, horrified.

Marianne shook her head. "I don't know. I left. It wasn't a pleasant sort of place, even before the old woman went odd. But I remember someone there saying she believed the pox had gone to the old woman's brain."

"Pox? But you said she was retired."

"She was, but you know that sometimes the treatments don't take. I don't know, Sarah. I mention it because it's the only other time I've seen anyone so changed from her nature."

"Last winter, didn't the doctor suggest my aunt be treated for—"

"Pox? Yes. But she never was. She thought—we thought, Frost and I—that all the change in her was due to the apoplexy she suffered when she was feverish. But this—madness...."

"Do you think that is what this is? What are we to do?" Miss Tolerance regarded her friend with horror.

"I don't know. Wait to see if this brainstorm passes and speak to her if it does. I know she don't like doctors, but there must be someone who could see to her. Like that man that tried to help the King when he went off his head."

"Doctor Willis?" Miss Tolerance pursed her lips. "He died some years ago, I believe. And I don't believe we will easily persuade my aunt to see a physician."

The two women stopped at the door to the garden. "Then we must wait and hope," Marianne said. "To be honest, Sarah, I do not know what to counsel else. And I should go back." She looked over her shoulder toward the salon.

Miss Tolerance nodded. After a moment of uneasy silence, Marianne embraced Miss Tolerance. "We shall look after her and see she comes to no harm. Now, I'll have Jess bring some supper over, shall I?"

Miss Tolerance spent a bad night and felt thick-headed and useless the next morning. She dressed, and was lacing her boots when Keefe knocked at the door.

"You never ate your supper, Miss Sarah." He looked at the untouched tray on the table with disapproval.

"I beg your pardon, Keefe. I forgot about it completely."

The porter nodded, frowning. "These is worrisome times." He was not, she knew, speaking of the war or the Regency. He withdrew a fold of paper from his pocket, an object whose dignity did not merit being presented on a tray. "Them boys come this morning with your report, miss."

It took Miss Tolerance a moment to recall who "them boys" were and what they might be reporting on. Then, with more eagerness, she took the paper. "Thank you, Keefe. What did you disburse on my behalf?"

He named a sum; Miss Tolerance paid him. "Thank you, miss. I beg your pardon for asking, but…what's to become of the household?"

Oh dear. "I do not know, Keefe. I have very little power to do anything," she told him frankly. "But what I have, I shall use to make sure that my aunt does not forget her responsibilities to all of you."

Keefe nodded. "I knew you would, Miss Sarah, but it's relieving to hear it said. I'll tell the others."

The porter left. Miss Tolerance hoped she had not promised more than she could accomplish. She opened the paper Keefe had brought her.

As before, it took a little time to decipher Ted's scribbles. A sharper pencil and less inventive spelling would have helped, as would punctuation. Lady Brereton had visited in a house in Cork Street and returned after an hour. Mr. Henry Thorpe had visited, then gone on to his club in St. James's Street and stayed there late—too late for that spy to stay out, lest he get a whipping from his mother. Lord Lyne had been the busiest. He had gone to his club, to a haberdashery, then back to his home. He had then gone out again an hour later, to a shop in Fox Street in Shadwell. The business located there was (if she could trust Ted's scrawl) called Amisley and Pound Drayage, and Lord Lyne had spent half an hour there before returning home for the evening. The man to whom he had spoken, Ted wrote, was the same red-haired man in the green coat who had visited in Duke of York Street the day before. What business would bring a man from Shadwell to Lyne's house, or take the baron to Fox Street? If it were a simple matter of shipping, might it not as easily be handled by Lyne's agent or secretary? Somehow she had assumed the man in the green coat was an acquaintance of Henry Thorpe's, not Lord Lyne's. Decidedly this red-haired man was a person of interest. Miss Tolerance decided that a call at Amisley and Pound Drayage was in order.

An hour later she alit from a hackney coach on a lively thoroughfare lined with offices, most to do with shipping, and a few businesses there to provide sustenance and drink to the workers of the neighborhood. The street was no dirtier than most, and significantly less sordid than many, but it was close to the Thames. By full summer the river would emit the stench of a cess-pit; already there was a sweaty, oily ripeness to the air. The sign which identified Amisley and Pound was old enough that the gilt had faded and chipped; the business was some years established. There was a large window of many fly-specked panes, through which she saw three clerks bent over desks. Her curiosity increased. She entered.

Not one of the clerks looked up. Aside from the scratch of pens upon paper and tapping of points on the lip of inkwells, there was some noise from the street but no other sound. When Miss Tolerance cleared her throat all three clerks turned to look at her impassively.

"May I speak to Mr. Amisley, please?"

"In't one," the rightmost clerk said. "Can I be of some 'elp, miss?"

"Mr. Pound, then?"

"Died Trafalgar year." The clerk wrote something in his ledger, crossed it out, then looked back at her. He was a big man with broad shoulders, and looked as though he was crammed behind his desk when he ought to have been loading boxes onto a ship. His face was unfortunate: long, full-lipped and sneering, with a peppering of dark stubble on his cheeks; his eyes were almost hidden by the pouches below them. "Miss," he said as an afterthought, and with no indication of respect or courtesy.

Miss Tolerance held on to her temper and smiled. "Are you gentlemen the proprietors of this establishment, then?"

"Proprietor would be Mr. Huwe. *Miss*". The clerk

dipped his pen again, wrote another line, then looked at her insolently. "D'you want to speak with him?"

Miss Tolerance was polite. "I should like that very much. Thank you."

The clerk got up from his stool, exchanged unreadable glances with his fellows, and vanished through a door at the back of the room. The employees of Amisley and Pound were not in the habit of dealing with the public, Miss Tolerance thought. The two clerks still sitting returned to their work, and Miss Tolerance waited without comment, feeling that her best choice was to match their impassivity with her own. After several minutes the first clerk returned, still sneering, and invited Miss Tolerance to follow him.

The room into which she was ushered looked as if a bomb might have exploded in a paper manufactory. Shelves lined all the walls except for a door on the far side, and these shelves were filled with ledgers, papers piled on top of the ledgers and, as often as not, papers fallen in drifts upon the floor. In the middle of this flurry of paper a desk was nearly hidden by more ledgers, and papers skewered every which way on an array of spindles.

A man rose from behind the tower of foolscap to greet her.

"That will do, Worke. Back to your 'counts go you."

Mr. Worke shrugged his heavy shoulders as if to say that nothing that followed was to be considered his fault, and shambled out.

The other man bowed. "Now, madam, I am Abner Huwe, at your service." He did not invite her to sit, but stepped a few paces from behind his desk. "How may I be of assistance, Miss—"

Miss Tolerance had determined that she would not give her name unless necessary. She adopted the brisk tone of a woman accustomed to managing household and family members. "It is kind of you to see me, Mr. Huwe. I am trying to find a gentleman, and was told he might have called in here."

"Here, miss? Not likely, that. No." Mr. Huwe's accent was distantly Welsh, but with thick veneer of the eastern end of London. He was a stocky man and muscular, with a square head and blunt, pleasant features. His hair was that rusty color which had likely been true red when he was younger; it stood up from his head in tufts, as if he were in the habit of running his hands through it. His coat was of neat, fine broadcloth, bottle green. "We get few callers here in the usual way of business, you see."

"How very strange. I was told the gentleman called here yesterday in the afternoon. A man about fifty, sparse hair combed forward, blue eyes behind spectacles, heavy eyebrows and a square chin. He is a very commanding man; I don't doubt you would remember him."

Mr. Huwe ran a square, thick-fingered hand along the side of his jaw as if in aid to memory. "And if this gentleman had called upon us, miss, why would you be wanting to know of it?"

Miss Tolerance had provided herself with an answer for this question. "I am trying to find the gentleman, Mr. Huwe. He and my father had discussed some business, but my father is stricken in years and has forgot some of the details of the matter. My father had recalled that the gentleman said that he would call here yesterday afternoon, but cannot remember the man's name."

"Does your father business with men whose names he cannot recall?" Howe asked with polite doubt.

"They were at Watiers, sir, and happened to fall into a conversation. If my father ever knew the gentleman's name he had forgot it by the time he returned home. He does not like to ask at the club, sir, for fear it will get 'round that he is not as astute as he used to be." Her tone mingled sympathy with impatience.

"But he remembered *my* name?"

"The name of the firm, yes. It is the way with old men, sir. One name will stick with them, while another goes—" Miss Tolerance made a gesture with one gloved hand, meant to suggest a thought winging its way from her brow. "I would be very grateful if you could help me, sir."

"What sort of business is it?" Mr. Huwe asked. His expression was no less cordial, but Miss Tolerance was aware of a sudden acuteness in his gaze.

"My father has some interests in India, sir. His clerk is out of the city upon business with the family properties, and as my father was adamant that the matter could not wait, I have undertaken to find out the gentleman's name and direction."

"You are a very active young lady, it is certain." Huwe looked at his visitor for another moment, then shrugged. "From the sound of it, the gentleman you're describing is Lord Lyne. He came to inquire about shipping some goods from a plantation in the West Indies, but we were not able to agree upon a fee. As for his direction, your father may reach him in Duke of York Street."

"Lord Lyne, sir? Gracious, my father means to fly high. Thank you very much, Mr. Huwe. I shall be able to relieve my father's mind upon the matter."

"'Tis a pleasure to so easily be of help, Miss—" again the suggestion that she would supply her name. Miss Tolerance curtsied instead.

"I bid you good day, sir, and again, my thanks."

Huwe bowed and started around the desk to show his visitor to the door, but Miss Tolerance, still in the character of managing female, waved him back to his seat. "I shall show myself out, sir. I have already taken enough of your time. Thank you."

Miss Tolerance went out past the three clerks. Mr. Worke had his nose back in his 'counts book, but the other two— an elderly man and a younger, less robust version of Worke with a large strawberry mark on his left cheek and a grey and red scarf wound twice around his throat despite the April warmth, watched her go with no pretense of working.

She gained the street and looked about her for a hackney carriage. The mystery of Lyne's visit seemed resolved, but it occurred to her to wonder why Mr. Huwe had been so helpful as to tell her, not only who Lyne was and where he might be reached, but the business upon which he had come to Amisley and Pound. If one were of a suspicious mind, one might almost believe that Lord Lyne's visit there had nothing at all to do with shipping or estates in the West Indies. She strove to recall: Lyne had an estate in India, and one in the Americas, but was it the West Indies or somewhere else?

Once again Miss Tolerance took her questions to Joshua Glebb.

The taproom of the Wheat Sheaf was crowded today. Mr. Glebb was not at his accustomed table, but the evidence of a tankard and trencher with the remains of a meal suggested that he had only just left.

"Good afternoon, Mr. Boddick. Am I too late to find Mr. Glebb?"

Boddick shook his head. "'E's still got business waiting, Miss." He gestured to a cluster of people—three male, one female—waiting together at a table near the fireplace. "May hap 'e gone out to the necessary. Will you take something?"

It was only polite to order coffee she did not truly want, and to ask Boddick to pour something for himself. Normally such an exchange would lead to conversation—she was quite certain Boddick would have an opinion upon the Prince of Wales's elevation to the Regency. But the barman was in a curiously withdrawn humor; he merely said, "Thank you, miss," and rubbed away at the tankard he was polishing.

"How does your brother, Boddick?"

The tapster shook his head. "Not so well, miss. 'Ome in bed, weak as a kit and breaking 'is bones with the shakin'. Ain't no bark to be 'ad for him, and o' course the fever come back straight away."

Miss Tolerance was very sorry to hear it. "I had thought he looked improved yesterday."

Boddick was sour. "That was yesterday."

"And there is no cure for it?"

"Best cure would ha' been not to land at Walcheren. Or to 'ave sent them with enough Peruvian bark to keep 'em from getting sick in the first place. Not like them in the War Office is breaking theys bones with fever. Rich 'uns get the bark when no one else can. And there's Mr. Glebb, miss."

The old gentleman stood in the doorway, wiping his hands on a pocket kerchief. Miss Tolerance thanked Boddick and went to intercept Glebb before he returned to his table and the queue of anxious people waiting for him. It was perhaps unfair of her to break into the line, but she meant to ask only one or two questions.

"Miss T., back again? You like the taste of Boddick's coffee, I suppose?" Glebb smirked at his own wit.

"I came for a quick word, sir."

Glebb cast an eye at his table and the people waiting for him. "A short word's all I have time for, Miss T."

"Well, then: what do you make of the name Abner Huwe?"

Glebb considered. "Shipper, down near Shadwell Dock. Hard man, jewed one partner out the business so's he killed himself. Runs it tight. Had his reverses like everyone—year or two ago his business was looking done up, but he come through and appears very snugly fit these days. Not borrowin', that's certain."

Miss Tolerance nodded. "So he might have business with Lord Lyne in the West Indies?"

"Might. What, is Lyne planning on buying property in the Indies? I'd say his money was still safer in Venezuala than up near them American States."

"Lyne has no plantation in the West Indies?"

Glebb looked at her with impatience. "You know I told you yesterday. South America and India. Wasn't you listenin', Miss T? Now, if you're quite done—"

Miss Tolerance pulled herself away from the suddenly interesting subject of Lord Lyne's property and made her final inquiry.

"Gerard Tickenor?" Mr. Glebb cocked an eyebrow. "What are you messing about with him, miss? A bad lot, I'd say."

"How so?"

"All in with 'im, and the bailiffs sniffing at his door. Used to be a very warm man indeed, but lost it all, ran through the fortune he married. Bought himself a tin mine that was near worked-out, and kilt half a dozen men trying to get the last bits of ore out. Wife's dead, so maybe he's on the look for a new fortune. You ain't thinking of marriage, are you, Miss T?" Glebb regarded her as if this was a very good joke. "I'd not trust that Tickenor to hold my watch, if you take my meaning."

"I do, Mr. Glebb. You confirm my own feelings." *Damn.* "You have been very helpful, and I have kept you from your other customers." Miss Tolerance pressed a half-crown piece into the old man's hand, curtsied, and took her leave as Glebb continued back to his table.

Miss Tolerance arrived at Tarsio's in the wake of a party of gentlemen in a considerable state of merriment, who shouted instructions to Corton about the number of bottles they wanted delivered to them straightaway, even as they disappeared into the Library. It was necessary for Corton to confer hastily with one of the waiters before he could turn to greet her.

"You've a visitor waiting in the first little room upstairs, miss." He spoke with the manner of someone bearing great and confidential tidings. "A *lady.*"

"Thank you, Corton." Miss Tolerance pressed a coin on the porter. "Did the lady give a name?"

"Mrs. Brown, miss." Corton clearly believed it to be an alias. "She ordered tea, which I made sure to send up to her. I hope I done what you would have wanted, miss."

Miss Tolerance assured him that he had anticipated her wishes admirably. "The first withdrawing room, Corton? Thank you."

As she climbed the stairs to meet Lady Brereton she organized her thoughts. What good news had she to give? There was no evidence from anyone that Evadne Thorpe even had an admirer, let alone one who could have enticed her to elope, which only made finding the girl the harder. How could an inexperienced girl of sixteen have vanished so completely?

She entered the little room and greeted her guest. After an exchange of curtsies Miss Tolerance would have begun to explain where the case stood, but her sister-at-law advanced across the room with a paper in her hand.

"You will forgive that I came, I know, when I tell you that *this* was delivered this morning." Lady Brereton's voice throbbed with a little forgivable melodrama.

Miss Tolerance took the paper and unfolded it. The note was writ in a loopy schoolgirl hand, rather rushed and careless:

Clarissa—

I am well, but do not wish to see you. Please do not look for me. I have friends who are seeing to my welfare. I send you my dearest love, but beg you not to look for me!

Evie

Miss Tolerance read the note twice. "This is her hand?"

Lady Brereton nodded. The girl was alive. That was a relief.

"Ma'am, what do you make of it?"

Lady Brereton's face was pinched. "What *am* I to make of it?" she asked. "'Tis such a strange letter."

"Strange in what way, ma'am?"

Lady Brereton opened the note. "She does not want us to look for her. She said so twice."

"Is that what strikes you as odd, ma'am?" It was possible that Evadne Thorpe was not, as her sister and Miss Tolerance had both imagined her, regretting her elopement. That despite the opinion of the household, the girl had plotted her own disappearance. But how, Miss Tolerance wondered, would the girl have known that there was

146

a search for her unless the investigation had come closer than she herself had surmised?

"She called me Clarissa," Lady Brereton added. "She never does that. When she was a baby she called me Clary, and that has always been her name for me."

"Could it be that she is attempting to put herself on a more adult footing, now she is—" How on earth to finish that thought with any sort of tact? "Now that she is a woman grown?"

"Then would she not sign herself Evadne?" It was a reasonable question.

Miss Tolerance examined the note again. "You are certain the writing is hers?"

Lady Brereton nodded. "Yes. Although it looks hurried."

"Or forced?" Lady Brereton thought, then nodded. "That suggests that the persons who are so careful of her welfare do not intend that she should quit them any time soon. So, Lady Brereton, it appears on the one hand that your sister is alive, which is a very good thing. It appears, upon the other, that she may be held against her will, which is not good at all. Will you take some tea?"

Chapter Ten

Miss Tolerance filled her sister-at-law's dish with tea and pushed a plate of ginger biscuits—a specialty of Tarsio's kitchen—toward her. "How did you come to receive this note, ma'am?"

"It was brought to my father's house."

"Yes, ma'am, but by whom?"

"Oh, just a little boy. The sort of child you might see on any corner. I gave him a sixpence, which he seemed glad of—"

"What did the boy look like?"

Lady Brereton blushed. "I hardly looked at him. I asked his name, and told him he was a good boy, and gave him sixp—"

Miss Tolerance controlled an impulse to shake the woman. "You asked his name? What is it?"

"Would that help? Martin, he said."

The name stirred Miss Tolerance's memory. "He was young, you say? Ten?" Lady Brereton shook her head.

"Eight? Six?"

"He was small—perhaps six or seven years. His hair was dark, he was grubby but not—not filthy." To her credit Lady Brereton was clearly trying to recall the boy's looks. Miss Tolerance sighed. How often in a day did one really note the faces of servants or climbing boys or street-sweeps?

"That note had to travel from your sister's hand to your own. If we can trace it back to her—"

Lady Brereton paled. "I should have asked. I ought to have looked more carefully." She put her tea cup down with a rattle. "It never occurred to me."

"Of course not." Miss Tolerance was bracing. "You are not accustomed to deal with such drama, nor should you be. It is my daily meat, and I know how to use what you have told me. This is good news, Lady Brereton, I promise it." She found she had taken the other woman's hand in her own and pressed it reassuringly. "To be frank, I have had less success in tracing her than I had hoped. This gives me a new avenue to investigate, and new hope as well."

Lady Brereton nodded. Miss Tolerance was relieved to see that the tears which had been imminent were gone.

"Now, I hope you will forgive me if I do not linger. I am eager to be about your business. If you would care to stay for a few minutes?"

"You are very kind, Miss Tolerance." Lady Brereton took up her cup. "I think I will finish my tea."

Miss Tolerance rose and curtsied. "Please stay as long as you wish, ma'am. I hope to have good news for you soon." She turned to leave.

"Miss Tolerance?" Lady Brereton was frowning thoughtfully. "I do not know why you—who you once were, but I wish I *had* known you then. I very much admire you."

Miss Tolerance was moved, enough so to be momentarily tempted to reveal to her client their close relation. But she had given her word to her brother. Finding out that they were sisters-at-law might at once damage Adam's bond with his wife, and Miss Tolerance's own with her client. "You do me too much honor," she said. "I shall let you know when I have any news." She curtsied and was gone.

Again Miss Tolerance returned to the corner of Jermyn and Duke of York Streets. There was only one boy on duty at the corner, his broom tucked under his arm as he dug the toe of his boot into the join between two flags, trying to prise the stone up. This casual pose was misleading: Miss Tolerance saw that the boy's eyes were fixed firmly on Lord Lyne's front door. She stopped beside him and pretended to button her glove.

"Have you been here all day?" she asked.

The boy looked up at her in surprise. Between his focus on the house and the absorbing destructive work he was attempting with the flagstones, he had not sensed her there. "All day, missus."

"Very good. Did you see a boy—a little boy—go in to-day?"

"Smaller than me? I seen 'im. Looked a right figger, 'e did. Went in to the kitchen door—"

"Was there anyone with him?" Miss Tolerance knew the word *figger* had some criminal connotation but could not recall just what it was.

"When 'e went in? Nah, 'e gone and rapped at the door—I'll tell ye, might 'a bowled me down when they let 'im in. I wonner if they give 'im sommat to eat? So 'e stayed for mi' be 'alf a hour, then come off wiv the ol' woman—"

"Wait. There was a woman with him?"

"Din't I say?"

Miss Tolerance's control was admirable. "No, you forgot that part."

"Yeah, ol' fly-by-night wiv a face like Friday. She came wiv 'im, gave 'im a paper to take in, then 'e rapped and they took 'im in, and she waited there—" he pointed to a spot perhaps twenty feet from where they were standing; just across from Lyne's house.

"And can you describe the boy and the woman for me?"

150

The boy nodded. "'E was little, brown 'air, 'ad a nasty face 'til 'e knocked on the door, then 'e went all wheedlin'. She—'e called 'er Granny. Big ol' woman wiv gray 'air, maybe your 'ight, missus. All frowns 'til the boy come out to 'er. Then she put on a face like one 'o them you see in the park wiv the rich babbies, and off they went."

Miss Tolerance nodded. A tall, heavy woman with gray hair and the ability to put on a motherly face. It appeared that Mrs. Harris of Bermondsey and her grandson had re-entered the picture in a most unexpected way.

The bootmaker's on the ground floor of Mrs. Harris's building in Marigold Street was closed; a sign at the door read *Gone to dinner*. Taking advantage of the cobbler's absence, two elderly pensioners, almost insensible with drink, sat in the doorway to the upper stories. Miss Tolerance begged their pardon and stepped past them, sending both old men into paroxysms of laughter. The smell of stale beer rose off them to follow her into the hall. One of the doors on the ground floor was open, and another on the first floor, which provided a sullen glow of light as Miss Tolerance approached Mrs. Harris's door.

Her first knock drew no response from within. She knocked again, waited, and was about to knock once more when she heard a low groan from within. This moved her to push urgently on the door, which yielded at once. In Miss Tolerance's experience doors which opened too easily were cause for caution. She paused to take the pistol from her reticule, then proceeded, quite prepared to find bodies on the floor.

They were not on the floor. Mrs. Harris and her grandson were slumped together on the sofa. Miss Tolerance's first thought was that some violence had come to them—it would not be the first time in her experience that she had arrived to find a witness hurt or dead. A moment's examination, however, revealed that Mrs. Harris was merely drunk, profoundly so. Her grandson appeared to be in the same condition. Three square bottles of blue glass stood on the floor, two of them empty, the third, just out of Mrs. Harris's lax reach, with little more than an inch of gin left in it. If the two of them had been in Duke of York Street no more than three hours before, they had been mighty efficient in pursuit of oblivion.

Miss Tolerance returned the pistol to her reticule, stepped round the end of the sofa, and bent to deliver the old woman a sharp slap. Mrs. Harris moaned, low, and slumped a little farther over her grandson. The woman's cap was half-untied, and had slipped down to cover the side of her face. Her pink scalp shone dully through thinning hair. Miss Tolerance struck the woman again.

"Whozza?" Mrs. Harris opened a gummy eye. "Whoz?"

"Mrs. Harris?"

The woman mumbled a string of half-comprehensible oaths and plumped at her grandson as if he were a feather pillow, trying to make him conform to her body's shape. The boy snorted and stayed asleep.

"Mrs. Harris, I need a word with you."

This time the woman struck out blindly. Miss Tolerance caught the flailing arm with one hand; with the other she slapped Mrs. Harris once more.

"Damn your eyes! What business you got a-hittin' me?" The woman sat upright and glared at Miss Tolerance. The effect of her outrage was spoiled by the cap, which slid down completely to cup the lower half of her face like a drooping mask. Mrs. Harris swiped at the fabric, squeezed her eyes shut, then opened them again as if doing so might change what she was viewing. Then she scowled. "Whot you want?"

"You may not recall me, ma'am—"

Mrs. Harris leaned forward, peering. "I ain't that jug-bit. I know you. You're that—" she faltered, belched foully, and sat back as if puzzled. "Who are you? If you're here on b-business, I ain't open for—"

No, Miss Tolerance thought. *You most certainly are not.*

"We have met before, ma'am. My name is Sarah Tolerance—"

Comprehension lit dimly in Mrs. Harris's rheumy eyes. "Oh. Miss Wozzit. If you go knockin' people up in the middle of the night it ain't no wonder you din't need my services." She belched again. "No man in 'is right mind'd 'ave you."

"It is not quite three in the afternoon. You and your grandson delivered a note in the Duke of York Street this morning," Miss Tolerance said. "Where did that note come from?"

An expression of startlement and anxiety crossed Mrs. Harris's face, immediately erased by a look of studied stupidity.

"Duke of York Street? Never bin there in all my life, nor 'ave Martin." She nudged the unconscious child as if he might corroborate the story. "Lookin' up the wrong skirt, you are." Mrs. Harris untied her dangling cap and used a corner of the muslin to scrub at the gummy corners of her eyes.

Miss Tolerance was not distracted. "I have several witnesses. You brought the boy, gave him the note, and sent him to the kitchen door. Your grandson was admitted to the house and brought up to Lady Brereton, gave her the note, and was given a coin for his trouble. He then returned to you and you left—apparently for the nearest gin shop."

"Martin 'as a cold, poor lamb." The old woman crumpled the besmirched cap in one hand and regarded her grandson with a parody of maternal fondness. "Gin's good for what ails 'im."

"I do not think insensibility is a specific for head colds," Miss Tolerance said. "Mrs. Harris, I do not care where you went afterward, or what you did with the money you received. But I must have the direction of the person who gave you the note."

"Or you'll do what?" The older woman's eyes narrowed, but there was apprehension, too, in her demeanor.

"One of my friends is a magistrate." Miss Tolerance was bland. "I am sure he would be interested to know—"

"No call for magistrates, Miss Wozzit!" Mrs. Harris

153

waved the cap in her hand and smiled. It was a smile meant to ingratiate, but failed in its object. "Beside, what would you say to your magistrate-beau? 'Ere's Mrs. Harris, who let 'er little grandson earn a penny bringing a note to a lady—"

"Sixpence," Miss Tolerance said.

Mrs. Harris frowned. "Little bastard tol' me 'e'd got a penny. Well, that's for later. But there's nothing 'gainst the law in that."

The time had come for a show of force. "Mrs. Harris, the man who gave you that note is holding a gently-reared girl against her will. I do think my friend the magistrate will be interested to know you are in league with a kidnapper—"

"I never did." Mrs. Harris's voice climbed in pitch. "I 'elp young ladies, that's my work. I don't 'arm 'em. As for the magistrate, I tol' you there's no call for that. Can't we 'ave this out civil-like? You ask your questions and I shall answer 'em." Mrs. Harris attempted to establish anew her professional dignity and maternal authority. "Ask your questions," she repeated.

"Very well. Was the note given to Martin or to you?"

Mrs. Harris's lip twitched, then she shrugged and said, "To me."

"When?"

"Oh, this morning. Martin and me was in Throgmorton Street early; there's a 'pothecary there I do some business with. Man come up to me and asked if my boy could deliver a note for 'im. Offered me a coupla bob for the service. 'Ow was I to know there was any 'arm in it?"

"This was not a man known to you?"

"Never seen 'im before."

"Then why would he approach you?"

The old woman counterfeited careful thought. "Because I 'ad the boy with me, I spose."

"Where were you when the man approached you?"

"I tol' you: Throgmorton Street."

"In the street? In the apothecary's shop?"

"In the 'pothecary's."

"And the name of the shop?"

"Jos. Halford and Son It's the son runs the place now."
Mrs. Harris was comfortably on familiar ground.

"Can you describe the man who gave you the note?"

She shrugged. "I dunno. Medium sort o' fellow, banty-legged, short. Brown 'air, brown coat. Nothin' remarkable about 'im at all."

Of course not. "Perhaps the apothecary would recognize him."

Mrs. Harris was cagy. "I don' think so," she said at last. "Prob'ly not. It was mighty busy."

Miss Tolerance suspected that the abortionist was not considering the truth so much as weighing what was her most believable lie. "Well," she said briskly. "I will have to talk to this apothecary. I must find this girl, and the note— and the man who gave it you—are my best links to her."

The older woman muttered something.

"I beg your pardon, ma'am?"

"Why d'you even care? Not like she's your sister or your daughter. Nor, for all the gentry talk of ruin and fate-worse'n-death, ain't so bad like to 'appen to 'er that ain't 'appened to a 'undred before."

"I cannot rescue that hundred, ma'am, but I do intend to rescue this one. And I gave my reason when we first met, Mrs. Harris. I have been hired to find her."

"Money." Mrs. Harris nodded sloppily. "That's the thing, ain't it. They'd as well to keep their sil'er, though. Do they think she'll be returned to them in the same condition she left?"

Miss Tolerance felt a cold prickle of dismay. "You know something of her condition, ma'am?"

Mrs. Harris was still very drunk, and the gin seemed to have renewed its pull upon her. She shrugged. "Stands to reason they'd 'ave 'ad the use of 'er. Nor kidnappers 'd 'ave reason to treat her gentle. She'll go 'ome knowin' a few new tricks. Mayhap her family will think better of bringing 'er 'ome."

"I will take that chance. " Miss Tolerance turned to go.

"Wait! Ain't I goin' to get something for me trouble?"

Miss Tolerance thought briefly but powerfully of how she would like to reward Mrs. Harris for her trouble. "There's still a little drink in that bottle," she said. "Good afternoon."

She retreated down the dark corridor, aware of shouted insults behind her, and emerged gratefully into the light. One of the two drunkards on the step had fallen asleep, mouth agape and face turned to the sun. He reeked of piss and beer. Miss Tolerance stepped over him and hailed a hackney coach to take her to Throgmorton Street.

Jos. Halford and Sons, Apothecary, had a storefront with fresh black paint and a recently cleaned window. The shop occupied the ground floor of a less well-kept wooden structure, very like its fellows in the street. The street was busy with wagons, carriages, and pedestrians. Miss Tolerance, let down from her hackney on the corner where Throgmorton met Bartholomew Lane, took a turn up and down the street before entering the apothecary's. The shop smelled pleasantly musty and green; the interior was as well kept as the outside. It was a small space and crowded; on either side rows of small drawers reached to the rear of the shop and up to the ceiling; the back wall was lined with shelves of brown-glass jars and decanters, each neatly labeled in spidery Latin. A counter to the left held a scale and tools for the making of remedies: a mortar, pestle, pill-forms, and a stack of clean white paper ready to be folded into packets. The counter straight ahead held the same objects as well as a ledger, inkstands, and pens. One of the drawers from the wall had been pulled down and rested, empty, on the counter. The label said *Cinchona pubescens:* a placard had been placed inside the drawer which said, in large red letters, *Sorry. No Bark.* Miss Tolerance thought with pity of Mr. Boddick's brother.

Behind the counter a young man in a fresh apron and gartered sleeves smiled expectantly.

"G-good afternoon, miss."

"Mr. Halford?"

"S-second of that n-name, miss." The man was perhaps Miss Tolerance's age, fair haired, plump and amiable. "H-how may I h-h-help you?" The stutter was evidently a permanent affliction.

Miss Tolerance stepped to the counter. "I am afraid I do not need any pills today, sir. Just a moment of your time, and some information."

Halford nodded encouragingly.

"Is a Mrs. Harris known to you, sir? An older woman, often with her grandson?"

Halford frowned. "I kn-now her, yes." His expression suggested he took no pleasure in the acquaintance.

"Was Mrs. Harris here this morning?"

The apothecary's frown deepened. "She w-was. Might I inquire w-why you ask?" His manner had cooled with the mention of the abortionist's name.

"I am seeking a man with whom Mrs. Harris spoke while in this shop. I do not think she is a very reliable witness—" Miss Tolerance permitted her opinion of the woman to color her tone, and Halford relaxed in response. "As it is very important I find the man, I knew I must speak to you. She said the shop was busy and you might have been too occupied to notice him, but—"

Halford waved his hand. "I k-keep a close eye on my shop, miss. Mrs. Harris came for alum and oil of p-p-pennyroyal. I was d-decanting the oil when a man approached her. They sp-oke a few minutes. By the time I had d-done he was gone."

"Thank you, sir. Do you recall what he looked like?"

"B-big fellow. Young. N-not a gentleman. Ill-shaved. He g-gave her something."

Miss Tolerance sighed. It was not much more than Mrs. Harris had told her—save for the physical description. "You can tell me nothing else about him?"

The apothecary shook his head. "He was the sort I'd k-keep an eye on: a shifty look about him, if you t-take my m-eaning."

"I see. Thank you, sir." She took her pocket-book from her reticule. "Will you permit me to show my thanks—"

"N-no." Halford was quite definite. "There is n-no n-need for th—" he stopped. "Wh-when you need a remedy—"

Miss Tolerance smiled and returned the pocket-book to her reticule. "I shall come to you straightaway. Thank you, Mr. Halford." She inclined her head. For a moment the shopkeeper seemed uncertain whether to accept the courtesy as his due from a woman of peculiar status, or return it as to an equal. Finally Halford bowed to her. It appeared that he was ready to give her the benefit of the doubt, despite her connection to Mrs. Harris.

When she left the shop Miss Tolerance walked for a few minutes, thinking. Mrs. Harris had told the truth, in that she had been approached in the store by a man who had given her something—presumably the note to be delivered to Lady Brereton. But her description of the man had varied from Halford's. Miss Tolerance was inclined to trust the apothecary—but his description had left her, once more, at a dead-end.

She turned down Broad Street to Threadneedle Street, seeking to avoid the crowds around the looming Bank of England. There was still a good deal of traffic both on foot and by vehicle. She stepped past a knot of aproned tradesmen who were engaged in noisy consultation over an open barrel, and waited in a crowd at the corner of Bishopsgate for a wagon to pass. Sir Walter Mandif's house was a little to the south, she knew. She had not spoken to him since their visit to Covent Garden, the memory of which was a pleasant distraction for a moment. To her right three massive women, very fine in satin dresses totally unsuited to the weather, the hour, or a stroll along city streets, were discussing hats. To her left, an elderly man was fiddling with his cane, impatient for the chance to cross the street. A group of boys, too well dressed to be sweeps or other working children, ran along the street making mischief. One of them dodged around the old man and swept his hand up to knock Miss Tolerance's bonnet forward over her eyes. She put her hand up to right the bonnet and in a moment found herself lifted off her feet and pitching forward.

It happened with such suddenness that for a moment, even as pain blinded her, she wondered what had happened. She did not lose consciousness, but briefly lost the ability to do anything but fall. Her arms would not extend to catch her; she fell toward the fat women, whose squawks of dismay were much magnified and distorted by the ringing in Miss Tolerance's head. The woman nearest her pushed her away and she fell to the ground, catching the side of her jaw heavily on the curbstone. She lay there for a moment trying to catch her breath and make her arms and legs obey the commands of her mind; the smell of the muck in the gutter, inches from her nose, was as good as a vinaigrette in clearing the fog from her brain.

Something was poking her in the side. Miss Tolerance moved her head enough to see the elderly man prodding at her with his cane. *He has found a use for the thing, at least,* she thought. She recognized the thought as a product of shock and knew she must pull herself together. She wriggled her fingers and was pleased, in a detached way, to find that they moved. When she opened her eyes again she saw her bonnet in the gutter, floating half-full on the muck there.

"Damn," she murmured. She closed her eyes again.

"Well, lady, shall we get you to your feet?" She felt a large hand grasp her wrist and pull. "Tripped, did ye?" Another hand moved to her shoulder and tugged upward. The jar this gave to her head nearly caused darkness to swallow her. She managed to stay conscious, and to open her eyes.

"You old chub, she's hurt!" A woman's voice, perhaps one of the satin-clad women. "See there on her spencer? That's blood!"

This caused a considerable stir, and more echoing inside Miss Tolerance's head. "I will be—if someone will only help me to stand—" she began.

159

Her rescuer hauled her upright and set her on her feet. At once Miss Tolerance felt her knees give way, and the man caught her again. She opened her eyes to discover that he was one of the aproned men she had seen peering into the barrel.

"Thank you," she murmured.

"Someone fetched you a good clout, lady. Footpads, I don't doubt, looking to take your purse." She realized the man was holding her carefully so as to avoid getting blood and muck upon his shirtsleeves. She could hardly blame him.

There was a general outcry against the state of affairs in London, which did Miss Tolerance no good but appeared to relieve the feelings of the crowd a little.

"Sir, if you will help me to a step where I may sit down?" Miss Tolerance asked quietly. The aproned man nodded and called for the crowd to step away. Within a moment she was seated on the stone doorstep of a chandler's shop. The crowd closed in around her, full of questions.

"Was your purse taken? We'd ought to call the Watch."

Miss Tolerance, at the cost of a little pain, looked down to see that her reticule still hung at her waist. She made the mistake of shaking her head. "They did not rob me. Did anyone see who struck me?"

Again there was a general murmur of dismay but no information. "You're bleedin' something narsty, miss," someone said. "Might be you need us to fetch you a carriage."

"Did anyone see who struck me?" Miss Tolerance asked again. She raised a hand to the back of her head; it was sticky, but the blood appeared to have stopped flowing. She could feel a very substantial knot growing there. "The boy—"

"What boy?" That was her rescuer, who was standing, arms akimbo, frowning at her.

"There was a group of boys chasing down the street. One of them pushed my hat off over my eyes; a moment later I was struck."

"But they din't take your purse." The second man tssked. "Ain't safe for a soul on these streets, and here 'tis broad daylight. You need a carriage, miss?"

Miss Tolerance was nauseated; her hands shook. She did not think she could stand to ride in a hired coach back to Manchester Square, but what was her alternative?

"If you would, sir."

"I thought them boys was just larkin' about," one of the women in satin announced to the crowd. "They was gone so fast."

"It's a scandal is what it is," another satin-clad woman announced. "You'd ought to tell the Watch. Or Bow Street, even."

The mention of the magistracy gave Miss Tolerance an idea. She raised her head and saw a carriage stopped by the corner with a crowd of people around it.

The aproned man put his hand out to take her elbow. "Here, I'll put you in the coach," he said. "I don' know what this country is comin' to."

The second man, who had stepped in to support her other elbow, chimed in. "Ain't no one ought to be struck down on the street."

"Thank you, sir." Miss Tolerance reached the carriage. Bile rose in her throat, and she had to work very hard not to be sick all over her rescuer's front. When she turned to thank her rescuer it appeared, for a moment, that there were twin aproned men on her right, supporting her into the carriage.

She was stopped by a man's voice crying, "I got 'im! I got 'im right 'ere!"

Miss Tolerance leaned on the carriage for support and turned her head. A short, bandy-legged man in an old-fashioned skirted waistcoat was dragging a boy toward the carriage. The boy was not struggling, but was shouting almost as loudly as the man himself.

"All I did was knock her hat! We thought it was a lark! Let go!" From his speech and his dress the child was clearly better born than his captor, who pulled the boy up

161

in front of Miss Tolerance. "I thought it was a game. He said I was just to knock your hat off! I didn't think to hurt you!"

In an instant Miss Tolerance's mind was marvelously clear. "Who told you?" she asked the boy.

"The man down there—" the boy shook off his captor's hand and pointed down Bishopsgate. "He said he was a friend of yours, and would I knock your hat off for him. He was right behind me, I thought—"

Miss Tolerance nodded encouragingly, then regretted it as a wave of pain almost made her faint. "What did this gentleman look like?" she asked.

The boy looked puzzled. "He's your friend. Don't you know him, miss?"

The aproned man, who had taken a proprietary interest in the case, asked the boy what sort of friend would clout a lady on the head. The child considered.

"But he was most particular, said it would be a very good joke if I would knock your hat, that you were very fond of that hat—"

Miss Tolerance reflected that she had indeed been fond of the bonnet, and fonder still of the skull it covered. "What did the gentleman look like?" she asked again.

The boy shrugged. "He carried a stick with a handle carved like an elephant," he offered.

And bashed my head with it. "Thank you. Next time a stranger asks you to assault another stranger you will think better of it, won't you?"

The boy nodded.

"Ain't you going to punish 'im, miss?" The bandy-legged man who had brought the child back was disappointed.

"I think he meant no harm, sir. But thank you for finding him. Now, if you will forgive me—" Miss Tolerance turned carefully back to the carriage.

The aproned man helped her in. "Where are you wishing to go, miss? I'll tell the jarvey." Unable to face the ride back to Manchester Square Miss Tolerance gave him closest direction she could think of; her rescuer closed the door and struck the side of the carriage to let the driver know he might move on. The sound made Miss Tolerance's head hurt anew.

Within a few minutes the coach drew up in Gracechurch Street, before the house of Sir Walter Mandif.

Chapter Eleven

Perhaps the greatest stroke of good fortune Miss Tolerance had experienced in a singularly luckless day was to find Sir Walter Mandif at home when she arrived. The jarvey, inspired by the promise of a lavish tip, had stepped to the door to inquire there. Miss Tolerance, for whom even the short ride had been as horrid as she had imagined, leaned out at the door of the coach in time to see Michael, Sir Walter's manservant, open the door. She waved, the jarvey explained, and Michael ran to fetch his master.

A moment later Sir Walter was at the door of the coach, paying the jarvey and assisting Miss Tolerance into the house. He said nothing, for which she was very grateful, but his face was pale and his lips pressed together. Miss Tolerance was brought into a small front parlor which, from its mustiness, she suspected was rarely used, and placed in a winged chair by the fireplace. Michael, who normally bounded about with the energy of a half-grown hunting dog, knelt to catch the fire and then, after a murmured consultation with Sir Walter, left the room.

"I have sent for a surgeon," Sir Walter said, low. "Have the goodness to sit here quietly while I find bandages and tea and—"

"I shall not move," Miss Tolerance promised. "You might wish to put a rag upon the back of the chair. I should not want to bleed upon your cushion."

"The cushion is not of the least consequence," Sir Walter said, and left the room.

Miss Tolerance, who had begun to feel that chill which sometimes accompanies a sudden injury, sat quietly by the fire, her eyes open but unfocused. She was not aware of how long it took for Sir Walter to return; he was heralded by the clink of china on a tray and the smell of smoky tea.

"First, let me make you more comfortable," the magistrate said. "Would you prefer to do this yourself, or will you permit me?" He held a damp scrap of linen in his hand. Miss Tolerance bent her head forward, wincing as she did so, and silently offered the back of her head to his ministration. Sir Walter took the remaining pins from her hair and pushed the mass of it forward, away from the wound. He dabbed carefully and inexpertly at the lump.

"I think the bleeding was caused by your hairpins, which the blow drove into your scalp," he told her. "The worst of that is stopped. But there is some very nasty swelling. You are lucky your hair is so thick; I believe it absorbed some of the blow."

"I am a lucky woman," Miss Tolerance muttered. She was beginning to feel drowsy.

Sir Walter cradled her head and guided it back against the chair. "The surgeon will be here soon. Michael has just come from summoning him. May I give you some tea?"

He might have been speaking to her at the punch table at Almacks. Miss Tolerance fought an inappropriate giggle. "Yes, please."

The hot tea—smokier than the blend Miss Tolerance

165

normally favored—settled her stomach and helped her to focus her thoughts. She was sitting in drowsy silence with Sir Walter, her hands curled around the cup, when the surgeon arrived a few minutes later.

He made quick, brutal work of his examination, and equally quick work of the stitches that closed the gash on her scalp. He echoed Sir Walter's congratulations upon the thickness of her hair—"'Tis likely what saved your life, ma'am."—and fixed a bandage over the wound. When it was done Miss Tolerance was trembling and soaked with sweat. She had not cried out, of which she was pardonably proud, nor had she given in to the profound nausea which had returned at the surgeon's touch.

Sir Walter saw the surgeon to the door. Miss Tolerance could hear the murmuring of consultation between the two men, then he returned to her.

"Mr. O'Leary says you are on no account to be moved."

"What, never? How exceptionally inconvenient." Miss Tolerance attempted a humorous tone.

"For at least two days. May I send a note to your aunt to apprise her of what has happened? I shall, of course, retire to an hotel—"

Miss Tolerance's head came up too fast. She winced. "Pray do not be foolish, Sir Walter." She sucked in her breath. "I am Fallen. Do you think I can be further ruined? If I had thought, when I told the coachman to bring me here, that you might be so silly as to—I appreciate your scruples, but I assure you, in this case they are needless. Unless, of course, it is your own reputation that concerns you—"

Sir Walter smiled for the first time, although the crease of worry between his brows did not vanish altogether. "I think I can withstand any gossip. And if you will not mind my presence I am happy to be here: Mr. O'Leary says you are to be closely watched. My cook might have done it, but it would have taken considerable persuasion—Mrs. Yarrow likes her own hearth of an evening, as she has often told me. Now, are you able to tell me what befell you?"

Miss Tolerance proceeded to explain the circumstances of the attack.

"You are certain the boy knew nothing more than he said?"

"I think he was honest—he seemed too frightened to be elsewise. And he was not the sort of poor child who might have been sold to a cutpurse for lookout or climbing jobs. He was well-dressed and well-spoken, neither of which are proof of virtue, I know, but my instinct is—"

"For the moment let us trust your instinct," Sir Walter said. "More tea?"

Miss Tolerance was later to look back upon that evening as remarkable. She had come to rely upon Sir Walter Mandif's friendship, but these were extraordinary circumstances, and Sir Walter, in his unassuming attentiveness, behaved like an intimate of much longer—and closer—standing. He dispatched Michael to Mrs. Brereton's house with a note for Marianne Touchwell—she did not think it wise to tell her aunt what had befallen her at this chancy time. Then, when Sir Walter had assured himself that his guest was as comfortable as her injuries would permit, he brought a book and read to her from Mrs. Edgeworth for an hour. Miss Tolerance was surprised he had such a work in his library, but his voice was soothing. She dozed for a while and woke to find Sir Walter watching her. Had she been well, this sudden intimacy would have oppressed her, but on this evening it was a comfort.

"Have you no work to do? I am very sorry to keep you here if you had ought to be in court or—"

"Do not trouble yourself. I have arranged to be my own master today. Now, I shall check the dressing on your wound and then we shall dine, if that is agreeable."

Miss Tolerance remembered in time not to nod her head. Sir Walter rose and came around the back of her chair. Again he pushed the heavy fall of her hair forward, off her neck. He pulled back the dressing, touched the swollen lump, and returned the dressing to its place.

The sensation of his fingers grazing lightly across her neck was both pleasant and unsettling. She tensed for a moment, which brought the pain again. She flinched.

"I beg your pardon—"

"No, it is nothing. You have gentle hands," she said lightly, and relaxed into their comfort.

"I do not wish to hurt you." Sir Walter came around the chair so that she could see him without turning her head. "There is no bleeding, the stitches Mr. O'Leary put in appear clean, and the lump on your skull seems a little smaller to my eye. How is your appetite?"

"Not very sharp, but I suppose you will say I must eat something to keep my strength up. At least you have not yet required me to drink spirits for their curative powers."

"If I thought they had any—" he began.

"Mrs. Harris dosed her grandson insensible with gin this morning," Miss Tolerance said. Sir Walter frowned at the non sequitur. "No, I am not wandering in my wits! By all means, let us have dinner, and I shall explain about Mrs. Harris."

So they dined. It was bachelor fare, a loin of pork fragrant with apples, and roast potatoes, served to them in the parlor by a large, silent woman whom Miss Tolerance took to be Sir Walter's cook. Miss Tolerance managed the broth that was placed before her first, and ate a little bread and, at Sir Walter's urging, a few bites of the roast. But she was too queasy to eat more, and contented herself with describing her visit to Mrs. Harris's rooms and what she had found there. She did not mention the woman's occupation; Sir Walter might have been forced to take official action against her, and while Miss Tolerance disliked the woman she did not wish to see her transported.

"So it was by her suggestion that you were in Threadneedle Street?"

"By her suggestion that I was in Throgmorton Street. After that I walked about the neighborhood to think. But yes: if anyone would know I should be in that neighborhood it would have been she. My first order of business, when I can stand up without pitching onto my face, will be to call on Mrs. Harris, you may be sure."

"Perhaps I should do so—or have Hook and Penryn do so—"

Miss Tolerance entertained briefly the notion of Sir Walter's two Runners, the Bow Street investigators who worked with him, calling upon Mrs. Harris. Bow Street, while well intentioned, was rarely discreet, and Miss Tolerance had promised her sister-at-law discretion. "I beg you will not. I can just imagine those gentlemen muddying the waters of that particular stream—which is none so clear as it is. I thank you, but will manage the matter myself in a day or so."

Sir Walter's eyebrows rose. "You expect to be up to managing matters in a day or so? No—" he held out a hand. "I will not argue with you. Not tonight. Mrs. Yarrow has made up a bedroom for you, if you are up to managing the stairs, and I will send her up to help you undress—"

"I have been dressing myself for years, Sir Walter," Miss Tolerance said mildly.

"Indulge me." His tone was dry. "I have sustained a considerable shock today."

Miss Tolerance smiled and winced. "You do not have injured women descend upon your doorstop every day? I shall defer to your injured sensibilities, of course."

In the middle of the night Miss Tolerance woke in an unfamiliar bed with a ferocious ache in her head. She could discern the outline of a figure slumped in a chair by the banked fire, but could not think who it might be. She sat up and regretted it, as the pain increased tenfold. She moaned, and the person in the chair stirred and unfolded himself, poured something from a jug on her bedside table, and supported her while she drank it.

"It will help you sleep," Sir Walter murmured. He lowered her back onto the pillows and Miss Tolerance closed her eyes. She felt his hand on her brow, smoothing her hair away from her face.

A few minutes later, when she looked again, Sir Walter had returned to the chair and was, to all appearances, fast asleep.

In the morning Miss Tolerance received a note from Marianne Touchwell which urged that she take care of herself, and added that Mrs. Touchwell had told a politic story to Mrs. Brereton, both to keep her wondering where her niece was and to keep Sir Walter's name from the matter.

"It is very kind of your friend, but I don't think my reputation needs to be guarded." Sir Walter handed the note to Miss Tolerance.

They were sitting in the parlor again, where Miss Tolerance had been able to eat a little more than she had done the day before. The curtains were drawn, as she found that light made her head hurt; they muffled the peal of bells from a dozen churches, calling parishioners to worship. Sir Walter was looking through papers which he had neglected yesterday.

"I do not think that was her chiefest concern. My aunt has been a little *notional* of late; she seems to resent the time I spend with you."

Sir Walter was amazed. "Really? We do not meet so frequently—this is, of course, a highly unusual circumstance."

Miss Tolerance sighed. "You know that my aunt was ill last winter? She has not been entirely herself since. Her jealousy, her betrothal—"

One of Sir Walter's sandy brows rose. "Her *betrothal?*"

Miss Tolerance nodded—she could do so now without too much pain. "To a man named Tickenor." Miss Tolerance strove to remember what Mr. Glebb had told her only yesterday, but it seemed to her that the blow to her skull had rattled a good number of memories loose. "He was helpful to my aunt some years ago in setting up her business."

"Do you know anything about the man?"

"Only that, and—" the memory came back to her. "I am

170

told he is not so deep in pocket as once he was. Which makes me fear that he may be taking advantage of my aunt."

"It does seem a curious about face for a woman who has been so independent for so long. I thought you had told me she had no use for marriage."

"She has said as much to me. This has taken us all aback, and I must say I am uneasy about the match. But I can say nothing to my aunt—"

"Surely you would be the most suitable person to speak."

"I am afraid if I do so she will defend him by saying I am only interested in her business."

"Her business?" Sir Walter put his papers, tidily stacked, to one side. "And are you?"

"No, Sir Walter, I am not. I have told my aunt often enough that I have no ambition to run her establishment."

"When you give up your present employment—"

"Give it up? How should I?"

Sir Walter set his jaw as one determined to face an unpleasant task. "You are young now, but surely you cannot continue to face the hazards of your work indefinitely."

"The hazard is no greater today than it was yesterday. When I am an old lady I shall very likely retire to a cottage in the suburbs and call myself Mrs. Smith or Mrs. Jones, as most retired Fallen do, and live upon my savings. All the more reason to work hard now. But that is not likely to happen for many years."

Sir Walter frowned. "You were hurt yesterday."

"I was, but not more gravely than I have been before. The risk of what I do is not new to me, Sir Walter. I go armed for a reason. My work carries some hazard, but I am well able to defend myself. Most of the time," she added fairly, with a gesture to the lump on her head.

"Until you grow eyes in the back of your head, your friends will continue to worry about you," Sir Walter said quietly.

"And I thank my friends for their concern—and their

friendship! I am well aware how I put you out by arriving here, uninvited, to make a sickroom of your parlor."

Sir Walter shook his head. "I only wish I could do more."

Miss Tolerance looked at her friend's narrow, foxy face and read a fleeting, and disquieting, tenderness. But the expression lasted only a moment before he asked, "Would you like me to make inquiries about this Tickenor?" She was able to smile with genuine appreciation.

"I would like it very much. Now: as it is Sunday, perhaps you mean to go to church? I beg you will not permit my presence here to keep you from that. Frankly, the matter of dressing and eating breakfast has quite done me up."

Sir Walter left her to doze before the fire, where Mrs. Yarrow occasionally appeared with tea and delicacies intended to tempt an invalid's appetite. Miss Tolerance found she could not read for more than a few minutes at a time before her headache returned. She had no other occupation: her concentration was too scattered to spend time in rumination upon Evadne Thorpe's whereabouts. In consequence, by the time Sir Walter returned that afternoon Miss Tolerance was bored and impatient. It was a considerable effort to be cordial.

Rather than take offense, Sir Walter appeared to understand without saying the effect of enforced idleness. "Mrs. Yarrow says you have not eaten enough to keep a sparrow alive, by which I think she means she has been plying you with cakes you did not want all day long. Let us dine— and let her go home—and perhaps we will have a hand of cards." He set about amusing her with such easy kindness that Miss Tolerance was soon in a better frame of mind. They dined, and after dinner played piquet for paper stakes; Miss Tolerance was pleased to find that her thoughts were becoming orderly enough to permit her to beat Sir Walter.

"Unless, of course, you permitted me to win."

Sir Walter shook his head. "I would do many things to

172

preserve our friendship, Miss Tolerance, but to cheat at cards is not one of them. I believe this is my deal."

Miss Tolerance handed him the deck. "What new tales of Bow Street?"

"The usual sorts: thievery in the main. A woman brought a complaint that the cook at a chop house had put broken glass into her dinner, but it was proved that she hoped to extort money from him."

Miss Tolerance declared *tierce*. "How does anyone think of such things? I never should."

"You have an honest soul. *How high?* I wish you might have been there—the woman brought her family, all ready to swear she was made of truth. Mrs. Bread—"

"*To ten.* Bread was her name?" Miss Tolerance chuckled. It made her head ache, but only a little.

"Good. And a half dozen little Breads, and an Aunt Bread and Uncle Bread and a dozen neighbors who might well have been Butters for all I could tell."

"I take it you are not always so amused by the people who come before you?"

"Very rarely. But this has been a week for eccentrics. I had to sentence a man who broke into an apothecary's shop to steal medicine to treat his son's ague, and an old woman accused her neighbor of stealing her cat, and told me she knew it was her cat because she had given birth to it."

"To the cat?"

"To the cat." Sir Walter looked at her over his cards. "The animal was brought to court to testify for the plaintiff, but it stood mute, and I confess I could see no resemblance between the old woman and her putative child—"

Miss Tolerance laughed hard enough to make her head hurt, and all at once she found herself near to tears. She pressed her lips together to contain an expression of her pain and fatigue.

Sir Walter observed it at once. "You are tired." He put his cards aside and got to his feet. "Please let me help you upstairs."

Miss Tolerance was certain she could climb the narrow stairs by herself, but permitted Sir Walter to take her elbow and assist her to her chamber. The hand supporting her was warm and solid; she was again conscious of an intimacy in Sir Walter's gaze. When they reached the door of her room, however, Sir Walter released her elbow. "You will be all right without assistance?" he asked.

She assured him that she would, and thanked him gravely. There they parted as chastely as could be imagined, and Miss Tolerance went in to lay her aching head on the cool pillow.

Miss Tolerance woke in the morning determined upon returning to Manchester Square. "I have trespassed upon your kindness long enough. My aunt will be wondering if I am lying dead under London Bridge, and my client will wish some report of the inquiries I have *not* made while I have idled here."

"I wish I could persuade you to idle a little longer." Sir Walter looked disapproving but did not attempt to persuade Miss Tolerance against her plan. He only requested that she break her fast there, and that he be permitted to take her back to Manchester Square before he went to Bow Street. "I hope you will not exert yourself too greatly for the next several days," he said mildly.

Miss Tolerance's stomach had finally settled, and she set to the food Mrs. Yarrow provided with an appetite. She was aware of a certain tension between Sir Walter and herself which she thought was inevitable, coming at the end of this period of enforced intimacy. She did not directly address it, but made a point of thanking Sir Walter again for his kindness, and of apologizing for the disruption of his household.

"I hope you will always come to me when you need assistance." Then, as if he too felt the awkwardness of their situation he joked, "Your arrival has inestimably improved Michael's bragging rights among his friends."

"Has it? I am delighted to help Michael—"

Miss Tolerance was interrupted by the arrival of Mr. Penryn, the younger of Sir Walter's investigators. He was a Cornishman, short and wiry, his coat loose on his frame, his dark hair falling untidily around his unshaven face; Miss Tolerance knew him to be clever.

"Beg pardon, Zor Walter—" the Runner stopped short, took in Miss Tolerance's presence at the table, bobbed his head in her direction and tactfully did not remark upon it. "Miss, Zor Walter, there's been murder done in Primroose Street. Will ye come?" Penryn looked at Miss Tolerance; did he fear that she would keep Sir Walter from his duty?

"You must go at once," she said. "You must not wait for me."

Sir Walter was as composed as if murder at breakfast was quite a usual thing for him. "Penryn, please fetch a hackney carriage. Miss Tolerance, if you will go so far out of your way as to accompany us to Primrose Street, I will return you to Manchester Square afterward."

"There is no need—"

"There is every need. I told you I would take you home, and I will not be forsworn. And you may be of help to me. I should value any opinions you may form upon seeing the scene of the crime. You have a unique eye."

Miss Tolerance was a woman working in a man's world, and her vanity was not immune to an such an appeal. She smiled, and Sir Walter sent Michael upstairs to fetch down their visitor's few possessions.

Primrose Street was little more than a dozen streets from Sir Walter's house. The coach Penryn had hired was new and passably comfortable for a public conveyance, but it was small and crowded, the cobbled streets full of ruts, the ride a series of starts and stops, and the sunlight very bright in her eyes. By the time they arrived in Primrose Street Miss Tolerance was forced to acknowledge to herself that she was not completely recovered. She said nothing, and whatever Sir Walter suspected, he did not offer sympathy or coddling. They alit at the corner of Bishopsgate and pushed through the inevitable crowd, with Penryn to the fore bawling, "Make way! Clear way for Magiztrate! Oot the way there!"

They won through the crowd and found Hook, Penryn's partner, standing protectively over the body, which lay face-down in a puddle of blood and gutter-muck. Hook was a little taller than Penryn and very thick through the body. He stood with his chest puffed out as if the red waistcoat he wore—the uniform of the Bow Street runners—might itself hold the crowd at bay. The crowd seemed unimpressed and an elderly woman was screaming something at Hook as Sir Walter's party arrived.

"Took yer time," Hook growled at Penryn. He turned to Sir Walter, but was stopped, apparently by the sight of Miss Tolerance beside him.

"What report can you make?" Sir Walter asked.

Miss Tolerance saw Penryn exchange a look with Hook that offered sympathy but no explanation, then he stepped in to push the crowd back. Hook turned to the magistrate. "Watch reported this man 'ere found dead about an hour ago on 'is rounds, sir." Hook took out a small book and thumbed to a page where he had written some notes. "Being as the Watch is known to me personally, he come fetched me, and I been 'ere wiv the body since—sent Penryn there to bring you. Nobody in this crowd knows 'im— he gestured at the corpse. "'E seems to 'ave been right clawed-off, like someone 'ated 'im particular. I waited for you to turn out the pockets, sir."

Sir Walter nodded and bent to examine the corpse.

Miss Tolerance, very much aware that she was here as an observer, stood to one side and watched as Hook and Sir Walter bent to roll the dead man over on his back. He had been beaten so severely that his face looked like something better suited to a butcher's stall, and there were marks of throttling on his neck. Half-dried blood mixed with muck oozed sluggishly from one ear. Miss Tolerance swallowed hard, then leaned forward to point at something.

"He was struck there," she said, indicating a swollen

area behind the ear. "Perhaps that was the first blow, which rendered it easier for his assailant to continue?"

Hook opened his mouth, then closed it. Sir Walter nodded thoughtfully.

Hook sank to his haunches and began to pull out the pockets of the dead man. Each article he removed, he handed without comment to Sir Walter: a small purse of red leather stamped with a fading gilt design, containing six shillings fourpence halfpenny; a broken clay pipe; a pocket knife; two pocket handkerchiefs, one ink-blotted and the other incongruously clean; a pouch of tobacco; and a knitted scarf in stripes of gray and red. There was a wallet with a dozen more scraps of loose paper, most with figures written on, a few with names or addresses, all of which Hook read to Sir Walter before handing them over.

"I beg your pardon, what was that last?" Miss Tolerance asked.

Hook looked at her with frank dislike, clearly wishing that she would go away and leave the business to the men. His eyes flicked to Sir Walter, then he sighed and repeated, "An address for someone name o' Thorpe, at Squale 'Ouse in Pitfield Street."

Miss Tolerance frowned. The sunlight was making her head hurt, the smells of urine, dung, and blood made her queasy, and she felt stupid and slow. Something about the address—it meant something to her. Squale House.

"May I see the paper?" she asked.

Sir Walter nodded to Hook, who handed it to her, scowling.

The note was written in tidy clerk's script on a scrap of vellum: *Thorpe, Squale House, Pitfield Street.*

"In that neighborhood, Squale House ain't no mansion," Hook said.

"No, it's an almshouse," Miss Tolerance said vaguely. For a moment she could not recall how she knew that, and yet she saw the place in her mind, and a plaque: *Squale House for the Relief of the Poor.* She had wondered who Squale was.

And then the threads knitted themselves together. But what was the name and direction of Lord Lyne's younger son doing in the pocket of a nameless corpse?

Chapter Twelve

It is a curious feature of a blow to the head that, for some time after the injury itself occurs, the thoughts and memories of the victim may be considerably disordered. Miss Tolerance had made this discovery on earlier trials and found it no less true, or frustrating, now. Her limbs would take her where she wished; her stomach had settled, the pain was abating. But to her disgust she found that she began sentences and forgot how she meant to end them; that where she sensed a connection between two thoughts she could not always articulate it. Riding with Sir Walter from Primrose Street to Manchester Square, Miss Tolerance struggled to explain.

"I know—I *know* that I know something more than I can put my finger upon. The paper—"

"There were a great many papers in that unfortunate man's pockets," Sir Walter pointed out. "I wish you will not distress yourself. You are still far from well—"

"I beg your pardon, Sir Walter, but I am not an invalid! I

thank you very much for your care—indeed, I can hardly express my gratitude!—but please do not tell me not to distress myself. When I know there is something I am forgetting, it does not help to be treated like a pretty simpleton."

"I would never presume—" Sir Walter began.

I have hurt him. "I know." Miss Tolerance made her tone conciliatory. "I am sorry, Sir Walter. My irritation is with myself, with my uncooperative brain, which will not tell me what it has locked away. And I, all ungentlemanly, lash out at you when you have naught but concern for me."

To his credit, Sir Walter took Miss Tolerance's apology and her assertion seriously. With a little humor he pointed out that Miss Tolerance had time to wait until her thoughts re-arranged themselves. "There is no hurry. The poor fellow will not become more dead."

That made good sense as far as the dead man himself was concerned. But Miss Tolerance was certain that the man must be connected to Evadne Thorpe—and for Miss Thorpe time might be of the greatest concern.

The coach set her down in Spanish Place. Sir Walter walked with her to the gate and waited until she had unlocked it and passed through to the garden. "You will let me know if there is any other assistance a friend may offer?"

"I will." She thanked him again. They parted cordially, but Miss Tolerance sensed that Sir Walter might have more to say at another time, and was not certain whether she entertained that thought with pleasure or dismay.

Her cottage was cool and orderly, as she had left it. Miss Tolerance changed from her walking dress—which had sustained a good deal of dirt and damage over the past three days—into a round gown of blue and white calicut suited to the warmth of the day. Thus refreshed, she walked across the garden to relieve Marianne's mind about her absence, and to hear the newest household news.

Cook greeted her with a look, and then a second look, pronounced her worn to death, and threatened to feed her until the roses returned to her cheeks. Keefe, on his way out of the kitchen with a tray, stopped long enough to welcome her home. "We're always a mite concerned, Miss Sarah, when you're off adventuring. Them boys have been coming regular."

"To the kitchen door, I trust." Miss Tolerance accepted a scone from Cook, since she could see it would do her no good to refuse.

"Aye. Miss Sarah. With bits of paper they called reports. I have them here—"

Miss Tolerance demurred. "Your hands are full; I'll collect them later. Have I missed any important business here?"

The porter looked as though he would say something if only he could. "Excuse me, they're waiting in the salon for their coffee, Miss Sarah."

"Of course, Keefe. Thank you."

When the porter was gone the cook was more forthcoming; as she did not serve, or mix with, Mrs. Brereton's clientele, Cook considered that she had license to talk as she would—although she would have beaten her kitchen staff raw had they taken the same license. Cook was beating egg whites in a copper bowl, standing over the table where Miss Tolerance was eating her scone. "Things is been all sixes and sevens for days, Miss Sarah. Since that man— you know, 'e come poking all round the house, talking about economies and making sure we ain't taking advantage of Ma'am."

"Mr. Tickenor?"

Cook nodded. "He's got his nose into the whorin' too, if you see what I mean—"

Despite the evocative image, Miss Tolerance was not entirely certain she did. "He is interfering with the staff?"

"It's all a hubble-bubble. He don't think Mrs. B should be serving the molly trade, and that's scairt young Harry to death, fearing Ma'am will turn him off. Nor Mr. Tickenor don't hold with hot water for the girls to be cleaning up with after, and he tol' Emma she was letting her gentleman take too much time—"

181

"Has Mr. Tickenor spoken to my aunt of his concerns?"

Cook whisked her eggs ferociously. "Ma'am's all took up with wedding plans. Left all the business to Miss Marianne—"

And Marianne had no authority to stop Tickenor's interference. "Perhaps my aunt needs to know how unsettled the staff is, and how like that is to disrupt the custom."

"*Do* you say something, Miss Sarah. We's all been hoping you would."

Miss Tolerance remembered the public slap her aunt had given her the last time she had tried to speak for the staff, but what was she to do? "I shall, Cook." She did not look forward to the conversation.

Upstairs she learned that Marianne was engaged and Mrs. Brereton going over her accounts in her salon. Miss Tolerance was aware of the headache in the back of her head; she ignored it and started up the stairs.

"My dear niece, how delighted I am to see you!"

Gerard Tickenor's voice boomed in the quiet of the hall.

Not niece yet. Miss Tolerance curtsied. "Good morning, sir. How do you do?"

"Very well. Learning what I can of your auntie's business. With my business experience I hope to be a help to her." Tickenor smiled at Miss Tolerance; the smile put her in mind of the grin of a large dog.

"I'm sure my aunt will appreciate your help, sir. What sort of experience is that?"

"Tin mining, my dear. Very lucrative."

"How fortunate for you." Miss Tolerance did not mean to antagonize the man, but she heard herself saying, "Of course, this is not a tin mine."

Tickenor made a gesture to brush her objection away. "Business is business."

"As you say, sir." Miss Tolerance's head was hurting, and that, with her dislike of the man, seemed to compel her to say more. "I believe with a tin mine the objective is to take as much of the ore out of the ground as possible. With a brothel, the objective is to serve the custom so well that they return—and with a custom such as my aunt has built up, that is a complex business. One spends money, as I understand it, to bring in more money. Or so my aunt has often said."

"You seem to have given the matter much thought, niece." The last word had an unpleasant emphasis. "Are you perhaps more interested in the house than your auntie believes?" Tickenor moved a little closer to her, as if he meant to intimidate her by his nearness.

"La, no, sir." Miss Tolerance was bland. "I have my own business to attend to. My aunt knows that I have no interest—"

"Mrs. B has told me about your business. Dressing up like a man and nosing into questions that don't concern you. No sort of work for a woman. Dangerous."

With the lump on the back of her head Miss Tolerance could hardly disagree, and yet, "I would be very bad at my aunt's business, sir. But I do care for my aunt, and for her people."

"Her people?" Tickenor's smile had slipped. "Your aunt's *people* are very much indulged."

"Are they? I should have said it was the clientele that was indulged. But my aunt's people are very loyal, and know how lucky they are to have an employer who appreciates their work. I do hope you will take the time to learn about the business before you make changes, Mr. Tickenor. Good morning." Miss Tolerance curtsied and made to step past him, but Tickenor's hand came out and grasped her wrist painfully.

"You will not fight me, *niece*."

"Why, what gives you the notion that I am fighting you, sir? When you are my uncle I am sure we will deal very well together." Miss Tolerance reached down and grasped the hand holding hers, pressing her thumb hard into the joint below Tickenor's thumb. His hand opened and Tickenor pulled it away, cursing. "I beg your pardon, sir. You were hurting my arm." Miss Tolerance curtsied. "Excuse me. I am overdue to make my duty to my aunt."

Miss Tolerance was up the stairs and out of Tickenor's reach before he could stop her again. At the door to Mrs. Brereton's salon she paused to compose herself. Tickenor must be very certain of Mrs. Brereton, to show his hand so baldly. The conversation she must have with her aunt now would require tact and a nimble wit; Miss Tolerance hoped that her injury had not rendered her too dull to say what she must.

Mrs. Brereton, neat in an ivory gown, sat at her writing desk perusing ledgers.

"Sarah! Come in!" She closed the top book. "Marianne said you were in the country, but you hardly look as if you have been enjoying country air. You look pinched. Come have some tea." Mrs. Brereton rang for Frost and ordered a tray. Frost looked warily at her employer, and at Miss Tolerance without her usual glare of dislike. If her aunt's behavior was shifting Frost's loyalty, matters must be dire indeed.

"What have you been about?" Mrs. Brereton pushed the counts-books on her writing table aside.

"My client's business, Aunt Thea."

"So you will say nothing more about it. Well, you look as green as grass."

"Only tired. This will be restorative. Thank you, Frost." Miss Tolerance poured out tea. "How do you do, aunt?"

"Very well." Mrs. Brereton took the cup her niece offered. "But so busy! I have a wedding to plan for as well as the house to run. It is so fortunate that Gerard is taking an interest."

"Very fortunate," Miss Tolerance agreed. "And Marianne is making herself useful, I am sure."

"I suppose so." Mrs. Brereton sounded doubtful. "Gerard says she resents his involvement."

"Perhaps they simply misunderstand each other, Aunt Thea. Perhaps the way they manage is different."

"What do you mean?"

Miss Tolerance trod carefully; her aunt was not ready to hear criticism of her betrothed. "Marianne is used to the way you have always done things, ma'am. Too, she is a

184

woman, accustomed to doing things quietly. Mr. Tickenor is a *man—*" she made her tone admiring. "He is forceful. Of course the staff are a little anxious as they do not know what to expect of him."

"What to expect? That he will be a husband to me and help in running the house. What else should they think? What do *you* think?"

I think you have no idea of what Mr. Tickenor plans, once he has married into your property. "It is only that your people have been so much accustomed to looking to you for their guidance; it will simply take a little time for them to look to another."

"Look to another? Don't be stupid, Sarah." Mrs. Brereton was becoming agitated. "I know you are not happy about my marriage—do not bother to deny, it is writ upon your face—but I will not have you sowing discord here. You and Marianne and Frost have had the ruling of the roost for long enough. It is high time that I took back the reins!"

"And handed them to Mr. Tickenor?" Again, Miss Tolerance cursed her too-ready tongue. "I am sorry, aunt. I am tired, and saying I know not what. But may I offer one small piece of advice? Tell the staff—above and below-stairs—that they have naught to fear from this change."

"They know it."

"No, aunt, they do not. Something beyond their control is happening, and they fear it. Your word is law here: tell them there is no need to worry."

"You may tell them I said it." Mrs. Brereton sounded pettish.

Miss Tolerance's head hurt, and it was increasingly hard to be civil. "As you have pointed out, ma'am, Marianne and I have no power to make such assurances. Your people wish to hear from you."

Mrs. Brereton pursed her lips. "It is indulging them shockingly. Tickenor says I am far too lenient with them—"

"And yet your business has done very well under that lenient rule."

That thought pleased Mrs. Brereton. "Yes, it has." She simpered: Miss Tolerance could not remember seeing her stately aunt simpering. "Very well. I shall speak to them. Now, pour me more tea, Sarah, and let us talk of something else. You know that many festivities are planned to celebrate the Prince's elevation to the Regency? It should bring everyone to London."

"And every man to Mrs. Brereton's?" Miss Tolerance said lightly. "How fortunate." They spoke of politics for a time, or rather, Mrs. Brereton spoke and Miss Tolerance made appropriate noises. Her mind had returned to her own work and the whereabouts of Evadne Thorpe. "I beg your pardon, Aunt?" Mrs. Brereton had asked her something.

"Where are your wits, girl? If two days in the country makes you so dull, you should never go there at all. I said, do you find it chilly? April is always so: too warm to keep the fires lit, too cool to be comfortable." Mrs. Brereton took up a light shawl of banded silk and arranged it about her shoulders.

Miss Tolerance's attention was caught by the shawl. It was woven in stripes of silver and burgundy, with a narrow stripe of gold at each end. "Aunt, thank you for the tea. It has left me feeling very much better," she lied. In fact, her head was pounding. "I have two days' work I must make up. I hope you will not mind if I take my leave."

The April sunlight dazzled as she walked across the garden, and she was grateful to reach the dimness of her cottage. There, despite the headache which had caused her to speak so intemperate to her aunt and Mr. Tickenor, Miss Tolerance had one task before any other. How had she left matters with Lady Brereton? That she would communicate any news she had of Miss Thorpe. And then she had fallen off the Earth's face. Lady Brereton was likely eager for news, and while Miss Tolerance had little of use to tell her, she took up her pen and wrote a brief note.

I regret that a stupid indisposition has taken me from pursuit of your business for the last two days, but I am now recovered and promise to return to the matter with renewed energy. I hope to be able to report something useful very soon.

Miss Tolerance sanded and sealed the note and brought it across the garden to Cole, who promised to have it delivered at once. She had been optimistic in the note; by the time she had returned to her cottage again, her head hurt so badly she could barely keep her feet. Miss Tolerance was forced to acknowledge to herself that she had no energy to speak of, that her thoughts were still far too disorganized to admit of deduction, and that only thing she was about to pursue was a nap.

Dark had fallen when Miss Tolerance awoke. She lit a candle and went downstairs to find that someone from the kitchen had left a tray for her: half a roasted chicken, new bread and butter, some cheese and an apple. Miss Tolerance did not want to light the fire for tea, so she poured a glass of wine which she forgot to drink, and sat down to her meal. Afterward she took out her writing desk and attempted, as she often did when the disparate threads of an inquiry stubbornly refused to come together, to make sense of what she knew.

At last she concluded that either the information she had was not sufficient to tell her anything about Evadne Thorpe's whereabouts, or her brain was still too rattled to discern the pattern. Unhappy, Miss Tolerance locked her door and went upstairs to bed.

She was wakened sometime later by a powerful pounding downstairs. A glance out the window told her it could not be very late; light still streamed from Mrs. Brereton's house. The pounding came again. It was either an emergency or some drunken patron of her aunt's had slipped his leash and come to see who lived in the little house. Miss Tolerance threw a woolen shawl over her nightdress and went downstairs bare-foot. Before she pulled the bolt she fetched her pistol and made sure it was primed.

When she opened the door she was astonished to find it was Sir Adam Brereton who had been knocking so vigorously. Behind him was Cole, wearing an expression of abject apology.

"Ad--*Sir* Adam?" Miss Tolerance replaced the pistol on the shelf nearest the door.

"Mrs. B said to bring him over, miss."

"You are hurt!" Sir Adam informed her.

"Yes, and tired, too. It is all right, Cole. I know the gentleman. It is perfectly safe to leave him with me."

"Perfectly safe! What do you mean?" Sir Adam looked from her to Cole and back again.

"Come in, Adam. It is chilly, and at least one of us is not dressed for talking on the doorstep by moonlight." Miss Tolerance stood back to admit her brother, then closed the door. "To what do I owe this extraordinary honor?"

"What do you mean, perfectly safe?" Sir Adam asked again.

"I know my life seems to you quite irregular, but I do not generally make a habit of entertaining men at this hour. My aunt's staff are a little protective. And you did appear distraught."

"They thought I might..." Sir Adam shook his head. "I came only to see if it was true you had been hurt."

It was now Miss Tolerance who was surprised. "Yes, it is true. But how did you know of it? And why—if I may ask—do you care?"

"Why do I care? You're my sister, for God's sake! Do I need any more license than that?"

Miss Tolerance began to laugh. "You come and rouse me from my bed in order to express your concern?"

"You were struck down in the street! I thought you were at death's door." Sir Adam was sulky now.

"Good God, Adam, a week ago you were disappointed to know I was not dead! I was struck a blow to the head, but thanks, as I am assured by the surgeon who attended me, to the weight of my hair and the thickness of my skull,

I am only a little the worse for it. 'Tis the nature of my work; sometimes people object to what I am doing and attempt to stop me."

"But to hurt you—"

Miss Tolerance regarded her brother with impatience. "I am no longer a lady, Adam. I am a Fallen Woman, and the world uses such as rudely as we will suffer them to do. I am not brutalized; I am not starving; I do not swill gin to numb the pain of blows from a whoremaster or the itch of the clap. When I ran away with Connell my life changed. *I* changed. If it makes it easier, you need no longer consider me your sister. Indeed, I thought that had happened long ago."

Sir Adam's horror had give way to bewilderment; now it seemed that was to be replaced with anger. "If you force the new acquaintance upon me, do you expect me to have no feeling for you?"

"I did not—" She stopped and sighed in frustration. "Adam, I told you who I was because it seemed unwise not to do so. Had the secret come out through no work of mine or yours, would you not have felt ill-used? I did not identify myself in order to curry favors from you. I am what I am. I do what I do. And sometimes someone takes a sword or a stick and makes an attempt to stop me. They have not yet succeeded."

"And I still have a sister."

The declaration moved Miss Tolerance. "You do, and shall, if you choose to claim her. No, not publicly! I do not intend to force your acquaintance. I stand by the assurances I gave you when we first spoke: your wife will never learn from me who I am. But now you know that I am alive and where I am, I certainly shall not turn you away if you choose to call upon me. Although—" she gestured at her nightdress and cap—"perhaps at a more convenient hour."

Sir Adam made a sound somewhere between a snort and a laugh. "Perhaps. But Sal—Sarah, you were not badly hurt?"

"Not badly, no. I lost most of today to a wretched head-ache—"

"Well, yes, you would do. D'you remember when I was thrown during the hunt? I laid abed for a week, could barely open my eyes—" Sir Adam broke off his reminiscence. "Should you not still be abed?"

Miss Tolerance smiled. "I was. No, no, Adam. It is now several days since I was struck. I am much recovered. But tell me: how do you come to be here? Yes, I know you heard I was hurt. But how? In my note to Lady Brereton I did not say I had been attacked."

Sir Adam considered. "I thought Clary—Lady Brereton—I thought she—" he sat heavily on the settle before the dark hearth and counted on his fingers as if numbering actions there. "The family was all together in Lyne's drawing room. My wife was playing on the pianoforte, and Lyne and I were playing backgammon." That was the thumb. "Your note was delivered—" the forefinger. "Lyne asked what it was and Clary—Lady Brereton—told us it was a report from you, that you apologized, that you had been unable to pursue inquiries for several days—" that was the third finger. "She went up to dress for dinner." The fourth finger. "Lyne and I stayed to finish our game. Henry and John were watching. Someone said something."

"Something?" Miss Tolerance suppressed her impatience. "About me? "

"Yes. The mention of you put Lyne all out of temper, then Henry said something very coarse about women who went out looking for…looking for trouble." Miss Tolerance was certain that *trouble* had not been the word Henry Thorpe had used. "Of course John took exception, and the two of them began to bicker. Who was it? Someone said something, but as to who it was—"

"What did they say?" Miss Tolerance pressed.

"I don't recall exactly. It's the devil of a thing. But I was left with the notion that you had been injured. Struck down in the street."

"Did someone say those words?"

"I don't know. Dammit, Sally, I wasn't taking it all down like a damned clerk." Sir Adam had lost the count of his fingers and looked up at his sister. "But when I went up to change I had begun to worry."

"This was all before dinner?"

Sir Adam nodded. "We had no engagement tonight, so I waited until Clary—Lady Brereton—went up to bed, then I came here."

"And you cannot recall who among them—Lord Lyne or his sons—suggested that I had been struck down, or how they learned of it." Miss Tolerance did not want to call attention to the question with her brother, whose discretion she did not entirely trust. "Perhaps there was a note of my injury in the *Times*," she said at last.

The cloud upon Sir Adam's brow lifted. "Oh, very likely," he agreed. For the first time since he had entered her cottage he looked about him, taking in the tidy room: sturdy furnishings with no pretension to elegance, two rag-rugs made by Miss Tolerance's own hands, a shelf of books and ledgers on the far side of the tiled fireplace. After the elegance of Lyne House and the sensual luxury of Mrs. Brereton's establishment it doubtless seemed meager to her brother.

"What's that?" Sir Adam had spied the pocket watch Miss Tolerance kept upon the mantle. "Connell's watch! I remember he used it to time my footwork; I hated the damned thing. How come you to—" he stopped, blushing.

"He left me the watch, and his sword and hanger, and his riding crop," Miss Tolerance said softly. "Everything else I had to sell in order to return home."

Sir Adam appeared to have been struck by an original and peculiar thought. "Sally, were you happy?"

"Yes, Adam. Despite the inconvenience and the danger we were very happy."

Sir Adam had asked the question, but now seemed uncomfortable with so straightforward an answer. "Well," he said at last. "You seem to be comfortable enough here. And

191

you have seen a doctor for that bump on the head?"

Miss Tolerance began to nod and stopped herself. "In a day or so I shall be quite recovered. What I chiefly need is rest."

Her brother took her hint. "I shan't keep you from your bed, then. Good night, Sally."

Miss Tolerance followed him to the door. "Good night, Sir Adam." She closed the door behind him and locked it.

In the middle of the night Miss Tolerance woke, panting, from a violent dream. She sat upright in her bed, staring at the shifting patterns of silvery moonlight on her counterpane and attempting to quiet her breathing and slow her heartbeat. There was something in the dream, something her sleeping mind had teased out of her, but waking had driven the thought away. She took long, slow draughts of cool air. A scent, not a real scent but a remembered one, lingered with her: coppery and warm, dangerous. Blood. Had she been dreaming of blood? It would not be the first time.

Miss Tolerance slid her feet from under the blankets, lit a candle, and went to fetch a notebook and a stub of pencil. Like many young women of good family she had spent some of her youth under the authority of a drawing master. She was the first to acknowledge that she had little talent. Still, the habit of making tiny sketches in the margins of her ledgers, or of essaying larger composition as a way of recalling something, had not left her. She returned to the warmth of her bed with the notebook upon her lap, put pencil to paper, and waited for inspiration.

She drew a series of arches and rectangles which, with the suggestions of heads and arms attached, became a large room filled with clerks seated at desks, applying themselves to their work. Rows of desks and clerks stretched into the distance, but in the foreground, as she added details, Miss Tolerance realized that one of the desks was empty. On what would have been the ground before that desk she drew a man. He lay on his back, one arm thrown up, the other drawn across his belly. In the throes of inspiration she drew a scarf around the man's throat in light and dark bands which she realized were the same colors she had noted earlier on Mrs. Brereton's shawl: red and gray. She sketched in the man's features lightly, the suggestion of a nose and cheekbones broken and swollen, the eyes closed, the mouth gaping and bloodied. On the man's left cheek, a mark.

The pattern of leaf and shadow danced on her bed. Miss Tolerance stared at her drawing. What was there she had never seen in life, she was certain. Had she seen a man bludgeoned to death under the unconcerned gaze of his fellows she would have remembered it. Who was the man, then? After a moment she realized it was the poor corpse she had seen that morning with Sir Walter in Primrose Street. The sight must have made a far greater impression upon her than she had realized.

Her pencil went back to his face. She blackened the mark upon the cheek, damning her disordered memory. There was something she should know. Had the victim in Primrose Street had such a mark on his face? And if he had not, had she seen anyone of late who did? Slowly, as if spinning threads together into a skein of yarn, she pulled the memories into a coherent whole. An office indeed, but with only three desks. An old man; a large, brutal looking one with a sneering lip; a younger one with a strawberry mark on his left cheek and a gray and red scarf wrapped twice around his neck. The man in Primrose Street, the man with John Thorpe's direction in his pocket, had been Mr. Abner Huwe's clerk.

Chapter Thirteen

Miss Tolerance woke early and sent a note to Sir Walter Mandif, inquiring if the man killed in Primrose Street had had a strawberry mark on his left cheek. "If he does, I may be able to offer some assistance," she wrote. Best not to be too certain upon the evidence of a dream. She signed and sanded the letter, sealed it, and brought it to Keefe for delivery.

"I have your mail, Miss Sarah," the porter told her. "I didn't want to trouble you with it yesterday as you looked right done up." He offered her two letters and two grubby twists of paper. "From them boys."

Them boys. Well, nothing was so likely to give her a sense of what she had missed—or not--as the reports from her street-sweeps. Miss Tolerance thanked him and took the mail back to her cottage.

Miss, the first report began.

The ol Lorchip gone to his club on St James Street and stad

there until dinner. The Ladychip wint to bond Street to a glover
shop, and to a sparkers (what could that mean? Miss Tolerance wondered. A jeweler was her best guess). *She come*
ome and then gone out later wiv her usband in a coash, dressed
to turn out yer eyes. Han't seen sign of the young gennelmens.

Nothing remarkable in that report except the spelling,
Miss Tolerance thought. She uncurled the second one.

Miss
The ol Lorchip wint out early to a coffe ouse in Fleet street to
drink coffee wiv that red hared man. His coat was brown today.
Then the ol lorchip wint to a bootmaker in St Jams street and to
his club.
The young Ladychip gone out to visit friends in Duke Street.
When she come ome the two gents come to visit too. Then the
yonger gent gone back to Pitfield Stret. The mean young gent
gone off wiv the Lorship to Durry Lane, but Charlie ad to be ome
afore they left it.

Again the red-haired man, who was apparently Mr. Abner Huwe.

Miss Tolerance took up slate and chalk from her writing
desk and began to make notes. Abner Huwe, the proprietor of a shipping business; Lord Lyne, owner of properties
overseas. There was no reason why the two men should
not meet, although it still seemed odd to her that Lyne
himself would meet so often with a man such as Huwe—
Lyne seemed to keep himself well above the company of
tradesmen. Miss Tolerance considered further. Had Huwe
lied, or merely been mistaken, about where Lyne's property was located and what his business might have been?
It was possible he had genuinely confused Lyne's holdings
in South America for the West Indies, but Huwe struck her
as the sort of man who rarely forgot anything. It was also
possible that he had misled her out of some desire to protect the privacy of Lyne's business. This desire Miss Tolerance could sympathize with, and yet she had a hard time

ascribing such scruples to Huwe. And why would Baron Lyne meet the shipper in a coffeehouse in a neighborhood which neither man was likely to frequent? It smelled wrong to Miss Tolerance's nose, and she was inclined to trust that organ.

And there was the matter of the man in Primrose Street. She was waiting to hear from Sir Walter, but if the corpse had, in life, been Mr. Huwe's clerk, there was another and curious link back to Lord Lyne. Or at least to Squale House and Mr. John Thorpe.

There was a knock on the door and Marianne entered.

"There's a Runner at the door for you, Sarah." The whore sounded more amused than concerned.

"Did he give a name?" Miss Tolerance put her papers into a desk and closed it.

"No, but I believe he was sent by your friend Sir Walter."

Miss Tolerance smiled. "I am very glad to hear it. I will walk across with you." She closed the cottage door and linked her arm through Marianne's. "I had been wanting to tell you: I had an encounter with Mr. Tickenor yesterday."

"Ah." Marianne appeared enlightened. "I thought you must have had a talk with someone. Mrs. B called us all in to the salon last night before the evening properly began, and told us that we had naught to fear from her marriage, that we should all be happy as turnips."

"Did she say *that?* Well, if she has put the staff's fears to rest I am very glad of it."

"Yon Tickenor did not seem so pleased. He smiled like his teeth hurt him."

Miss Tolerance nodded. "Mr. Tickenor showed me those teeth. Evidently they are not so sharp as he had imagined."

"You'll want to be careful of him, Sarah. I don't think he's a man cares to be thwarted."

"What man does?" Miss Tolerance was satisfied that, whatever Mr. Tickenor's feelings, she had made her point with Mrs. Brereton. "And just how happy is a turnip?"

Marianne shrugged. "When it's in the ground I should think it was happy enough. Uprooted and in the soup—

who's to know? I've put your visitor in the little front room."

Miss Tolerance found Mr. Penryn looking very much as he had the morning before, his hair disheveled in the same degree, the precise amount of dark stubble present on his chin, and the same spot of grease on his red waistcoat. He stood by the window in the little withdrawing room, his hands clasped behind his back, rocking back and forth on his heels.

"Good morning, Mr. Penryn."

The Runner turned on one heel. "Good morning, miss. Zor Walter's compliments, and would you come w' me, please? 'E'd be grateful for a word."

"In Bow Street?"

"Yes, miss."

Miss Tolerance tarried long enough to send for her bonnet and wrap, and let Penryn escort her from the house, where a carriage waited. "Zor Walter's orders, miss, was to treat you gentle-like on zircumstanz of your injuries."

"I appreciate his care, and yours," Miss Tolerance said gravely.

They rode in silence along Oxford Street, skirting Seven Dials, thence to Drury Lane and, finally, Bow Street. Under Penryn's escort Miss Tolerance moved quickly through the crowds inside the offices, and was delivered to Sir Walter's office, where she found Hook and Sir Walter in conversation.

"Ah, Miss Tolerance." To the obvious impatience of Messers Hook and Penryn, Sir Walter asked no questions until he had seen her settled in a chair and had inquired as to her health. Miss Tolerance was only a little less anxious than the Runners to reach the reason for the meeting, and kept her answers brief.

At last, "May I ask how you knew that our victim yesterday had a mark upon his face? I do not believe the mark was visible due to the—er—the gore."

"I apologize that it took me so long, Sir Walter; gentlemen." She bowed her head, acknowledging the Runners.

"It came to me yesterday that I had seen the man—my memory has been a little disordered since that blow. I believe he was a clerk in a shipping office, Amisley and Pound, in Shadwell."

"'Ow you come to know that, miss?" That was Hook, who generally regarded the public—of which, despite her friendship with Sir Walter, Miss Tolerance was emphatically one—with deep suspicion.

"I had occasion to visit the office a few days ago in pursuit of an inquiry. I know nothing about the man himself; indeed, if he had not worn that scarf I should likely not have remembered him at all."

There was a stir of activity as Penryn and Hook conferred over a list of the deceased's property. "Red and gray scarf, stained with blood," Mr. Hook read. "'E was a-wearin' of it when you saw 'im?"

"Yes. As it was a warm day, I was surprised to see it, and noted it particularly." Miss Tolerance did not feel it necessary to mention her dreams or her aunt's silk shawl. "If you intend to send someone to interview his employer, Sir Walter, might I be permitted to accompany him?"

A look passed from Hook to Penryn to Sir Walter and back again. Sir Walter cleared his throat. "I think I will go myself, as we will need to learn if the man had any kin, and they will need to be notified. If you wish to accompany me I shall, of course, be pleased to have your company."

It was thus agreed upon, and in half an hour Miss Tolerance and Sir Walter were in a coach rattling toward Fox Street, Shadwell, and the offices of Amisley and Pound. Hook had stayed in Bow Street, and Penryn had opted to ride on the box with the jarvey.

"Have I caused trouble by asking to come?" Miss Tolerance murmured.

"For me? Not in the least."

"Mr. Hook seemed less than pleased."

"He is not paid to be pleased by my decisions."

"Why *did* you permit me to come?"

Sir Walter smiled. "Because I was certain that, if I did not, you would go by yourself at another time. You are not yet well enough to make such inquiries on your own."

Miss Tolerance was unsure whether this more irritated or amused or touched her.

As on the occasion of her last visit to Shadwell, Fox Street was busy with tradesmen and carriers. By contrast, when Sir Walter led the way into the offices of Amisley and Pound there was a hush broken only by the scratch of pen on paper. Only two of the tall desks were occupied, and it took a very long minute for the large man, whose name, Miss Tolerance recalled, was Worke, to look up from his ledger.

"Their employer's name is Huwe," Miss Tolerance murmured to Sir Walter.

"Good afternoon. Is Mr. Huwe available?"

Worke looked at Sir Walter and his companions; his eyes widened slightly at the sight of the Runners' red waistcoats. He did not appear to notice Miss Tolerance at all. "This a law matter?"

"I shall need to speak with Mr. Huwe." Sir Walter was firm.

Worke edged himself off his stool and went into the office. He was gone rather longer than seemed necessary to announce the presence of the magistrate and his officers, and when he returned his face was red.

"Walk in," he muttered.

Sir Walter led the way into the office, which was no tidier or less congested with paper than it had been upon Miss Tolerance's last visit. The only difference of note was that a chair, piled with ledgers and loose paper, had been moved to the back of the office against the door to make space for the visitors. Miss Tolerance stayed at the rear of the group, not wishing to draw attention, but it seemed this was a bootless effort. Abner Huwe rose, circled a few steps from behind his desk, and bowed cordially to her before he addressed himself to Sir Walter.

"I see you are returned to us, miss. Was your father able

to speak with—"

Before he could speak Lyne's name Miss Tolerance shook her head. "No, sir. After all my trouble it appears that the business was no longer so pressing. But we are here upon a very different errand."

"Indeed, very distinguished company you have brought to us! Nothing is amiss, I hope." The Welsh inflection was more in evidence than it had been before.

Sir Walter evidently felt it was time he took the lead. "This lady is here to help us in pursuit of an investigation. Do you have in your employ, Mr. Huwe, a young man with dark hair and a birthmark here—" he indicated his left cheek.

"Such a man, Tom Proctor, I had as clerk. But as he has not seen fit to come to work, nor sent word of where he is, he will find there is no employment for him here." There was no anger in Huwe's voice.

"About that, sir. I regret to tell you that Mr. Proctor has been the victim of an attack. He is dead, sir."

"Dead, say you! Dead! Poor young man." Huwe took a step back as if he meant to sit in the chair there, then realized it was too full of papers to accommodate him. Despite this show of surprise there was neither shock nor sorrow in his words. "Poor fellow, I did wonder why he had not come on his time."

"Did Mr. Proctor have family, sir, that we might notify?"

Huwe craned his neck as if to look around Penryn, who stood in the doorway. "Hi, Worke!"

Penryn stepped to one side. The big clerk showed his face behind the Runner.

"Poor Tom Proctor's dead. Had he any family? Wife or old Dad or such?"

Worke shrugged. "Nah." With which expression of sympathy he went back to his desk.

"You must advertise for a new man, Mr. Worke," Huwe called to his back.

He turned his attention to Sir Walter again. "This is a shocking thing, to be sure."

"Yes, sir. Murder always is."

"Murder, do you say? I thought you said the poor fellow was robbed."

"I said he was attacked, sir. Not quite the same thing. Did your Mr. Proctor have any enemies, sir?"

Huwe ran a hand through his disordered red hair and frowned. "I do not know of any. He seemed a good, sober fellow, did the work he was set, which is all I care for. What he did at day's end I cannot say."

Sir Walter nodded. "Do you know where he lodged, Mr. Huwe? Perhaps his landlord will tell me more."

"Indeed, sir, I have told you what I might." Huwe put his forefinger to the side of his nose and frowned. "I remember me that the boy lived in a boarding house in Well Street, not so far from here. But it is one of those helter-skelter places with six to a room. I do not know if the landlord could tell you more."

"We shall make enquiries." Sir Walter was mild. Miss Tolerance remembered what it was like to be quizzed in that bland, polite manner, and she did not envy Abner Huwe. "Do you recall the number of the house, Mr. Huwe?"

Perhaps to suggest the urgent business of a man who cannot be all day dealing with the affairs, however sad, of a former employee, Mr. Huwe took up a sheaf of papers from the chair behind him and began to run his thumb along the edge of the stack, as if he could barely restrain the urge to rifle through them. "I think it was at the corner of the Ratcliffe Highway, but I cannot be certain."

"Thank you, sir. If you recall anything that you believe material to Mr. Proctor's death, I would appreciate—"

"Oh, indeed, indeed. I shall be in touch with you directly. I wonder, though—" He tapped his thumb on the pile of papers and smiled. "Might I be asking one question?"

Sir Walter inclined his head politely.

"How is it you determined that the poor young fellow was in my employ?"

201

Sir Walter glanced at Miss Tolerance. "This lady was in the vicinity of the incident and recognized him."

"Did she so? She is a very observant lady, then." Huwe's tone was all admiration. He turned his regard to Miss Tolerance again. "It is fortunate that she was in that vicinity, I think." His smile was polite but there was a curious edge to it.

"Fortunate indeed, and fortunate that she understood her civic duty so well as to bring the information to my attention," Sir Walter agreed. Miss Tolerance realized he did not like Huwe any better than she did. "Mr. Huwe, as I said, if you—"

"I beg your pardon, Sir Walter." Miss Tolerance was forceful. Sir Walter paused, then deferred to her. "Perhaps Mr. Huwe will answer one more question?" In fact she had several, but only one could be asked now without giving away her surveillance of Lord Lyne.

Mr. Huwe smiled condescendingly.

"Sir, do you know why Mr. Proctor should have had the direction of the Pitfield Street almshouse run by Mr. John Thorpe writ on a slip of paper in his pocket?"

Miss Tolerance thought that whatever Mr. Huwe had expected, this was not it. His eyes widened slightly and his ruddy complexion darkened; the smile straightened into the beginning of a frown. *I should not like to have this man angry with me.* Then his expression became again as bland and jovial as that of an alemonger at the village fête. "A Mr. John Thorpe, say you? That I cannot tell. Perhaps my man and Mr. Thorpe drank a pot of ale together, or meant to do."

"Perhaps so. Thank you, sir."

"You are most welcome, miss. I hope you will give my lord Lyne my kindest regards when you see him next."

"Lord Lyne, sir? I am not likely to see him at all. I wonder you should think it."

"Ah, yes. It was your father who was seeking Lyne." Huwe's smile broadened. "Do not mind it, then."

Sir Walter broke into the peculiar current that was building between Huwe and Miss Tolerance. "Thank you, Mr. Huwe. We will take our leave." He bowed. Miss Tolerance curtsied. Penryn waited to follow after until they had left the office.

Penryn joined them in the coach, pointed now to Well Street, and offered the opinion that there was something not right about that Welsh bastard.

Forestalling Sir Walter's admonition about language, Miss Tolerance voiced her agreement. "He was curiously unmoved by his clerk's death."

Penryn shook his head. "T'ain't that, miss. Man like that 'un, clerks is thruppence the brace. But he doon't like you, and he din't like you bein' there."

"He was surprised by your question, I thought," Sir Walter said. "Who is John Thorpe?"

"He manages an almshouse in Pitfield Street. I was lately involved in an inquiry in which his family was named."

"Well either he doon't care for it that you knew this Thoorpe, or he din't loike that his clerk did," Mr. Penryn said firmly. "Eyes bugged out like he'd et a frog."

At Well Street Miss Tolerance would have made to alight, but Sir Walter stayed her and sent Penryn to inquire for the boarding house patronized by the late Mr. Proctor.

"Now, what was that about?" Sir Walter asked when the Runners were clear of the carriage.

"You know I cannot—" Miss Tolerance began.

"I know that your investigation appears to be rubbing shoulders with mine. I only wish to know to what degree."

"Mr. Thorpe, whose name appeared on the paper we turned up in Proctor's pocket, is peripherally related to my current inquiry," Miss Tolerance told him. "I do not know if the two matters are connected—"

"Then you have a stronger regard for coincidence than I do," Sir Walter said lightly. "Is it not likely that the murder of a man who is connected to your investigation should be related to that investigation?"

"Alas, quite likely." Miss Tolerance was unwilling to involve the magistrate in her search for Evadne Thorpe, at least until she had had time to learn if Proctor's death could be factored into Miss Thorpe's absence. "And I wish I could be more useful to you, Sir Walter, but—"

"I understand your scruples. I hope you understand that at some point it may become impossible for me to honor those scruples."

Her head hurt and despite her regard for Sir Walter Miss Tolerance found herself wishing she were elsewhere and alone. "I do understand, Sir Walter. I hope you understand that I may not be able to accommodate your curiosity in the matter." She looked at him directly; Sir Walter returned the gaze.

"We must hope it will not reach that point," Sir Walter began. Any further comment was cut off by the return of Penryn. The Runner had his face screwed up as if he had smelled something foul.

"Well, Zor Walter, I found it." The Runner pointed an accusatory finger at the third house, a four story frame building that listed slightly toward its left-hand neighbor. Two elderly men sat upon the stone steps to the doorway, watching Penryn with a combination of curiosity and amusement. One man had a square blue gin bottle in his hand, the other a flyswatter which he plied vigorously and at some peril to his fellow. Behind them the door, frame as much askew as the building, opened inward on a hallway of Stygian emptiness.

"Do you wish to come in?" Sir Walter asked.

"Yes, very much."

The two men at the door, as Sir Walter's party approached, leaned away from the entrance as if to give easier access; the man with the gin fell backward and off the steps, where he lay, giggling weakly. His fellow paused in his fly-swatting and reached out a hand to touch Miss Tolerance's dress as if it were a relic of some sort. Miss Tolerance reached one gloved hand down and pushed the man's fingers away gently.

"Is the landlord in?" Sir Walter asked.

The old man screwed up his face in a moue of denial. "Out on business. Lef' 'is boy 'ere. Donal'. Be in the orfice." He reached for Miss Tolerance's dress again. "H'aint seen noffin' this pretty since Aboukir year."

Miss Tolerance reached again to disengage the man, but Sir Walter was there before her. "Do not presume to touch this lady." He was icy. "The office is to the right?" He stepped back, blocking the old man, to let Miss Tolerance pass into the building before him. She did not know whether to be touched or annoyed by his protectiveness.

The hallway was hot and fetid. Penryn slipped past Miss Tolerance and pounded on the office door. There was a muffled "Come on, then!" from the other side.

A youth of twelve or so years sat with his boots upon the table, cleaning his nails with a pen knife, a task to which he was giving his whole attention. His face was spotty; his dark hair fell around his face disorderly. He did not look up. "Whot?"

Sir Walter stepped into the room with an air of command. Miss Tolerance stood to one side and Penryn stationed himself full in the doorway as if to discourage flight. "You have a lodger here named Thomas Proctor?"

The sound of Sir Walter's voice, both more authoritative and more gentlemanly than he had apparently expected, startled the boy. He jabbed himself with the knife, swore, slid his feet off the desk and looked up at his visitors. He put his finger, which was bleeding slightly, into his mouth.

"You wan' who?" he asked around the finger.

"Thomas Proctor."

The boy looked at Penryn, then back to Sir Walter. "He ain't no kin o' yourn, I reckon. Whoz 'e done?"

"He has been murdered." Sir Walter's voice was matter-of-fact, but the effect on the boy was immediate. He took his finger out of his mouth and stared at Sir Walter as if he were a Drury Lane melodrama in and of himself.

"Murdered? Where? 'Ow? Z'ere going to be trial?"

"When we find the man who did it. What can you tell me about Mr. Proctor?"

The boy snickered. "That 'e's dead? I dunno. Paid 'is rent on time. Slep' in—" he paused and thought, visibly, frowning as if it hurt him. "Slep' in number four, on the first floor, wiv five other gents."

"And his personal belongings?"

The boy shook his head. "Dunno. They's cupboard up there, but I don't know 'e ever used 'un."

"Perhaps you should show us Mr. Proctor's room."

"Yes, sir. My da would know more'n me, sir."

"You know enough to show us to number four, do you not?"

The boy nodded. He peered past Sir Walter and Miss Tolerance to regard Mr. Penryn with interest. "Zat a real Runner, sir?"

"He is. The room, boy."

In near darkness the boy led Sir Walter's party up narrow stairs that, like everything else in the house, listed to the left. At the top of the stairs he opened a door and went in. Miss Tolerance heard him fumble with the tinderbox, then there was a glow of candlelight. The boy returned to wave his visitors into the room. Three of them could barely fit in it: in the yellow light Miss Tolerance could make out a windowless space containing two beds, and a large chest with six cupboards fitted with dull brass plates. The beds were not overlarge, and she tried to imagine three grown men sleeping in each of them. At least they had beds to sleep upon; some lodging houses did not provide even that sort of amenity.

"'At's the cupboard, sir." The boy jabbed his finger toward the chest.

"And do you know which of the cupboards would have been Mr. Proctor's?"

The boy shook his head. "Me da might, sir. "E keeps a book wiv numbers of the keys boarders take out. So 'e can charge for the service, like."

Miss Tolerance saw an expression of impatience fly across Sir Walter's face; he kept his voice admirably impassive. "Would that book be in the house?"

The boy nodded.

"Then perhaps, if I send Mr. Penryn down with you, you can discover which of these cupboards, if any, was claimed by Mr. Proctor." The notion that this was a suggestion was belied by Sir Walter's voice and Penryn's demeanor. "We will await your return."

Miss Tolerance advanced to the chest, took out her handkerchief, and rubbed at the brass plate on the first cupboard. Gradually the number 1 could be perceived. The kerchief came away blackened with tarnish.

Penryn reappeared in the doorway, his narrow face eloquent of irritation. "That beetle-headed boy! Found the ledger at last, Zor Walter, but he doon't read, zo spent five minutes gazin' at the page 'zif it would speak to him."

"Did it speak to *you?*" Sir Walter asked.

"Yon Proctor rented a key to number five. But no key was there here. Nor did he have a key 'pon his person when we inspected the body, Zor Walter."

Miss Tolerance reached out and attempted to pry open cupboard number five with her gloved finger, but it was locked.

"Shall I break it down, zor?" Penryn asked hopefully.

Sir Walter shook his head. "Whatever is there will wait until the landlord has returned." He directed Penryn to stay and oversee the opening of the cabinet. "I do not want anyone to anticipate us in doing so. Anything of interest that you find should be brought straight away to Bow Street."

Penryn nodded dourly. Miss Tolerance doubted he was enthused at the prospect of sitting in the fetid heat waiting.

"There is one other thing we might try, Sir Walter," she offered.

Sir Walter raised an eyebrow encouragingly. Miss Tolerance reached up and removed a hairpin which she held up to the candlelight and bent. It took her several minutes working at the keyhole with the pin. At last it yielded to her efforts with a click, and she prised the cupboard open.

Penryn shouldered her out of the way and removed

from the cupboard, cataloguing as he did so, three pairs of stockings, two shirts, a leather wallet, a pair of shoes in good enough repair to have been Proctor's Sunday best, a small knife, a half-carved figure of a soldier. At the bottom was a small coffer of dark wood banded in copper. It was locked. Without comment Miss Tolerance offered her hairpin to Penryn and he attempted to pick the lock. When he failed, Miss Tolerance tried as well, with no more success.

"We will take it with us," Sir Walter said.

Penryn tucked the coffer under one arm and led the way out of the room and down the stairs. "Nasty place," the Runner muttered. "Not a breath of air. Three men to a bed, packed close as African cargo. You lie down here, you wake w' the fleas."

Yet it was no worse than many such places in the city and—depressingly enough, Miss Tolerance thought, rather better than some. The party reached the ground floor and the little bit of fresh air that stirred through the crooked front door. Sir Walter paused long enough to make sure the boy in the office understood that he expected to see the landlord in Bow Street at his first opportunity. Then, gratefully, they reached the street and their hired coach.

"I have known you for a twelvemonth and still you surprise me," Sir Walter said to Miss Tolerance as the carriage rolled away from Well Street.

"How is that, sir?"

"Your...*skill* with a hairpin. I am not certain I should take official notice of it."

Miss Tolerance laughed. "I should certainly never exercise it except under the aegis of the law."

"But where did you learn such a thing?"

"From a man in Amsterdam who could not pay for his tuition in our *salle* any way but in kind. He wished to learn to fence."

"I would have thought the sort of man who could pick locks would have been well able to defend himself."

"The man was working for British Intelligence, Sir Walter. There are times, I gather, when a pistol is too loud."

Penryn, again seated opposite Sir Walter and Miss Tolerance, pursed up his mouth consideringly, then gave a bark of laughter. The coffer, which rested in his lap, jumped.

"Will you open the box?" Miss Tolerance asked.

Sir Walter nodded. "A wedge and mallet should take care of the matter. Do you wish to stay to see what is inside?"

"I should like to, just to satisfy curiosity. Do you mean to open it at once?" Sir Walter nodded. "Then, if you do not mind it, I will stay. Once we have discovered what is in the coffer, I must return to my own business."

"You do not think this business is in any way connected to your own, then?"

"At this moment I do not. Still, I am of a curious nature, and a locked box belonging to a murdered man must always command some interest."

Chapter Fourteen

When the carriage drew up in Bow Street, Mr. Penryn led a small procession through the thronged foyer of the court, holding the coffer clutched to his chest as if it contained rubies. Miss Tolerance and Sir Walter followed into Sir Walter's office, where Penryn placed the box on the desk and went to find tools. Miss Tolerance and Sir Walter stood across the desk from each other and bent to examine the box. She was aware of his nearness; the brim of her bonnet seemed to envelop him as well as herself.

Penryn returned. Sir Walter and Miss Tolerance stepped back and watched as the Runner applied wedge and mallet to the lock. It took two blows to splinter the hasp from the coffer.

Sir Walter stopped Penryn from striking again. "No need to destroy the box itself, man." The magistrate lifted the lid and all three, Sir Walter, Miss Tolerance, and Mr. Penryn, stared at the contents.

"Dirt!" Penryn wrinkled his nose.

It was not dirt, in fact, but a powder, like in color to snuff but too fine and in too great quantity. The coffer was nearly half full of reddish-brown dust, motes of which skirled into the air and made Miss Tolerance's nose itch.

"What soorta cod's head keeps a box o' dirt?" Penryn stalked from the room, shaking his head.

"A fine question." Sir Walter put a finger into the dust, sniffed it, licked it, and spat. "Foul stuff. I wonder what it is."

Miss Tolerance refrained from pointing out the unwisdom of tasting an unknown substance, particularly one found in such unwholesome surroundings. Instead she took a scrap of paper from her reticule and twisted a bit of powder into it. "Perhaps Mr. Penryn's question is more to the point. Why would your dead man keep a locked box full of—whatever it is?" The air was full of dust motes; she found she wanted powerfully to be away from the musty, acrid smell. "My curiosity has been allayed—if rather inconclusively. Unless you have further need for me, Sir Walter, I must return to my own inquiry."

Sir Walter closed the box and bowed over Miss Tolerance's hand. "Thank you for your help. You will let me know if there is any way I may be of assistance to you."

Miss Tolerance smiled and curtseyed, and turned to make her way through the outer offices to the sunny street.

Miss Tolerance hailed a carriage to take her to Squale House in Pitfield Street. Her thoughts strayed to the note Lady Brereton had received; even if Evadne Thorpe thought she did not wish to be found, she might not know her own best interest. It was still Miss Tolerance's belief that the girl had written the note under compulsion.

In Pitfield Street the door to the alms house gaped open. Miss Tolerance stepped inside. To her left behind a closed door she heard the voices of children raggedly chanting their ABCs. Further along the hall in the room in which she had spoken with Mr. Thorpe she saw three very young women, babies in their arms, clustered around a matron

211

with a tin basin. "Never put your babe in the basin without you check how hot the water is first," the woman said. From the expression on the faces of the young mothers, the notion of immersing a baby in water at all was new and unsettling.

"May I help you?"

Miss Tolerance turned. Her interlocutor was a stocky tow-haired man of middle years. His expression was patient rather than kind; his dress and manner were gentlemanlike. Miss Tolerance strove to call his name to mind.

"You are Mr. Parkin?" That was the name of Thorpe's partner in benevolence.

The man inclined his head in lieu of bow. "You have the advantage of me, madam. I am Parkin. How may I be of assistance?"

Miss Tolerance curtsied. "I am Miss Tolerance, sir. I am seeking Mr. Thorpe."

Hearing her name, with its implication that she was not one of the *virtuous* poor, Parkin's manner became more distant. "I regret, Mr. Thorpe is not here. Is there some way in which I may help you?" His tone suggested he hoped there was not.

"Perhaps, sir. Can you tell me if a Mr. Tom Proctor ever called upon Mr. Thorpe?"

Mr. Parkin looked blankly at Miss Tolerance. "Proctor?" He shook his head. "I don't know the name. We've a good many visitors in the course of the day, but most of them are women and children—" he waved his hand vaguely in the direction of the classrooms. "Some visitors must be kept away; men who visit are sometimes seeking the victims of their own brutality—"

Miss Tolerance detected the beginning of a well-rehearsed sermon. "I don't believe that Mr. Proctor is one such, Mr. Parkin. That is really all I needed to learn. When Mr. Thorpe returns, would you tell him of my visit and my question? He will know how to contact me. It is a matter of some urgency," she said.

Parkin, seemingly untroubled that his lecture had been

interrupted, nodded. Miss Tolerance curtsied and turned; Parkin did not trouble himself to see her to the door. As she left, Miss Tolerance reflected that were she in need, assistance would have come more palatably from Mr. John Thorpe than from his colleague.

Until she could speak with Mr. Thorpe it was impossible to tell what importance to put upon the paper found in Tom Proctor's pocket. Had the man spoken to Thorpe? Upon what business? When? Miss Tolerance picked her way carefully down the steps and came face to face with Hettie the pickpocket. Without thought Miss Tolerance put her hand to her reticule.

"Ooo ye wantin' this time, dearie? An' wossit worth to ye?" Hettie reached out her hand to Miss Tolerance, up.

Miss Tolerance considered. "Are you here most days?"

Hettie nodded vigorously. "When I'm not dining with the Prince o' Wales, I'm 'ere rain or shine and fog betwixt 'em."

"Do you know Mr. Thorpe, who runs the alms house?"

"Which, the sourish fellow wiv the yellow poll or the nice liberal gent?"

"I believe," Miss Tolerance said, "he would be the liberal gent."

Hettie licked her lips. "Lovely. Nice manners, sometimes 'as tuppence for an old woman, too. Din' even 'old it agin me when I tried the dip on 'im."

"A true philanthropist. Tell me, do you see who comes and goes at the alms house? Excellent. Did you ever see a young man—"she struggled to call more of Proctor to mind than his birthmark and scarf. "A young man, tall, dressed like a clerk. Dark hair and a strawberry mark here—" she pointed to her own left cheek—"very likely wearing a red and gray scarf."

"Straw-bry mark, miss?" Hettie mimed thought with a finger to her brow. The odor of stale hops and juniper berry clung to her; each time she opened her mouth there was a whiff of decay: one of her teeth was rotting in her head. "Straw-bry mark an' a scarf. Might be I did, miss.

213

Lemme think on it a moment." She scratched her scalp audibly. "Coupla days ago, this'd be? Great gawk wiv 'is 'air floppin' down so—" one gnarled finger sketched a diagonal line across her brow—"an' the mark right there, shaped bottle-like." She grinned. "Ye might say that's a shape I got a familiarity wiv, miss. 'E gone into the alms house, then come right out again. Matter of a minute 'r two."

"Do you know if he spoke with Mr. Th—the liberal gent?"

Hettie looked affronted. "I ain't the damned val-let, keepin' track of who's jawin' to who."

"Of course not," Miss Tolerance said. "I only wondered. And this was two days ago?"

Again the woman scratched her scalp. "One day's like the other 'ere. No, the bell was ringin' for church, so p'raps it was Sunday. It wun't raining, that I know."

It had not rained for a fortnight. Miss Tolerance sighed and gave Hettie a pair of tuppenny pieces. Before she could thank her the woman had scuttled away in the direction of the gin shop.

All very suggestive, but nothing conclusive. Somewhere, she thought, must be the thread to pull to unravel this mystery, but whether Evadne Thorpe would prove to be at the center of it she was not sure. Miss Tolerance thought of the twist of paper she had taken away from Proctor's box, and decided to seek professional assistance.

If she felt any trepidation in visiting Mr. Halford's apothecary shop, so near the site of an attempt upon her life, Miss Tolerance did not mean to let anxiety rule her. She did survey the street before alighting from the hackney carriage, and gave instructions to the driver to wait for her.

Mr. Halford, again neatly turned out in apron and cuffs, was making pills from an ivory-colored powder. He was finically careful, measuring out the powder over a piece of paper, wiping out the pill-form and filling it, flipping the lever to compress the powder into a lozenge, and carefully removing the resulting pill to a paper packet he had ready-made on the counter. Miss Tolerance thought it a shame to interrupt him, but Halford looked up from his work and smiled.

"How m-may I help you, mmmiss?"

His expression was blankly courteous; he did not remember her from her previous visit. Miss Tolerance took the twist of paper from her reticule and offered it to the apothecary.

"I wonder if you might tell me what this is, sir. Going through my—" she thought rapidly. "My late grandfather's effects, we found a jar with a good deal of this substance, and wonder what it is. My brother says it is *not* snuff—"

Halford touched gingerly at the caked powder, stirred it with his finger, then, as Sir Walter had done, raised his finger to his lips. *Am I the only one who thinks that unwise?*

"You h-have a g-good deal of this substance, miss? I w-would be happy to p-pp—to *buy* it from you—"

"Tell me first what it is, sir, if you please."

"*Cinchona pubescens.* Often called Jesuit's bark or *quinina*. Good for lowland fevers caused by bad air. Since the W-walcheren exp-p—"

"It is in very short supply, I believe. But surely you must be adequately supplied with the stuff?"

"Sadly, no. B-b-bark is often hard to c-c-come by, p-p-articularly now. If you w-wish to sell your supply—" Halford's expression was hopeful. Miss Tolerance felt a moment of remorse at having raised his expectation.

"I must consult with my family first, sir. But I thank you very much for your assistance. When I next have need of a remedy you may be assured I shall come to you," she added, to save the man the trouble of making the request himself.

Halford gave the slightest of bows, already turning back to his pill press. Miss Tolerance returned to her waiting hackney coach and gave the direction of Tarsio's. The carriage, fortunately, was fairly new and well sprung; it made the journey from Throgmorton Street to Henry Street without too much juddering, which permitted Miss Tolerance to doze. It was four days since she had been attacked, and she had not really been free of headache in that time.

At Tarsio's Miss Tolerance ordered a pot of tea and went directly to the Ladies' Salon. There she sat at a desk and occupied herself for some little time in writing letters: a second request for payment from a client, then a brief note to Sir Walter Mandif, explaining what the contents of Proctor's box had been. She was sealing this second missive when her tea, and the mail, arrived. A former client had, she was delighted to see, at last sent a bank draught which had been promised for some time. Miss Tolerance suspected that a run of luck at the faro bank had coincided with the arrival of her last dunning letter, but however the funds arrived, she was happy to have them. The second note was from Mr. Joshua Glebb, whose handwriting was narrow and excessively curled; it took her several minutes to be certain of the contents. He had new information regarding Mr. Abner Huwe; he would be at the Wheat Sheaf until dark fell or the custom died away; he was her earnest servant.

Earnest? Miss Tolerance finished the tea in her cup and left to return to the Liberty of Savoy.

Even so late in the day it was mild, but Miss Tolerance found Mr. Glebb alone at his table near the fire, hunched forward as if against a deep chill. She saw why at once; he had a cold. His long nose was red with mopping and his eyes were watery. Whatever he drank from the tankard before him, it steamed and smelled of rum. "Glad to see you, miss." His voice made Miss Tolerance want to clear her throat.

"My dear Mr. Glebb, should you be away from home in this condition?"

He shrugged his narrow shoulders. The yellowing fringe of hair on his collar stirred and settled, and Glebb leaned over his tankard as if to summon warmth from it.

"You order something for yourself, miss. Then we can talk."

Miss Tolerance raised a finger at Mr. Boddick, mouthed *coffee*, and turned back to Glebb. "I hope this information is important enough to risk your health for, Mr. Glebb."

"I'd no notion I'd be taken so bad, nor so quick. After our business is complete I'm for home and my bed, no mistaking. Mrs. Glebb can put a hot iron to my feet and give me gruel and toddies until I feel better. But I had other business to—" he coughed deeply and spat into the fire. "Other business to tend to than yours, so don't go putting this to your own account."

"At least tell me what you have learned so I may release you to your wife's care, sir."

Mr. Boddick put her coffee down before her and was gone before she could thank him. Miss Tolerance took a sip of her coffee—unfortunately watery and burnt—and gave her attention to Glebb.

"I did a little more asking about Huwe. He's a nasty piece of work; bad temper, and mutterings everywhere about shady doings. Nothing as you could point a finger— or a magistrate—at, though." He stabbed at the air with his forefinger. "What I did learn—did you know that two of his ships was first on the scene bringing shipments to Walcheren?"

"Provisions?" Miss Tolerance was perplexed.

"Cinchona bark. There's hundreds of men fell sick almost as they landed, and the Navy with no more than a teaspoon of the stuff to hand. Then on the horizon privateers appeared with chests full of the stuff. *Providential* like."

His tone was not lost on Miss Tolerance. "The privateers charged hefty prices, I take it. The commission investigating the Walcheren debacle has not looked into the role of those privateers?"

"Not that I know of. But look you, Miss T: a man owns a ship filled to the rafters with just what's needful, and sends it along to make a profit, that's reasonable. A man owns

217

two such? Just at the right time? That's *speculation* in time of war. They brought in *tons* of the stuff, miss. The bark. Where'd he get it, when it's hard to come by? How'd he know it was going to be needful? I ain't the sort sees plots, but this is the sort of thing begs a little attention, don't you think?"

Miss Tolerance nodded. Glebb rose unsteadily to his feet. "Well, I've passed that along to you to fret over. I don't mean no unseemly haste, Miss T, but I'm for home and my bed." As he started to bow his pear-shaped body was racked by a spasm of coughing. When he recovered himself Mr. Glebb made his way out of the taproom without further word to Miss Tolerance or Mr. Boddick.

Miss Tolerance sipped her coffee, thinking. She did not like Abner Huwe and was quite ready to believe him capable of villainy, but dislike was not proof. Nor was she certain what this new information had to do with her own business. If Huwe was involved in a scheme to drive up the price for Peruvian bark, that might explain why his employee Mr. Proctor had died with so much of the stuff in the box. What it did not do was concern Lord Lyne or his missing daughter. Without making something up from whole cloth Miss Tolerance could see no connection.

She settled with Mr. Boddick and was favored with his opinion on the Army's late success in the Portuguese town of Sabugal for several minutes before she was able to excuse herself and start for Manchester Square. It had been a day, Miss Tolerance thought, in which a good deal of effort had been expended to little purpose, but she was tired and her head was hurting. She would beg some supper in her aunt's kitchen, darn a stocking, and go to bed.

The carriage left her in Manchester Square. Miss Tolerance walked along to the gate in Spanish Place and entered there. There was a rosy gilding of light on the upper stories of Mrs. Brereton's house, but the garden below was blue with shadow. As Miss Tolerance started along the path to her cottage she heard an unaccustomed sound from the farthest corner of the garden, by the necessary house. Someone was weeping.

"Hello?" She kept her voice low. The sobs, raw and coarse, continued.

Miss Tolerance stopped to the left of her house, stepping as carefully as she might among flower beds that were just beginning to green and send up shoots. The necessary house was, by design, in the most shadowed corner of the garden; beyond a flash of white—stocking? scarf?—she could see nothing of the author of the noise.

She essayed again: "Hello?" This time the sobs stopped. Who would choose such an unlikely, not to say noisome, place in which to relieve her feelings?

And then, as she looked around the corner of the privy, she saw that it was not *she* at all. A boy sat behind the necessary house, heedless of the stink and of the dirt that sullied his fawn breeches. He had his arms looped around his knees and his face forced down between them; in the dimness she could tell only that his hair was light and his legs were long. A shudder shook the boy, and a small hiccup.

"You cannot stay there all night, you know," Miss Tolerance said at last, gently. "I had planned to make a pot of tea. Will you come share it with me?" When the boy made no move she added, "I may have some toast as well. With butter and jam."

Whether it was butter or jam that persuaded the boy, she did not know. He raised his head; what light there was caught on the smear of snot and tears across his cheeks. It was Harry, Mrs. Brereton's new boy, who had been hired to take the place of Matt Etan.

Matt had been Miss Tolerance's friend, and she had resisted close acquaintance with Harry for that reason. Where Matt had been frank, humorous, and bawdy, Harry appeared anxious and curiously refined for a male whore. Mrs. Brereton, one of the very few Queens of a London brothel to keep such a boy among her females, believed the boy would season and add luster to the establishment. Seeing him now, Miss Tolerance was doubtful. But lack of engagement with the boy was not the same thing as lack of sympathy.

"Come, Harry. Some tea and bread-and-butter will help put things to right. And perhaps you will tell me if I can be of any assistance?"

The boy—young man, rather—got to his feet, telescoping like a spy-glass. He was very tall and slender, towering over Miss Tolerance and swaying. She led the way to her cottage, unlocked the door, waved Harry in. Then she went about making tea: stirring the fire, filling the kettle by the cistern kept by the dresser, putting out cups, cutting bread in thick slices. She did not talk, and Harry, who had seated himself on the settle and hunched toward the fire as if to warm himself, said nothing.

At last, when the tea was steeping and the toast ready, Miss Tolerance sat and regarded her visitor. "Is it so difficult, then, working in my aunt's house?"

Harry's head jerked up. "No! They're all kind as can be, Mrs. Touchwell, Emma and Chloe and the other girls, Mr. Keefe and Mr. Cole. I thought to be afraid of Mrs. Brereton—she's imposing, but she's kind."

Imposing? Miss Tolerance recalled that the boy's first lover had been a country clergyman. He had certainly learned a formal way of speaking. She poured out tea and passed a cup to him.

"There is milk for you there. Harry, I hope you will not take it amiss if I tell you that most of the folk in my aunt's employ do not spend their free time weeping. Particularly not weeping where I found you." She regarded him sympathetically. His breeches were grimy. He wore no coat and his shirt was similarly smudged; he had used one sleeve as a handkerchief. His brown eyes were red-rimmed from crying. He was unlikely to be the object of any man's desire in this state. "Is there some way in which I may assist you? Is it that you are not cut out for the work? You need not feel it is your only choice—"

"No, the work's—" Harry blushed. "The work's—I don't mind the work at all. I know there's some miss the old boy

Matt, but I'm trying to win them over. And there's some of them, my gentlemen that is, that are very kind indeed."

Kind was to be the word, then. "Harry, if Mrs. Brereton is kind and her people are kind and your clients are kind and the work does not distress you, there yet was something had you weeping behind the outhouse. I won't demand that you tell me, but I assure you I will not tell anyone what you say to me, and I might be able to help."

The boy shook his head. "I can't. He said he'd—"

"He?" Miss Tolerance poured more tea into his cup. "What did he say he would do?"

The boy's chin trembled. "He said he'd beat me til my looks were gone, then throw me out the door, and that I'd die in a stew on the waterfront with weeping sores on my—on my mouth—and—" he broke off, horrified by the enormity of the threat. Miss Tolerance was grateful to be spared further details.

"Harry. He was looking down again, threatening tears. "Harry. Listen to me, please." She used the tone that had proved so effective when her own nursery maid had used it. "Listen to me. No one will beat you. And for the rest, if my aunt has good reports of your—your work from your gentlemen, there is no reason you need ever leave if you don't like to do."

"He said." A low, urgent whisper.

"Who said?"

Harry shook his head again.

"Harry, you know very well that my aunt has rules for her clients as well as for those who work for her. If one of them is making threats, she will put a stop to it." Miss Tolerance suspected her aunt would not care so much for Harry's feelings as for the lack of respect shown to her and her house, but in the end the result would be the same. "Tell me who has put you in such a state?"

Had it been possible for Harry to draw his head entirely between his shoulders, turtle-like, she suspected he would have done so. When he could retreat no further in that way, Harry whispered, "Mrs. B's—Mrs. B's man."

Her man? Keefe? Cole? They were the only men regularly upon the premises, and Miss Tolerance would have laid odds against either of them abusing their places so. Then a singularly unpleasant notion occurred to her. "Why would Mr. Tickenor make such a threat?"

Hearing the name of his tormentor made Harry tremble further, and the whole story came haltingly forth. That afternoon Mr. Tickenor had happened to see Harry in the parlor and, perhaps displeased that the boy had no engagement in that minute, asked him to follow, "and help me for a moment." Harry followed Tickenor to one of the smaller withdrawing rooms long the hall where, instead of required him to assist in unsticking a drawer or moving a table, Mrs. Brereton's fiancé had pushed the boy to his knees.

"He wanted me to—he said I had to—" Harry could not bring himself to say the words, but Miss Tolerance was quite able to imagine what Mr. Tickenor had wanted.

"What did you do?"

"I did what he said. I told him Mrs. B has rules against, but he said he was checking the quality of my w-w-work. And then when I was done he gave me a smack—" he gestured to the fading mark of a hand near his left ear. "Then he said if I said a word he'd—what I told you before."

"He threatened to beat you and expel you from the house."

Harry nodded.

"Harry, he has no power to do so." Even as she said it Miss Tolerance wondered if that was so.

"But Mrs. B means to marry him."

"Then he had best learn beforehand that there are limits to his authority here. Come with me and we'll sort this out with my aunt."

Harry's slender body reared back. "No! No, Miss Sarah. I don't want to leave, even if he don't beat me he'll still—"

She took Harry's hand and drew him to his feet. His tea cup, sitting at the edge of the table, rocked and Miss Tolerance put her hand out to push it to safety. "Harry, if Mr.

Tickenor has done this once, do you think he will not do it again? And if he has done it to you, do you not think he might try it with someone else in my aunt's house? If you are afraid to tell my aunt, let us at least talk with Mrs. Touchwell."

Faced with that alternative Harry became more cooperative. Marianne, he seemed to think, would not throw him at once to Mr. Tickenor's mercies. Silently he followed Miss Tolerance across the garden to Mrs. Brereton's house. In the kitchen Cook looked at the boy and observed that he looked as if he'd combed his hair with a holly bush. Miss Tolerance suggested Harry take a few minutes to render himself presentable. "Come back here when you are done," she suggested. She did not want to have this conversation upstairs where anyone might enter the room. "I'll ask Mrs. Touchwell to join us."

A quarter hour later Marianne Touchwell had been summoned and Cook had given over her own bedroom for their discussion. Marianne listened as Harry repeated his story, nodding now and again.

"Well, Harry, you're a good, brave fellow to have come to me," she said comfortably. "Now, unless I am much mistaken, you have a gentleman due to arrive in just a short while. So you go and entertain him. Don't worry, dearie. Miss Sarah and I will make all right."

Harry left Cook's room. With the burden of his secret lifted and his worst fears assuaged, his step was lighter and his shoulders unstooped.

"Poor idiot boy," Mrs. Touchwell said sadly. "Do you think I ought to look him out a place in another house?"

"Would that solve the problem?" Miss Tolerance asked. "I think rather you should ask, if Mr. Tickenor has tested the waters with Harry, has he done similarly with any of the others?"

"Oh, God, that'd put the fox in the chicken house for sure. But even if he has, what am I to do then?"

"Tell my aunt."

"And find myself working somewhere else? Sarah, this

is my home as much as it is yours. The boy's got a point: it's a fearful thing, even for a successful whore, to suddenly find herself with no followers, no home—"

"Do you think I don't know that? It's a fearful thing for any woman to find herself homeless, without family to support her. Marianne, I cannot imagine that, once he has found power over Harry or—anyone else in the house—Mr. Tickenor will abandon it. Do you think my aunt is so lost to good business sense that she would wish all of her workers reduced to fearful shadows?"

From the kitchen there was a homely rattle of spoon against copper bowl, and Cook's voice instructing the kitchen maid to bring the salt box from the dresser in the pantry. Marianne Touchwell thought and Miss Tolerance watched her. At last, "Let me find out first if yon Tickenor's been troubling the rest of the staff. Then—you must help, Sarah. No matter how much she trusts me, I'm still a servant to your aunt. You're family."

"I will help if I am able," Miss Tolerance agreed. Privately she wondered if, in such a negotiation, her relation would be as useful as Marianne believed.

Chapter Fifteen

The next day dawned gray and cold; even the half-bloomed flowers in the garden appeared to have thought better of emergence and furled into green shoots again. Miss Tolerance rose with the resolve to find Mr. John Thorpe and determine for once and all whether the matter of the late Mr. Proctor had any connection at all to Evadne Thorpe's disappearance. It was early when she left the house; perhaps he was still at his father's house in Duke of York Street.

She was pleased to spy one of Bart's squad of sweeping boys already at his post on the corner at Jermyn Street. They exchanged no sign; the only others abroad at this hour appeared to be milkmen and grocer-boys. Miss Tolerance approached Lord Lyne's house with a little trepidation: the baron had made it clear that he disliked her involvement, and any encounter with him was like to be unpleasant. Still, she could not lurk in the street waiting for Mr. John Thorpe to emerge. She had steeled herself to knock on the door when another figure appeared at the corner, walking unsteadily toward her.

Mr. Henry Thorpe had clearly drunk deep the night before and had not yet returned home. His gaze was bent on the paving stones beneath his feet, all his attention upon maintaining his balance. He did not look up to notice Miss Tolerance until he was five feet from her.

He squinted. "Miss—whatsit. Miss Chastity?" He giggled weakly and winced.

Miss Tolerance forbore to mention that he was not the first to make a game of her name. "Good morning, Mr. Thorpe. I was hoping to speak with your brother."

"What's the hour?" Thorpe patted at his coat, clearly hoping to find his watch. "Damn. Pawned it. What's the hour?" he asked again.

"A little before nine, I believe."

Thorpe made an exaggerated gesture of dismissal. "You'll have missed him, then. John is up and saving the unfortunate before dawn."

"Ah." Miss Tolerance sighed: back to Pitfield Street, then. "Good morning, then, sir." She turned toward Jermyn Street.

"Wait." From the expression in his face Mr. Thorpe could not believe himself that he had called her back. "Evie—my sister."

"Have you recalled something that might help me find her, sir?"

His shoulders slumped. "No word of her, then."

"Had I word, do you think I would withhold it?"

"No, I—" Thorpe raised both hands to his face and scrubbed mightily. "God, I can barely think."

Miss Tolerance made a rapid calculation of time and benefit. "Mr. Thorpe, will you permit me to offer you a pot of coffee? I have often found that helpful in…cases such as yours."

She was surprised to see the man grin lopsidedly. "With the jug-bit? I'm not drunk anymore, Miss Whatever, just have Hell's own head."

"Coffee may help there, too, sir," Miss Tolerance said sympathetically. "Surely it will not hurt. And we may talk about your sister."

They found a coffee house a few streets distant; the proprietor looked at Miss Tolerance a little askance, as such establishments were still largely the province of men, and today Miss Tolerance wore the garments of her sex, including a becoming straw bonnet. She ordered a pot of coffee and some rolls, then joined Mr. Thorpe, who looked relieved to find himself indoors, out of the glare of gray morning light and away from the worst noise of the street.

"No word of my sister," he said grimly. "I thought of what you said the other day. That Evie might wish to be rescued from what she—from her situation."

"I confess that I was surprised you so easily believed otherwise, Mr. Thorpe. Did your sister ever give you reason for it?"

"Not—No. But I've never been much in the way of seeing the best in people."

"Perhaps it is just that you too easily believe the worst."

"Aren't they the same thing?" Thorpe ran his thumbs along the crease between his brows. "I never thought to see the old man in such a rage at Evie. John displeased him with his charities, and he thinks Clary's husband's a wealthy fool, but I thought all his fury was reserved for me." Thorpe smiled crookedly. "If he could be as angry at Evie as ever he has been at me—I suppose I thought she must have committed *some* sin."

"So you judged her by your father's reaction."

"The old man's stiff as a poker, but I've never seen him truly angry except for cause. When *I* was—" the coffee and rolls arrived, and Thorpe was distracted.

The coffee dispensed, "You did something that angered your father?" Miss Tolerance prompted.

"Angering—that seems to be my genius. But enraged! An entirely different category. A few years ago I got myself mightily embarrassed: gambling debts, a woman—" he shrugged. "The old man had found me work in the War

Office through one of his cronies—my father's a great one for the military—and thought it would steady me. Give me a sense of responsibility." From his sour tone Miss Tolerance understood that the last words were not Thorpe's own. "I outran my income and my salary and had to go to the old man for help. He was—" Thorpe took a deep draught of his coffee as if it could blunt the memory. "He was mad with anger. Hadn't told me about the property in Venezuela, y'see."

"I'm sorry, sir, but I do not follow."

"My father had had reverses about that time too: damned Bonapartists in Venezuela were threatening to take over the plantation for the good of the damned nation. Trade with the rest of the continent was disrupted. Damned war, you see: *his* income was affected."

"The well was running dry," Miss Tolerance suggested.

"Aye. When he told me, I tried to find the money myself—only made things worse. Before it'd been mere debt, but now—I think if he could have cast me off me then without a farthing he would have done. But there's the name, the damned family name, had to hush it all up, my gaming debts had to be paid. He found the money somewhere, and it all would have been well except somehow someone had noticed—and it all came out—"

"What came out?"

"At the War Office. Never play cards with a man you work with. I marked my cards, see. Only the once, when I didn't see any other way out of my debt. But cheat once and you're a cheat forever. Can't have a cheat in the War Office. Drunk or whoring or on the lookout for the Bailiff is no scandal, but cheating! I was asked to leave the post. Quietly." Thorpe shrugged. "The old man can barely look at me. I haven't touched cards since," he said, like a boy offering mitigation. "But he won't forgive me. He set great stock in my holding that post."

For the second time in as many days Miss Tolerance felt the teasing sensation that some bit of clarity was just beyond her reach. "It was the loss of your position at the War

Office that distressed him?"

Thorpe shrugged again. "Damned odd man, my father. All about the family name for him. I nearly brought the family to scandal; I suppose his cutting Evie off is his way of seeing it don't happen again."

"You make it sound very cold-blooded, Mr. Thorpe."

"Say hot-blooded, rather. If you had seen him, all anxiety that the news would out and all the world be privy to the disgrace! And then Clary invites a stranger into his business!"

"Sir?"

Thorpe inclined his head in a sketch of a bow. "Yourself, ma'am. When my father says something is at an end, it is. And yet there you were, refusing to let the matter die."

As if his choice of words struck him as unfortunate, Thorpe addressed himself to his coffee. Miss Tolerance considered the web of information and impression in her mind. Finally, "Mr. Thorpe, was there some benefit that accrued to your father from your position at the War Office?"

"What? Can't think of any. He liked knowing what was being planned—he'd grill me on it, approve or disapprove based on what happened a hundred years ago. I think he hoped I'd give Castlereagh a scolding on his behalf, or at least pass along his advice. My father believes England would have been done with Bonaparte by now were he prosecuting the war."

Miss Tolerance thought of Mr. Boddick at the Wheat Sheaf and smiled. "So do half the men in this city, Mr. Thorpe."

"Half the men in the city don't have an ear in the War Office."

"Are you saying you told Lord Lyne things he should not have known?"

Thorpe looked up from his coffee with an unexpected glint of steel in his expression. "I may be a drunk and a cheat, but I'm neither stupid nor a traitor. I gave the old man no secrets. Half the nation knew of the plan to sink Bonaparte's fleet before it was rebuilt; the damned ships were sent off with bands and ladies waving kerchiefs."

"Chatham's expedition?" Everywhere she turned of late there was Walcheren or its vestiges.

Thorpe had not heard her. "...and I told him so. The old man got properly exercised, muttering about the lessons of history."

"He was distressed?"

"More incensed. Wrote a long letter out, told me to give it to Castelreagh. Who, I don't doubt, threw it in the fire. I certainly never heard that the Secretary said aught to my father." Thorpe's coffee was gone. He hefted the coffee pot, put his hand against the side. "Cold. What has all this to do with Evie?"

"I do not know yet, Mr. Thorpe. Perhaps something useful. It is my experience that seemingly unrelated events do, sometimes, when laid together properly, tell a story."

"And that story will answer all?" With increasing sobriety Mr. Thorpe's habitual sneering demeanor was reasserting itself.

"I trust my intuition, sir, and my intuition says it will."

Henry Thorpe pinched the top of his nose and closed his eyes. "Then find my sister, Miss Tolerance."

A mist too fine to be rain but too wet to be fog had settled over St. James's Square. Miss Tolerance pulled the collar of her half jacket tight, wishing she wore the Gunnard greatcoat that fell to her ankles. She had donned a favorite walking dress, hoping the day would turn fine. That hope defeated, she decided to return to Manchester Square, change into men's clothes, and hire a horse to ride in relative comfort to Pitfield Street. Mr. John Thorpe might not like the example she set for his charges, but she would be warm and dry and more attentive to her day's work.

A hackney carriage delivered her to Manchester Square. As her aunt's house would at this hour be bustling with the tumult that followed a night's successful business, she decided to avoid the brothel altogether. She went down Spanish Place to the garden door. Or would have done, but an electric sensation between her shoulder blades told her she was being followed close by. She turned. The man blocking her return to the square was tall and broad-shouldered; he wore a greatcoat of brown wool, stained and rumpled, and a shapeless hat pulled over his eyes. The fellow did not mean to be recognized or described to any other party, but Miss Tolerance knew him.

"Mr. Worke?" She kept her voice as level as she might.

Worke's full, sneering mouth twitched. "Know me, d'you?" He hefted a walking stick in his left hand.

"I have a memory for faces." Miss Tolerance looked past Worke to see that the street was empty. He had no confederates waiting to assist him, which was good; she saw no one she could summon to her aid, which was not. "What brings you to Manchester Square?" The ivied garden wall rose beside her, the gate to the garden too far to reach before he overtook her. Calling out *might* bring assistance, *if* someone chanced to hear her cry.

Worke scowled at Miss Tolerance.

"Is it a coincidence that we meet today, sir? Or is there some way in which I can be of assistance?" She had no knife or sword, and—she damned herself—she had come out without her pistol in her reticule. It would have to be her wits. Miss Tolerance took a step back toward Spanish Place. "I do not generally conduct business here; perhaps if you will accompany me to Tars—"

Worke stepped forward. He reached for Miss Tolerance's shoulder, his hand meaty and strong; blocking it would be as good as a declaration of hostilities. "You're goin' nowhere," he said. "Not without you tell me what I'm wishful to know."

Ignoring the hand on her shoulder Miss Tolerance drew herself up and said crisply, "This mysterious manner does neither of us good, sir. State your business and perhaps I may assist you."

"You'll tell me." Worke squeezed her shoulder. The pressure was so painful it was all Miss Tolerance could do not to cry out. "You will tell me." He was as much interested in causing pain as in answers, she thought. If she pretended her shoulder did not hurt he would doubtless redouble the pressure. If she squealed it would please him, no doubt, but how would that benefit her?

"Take your hand off me," she said quietly.

Perhaps without realizing it, Work relaxed his hand just a little; Miss Tolerance dropped her shoulder, twisted out of his grasp, and retreated a few feet toward the gate. The big man looked at his hand as if it had betrayed him, and stepped forward.

"I have friends just beyond this wall," she told him. "Can you say as much? I dislike to disturb my neighbors, but I will cry out if you force it."

The big man looked to his left and his right. Then, startlingly, Worke grinned. His teeth were uneven and yellow; the smile ferocious. "No one to hear. Now, missy, what you done with my box?"

"Box?" Miss Tolerance's bewilderment was genuine.

Worke stepped forward again. "Don't play the innocent. You took a box from Tommy Proctor's crib an' I want it back." He moved to grab her shoulder again. Miss Tolerance dodged out from under his hand, but in so doing she fetched up against the wall of Mrs. Brereton's garden. Worke's hand came out to bar her way, and he loomed over her, confident in his ability to intimidate.

"I took no box." It was only the truth.

"Hell you say. I went round to Tommy's and they tol' me *you* come took away the box of—of mine. I'll have back."

Miss Tolerance suspected that the news that his box was safe in the hands of a Bow Street magistrate would enrage Worke further. The big man took a step forward. Then Worke reared up and spun, shaking his shoulders violently. Miss Tolerance jumped away and for a moment saw a shaggy head just behind Worke's own. With a great shrug he shook his attacker off, but now something—it appeared to be a large dog—hung from Worke's leg. He pivoted on one foot, shaking the other to free it from what she saw now was a boy. Bart, the leader of the crossing-sweeps, clung ferociously to Worke's leg with arms, legs, and—yes, with his teeth, too. Worke, bellowing, swung his leg around until he could smash it, and the boy, against the garden wall. With his next kick Bart went flying, hit, and dropped to the base of the wall. His eyes were open and he was conscious, but blood flowed from under his hair and curtained his cheek.

Worke bent over his leg, where the trouser was torn and there was blood. Miss Tolerance dodged past the man to get to the boy; his hand swept out to grab her in vain.

Bart was panting; blood slid into his mouth, but when he looked up at Miss Tolerance his eyes focused. "D'I stop 'im, miss?"

Miss Tolerance would have reassured him, but there was no time. Worke straightened up and brandished his walking stick. "The box, you whore, or I'll finish dashin' that-un's brains out."

Miss Tolerance placed herself between Worke and the boy. "You will have to kill me to do it, and then how will you know where your box of bark is?"

At the mention of the contents Worke checked. Then, "You'll gimme that box or I'll murder ye both!" Worke lumbered forward. Miss Tolerance did the only thing left to her: she kicked the man as solidly as she could between the legs. It was not a direct strike: she had enough experience with such tactics to know that. It hurt him, though. Worke staggered back, the stick in his hand fell with a clatter, and he crouched over his pain. Rather than stay to see what damage she had done, Miss Tolerance pulled Bart to his feet and made for the garden door, hoping to be through it before Worke recovered.

She did not see what occasioned the sudden bellow behind her. Not until she had the door open and Bart pushed before her into the garden did she turn. Keefe, with Ted behind him, held Worke by the scruff of his neck like a truant schoolboy.

"Everything all right, miss?" Keefe, unruffled, might have been asking how the weather did. Worke, on his knees before Keefe, hung there. The flesh round one eye was swelling and his lip cut open.

"Thank you, Keefe. It seems you have matters in hand."

Ted circled round the two men to peer into the garden. "Bart! Your 'ead's busted!" He pointed with delighted horror at his friend's gory crown.

"Not broken, I think," Miss Tolerance said. "But in need of bandages and a beef steak. Keefe, may I leave this—" she gestured at Worke—to you?"

"Aye, miss. I'm happy to take him off your hands." He shook Worke gently. Worke glared about him, and Miss Tolerance suspected that very soon his belligerence would return unless he was made aware of the uselessness of it.

"The box, Mr. Worke? Did your informant tell you I was only one of a party who went to Mr. Proctor's rooms? The others were a magistrate and a Runner. The box is at Bow Street; if you inquire there I'm certain they will be delighted to discuss the matter—and Tom Proctor's death—with you."

This information appeared to knock the remaining air from Worke; his mouth worked soundlessly and he looked side to side as if he feared someone else might have heard the news. Keefe hauled him to his feet unresisting and turned him toward the Square.

Miss Tolerance urged Ted before her into the garden. Looking back, she saw Bart's cap and Worke's walking stick lying on the walk; thoughtfully she collected them, locked the garden gate, and shepherded the boys into her cottage. There, over his protests, she stanched the bleeding from Bart's head wound, urged him out of his jacket, and inspected him for other damage. Ted, awed by his leader's bravery as much as by his injuries, kept up a delighted patter about the bully's size and ferocity, until Bart told him curtly to give over.

There was a moment where Miss Tolerance thought violence would break out again. To forestall it she sent Ted to ask for a piece of steak for Bart's eye.

"Thank you for coming to my aid," she said gravely. She

had put the kettle on, and now poured a little warm water into a basin and took up a rag to clean his face.

The boy shrugged away, but Miss Tolerance held him firmly in place.

"Y're welcome to it." He was sullen. Then a grin broke across his face. "We're in business t'gether, like. Can't let 'im 'urt a partner."

"Very true. Speaking of business, I collect you had come to bring a report?"

"Yes, miss. Nothin' much yesttiday except the red-haired man come in the evening and got turned away."

Miss Tolerance stopped dabbing and regarded the boy. "Did he?"

"Yes, miss. Round about lightin' time. 'E come stumpin' down the street, mad as the duck's dinner." The boy's eyes gleamed through the gore. "An' that was before 'e even clapped the knocker. Footman come to the door, tuck a look at the ginger-man, shook 'is 'ead and woulda closed the door, only the ginger-man put 'is boot in the way, like. Couldn't 'ear what was said, but the red-headed man was that angry. So the servint got the door closed, but the ginger-man slammed on the knocker so 'ard I thought 'e'd strike it straight through the door. Servint come and opened the door again, wiv another bloke be'ind, both shakin' their 'eads. Dunno if the Lord was out, or just wan't in to Ginger, if you take me."

Miss Tolerance assured Bart that she did. "Did you see all this yourself?"

"'Appen I did," he said proudly. "Ted wrote it all down for you, miss." Bart pulled a grubby twist of his paper from his pocket and offered it to her.

Miss Tolerance put it aside as, at that moment, Ted returned Keefe just behind. The porter carried a large tray with cheese, bread, several small pies, a pitcher of milk and, in state on a china plate, the requested beefsteak.

"Thought as how the young'uns might like something to eat after their exertions, miss."

"Very well thought of, Keefe. I thank you." It was clear

that a bond of some sort had been forged between the porter and her spies. Miss Tolerance put aside the stained rag, having done as much for Bart as she could, and offered him the steak, which he clapped to his face at once.

"Please eat, boys," Miss Tolerance urged.

It was not to be thought that any conversation might be had while the youngsters applied themselves to their meal. Bart's wound began to bleed again as he ate, and it was all Miss Tolerance could do to keep the gore from mixing with his milk and meat pie. She took the food from his hands, bound his crown in a rakish bandage, then let him reunite with his meal.

"You may tell your fellows you were a hero today. And you as well," she told Ted. "For fetching Mr. Keefe."

Ted, crumbs of cheese adhering gummily to his teeth, grinned. "Best adventure I ever 'ad, miss."

Miss Tolerance poured him more milk.

When the boys had finished everything on the tray to the last crumb of pie crust, Miss Tolerance paid them their stipend with an additional vail for heroism. This new source of income impressed Bart despite the shaking he had sustained.

"P'raps you'd like to 'ire us on full time, Miss. As—" he sought for the word. "Some'un to guard you, like?"

"You propose yourself as my bodyguard?"

"Done good for you just now, ain't we?"

Miss Tolerance regarded Bart's bloodied collar and the bandage on his crown and wondered what his mother would make of the idea. "I cannot waste your talents on brute force," she said. You are more useful to me in your present assignment."

Bart was determined. "There's the other'ns for that, Miss."

"But without your leadership—"

"Well, yeah. They'd be 'opeless wivvout I tell 'em what to do."

Miss Tolerance smiled. "Just so. Bart, I must ask you to remain my secret weapon."

"Secret weapon? Well, I might do, I s'pose."

The boys left; Miss Tolerance sent Keefe to bespeak a hack at the stables and changed from her walking dress to the breeches, coat and boots that were better suited for travel on horseback through the city.

"What did you with Mr. Worke?"

The porter looked pleased. "Told him if he ever come round here again or thought to touch so much as a nail in your shoe, I'd break his crown for him."

"I hope he was suitably chastened?"

Keefe nodded. "There's them that remember me from my prize-fighting days, Miss Sarah. Happen that 'un did. He won't come round no more."

Miss Tolerance thanked him. She did not doubt Worke would avoid Manchester Square. Thoughtfully she picked up the walking stick Worke had dropped and ran her thumb over the handle, a rough carving of an elephant's head. It was proof that Worke had already attacked her once, and well away from Keefe's observation. Striking at her on Threadneedle Street might have been the clerk's own idea, but she did not believe Worke had approached her here on his own authority. It was time to confront Abner Huwe and insist that he call off his dog.

She took the cane and set out, not for Pitfield Street and Mr. John Thorpe, but for Fox Street and Amisley and Pound Drayage. She wore her small sword and carried her pistol, half-cocked and ready, in the pocket of her Gunnard greatcoat.

Miss Tolerance urged her hired mount through the busy streets, east past Gray's Inn toward Shadwell, thinking of Worke's attack upon her and the reason for it. He had demanded the coffer of cinchona bark, and spoken of it as his own. But when he learned the box had gone to Bow Street his reaction had been fear, and not, she thought, fear of the Runners. Miss Tolerance thought he was afraid of what Abner Huwe would do when he learned where the box had gone.

Was the box Huwe's then? What had Joshua Glebb told her the day before? That the first two privateers to reach the Walcheren encampment had belonged to Huwe, and had providentially borne chests of cinchona bark. But Huwe made his business shipping goods that belonged to others; he was unlikely to trade in bark himself. Something tickled her, something elusive. How was it that Abner Huwe's ships had arrived at Walcheren so soon and with bark in such quantity? These were interesting questions, and might be important to her later. For the moment, however, she wanted only to tell Huwe to call his dog to heel so that she might return her attention to the matter of Evadne Thorpe.

The greasy, rancid smell which rolled off the Thames had a moldy note today. The mist had become rain, the light was gloomy, and people darted from doorway to doorway, holding papers or rain shields above their heads. Water guttered off the brim of Miss Tolerance's hat; she was very grateful she had decided to change costumes before coming to Fox Street.

She tied her mount to a post near Amisley and Pound; the fly-specked window was fogged with condensation, and from the street she could see nothing inside but the glow of lamps. Miss Tolerance gathered her courage, put Worke's walking stick under her arm, and entered the office.

Only the elderly clerk she had noticed on her first visit was there. The old man, hunched miserably over the slanted top of his narrow desk, did not acknowledge her arrival. His nose was close to his work, and he dipped his pen in the inkwell and ignored her vigorously. The desk at which Tom Proctor had sat four days before was empty. So was Worke's.

Miss Tolerance cleared her throat.

The clerk wrote to the end of the line before he looked up. "Aye, sir?" Either his eyesight of his powers of observation were lacking.

"I must speak with Mr. Abner Huwe," she said firmly.

The old man shook his head. "Mr. Huwe is not avai—"

"My business is urgent."

"That don't put him here if he ain't here," the clerk said.

"When will he return?" *And will he be preceded by Worke?* Miss Tolerance had no ambition to encounter the big man until she had spoken to Huwe. "Truly, my business cannot wait." She underlined the sentiment by making a show of reaching for her pocketbook. That caught the old man's eye.

"Might happen he'll be available shortly," he admitted. "If ye'd like to wait for him?"

It was arranged, with the tactful exchange of half a crown, that she would wait in Mr. Huwe's office for his return. The clerk kept calling her "sir." Miss Tolerance did not enlighten him; she allowed herself to be seated in a chair in Huwe's paper cluttered office. The moment the old man left, however, curiosity impelled her to inspect the room. There was little enough to tell from it; the paper stacked on the desk and shelves, spindled or gathered into folders, appeared to be in the main bills of lading, maps, and correspondence. Miss Tolerance kept half an eye on the door to the outer office lest she be discovered in her investigation. She stepped to the rear of the office and tried the latch of the door. It was not locked.

The room beyond the door was windowless and unlit; what she could see was in shadow. By the light from the office she could tell that the room beyond was small. There was a table, a stool, and beyond that a cot. Perhaps Abner Huwe slept here when his business kept him late. Miss Tolerance turned away, then turned back. Something was wrong.

There was a pair of shoes under the table: ladies' slippers of kid or calfskin, pale cream or yellow, the sort of shoes a young woman might wear in her home but not robust enough for London streets. They were as out of place as a daffodil in a midden.

Miss Tolerance looked back at the door to the outer office, saw nothing, and decided the risk was worth the possibility of confirming a sudden, horrid idea. She stepped into the small room and picked up a shoe. It was neatly made, for a foot smaller than her own, embroidered on the toe with a wreath of white laurel leaves. It was meant for the foot of a young lady of quality.

Now she heard voices from the rooms beyond, the wheeze of the elderly clerk: "a gennelmun's waitin' for Mr. Huwe." She dropped the slipper into the pocket of her Gunnard coat and stepped back into the office, closing the door behind her. She had imagined before that the door led to an alley, an exit from the office. Now she knew it did not, and that the old man, and whoever it was he spoke to—stood between her and escape to the street.

The door to the outer office opened and the elderly man peered in as if he expected the visitor somehow to have vanished. Watching from behind him, as implacable as a wall, was Worke.

Chapter Sixteen

For several loud beats of her heart Miss Tolerance stood silent. Perhaps Worke, like the other clerk, would take her at her seeming and believe her to be a man. If he saw through the imposture perhaps he would not immediately know her for the woman he had twice attacked. But the big man was more observant than that; she saw as if it were drawn on his face his apprehension of who stood before him. Miss Tolerance put her hand on the hilt of her sword.

Worke licked his lips. "Look what we've here." His voice was soft. "Go on back to the books, Abel. I'll see to the guest."

Abel, looking from Worke to Miss Tolerance and back, withered visibly. He was clearly familiar with Worke in this humor and wanted no part of it. He circled Worke with a palsied shuffle and disappeared into the outer office, the door half closed behind him.

Keefe or Bart had done some damage to Worke earlier.

The flesh below one eye was plummy and swollen, and a cut had scabbed over by his ear. Miss Tolerance judged it best to pretend the fight had never occurred. "Will Mr. Huwe return soon?" she asked. "I need a word with him."

Worke grinned like a dog. "And you dressed like a camp follower? P'raps he won't speak with *you*."

"Perhaps he will not. I'm sure he would rather speak with me now than with the Runners later."

"An' why would Runners be comin' here?" Worke moved into the room, his hands half-clenched and held away from his body as f he were prepared at any moment to seize her. "You thinkin' to call them in?"

"Only if I cannot get satisfaction from Mr. Huwe."

"What, with that hatpin? He thrust his chin in the direction of her still-sheathed sword. "Come to fight a duel, maybe?"

Miss Tolerance ignored that. "If Mr. Huwe is not going to return soon I will have to come back later. I have business to attend to."

Worke drew a deep breath; he seemed to swell to fill the doorway. "You ain't thinkin' I'd let you leave?"

The pommel of her sword hilt was warm in Miss Tolerance's palm. She drew the sword with a fluid motion and stood in a relaxed *garde*. "I am not thinking that you will have much choice." She was pleased that her voice kept steady.

For a moment it appeared that the surprise of having a woman draw steel on him would win Miss Tolerance's point. Worke stumbled back a step, straight into the door frame. The impact recalled him to himself. He stepped forward before Miss Tolerance could close with him, and reached about him until his hand found the curved head of an iron tool leaning against the wall. The thing was as long as his forearm and, by the look of it, meant for prising open crates. He held it at arm's length in answer to Miss Tolerance's own stance: even with one end of the bar bent backward the tool gave Worke, with his longer arms, the advantage of reach. Miss Tolerance knew that her sword would not withstand a direct hit from the bar. If Worke hit *her* with it he would break her bones—or her skull.

Miss Tolerance retreated half a step. The iron bar was heavy; wielding it would fatigue even so big a man as Worke. His stance made it plain that the sword was not his usual weapon, which might give her some advantage. Still, he was larger, his weapon heavier, and she was certain he would not scruple to kill her if he saw the chance. She must let him tire himself, or draw him away from the door or, failing that, distract him. "You killed Tom Proctor," she said.

Worke licked his lips. "If I did? Tommy'd been stealing—"

"—Cinchona bark, I know."

As he had on the street, Worke reacted to the mention of the box's contents. He did not answer, but stepped toward her, moving his right hand, the hand that held the bar, from side to side, the forked tip at the height of her nose. Miss Tolerance extended her arm, her blade unwaveringly pointed at Worke's heart, and the big man retreated again.

"Did Proctor mean to sell the bark? It would have made a nice supplement to his salary."

"Nah, he was sick. Kep' it for 'imself."

"Thus the scarf on an April day," she murmured to herself.

"Too smart by half, Tommy was. Like you." Worke leaned forward, poking at her with the bar's tip. Heavy as it was, it was not a stabbing weapon, and while he was poking rather than swinging the bar Miss Tolerance could parry it on the forte of her blade. She was back *en garde* immediately. Worke swung the heavy bar back in line, but there was a tremble in his arm. The weight of the bar was taking its toll. "I've had *just* enough of you, you whore. I'll break your crown proper this time."

He raised the bar up and brought it down with crushing speed on the spot where, only a second before, Miss Tolerance had stood. His movement had telegraphed his intent. Instinctively she stepped to the side, let the bar glance off

243

the guard of her sword, then caught the bar with her blade to bind it down as if it were a blade. When the point of the bar neared the floor she stepped on its length, pulling it from Worke's hand. Worke, badly overbalanced, attempted to straighten up as Miss Tolerance cocked her wrist and brought the pommel of her small sword up to smash into his chin.

The big man stumbled back and crashed into the door-frame. He slid down along it until, top-heavy, he toppled into the doorway and lay like a fallen bear, quite unconscious.

"I cannot tell you how much I dislike being called whore," Miss Tolerance muttered. She kicked the prising bar under the desk, lest Worke come to himself and think to use it again. Her earlier plan of telling Abner Huwe to call off his man was gone. She would leave, find Sir Walter in Bow Street, and lay the entire matter of Proctor's death, and Worke's assaults upon her, in his hands. The Law could take responsibility for Worke and Huwe.

Worke made a sizeable barrier in the doorway. She would have to step over and around him, but at least the clerk Abel had not come to investigate the noise. Perhaps he was accustomed to the sound of conflict emanating from the office. Miss Tolerance glanced back at the door to the back room as if to assure herself no one was waiting there.

"You do not intend to leave us, surely?"

Miss Tolerance's head snapped round so quickly she was reminded that only a few days before she had been an invalid with a broken crown. Abner Huwe had appeared in the door to the outer office, just beyond Worke's prostrate bulk. He held a business-like pistol.

"You will put aside your sword, please." Huwe's tone was as pleasant as if he had asked that she close the window or pour the tea. Miss Tolerance's daily reading of the Dueling Notices left her with no favorable impression of the accuracy of pistols in general, but she was not tempted to test the weapon or Mr. Huwe's skill. She put her sword on the desk to her right and stepped away. Her own pistol was a solid weight against her thigh, but she doubted Huwe would let her extract it before he discharged his own weapon.

"I would barely have known you for a woman." Huwe gestured toward her with his pistol.

"If you must point, Mr. Huwe, may I ask that you do so with your hand alone?"

"Was I impolite? It's hard to know how to speak with a *lady* such as yourself."

"Do you think to distress me by reminding me I am no lady? I'm aware of it. As for my dress, these garments are more congenial in hazardous settings." She nodded to indicate that she included the offices of Amisley and Pound in that class. She kept her voice level and amused: a show of confidence was her best tactic. "My work sometimes takes me to venues where muslin and kid boots would be a positive hindrance."

"What work would that be? Nosing about, bringing magistrates to my door?" He tapped Mr. Worke's head with his foot. Worke remained unmoving. "Attacking my clerks."

"Your clerk attacked me, sir, in the street outside my home and, before that, in Threadneedle Street. I came to ask you what your design was in sending him to me. As for what my work is, I am paid to find things and answers and sometimes people."

Rather too quickly Huwe said, "I've no people here that oughtn't to be."

"You did have a visitor in that room recently." She did not take her eyes from Huwe, but indicated the door behind her with a quick jerk of her head. "A lady. I don't suppose you'd permit me further investigation?"

Mr. Huwe's lips twitched. "For a woman, you've a sense of humor, surely. No, I'm minded to stay where we are until it comes to me what I am to do with you."

"You might let me go," Miss Tolerance suggested. "My business is to find a young woman, Evadne Thorpe. As she

245

is not here, I must seek her elsewhere." She used the name to startle, and indeed Huwe's smile disappeared. "You know the name, sir?"

"Should I know it?"

"She is the daughter of your associate, Lord Lyne."

Huwe shook his head. "He would be no associate of mine."

"With all the visiting between you of late? Yes, I know of it. I think you and Lord Lyne had some business between you a few years ago that has its hooks in you to this day. Something to do with the box which was found by a magistrate in Mr. Proctor's room? Somehow poor Miss Thorpe became entangled in her father's business."

"Again this girl. What use would I have for a girl?"

"What use has any man for a young, pretty girl? And—" As the whole of an idea came to her she spoke her thoughts aloud. "Knowing you held his daughter would surely keep Lord Lyne from disclosing details of your arrangements."

"Our arrangements!" For the first time the pistol in Huwe's grip shook. "I say again, we are no associates. What business would his lordship conduct with such as me?"

"I am piecing it together. Lord Lyne has a plantation in South America with ties to trade there, and is, I believe, an enthusiast of military history. And his son worked in the War Office. I understand that Lord Castlereagh dismissed Lord Lyne's counsel regarding the insalubrious climate of the Dutch lowlands. And you have ships, two of which were the first to arrive at Walcheren, fortuitously laden with chests of cinchona bark when His Majesty's Navy had not more than a day's supply. It takes no extreme leap to conjecture that Lyne procured the bark which you sold. I imagine that you together made a very handsome profit. Almost an indecently handsome profit, the sort the Walcheren Commission might take interest in."

"Conjecture. Guesses." But Huwe's pleasant, snub-nosed face was stony. "How could you know such things?"

"As I said, sir: my work is to find answers. All I meant to do was find Miss Thorpe, but the looking has led me to a budget of other matters. Did you really hold Miss Thorpe here, sir? Where is she now? Did Proctor help her to escape? I imagine that would have angered you. Mr. Worke has already admitted to Proctor's death—"

Huwe kicked his clerk again. "He's a damned coarse instrument, Worke. I'd have done better to manage the matter myself."

"You would not have killed Proctor?"

Now Huwe stepped over Worke's shoulder into the room, testing the ground beneath him carefully. His pistol arm had dropped a little, enough to give relief to the fatigue of holding the thing at arm's length. He regained his smile. "Proctor's body would never have been found. The boy stole from me, and meant to help my little prize escape. I'd have killed him for either," he said easily. "I am not to be crossed."

"Not by clerk or business partner."

"That's the truth of it."

"You took Evadne Thorpe to use as a weapon against her father."

Huwe nodded as if this were a particularly clever thing. "It was needful to do something. There's still money to be made in the bark trade, but Lyne wanted to cry quits. Worried we'd be discovered. But the risk was all mine! They won't hang a peer for anything less than high treason. The old man kept whining on about the disgrace if we were found out. I meant to give him a taste of disgrace."

"By kidnapping his daughter?"

Abner Huwe's face was flushed, his expression a mix of anger and pleasure. His rusty hair stood on end as if he had been pulling it. Miss Tolerance heard a woman on the street selling hot potatoes. The rattle of carriage wheels, and a dog barking, and the sound of voices like a river's churning, all came to her from the distance. "Even then he was more fearful for his name than for the girl."

"How did you remove the girl from her father's house?"

"You're a deal too nosy for your own good."

"You are not the first to remark it, sir."

Huwe snorted with amusement. "It's a great waste to have to kill you."

"If you truly mean to kill me, sir, you ought at least to satisfy my curiosity. How did you take her?"

Huwe smirked. "A last request, you mean? Well enough. Mr. Worke went round, told the man at the door he'd a book for the girl from the library. Man went back to his dinner, Worke took the girl straight from her dad's hall, easy as cream." He shook his head.

"Will you satisfy my curiosity on another point, Mr. Huwe?" Huwe still blocked the door, and she was sure he would not permit her to push past him, leap over Worke's body, and depart. No one other than the old man in the front office knew she was here. Fortuitous rescue was unlikely. She must keep Huwe talking while she found a way out of her dilemma. "When did Miss Thorpe take leave of your hospitality?"

Huwe rocked onto the balls of his feet. "Only yesterday. I had business at the docks, and Worke—" he aimed another kick at the clerk—"he took it upon himself to seek the box Proctor had thieved from me. He left old Abel here alone." His nostrils flared, but whether his contempt was for Abel or Worke was unclear.

"Mr. Abel was not aware of her presence here?"

Huwe spat. "Mr. Abel's half deaf and sees naught beyond his nose. He's a fine hand at totting up numbers—a regular mathematician. For the rest, I'd not trust him to guard my hat, let alone a valuable property."

Valuable property. Miss Tolerance's stomach heaved at the thought. "So Miss Thorpe escaped Mr. Abel's indifferent care—"

"Not for the first time," Huwe interjected.

"--and she went...where?"

"How in Hell do I know? Crept out with my property and ran. I thought she'd gone home to her dad, and I went to fetch her back, but Lyne wasn't at home to me, if you please. Sent the porter to turn me away, as if I hadn't enough proof to turn his *name* to shit."

"How very frustrating for you, sir."

"Don't take such a tone, you." Huwe raised the pistol yet again. "I've the whip hand here, had you not seen?"

"I meant no disrespect, Mr. Huwe." Holding the whip hand was the great thing for Huwe, Miss Tolerance thought. "You did not regain Miss Thorpe?"

"*Miss* Thorpe? There's precious little *Miss* to her now, and naught she don't understand about the way of a man with a maid. No, I did not regain her. But if you're still looking for the piece it means Lyne has not got her," Huwe said with satisfaction. "I can still get her back—"

Miss Tolerance shook her head. "I will not let that happen."

Again Huwe snorted. "Look about you, woman. There's no one to help you. Though you're handsome enough. If I took you back to my little room, perhaps I'd let you persuade me to let you live."

"Without the least wish to be melodramatic, sir, I think I would rather die. And surely a pistol shot emanating from these offices would bring someone to investigate; you cannot kill every person who finds you out."

Huwe looked at the pistol in his hand. "Mayhap it's too noisy without I close the door, and this—" he kicked Worke in the knee—"blocks me from doing that. But it should be no great thing to dispatch you by hand."

Miss Tolerance was under no illusion that she could best Huwe with strength. If she reached for her sword quickly enough to keep him away he would likely fire the pistol regardless of noise; nor could she reach for her own pistol, still in the pocket of her Gunnard coat. She stepped back a pace, looked about her and saw nothing but papers—not even a convenient paperweight.

Huwe took a step closer, then another. He was almost within her reach. Could she kick him as she had Worke, hours ago that morning? But the damned man was sidling, making his groin a difficult target. *Think.*

249

He was on her, one hand circling her throat, the other reaching back to tangle itself in her hair like a lover's caress. She tried to stomp his foot but could not find it. She kicked, struck him, but not so hard as to make him drop his hands. As he squeezed and his flushed, contorted face swam before her eyes, she fumbled at her coat pocket and found—not her pistol, but Evadne Thorpe's kid slipper. She pulled it out and swung it against Huwe's head hard enough that he dropped his hands. She sprang backward, panting, and reached again, this time grasping the pistol which she cocked and thrust, with the same motion, at Huwe's belly.

He stopped, looking down at the muzzle that disappeared in the front of his waistcoat.

"Had a trick or two laid by, did you?" He was panting as hard as she and, she realized with disgust, was aroused. "Well, what are we to do now?"

She meant to give him no time to hatch a new scheme for her defeat. "Turn around, Mr. Huwe."

"Shoot me in the back, will you?"

"No, sir. Now, to your knees." With her left hand she pushed hard on his shoulder until the man went down, first on one knee, then the other. "Lie flat, now."

When Huwe was prone on the floor Miss Tolerance knelt over him, the bore of her pistol to the nape of his neck and her knee in the small of his back. "Do not move, sir, or you will not even know that I have killed you." With her left hand she pulled off the long black ribbon with which she had clubbed her plaited hair. "Now, put your hands behind your back, Mr. Huwe. Very slowly and very carefully."

One handed, Miss Tolerance tied his wrists together; not until she was confident that he could not loose himself from the weave of ribbon around his wrists did she rest her pistol on his back. Two handed, she tied several knots to secure the ribbon. Then she reclaimed the pistol and stood.

"I'll ask you to rise now, Mr. Huwe."

"What do you think to do with me?" The man rolled to one side and managed to get himself to his feet.

"I mean to bring you to Bow Street. Mind your step as we go through the door. Mr. Worke is a sizable obstacle." Left-handed, she regained her sword and returned it, awkwardly, to its sheath. She jabbed Huwe once in the shoulder with the pistol in her hand to encourage him to move. Huwe shuffled toward the door—who would blame him for his reluctance? Miss Tolerance followed, her left hand now on his shoulder, her pistol still aimed at his back. As they went through the door Huwe stepped with cruel weight on Worke's hand.

The clerk moved and groaned. Huwe staggered backward into Miss Tolerance, forcing her pistol back against her.

The pistol released its charge.

In the moment when the report seemed to hang in the air like a note of music, she was not sure if she had shot Abner Huwe. But the man reeled forward, away from her, still bound but unhurt. At that same moment Miss Tolerance felt a horrid pain radiate from her upper arm. She had shot herself.

Her first emotion was impatience: this had gone on too long, she was tired, she would needs have recourse to the surgeon again and she disliked surgeons. When Huwe rounded and charged at her like an angry bull she abandoned any thought of subtlety. She used the butt of her discharged pistol to smash him in the head. Unlike Worke, a single blow did not handle the matter: she had to strike again. Even then he was only stunned, not unconscious, when he slumped to his knees.

Miss Tolerance stepped carefully around both Huwe and Worke, into the outer office. Mr. Abel was still bent over his desk as if attention to duty could insulate him from whatever was occurring in the inner office.

"You!" Her voice was hoarse. "Fetch some rope." To underline the urgency of her request she pointed her pistol at him—he would not know it was empty.

Abel moved with an alacrity of which she would not have thought him capable, bringing rope and, at Miss Tolerance's direction, binding his master and then Worke. By the time he was done and Miss Tolerance was certain that neither man would easily get loose, Huwe was spitting obscenities and Worke was beginning to groan and shift.

"Now, Mr. Abel, one more chore." With the excitement of the moment ebbing she felt dizzy and sick; there was an ooze of stickiness on her left arm which she knew must be blood. "You must go to Bow Street and ask for Sir Walter Mandif. Go at once, give him Miss Tolerance's compliments, and ask him to come here straightaway."

The old man cast a fearful glance at Huwe, then looked back at Miss Tolerance.

"Don't think of running before you find Sir Walter, Mr. Abel. Given Mr. Huwe's temper, I think your best safety lies in making sure he is taken in to custody by the law, don't you?"

Thoughtfully, Abel nodded.

"Good. Now go." Miss Tolerance waved the pistol at him. Abel scuttled off with surprising speed.

Disregarding the threats and groans from her captives, Miss Tolerance put the pistol aside, shrugged out of her Gunnard coat and, with greater difficulty, took off the coat beneath to inspect the damage she had inflicted upon herself. The bullet had caught her in the fleshy part of her upper arm. In shirtsleeves, she pulled away the edge of linen that had been carried into the wound. That started a fresh flow of blood. After she had torn away her lower sleeve and clumsily bandaged the wound, she reloaded her pistol, sat upon the floor where she could watch her prisoners, and waited for her rescuers to arrive.

Sir Walter Mandif did not like it.

He had arrived with his constable Hook, and an exceedingly reluctant Mr. Abel. In the door to the street Abel froze, looking like a terrified horse, the whites of his eyes showing.

"Let him go, please, Sir Walter. He's served his purpose."

"My dear—Miss Tolerance! How do I find you?"

She got to her feet, wincing and shaky. "The worse for wear, I fear. But I have Tom Proctor's killers here. It is quite a tale."

Mr. Hook was circling the two bound men, inspecting them. "Ol' man said one'a these shot you, Miss?"

Miss Tolerance sniffed. "Mr. Abel was misinformed. I am afraid, Mr. Hook, that I shot myself."

Sir Walter's eyebrows rose. "Did you do this a-purpose?"

"No, Sir Walter, I did not." Her knees did not seem strong enough to bear her weight. Miss Tolerance leaned against the wall.

"I must get you to a surgeon," Sir Walter said. "Hook, fetch a carriage for me. Then you will take these men into custody. I will meet you in Bow Street shortly."

Miss Tolerance attempted to send Sir Walter away with Hook. "If you will be so kind as to put me in a carriage, I can take—"

"No." Sir Walter was firm upon the point. "I will not embarrass you by carrying you to the carriage—unless you force the point."

In fact, Miss Tolerance was more grateful than she liked, to be taken in charge, supported to the street, and helped into the carriage. Once there, however, Sir Walter gave the driver his own address, and Miss Tolerance was bound to protest.

"I have already trespassed too much upon your kindness, Sir Walter. Driver, Manchester Square, if you please."

Mandif did not argue, but his face took on a pinched expression. "If you think I mean in some way to take advantage—"

Miss Tolerance looked heavenward. "I don't think anything of the sort. I will be very comfortable in my own home. I hope you will believe that my aunt knows the name of several fine surgeons."

His expression became, if anything, more pinched. "You do not wish to be beholden to me."

"Good God, Mandif, are we characters in a play?" She glared at him half-serious. "I do not mean to bruise your feelings. I simply want to sleep in my own bed." Every jolt of the carriage made her arm hurt more ferociously. She was reaching the stage of exhaustion and pain where all she wished to do was sleep or cry.

"I apologize," Sir Walter said at last. "I fear the sight of a friend...*perforated* in such a fashion distresses me."

Despite her pain that won a smile from Miss Tolerance. "No more than it distresses me! This morning I was attacked, this afternoon I fought both of those men Mr. Hook so obligingly took away." She leaned back against the seat, closed her eyes, and recited what she knew of Huwe's and Worke's involvement in Tom Proctor's murder, of Worke's attack that morning, and of Huwe's attempt on her life. When she pulled aside her neckcloth to show the magistrate the bruising on her neck, Mandif drew in a sharp breath that told her just how nasty it looked.

"You said there was more. Are there other crimes to lay at their door? Not that murder, or attempted murder, is not sufficient—"

"For now, let it be enough. There are some matters on which I do not yet have sufficient evidence."

Perhaps because he was her friend, perhaps because he recognized that further debate would be useless, Sir Walter let the matter lie.

Miss Tolerance drowsed. When the carriage stopped in Manchester Square she discovered that her head was on Sir Walter's shoulder. She sat up, a little dismayed, and let the driver lift her down from the carriage. The man was clumsy, aggravating her pain until she was close to tears. Sir Walter insisted upon escorting her to Mrs. Brereton's door. There, however, she made him go.

"You have work awaiting you. I promise that my aunt's people will take very good care of me, and that I will let you know how I go on tomorrow. Yes, Cole, it's I," she said to the porter when he opened the door. "I'm afraid that I have suffered a little mishap. Thank you, Sir Walter," she said firmly. "Good night."

She was escorted gingerly into the house; it took some firmness on her part to keep Cole from carrying her, but she was grateful to be able to lean upon his arm all the way to her cottage. She asked him to send for the surgeon and went in to the blessed quietness of her own home. She had draped her coat and greatcoat over her shoulders. Once inside she let them fall to the floor and felt frankly too dizzy to pick them up. Instead, she dropped onto the settle before the cold hearth and succumbed to a doze that was not broken until Marianne Touchwell, with the surgeon Mr. Pynt behind her, came to inspect the damage.

Mr. Pynt was professionally disapproving. He took the ball from her arm, cleaned the wound, dusted the whole with calomel, and bandaged the site neatly.

"If you do not open the wound by some foolish exertion you should do well enough." He was grudging. "Is it useless of me to suggest that you wear your arm in a sling?"

"Not at all," Marianne answered for her. "I'll see to it she does." The face she turned to Miss Tolerance was comically fierce.

Pynt sighed, shrugged, took his payment and departed.

"Well, you have had an exciting day. I hear that Keefe had to rescue you from an attacker this morning. Now you come home shot! Your aunt—"

"Don't tell her!"

Marianne shook her head. "I won't. There'll be enough ado in the house without that. Here." She poured a dram of whisky from Miss Tolerance's small store. "You take this. Jess will be over in a little while with some soup— something not too challenging for your stomach, aye? Tomorrow, though, we need to talk about your aunt and Mr. Tickenor."

Miss Tolerance nodded heavily. She had contrived to

forget about Tickenor and Harry's revelations. "Tomorrow," she agreed.

"There's a plan, then," Marianne said comfortably.

Chapter Seventeen

With difficulty Miss Tolerance dressed herself to present a severely respectable appearance, in her steel-blue walking dress and a bonnet devoid of decoration. Her arm was swollen and bruised, but when she woke she had seen no redness on the flesh above the bandage that might indicate dangerous infection. This being so, she considered herself fit to work; although it was necessary to grit her teeth to put up her hair and tie her bonnet. When she asked Cole to summon a hackney carriage for her he did so, but not before he had presented her with a sling fashioned from a length of black silk. "Miss Marianne said you promised, Miss Sarah."

Miss Tolerance permitted Cole to assist her in putting the thing on. In truth, she was more comfortable with her arm thus supported.

She gave instructions to the jarvey for Pitfield Street. Circumstances had distracted her from her conversation with John Thorpe; she had discovered where Evadne Thorpe had been, but did not know where she now was. She must believe that any words between Tom Proctor and John Thorpe would have concerned Evadne Thorpe; it was time to learn if there had been such a conversation and what its outcome had been.

The carriage's heavy curtains smelled of dust and mildew; she pushed them aside and watched her fellow citizens going about their business. It was a warm, pleasant day; the scent of spring floated atop all the other less agreeable London smells. Against common sense Miss Tolerance allowed the sunshine to persuade her she would find Evadne Thorpe and restore her to her sister.

Even the dreariness of Pitfield Street was touched by light and warmth. The carriage stopped by the gin shop; a dedicated drunkard sat propped against the brick of the building, his face turned to the sun and a half-full blue bottle clutched in his hands. A woman in the pie shop who, by her voluminous apron, Miss Tolerance took to be the cook, came to the door to empty a basin of dirty water into the street; she smiled apologetically as the water lapped Miss Tolerance's boots. Old Hettie the pickpocket was nowhere to be seen; that in itself seemed auspicious.

The door to Squale House was closed and locked.

The shine upon Miss Tolerance's good humor diminished slightly. She lifted the knocker and let it drop. The noise this produced was loud, but summoned no one. She tried again, and then once more; still no one arrived. Miss Tolerance turned to survey the street. She was not to be balked of her object: she meant to talk to John Thorpe and she would do so, if it meant she must wait all day. She did not wish to wait on the doorstop, however. There was no coffee house or even a public house where she might sit for the price of a tankard; the gin shop appeared her only option, and that did not appeal.

Behind her, a bolt grated. Miss Tolerance turned to find, not Mr. Thorpe but his partner, the stone-faced Mr. Parkin. By the evidence she had roused him from napping: his hair stood on end, his collar was loose, and he had thrown a waistcoat on without noticing that it was inside out. When he realized who his visitor was his scowl deepened.

Miss Tolerance curtsied and asked for John Thorpe.

"You have missed him again, Miss—" he shook his head as if to shake her name into it. "You will have to call again."

"I am very sorry to have waked you, Mr. Parkin, but it truly is imperative that I speak to Mr. Thorpe. It is a matter of family business. If he is not here, can you say where I might find him?"

Parkin eyed Miss Tolerance grimly.

"Please, sir." She softened her tone and lowered her eyes, hoping a display of maidenly diffidence would persuade.

Parkin's scowl did not melt so much as fade, apparently defeated by Miss Tolerance's gentler manner.

"When John left last night he said he had some family business to attend to. Went off with Godwin. He—Godwin—might know where John has gone to. If you find him I wish you will send him back here; I was up until dawn with a sick infant." From his tone Miss Tolerance apprehended that he regarded babies with dismay.

"If I find Mr. Thorpe, sir, I shall certainly tell him. Where will I find Mr. Godwin?"

"Somers Town." Parkin began to close the door, but Miss Tolerance put her hand out to stop him. "The Polygon. Number 29, I believe," he added.

Parkin closed the door upon Miss Tolerance's words of thanks.

It was not a very great distance from Pitfield Street to Somers Town. The carriage rattled along the Pentonville Road and Miss Tolerance attempted to ignore the way the jolting made her arm throb.

Number 29, The Polygon, was a pleasant four-story house with a disheveled quality, as if its occupants would recall every now and then what paint or polish might be

259

required, but for the moment were very much engaged elsewhere. Miss Tolerance dropped the knocker with a sold *thwack* and waited.

A girl, perhaps no more than ten or eleven, opened the door half-way and peered around it.

"Good afternoon. Is Mr. Godwin at home?"

The door opened a few inches more; the girl appeared to weigh the question seriously. She wore a blue-striped gown with a too-large apron, a plain cap over a disorderly mass of pale hair, and the gravity of a scullery-maid promoted to serve upstairs. "I shall 'ave to ask," she said at last. She closed the door, leaving Miss Tolerance to stand on the steps. She waited.

"Ma'am says you're to come in. She likes visitors." The girl grinned as if this bit of information must amuse Miss Tolerance as much as it did her. The hallway into which she beckoned Miss Tolerance was pleasant and well lit, the walls painted a rosy color. There were pleasant smells of baking and blacking, and the sound of female voices from further down the hall. "Ma'am is in 'ere, with Miss Mary and Miss Fanny. I'll look about and see where Mr. Godwin's got to."

Miss Tolerance thanked the girl gravely. Whatever the Godwin household ran to, the traditional formality between servant and served was not much observed. She followed the girl down the hall.

"Beg pardon, ma'am. 'Ere's the guest. Oh!" The girl's hand went to her mouth. "I forgot. " She turned to Miss Tolerance and murmured, "What name shall I say?"

"Tolerance," Miss Tolerance whispered back, amused.

"Miss or Missus?"

"Miss."

The girl turned to address the room. "Miss Tolerance, ma'am."

The girl stepped back and waved Miss Tolerance forward like an ostler directing coaches. Miss Tolerance stepped into a small, old-fashioned parlor crowded with furniture and books. In a large, winged chair near the fire an older woman sat, very settled, as if this was her accustomed place. She wore a green dress of a style perhaps a dozen years old, with a shawl over her shoulders; another shawl lay across her knees, her hands folded unmoving on top of it. Her hair was abundant and gray, piled atop her head and bound there with a gauzy green scarf; she looked as if she might have frozen in the year '97 or '98. Her face, too, seemed half frozen. It was a handsome face with marked eyebrows, a strong nose, firm chin and well-formed mouth, but the left side of it was utterly without mobility. The woman's one-sided smile was uncanny.

"Mrs. Godwin?" Miss Tolerance curtsied. The woman in the seat inclined her head a little in response. Two girls, dressed in muslin gowns of more recent style, stood protectively to the right of Mrs. Godwin's chair. The taller of the two was perhaps seventeen years old; she stepped forward, curtsied and said "I am Fanny Imlay." She had a strong resemblance to Mrs. Godwin: the same mobile mouth, firm chin and dark eyes. She tilted her head up as if anticipating a quarrel. "This is my sister Mary Godwin."

The younger girl curtsied. She was several years her sister's junior, slight, with a long neck and a small, pretty face. Her hair was dark, her eyes large, observant and, Miss Tolerance thought, a little sad.

The woman in the chair mumbled something. Mary leaned forward to listen, then interpreted. "My mother asks that you sit, Miss Tolerance. How may we help you?"

Miss Tolerance sat upon the sofa which faced Mrs. Godwin's chair.

"I am looking for someone, ma'am. It was suggested to me that Mr. Godwin might be able to help me."

A look, and with it a communication of sorts, passed between Mrs. Godwin and the girls. Mrs. Godwin spoke again; it was impossible for Miss Tolerance to make out what the woman said.

"My mother was struck with apoplexy when I was born," Mary Godwin explained. "Fanny and I speak for her."

"I see." How must the poor hulk of a woman in the chair opposite feel, to depend so upon her children? The mobile side of Mrs. Godwin's face twitched briefly into a frown, then relaxed, and she muttered something.

"My mother asks how it comes that you are searching for this person," Miss Imlay said.

Miss Tolerance had a sense that truth was likely to gain her the most sympathetic hearing. "I earn my bread as an agent of inquiry," she said directly to Mrs. Godwin. "You may apprehend from my name, ma'am, that I am Fallen. There are very few occupations open to a woman such as I, and—"

Mrs. Godwin made a very urgent grunting sound. One of her hands stirred slightly in her lap, as if she wished to gesture emphatically with it.

"Mama says you must tell her more of this, Miss Tolerance." Miss Godwin looked as excited as her mother. "Mama is *very* interested in the careers of women who live outside the pattern of society. In her book *Vindication of the Rights of Women—*"

Miss Tolerance frankly stared. Mrs. Godwin was Mary Wollstonecraft? There was great intelligence in the woman's eye; what tragedy for so powerful an intellect to be trapped inside a broken body. She recalled herself: she had a task to do. "I would be happy to come again and speak of my history at length, Miss Godwin, but at the moment my work is urgent. If I might speak with Mr. Godwin for just a moment?"

Mrs. Godwin grunted.

"My mother says perhaps we may be of help. Mr. Godwin is occupied with a manuscript for publication and must not be disturbed." Miss Imlay moved behind her mother's chair and put a hand on the woman's shoulder.

Mrs. Godwin muttered at length. Fanny Imlay blushed.

"My mother asks who it is you are seeking, Miss Tolerance."

"Is that all she asked?"

Mrs. Godwin's right eye widened. Again she spoke.

Mary Godwin answered this time, with a hint of smugness. "My mother first said that my sister was to be careful to represent what she was saying without embroidery. Then she said that you were sharp to notice that Fanny had not conveyed—"

"I quite understand," Miss Tolerance said. Fanny Imlay's blush intensified, and she glared at Mary Godwin. If there was any useful information here, she could not make an enemy of either girl. "As to whom I seek—I was told Mr. Godwin might know where I could find Mr. John Thorpe."

"Mr. John Thorpe?" There was a silent exchange of looks between the three females.

Mrs. Godwin spoke. This time Miss Tolerance listened carefully and made out the gist of it. "You ask why I believe your husband would know where Mr. Thorpe is?"

Mrs. Godwin inclined her head. Miss Imlay frowned a little, but Mary Godwin smiled.

"You're very clever! Mr. Johnson has known Mamma since before I was born, and still he cannot understand what she says!"

Miss Tolerance returned the girl's smile. "To answer your question, ma'am: Mr. Parkin at Squale House referred me to him. I met Mr. Godwin there a few days ago when my inquiry first took me there. I am—" She paused, torn between discretion and the notion of encouraging information from the Godwins. "I am searching for a young woman—"

"Did she run away? Elope? How romantic! How very brave she must be!" That was Miss Godwin.

Mrs. Godwin growled something Miss Tolerance could not parse, and her daughter fell silent.

"I believe she *is* brave, Miss Godwin, but her story is not a romantic one."

"*Brave.*" The word, like a single crack of a riding crop, was spoken from the doorway.

Miss Tolerance turned. Mr. Godwin stood close behind a young woman whose face was familiar to Miss Tolerance from the portrait she carried even now in her reticule. She

263

rose and curtsied.

"Miss Thorpe."

In the portrait Evadne Thorpe's face was soft and round-ed, her eye merry. The girl who stood before Miss Toler-ance now was slender to the point of emaciation, pale, with a distant expression of anxiety and resentment. Her eye had been blacked some days before. There were other bruises, including a mottled ring of purpling marks around her throat that suggested someone had tried to throttle her. "I understand from John that my sister hired you to find me."

"She did. Lady Brereton most urgently desires to know, first, that you are well, and second, if you will come home to your family."

Mention of her sister's name softened Miss Thorpe's ex-pression, but only momentarily. Then her face became fixed and adamantine. "If Clary sent you she must believe you are not a danger to me, Miss—Tolerance, was it? I shall trust you this far: you may tell my sister that you found me, not well but better. You may tell her that I will *never* return to my father's house."

Mrs. Godwin said something. Mr. Godwin, who had thus far been silent, stepped forward. "Quite right, my dear. Fanny, Mary, I think you may find yourselves occu-pation for a little while. Mary, have you finished the essay I set you? Fanny, have you fair-copied your poem?"

The girls quitted the room with the air of people who are going to miss the last act of a good play. Mr. Godwin came to sit beside his wife; he took one of her inert hands in his own and looked on expectantly.

Miss Tolerance rose to seat Miss Thorpe beside her on the sofa, weighing how best to speak to her. The best coin she had to offer was her own history, and she would use that if she must.

"Miss Thorpe, I can only guess the nature of your or-deal," she began. "I know you have been foully misused. If you fear that your sister will not understand or sympa-thize—"

Evadne Thorpe's pretty mouth pinched. "She could not understand."

"Perhaps you wrong her—no, please hear me." Miss Tolerance extended her hand with her plea. "From my name you may infer something of my history." Godwin and his wife observed her with interest. "When I left my home my father made it plain that I was dead to him and to my family. But I have recently encountered—" she stopped, remembering that Sir Adam was Miss Thorpe's brother-in-law. "I have recently encountered a member of my family who is not so determined to cut the connection. I know as a fact that your sister and her husband will welcome you home. I think your older brother, perhaps even your father, will come in time to—"

"My father." The revulsion in those two words was shocking. "Why do you think my brother John brought me here, Miss Tolerance, rather than to my father's home? My father gave me to the man who raped me."

In the silence a door closed upstairs; there was a sound of footfall. Mr. Godwin rose to shut the door to the hall. He returned to his wife's side.

Miss Tolerance could think of no sentiment adequate to express her horror.

"These kind people—" Miss Thorpe gestured to the Godwins—"have not heard the whole of the tale. Perhaps they, as well as you, should know it. I did not believe it at first, no matter what He said. My captor. But then I escaped, and my father sold me back to him."

"Sold?" Godwin's tone echoed Miss Tolerance's own revulsion.

"Sold." Evadne Thorpe nodded. "I contrived to slip away from Him. I sent a message to Papa, thinking he would come for me. Instead I was delivered me back to Him. I don't know what the payment was, but He told me that I was bought and paid for, and if I tried to run again I should simply be returned again, like a run-away...mongrel bitch." The girl would not speak Huwe's

265

name; as she told the tale her tone became flatter and flatter, until she might have been discussing the weather or a new hat, except for her emphasis on *he, him, his.*

"Your captor told you this?" Miss Tolerance asked. "And—forgive me—you believe him? You do not think he said these things to distress you?"

"I know he did, but that makes them no less true. When I escaped the first time I ran—the people I passed in the street must have thought I was a lunatic, barefoot, in my shift with a blanket thrown over it, running through the most horrid streets. When I could run no more I took shelter in a cookshop—the woman there was wonderfully kind to me, and sent her son to my father to beg for help. A woman came, Mrs. Harris, and she was everything kind and comfortable—until she brought me back to Him again. How else would she have known where I was hidden? She brought me back; I saw Him pay her before—then He beat me. That was almost of no moment, not compared to what came next. When He was done with me he gave me to Worke." Despite a tremor in her voice Evadne Thorpe's face was as still and cold as alabaster.

"Worke?" Godwin looked puzzled.

"The name of his helper," Miss Tolerance told him. "Abner Huwe gave you to Worke?" The girl flinched to hear the name spoken aloud, but it was important, crucial, to be clear.

"Only for that once, to teach me a lesson. Worke's reward, He called it. When they had both finished with me He sent for Mrs. Harris again. To *patch me up* after their celebrations, He said. That was when He told me how he had known where to send her: that Papa wrote at once to tell him where I was hiding."

"It must have been a lie. No father could do such a thing." Mr. Godwin's expression was not of disbelief but of revulsion. "No man—"

"She was meant to be the means to ensure her father's cooperation," Miss Tolerance said quietly. "She was a hostage to her captor's greed and her father's pride. And the

266

damned bark," she added to herself.

"What?" Miss Thorpe, Mr. Godwin, even Mrs. Godwin regarded Miss Tolerance as if she had made a joke.

"I beg your pardon. I know what the matter was between Huwe and your father, Miss Thorpe. It could have meant ruin for both men, perhaps even charges of treason."

"I know." Miss Tolerance had not thought it possible that Evadne Thorpe could become any more ashen. "This time I brought away proof of it." Her smile was an awful thing.

"Proof?"

"My father's letters. Huwe's ledger. I thought if I had them they would be afraid of me, that they would leave me alone." Miss Tolerance thought the effect would be rather the opposite, but did not say so.

"Both Huwe and Worke are under arrest," Miss Tolerance told the girl. "You have nothing more to fear from them."

"But I would have to—bring evidence against them? I cannot see Him again."

Miss Tolerance took the girl's hands in her own strong grasp. "The charges upon which they were arrested have nothing to do with you: Worke killed a man at Huwe's instigation, and both he and Huwe tried to kill me." She gestured to the black silk sling. There was a murmur of shocked disbelief. "Your name need never be mentioned—I doubt they will give it out, as it would only lead to further, and more dire, charges against them."

After a long, thoughtful silence, Mr. Godwin said, "The question, then, becomes, what do you wish to do, Miss Thorpe?"

"Do?" Evadne Thorpe looked at the Godwins. "Sir, if you and Mrs. Godwin will permit me to stay a little longer, until my brother can find some employment for me, sewing or, or laundering—"

She was interrupted by Godwin's assurance of her welcome, and Mrs. Godwin's rumble of indecipherable agreement. Miss Tolerance let them finish.

"You have a very good and safe haven here for the moment. That gives you an opportunity to think upon the future. You have nothing more to fear from Abner Huwe."

"But my father's part will not be known. There is no way it *can* be known?"

"Not unless you make the accusation yourself." Miss Tolerance thought to soothe the girl's anxieties. Instead Evadne Thorpe's lips pressed together as if to contain an explosion. Her eyes were hot with fury.

"Then I must do so."

The Godwins regarded their guest with dismay.

"Miss Thorpe, I beg you will think carefully." Miss Tolerance kept her own apprehension strictly controlled. "With the evidence the magistracy has, Huwe will doubtless pay with his life. To implicate your father—would a man capable of the things he has done balk at lying? How if he said you had gone willingly with Huwe? Juries are made of men; they might take his word against yours." She paused to let the import of this penetrate. "The details of your mistreatment would inevitably become public."

"I have the papers I took," The girl's voice was tight as a fist. "Even if they did not persuade a jury of his complicity, his name, the name he cares for so much—"

"Your father's name would be tarred very black indeed. But you have already said you fear encountering your...kidnapper. If you bring these charges you might have to do so. Are you prepared to take that step for the satisfaction of ruining your father?"

The change her words wrought in Miss Thorpe was remarkable. She shrank back, her shoulders hunched, her voice reduced to a whisper. "No. Not that." Her lips twisted bitterly. "I am a great coward. It would make me very happy to see my father suffer for what he let Him do, but to face Him again—I think I would die."

Mr. Godwin left his wife's side and came to kneel on Evadne Thorpe's other side. "Miss Thorpe, there is no reason you should do so. This lady has told you that he will be punished for his other crimes. As for your father," he spoke earnestly. "I truly believe you are better served to leave vengeance to the Creator."

Miss Tolerance nodded. "A little time will convince you of Mr. Godwin's wisdom. It is your own future we must plan for. You are among friends here." She nodded comprehensively to the Godwins. "I hope you will permit me to tell your sister where you are—Lord Lyne will know soon enough that Huwe has been taken, and I imagine fear of exposure from that quarter will give him as much alarm as you could wish."

Evadne Thorpe nodded slowly. "I hope He talks," she said at last. "I hope He does."

Godwin disagreed gently. "For your sake, and for that of your sister and brothers, I hope he does not, Miss Thorpe. As for your father," his chin came up combatively. "I might speak to him of the wisdom of providing for you—"

A guttural noise interrupted him. Mrs. Godwin, despite the paralysis of half her face, wore an expression of disagreement so eloquent it stopped her husband from saying further.

Evadne, too, appeared appalled. "I do not want his assistance. I do not want anything from him, ever." Her voice was shrill, her hands fisted in her lap. She stared unseeing at some vivid tableau in her imagination.

"Miss Thorpe. *Evadne.*" Miss Tolerance spoke sharply. "No one will force you to take anything from your father." She made her voice quiet, almost singsong, as if she were telling a story to a frightened child.

She turned to Godwin. "Your kindness is undeniable, sir, but what would be served by attempting to secure Lord Lyne's help? I know Miss Thorpe's sister means to stand by her, as your friend Mr. Thorpe surely does. She need not ask her father for anything."

"But surely the man should be made aware—"

Again Mrs. Godwin gave a rumble of dissent.

"My dear, I mean only that he should have the opportunity to repent, to make apology. But as you feel so strongly, and Miss Thorpe as well, I will of course refrain."

269

Evadne Thorpe nodded. "I thank you for your concern. I know you mean kindly. But I am not able—I shall never be able—to forgive my father, no matter how he repent."

Godwin nodded, rising laboriously from his knees, to stand with his hands clasped behind his back. "All shall be as you wish. I hope you know that you are welcome to stay here as long as you wish it."

The atmosphere of revulsion, shock, and anxiety which had filled the room had begun to lighten. Evadne Thorpe, drained and weary, smiled at Godwin, then at his wife. Miss Tolerance thought it was time for her to leave.

"I have given you a great deal to think about, Miss Thorpe. I hope you will do what makes you most easy in your mind now: work, or a rest—"

"I agree. This has been a tiring interview for you, my dear. Would you not like to go sit with the girls and read?" Mr. Godwin had slipped back into his role as protector. Evadne Thorpe nodded. He escorted her, as carefully as if the girl had been a beldame, out of the room. A few moments later he returned.

"You will watch over her mood, sir?" Miss Tolerance asked. "I regret that I have raised some very powerful feelings in her."

"She is not as contained as she was," Godwin agreed. "That may be for the best. But we will watch her carefully." Mrs. Godwin, who had watched the scene unfolding before her implacably, nodded and added something Miss Tolerance could not make out. She looked inquiringly at Mr. Godwin; his mouth twitched into a small smile.

"My wife is of a fierce temper; we do not approve of public execution, but I think she would make an exception in the case of Mr. Huwe."

Mrs. Godwin gave a grunt of laughter. Her husband patted her hand. "I hope that, when this whole matter has been successfully arranged, you will come again to talk with us, Miss Tolerance."

Before she could say yes or no, Mary Godwin had appeared in the door.

"Papa, Fanny asks if you will come look at her fair copy."

Miss Tolerance rose. "Please go, Mr. Godwin. I take my leave of you, with thanks." She curtseyed to Mrs. Godwin, then to her husband.

Godwin bowed. "Mary, will you show our guest out? Good afternoon, Miss Tolerance. And good luck."

Mary Godwin took Miss Tolerance's hand in her own small one and led her from the room.

"Mamma likes you," she said seriously. "I hope you will come again."

"I will," Miss Tolerance promised with equal seriousness.

"Mamma was a very important writer before I was born," the girl continued. "Before her stroke. My birth was the great disaster of her life." She said this as if it were the most unremarkable sentiment imaginable.

"She gained you, which I am certain she does not regret."

The girl was not convinced. "Her work was important. We try to help her continue, but it is hard. Her eloquence was so deranged by the stroke. Even when we attempt to write down her words, the result is not what she wishes. My Papa is devoted to her. Her infirmity has been very hard upon him."

Miss Tolerance wondered how often these sentiments had been repeated in the girl's hearing.

"Hard upon you all," she suggested. "You and Miss Imlay as well."

"Fanny is a poet," Mary said, as if that explained the matter.

"Yours is a very literary family, then. Are you a writer?"

"I?" The girl looked surprised. "I write little stories, not essays or poems. Not like Mamma or Fanny."

"Writing stories is a gift," Miss Tolerance suggested. They had reached the door.

"I suppose it is. Please visit Mamma," the girl urged again. "It would make her very happy."

Chapter Eighteen

The disclosures she must now make were of such delicacy that a meeting with Lady Brereton at Lord Lyne's house seemed ill-advised. Even a meeting in the Ladies' Salon at Tarsio's felt unwarrantedly public. Thus at Henry Street, Miss Tolerance ignored the raised eyebrow her appearance occasioned—the black silk sling seemed to worry the porter considerably—and arranged with Steen to have one of the withdrawing rooms on the second floor held for her. When she gained the Ladies' Salon she wrote to Clarissa Brereton.

I have news, but of such nature that I will ask you to meet me here at Tarsio's club, where I may arrange for us to be private. I will be here all this afternoon and into the early evening. If a meeting today is not possible, please send a note to me appointing a time more convenient.

A runner was dispatched to Duke of York Street with the

note and stern instruction to give it to no one but Lady Brereton herself. Now Miss Tolerance, hungry and worn from the emotion of the interview in Somers Town, called for wine and cake. Despite the warmth of the day a fire had been lit in the Ladies' Salon. That, and the Jerez wine, combined to somnolent effect. When Miss Tolerance was wakened from her doze by Corton, the footman, she was at first unsure of where and when she found herself. The afternoon was advanced, the Salon had filled up with female members recuperating from shopping expeditions, and Corton wore an expression of concern.

"You've a visitor, Miss. Steen says you'll likely want her shown to one of the little rooms?"

Miss Tolerance agreed, dispatched Corton to escort her visitor to the second floor, and collected herself to meet her. She found the lady waiting in the hall outside the withdrawing room, wringing her hands and examining a still life which featured two apples, a tankard, and a very dead pheasant.

"Lady Brereton?"

The sight of her agent's injury appeared to overset all other of Lady Brereton's concerns. "My dear Miss Tolerance, is this the indisposition you wrote me of? You are hurt!"

It took Miss Tolerance a moment to recall that she had mentioned the first injury she had taken in the course of Lady Brereton's business. "That was something else, ma'am. As for this? A slight disagreement with one of the players in your sister's tale. I will tell you about it in course." To forestall oppressive concern Miss Tolerance held the door for her client. "Will you walk in?"

The withdrawing room was a small square; there was no fire lit, and a window was open to admit a breeze and the honeyed afternoon light. Rosebuds on Lady Brereton's straw bonnet stirred slightly. She wore a white muslin dress and dull pink spencer embroidered with more rosebuds. The effect was feminine, perhaps a touch frivolous. The lady's face, however, was drawn and anxious. She took a seat.

273

"What have you to tell me?" She knit her gloved fingers together in her lap, clearly braced for the worst.

"Let me set your mind a little at ease, ma'am. My first and best news is that your sister is alive and safe."

Lady Brereton sank back into her chair, as if relief had deprived her of all strength. She bit her lip and her eyes closed prayerfully.

"Miss Thorpe's situation for now is a good one—she is with respectable people who are happy to have her, and who concern themselves with her welfare. They are known to your brother—"

Lady Brereton's eyes snapped open. *"To Henry?* I am fond of my brother, Miss Tolerance, but I am fully aware of how irregular most of his acquaintance—" she seemed in danger of relapse into her former anxiety.

"You mistake me, ma'am. The acquaintance is Mr. John Thorpe's."

Miss Tolerance was not prepared to meet outrage. "John? *John* knows where Evie is? How long has he known? Why did he not tell me?" Lady Brereton's softly rounded chin took on an ugly, stark edge. Miss Tolerance would not in that moment have wished to be John Thorpe. "When I have been beside myself with worry? Why did he not bring her directly to me?"

Miss Tolerance raised a hand to stop the flow of words. "It is only a day ago that your brother would have heard from her. I assure you Mr. Thorpe has good reason for his reticence: your sister did not authorize him to tell you—"

"Not tell me? Evie did not want him to tell me?" Lady Brereton's wrathful expression gave way now to hurt and bewilderment. Miss Tolerance was aware of her own impatience and bit it back: Lady Brereton had no idea yet how her sister had been used.

"The situation is not a simple one. I hope you withhold your judgment about your brother's behavior and your sister's until you have heard the whole of the tale."

Lady Brereton's eyes glittered, but she squared her shoulders and nodded. "Of course. But where is she, if she will not come home? Is she—was she—" her pause was eloquent of questions she feared to ask. "What happened to her? Where has she been? Is she well?"

"The details are hers to share with you, ma'am. I will say that she met with very cruel treatment. The worst you can imagine will not be far off." Miss Tolerance paused meaningly. "You must be prepared to find she is no longer the girl you remember. She was a captive until a day ago, but as to who held her and how, that story is Miss Thorpe's to tell. If you are willing to see her—"

"Willing? Of course I am. But why will she not come home?"

Miss Tolerance regarded her client, her sister-at-law, and reminded herself that, for all the soft femininity of her appearance and the girlish flute of her voice, she had seen Lady Brereton face down her father's rage without blinking. Evadne Thorpe would need *that* sister to help her.

"Miss Thorpe believes she will not be safe in your father's house."

The effect of this statement on Lady Brereton was striking; all softness fled. She sat rigid, staring at Miss Tolerance. At last, "Is it my brother Henry she fears?"

Miss Tolerance would not be drawn. "Truly, ma'am, it is not my story to tell. I can bring you to her this evening, or in the morning, if you prefer it."

"Let me go to her now." Lady Brereton took up her reticule and made to rise. "I cannot know how to help her until I do." She looked around her as if to defy an imagined watcher. "I know Evie fears our father's temper, Miss Tolerance, but I am certain that when she is returned to him he will forgive her at once and—"

Again Miss Tolerance stopped her. "Ma'am, only let your sister tell her story."

Lady Brereton had come to Tarsio's in her own barouche. Miss Tolerance felt a shock of recognition on seeing the livery the driver wore: it was unchanged from her father's time. She gave the driver the Godwins' direction

275

and sat back. She was not often afforded the opportunity to ride in a clean, well-kept, well-sprung vehicle; given the various hurts which she had lately suffered, she appreciated the small luxury particularly. She and Lady Brereton did not speak much as they rode; Lady Brereton was lost in her own thoughts. It was left to Miss Tolerance to wonder how the rest of the family, including Sir Adam Brereton, would greet the news of Evadne's discovery and the story of her captivity.

At Number 29 the Godwins' door was opened by the child in the blue-striped gown, who greeted Miss Tolerance as a friend of the household, but frankly stared at Lady Brereton's superior finery. They were ushered into the hallway, where the earlier smell of baking had given way to that of roasting meat. The girl left them to inquire if "that young lady" would see them; when she returned a few moments later she led them, not into the sitting room where Mrs. Godwin held court, but up the stairs to a pleasant room with sofa and chairs upholstered in old fashioned fabric. The room faced the rear of the house and a pretty, small garden. The sun was low enough in the sky that the lamps had been lit.

"Ma'am told Miss Fanny I'm to bring that young lady here to you," she told them. The maid was one of those who preferred to narrate her actions as she performed them.

Lady Brereton looked out at the twilit garden, twisting a kerchief between gloved fingers.

"Clary?"

Evadne Thorpe's voice was husky and uncertain. She stood in the doorway, poised to run away if her sister should frown. Lady Brereton turned, arms extended to gather Evadne to her; the girl stumbled forward into them, and both began to weep.

Miss Tolerance left the room, closing the door behind her.

She spent nearly an hour downstairs with Mrs. Godwin, who asked, through her daughters, many questions about Miss Tolerance's profession and its origin. Miss Mary was captivated by the romance of her elopement; Miss Fanny and her mother were more interested in the practical aspects of her work.

"In men's clothes? Truly? Do you not feel—" Miss Imlay turned to her mother as if she might supply the correct word. "Do you not feel particularly exposed, dressed so?"

"I am quite accustomed to it. When I lived in Belgium and taught fence, it was practical. And safer. Now—my profession sometimes requires me to defend myself, which is far easier to do in breeches and coat than in kid slippers and petticoats."

Mrs. Godwin nodded slightly, the right corner of her mouth quirking upward. She mumbled something to Fanny.

"How much can you command in payment for your services?" the girl asked. She was apologetic: "My mother asked."

Miss Tolerance found herself deep in a discussion of fees, expenses, and investment. Mary, evidently finding this uninteresting, picked up a book and began to read. Mrs. Godwin, through Fanny, asked particularly about the treatment Miss Tolerance encountered from men of all classes. The woman's body was wrecked, but her mind was still sharp and her opinions unaffected.

So immersed in the conversation were they that it was almost a surprise when Evadne Thorpe and Clarissa Brereton appeared at the door. They were hand-in-hand; from the evidence of their eyes there had been many tears. Lady Brereton, shorter than her sister, looked the taller in her protectiveness. For her part Evadne seemed happy to lean against her sister, to enjoy that sororal protection and authority.

"I beg your pardon." Lady Brereton spoke to Mrs. Godwin. "I have come to thank you with all my heart for your care for my sister—"

Mrs. Godwin said something that was clearly a protest. At the same time Fanny Imlay said "I has been our pleasure to have her here—"

277

"—and to ask if she may remain with you for a day or so longer," Lady Brereton continued. "I must talk to my husband and my brothers, although I do not expect any objection to Evie coming to live with me."

Miss Tolerance thought of her brother, of Lord Lyne, of the attitude of common society to which Miss Thorpe would be subject, and wondered if such a solution would prove wise. She said nothing of it.

"My mother asks me to assure you Miss Thorpe is welcome to stay." Fanny Imlay's lips pursed, and Miss Tolerance wondered if the girl liked the idea of another pretty girl permanently resident in the Polygon.

It was time, she thought, to leave.

Before the witness of Mrs. Godwin, Miss Fanny, and Miss Tolerance, Clarissa Brereton embraced her sister, promising to settle the matter of her future as quickly as possible. This time it was Fanny Imlay who escorted Miss Tolerance to the door, with Lady Brereton, handfast with her sister, following after.

In the barouche Lady Brereton gave vent to her feelings in a burst of tears. Miss Tolerance kept quiet, passed her a kerchief when Lady Brereton's own lacy one became sodden, and waited out the storm. Her demeanor at last became more composed.

"You have some idea of what my sister suffered, and what she believes my father's part to have been."

Miss Tolerance nodded. "She told you the whole of it?"

"She did. Now I must think what to do. Remove from my father's house at once," Lady Brereton said, as if to herself. "Adam will understand. And tomorrow I will talk to John and Henry, and—" she kept up a quiet monologue which required no response from her listener, until at last the barouche arrived, not at Tarsio's or in Duke of York Street, but in Manchester Square.

"Is this not right?" Lady Brereton asked when she saw Miss Tolerance's surprise. "I thought perhaps you would prefer to go home."

"It is very kind of you indeed," Miss Tolerance assured

her. "I was only surprised that you were aware of my home's location."

Lady Brereton waved a gloved hand, making the matter of no importance. "I cannot thank you enough for restoring Evie to me, Miss Tolerance. In a few days will you call on me? I will send a note to let you know where my husband and I are staying."

Miss Tolerance recognized a dismissal. She thanked her client, bid her good evening, and descended from the carriage.

It had been a day of considerable emotion, even at second hand. Miss Tolerance looked around her carefully before she entered Spanish Place; Worke and Huwe might be in custody, but if either man had another confederate she was in no case to defend herself. But the street, and Manchester Square itself, were empty of all but a few menservants come out to light the lanterns hung by the doorways. She entered the garden from Spanish Place, thence to her cottage, where she stirred her banked fire. She could not raise flame enough to boil water; her arm was by now too painful to permit her to carry and arrange in the fireplace the fuel needed. Which meant, she reflected sourly, that she ought to have someone examine the hurt for her and perhaps change the dressing.

In the kitchen of Mrs. Brereton's house all was in what appeared to be chaos. Miss Tolerance, who had spent a good number of hours observing Cook's management, knew the pandemonium was more seeming than actual; that dishes for the lavish buffet Mrs. Brereton made available to her customers would be finished and brought up to the saloon; that pots and pans would be scrubbed and put away; and that the dire threats Cook made upon the life and limbs of her kitchen staff would never be acted upon.

"I'll have your liver for sausage if you let that sauce burn," Cook was advising Jess, the scullery girl newly promoted to cook's assistant. Cook turned—it was astonishing that so vast a woman could move so quickly—and greeted

Miss Tolerance, chiding that she looked half-fed and pale. "A cup of soup is what you need, Miss Sarah. And maybe a roll or two?"

"I was hoping to speak with Marianne for a moment," Miss Tolerance said mildly.

"Well, do you sit then. I'll send this'n off to find her." Cook elbowed the new scullery boy, who had just brought in a scuttle of coal for the oven fire. The boy did not quite drop the coal, though it was a near thing. "You, Jeddy, run tell Cole Miss Sarah wants a word with Mrs. Touchwell."

Jeddy gestured at Miss Tolerance with his chin. "This'n Miss Sarah?" He was a chubby boy, highly freckled, with a droopy eye; his left hand was pebbled with warts. Miss Tolerance nodded in acknowledgment. "Well eno'. Back in a tick."

Cook shook her head. "That'n'll take a lick of training up just to understand who's to be respecked, Miss Sarah. Don't you mind Jeddy's way." She pressed a cup of broth into Miss Tolerance's hands as Miss Tolerance was assuring her she did not mind the boy in the least.

Jed returned and went out for more wood; shortly Marianne appeared, dressed for the evening and draping an ivory-colored Norwich shawl about her shoulders.

"I was hoping you would have a few moments to dress my arm," Miss Tolerance said. "If it is inconvenient—"

"As it happens, it is entirely convenient. I've an engagement later; the gentleman has the whole evening and means to use it. Let me see." She asked Cook for some hot water, and took her friend into Cook's room for a little privacy.

The wound was still angry looking, the flesh above the dressing swollen and red. Miss Tolerance looked away as her friend worked, dabbing carefully at the wound, dusting it with calomel powder and, at last, binding it up again. It was just as well, Miss Tolerance thought, that she had eaten nothing more than broth.

"I suppose I cannot persuade you to lie abed for a few days and give this a chance to heal?" As Marianne finished the question another whore looked in at the door. Mrs. Lisette Lipper, short, plump and usually rather lazy and amiable, was all a-rage. Her dark eyes were wide under scowling brows, and her diction was decidedly less elegant than was required upstairs.

"Mary, Mrs. B's man was at me just now. I told him I had a man coming and he done this to me!" Lisette extended her arm to display a fierce ring of red flesh. "Twisted it proper, like. Then give me a kiss and said he'd take his due later!"

Marianne and Miss Tolerance exchanged looks.

"It was Mr. Tickenor?" Marianne asked carefully.

"I just said so, didn't I? You ast—asked—the other day if I'd had any problem with 'im—him—and I hadn't, then. But tonight—And I know Annie has too, only she just lifted her skirts and let him take what he wanted."

"Mrs. B's rules—" Marianne started.

"I know, but he's got Mrs. B's ear, and what was Annie to do? Spit in his eye? Call for Keefe?"

Miss Tolerance was conscious, first, of Marianne's eye upon her, and second, of her own exhaustion. "Now?"

Marianne was regretful. "I really think so, and Sarah dear, we need you by. I know your aunt has been tetchy of late, but she does set store by what you tell her, and this ain't going to be a pleasant conversation at all."

Miss Tolerance nodded. Marianne had finished bandaging her arm. Returning her arm to her sleeve cost her a moment of pain severe enough to fill her mouth with the taste of it. Then she was dressed and buttoned and ready. She took a moment to summon her resolve, then: "Let us go up," Miss Tolerance said. "We'll need Harry as well."

"I'll fetch him," Lisette offered, and went ahead.

The four: Marianne, Lisette, Harry and Miss Tolerance, met outside Mrs. Brereton's sitting room. Harry was dressed for the evening custom in shirt and waistcoat, a kerchief knotted romantically round his throat like a highwayman; he attempted to carry himself bravely, but he could barely raise his eyes from the floor, and rubbed his thumb and forefingers apprehensively.

Miss Tolerance arranged her features as sympathetically as possible. "Come, Harry." She put her arm through his in a friendly manner. "Mrs. Brereton needs to know what has been happening. Come," she said again. "I will not let anyone hurt you."

The boy looked down at her from his spindly height, his lips twisted in a sad smile.

Mrs. Brereton was taking tea with Mr. Tickenor at the small round table near the window. The drapes were drawn, the candles lit, and the chiffonier nearby was piled with evidence of the meal just past. The bawd regarded the group in her doorway with no little amazement.

"Should I say good evening?" Her voice was dry.

"I hope so, aunt." Miss Tolerance said nothing to Tickenor. At the sight of the older man Harry took a step back, but Miss Tolerance had prepared for his anxiety. She hugged the arm looped in her own closer and led him into the room. On her other side Marianne and Lisette stepped forward.

Tickenor's face became blank and watchful.

Mrs. Brereton appeared to be in a reasonable state of mind; she saw Harry's distress at once. "Well, Harry? What's amiss?"

Harry shook his head; his skin had taken on a mottled, unhealthy color. Miss Tolerance doubted he would say anything unless force to do; it was enough that he was here.

"Two nights ago I found Harry behind my house, ma'am. Weeping. He was afraid he would be beaten and turned off."

"Turned off?" Mrs. Brereton's tone made the idea ridiculous. "Good God, boy, unless you have been brawling in the street or stealing the plate, why would you think any such thing? Now and again a patron may become...too enthused, but as for *beating*, this is no birching house. You are not required to cater to such tastes if you dislike it; I only ask you be polite in your refusal. Why would you be turned off? Has someone threatened you? Who?"

Harry shook his head again.

"It was not a patron, aunt." Miss Tolerance looked deliberately at Tickenor. "Nor is Harry the only one to experience this gentleman's attentions."

Mrs. Brereton followed her niece's gaze and her own expression hardened.

"I know you do not like Mr. Tickenor, Sarah. Perhaps you feel he has cut your expectations in half. But to concoct a tale—"

"Aunt, I am here only because I found Harry weeping behind the outhouse, afraid he would be punished for what he had been forced to, and fearful of what would happen if he spoke up. I think if you talk to Emma or Lisette—" Miss Tolerance turned to nod at Mrs. Lipper—"Or Annie? Yes, Annie, you will find that Mr. Tickenor has been very even handed in their attentions."

"His attentions. But they know my rules. They would have come to me."

"They are coming to you now. They might have come earlier, but you have made it plain you do not wish to hear a word against your betrothed. So you have pitched one rule against the other; how were they to know which rule trumps?"

Mrs. Brereton turned from her niece back to Harry. "Tell me what happened, boy." Her voice was gentler now.

In broken sentences Harry related his story: Tickenor, the closet, the threats and the sex that followed them. Throughout the whole Tickenor looked out the window as if nothing being related was the slightest bit out of the ordinary. Harry finished with, "It's the truth, ma'am, as God is my witness."

"Yes, Harry. I'm sure you think it's so," Mrs. Brereton said absently. Miss Tolerance had a moment of fear; hearing this, would her aunt still side with Tickenor? "Lisette? You have something to tell me?"

The whore stepped closer to her mistress, her wrist extended. The circle of bruised flesh was still visible. "Not an hour ago Mr. Tickenor tried to have me, too, ma'am. When

I told him I wouldn't—I've a caller coming soon, even if I wanted to break your rule, which I do not—he did that, ma'am. Then told me he'd take me later."

There was silence except for the whickering of the candles near the window.

"Very well. If you expect a caller, don't keep him waiting. I'll speak to you later if I have need." Mrs. Brereton spoke to her fiancé. "Gerard? What have you to say of all this?"

Tickenor smiled and raised an eyebrow. "Say? What is there to say? Are you going to take the word of a whore— and a molly-whore—over mine?"

"My dear, I deal with whores all day long. I find my people are generally truthful. If I call Anna and Emma to ask them about this, what will they tell me?"

"Oh, for Christ's sake!" Tickenor rose and stalked to the curtained window. "If you mean to be jealous—I was merely—"

"Merely sampling the wares to test for quality?" Miss Tolerance murmured.

"Oh, well, *you*, you quean," Tickenor was venomous. "Your auntie knows better than to believe a word comes out of your mouth."

"Does she, sir? That would make me sad."

"Be quiet, Sarah. You will muddy waters that are suddenly becoming quite clear." But Mrs. Brereton did not sound angry, merely impatient with distraction. "Gerard, as you have acknowledged sampling the wares—"

"They came to me, all of them, offering it—"

"And you slapped Harry and wrung Lisette's wrist for their presumption?" Miss Tolerance could not restrain herself.

"Sarah, I asked you to be quiet. I am able to draw my own conclusions. Gerard, why would any of my people impose upon you in such a fashion?"

He shrugged. "To get upon my good side, I suppose. What is the to-do? They're there for the taking. Perhaps they fancied me."

Harry, still at Miss Tolerance's side, shook his head. "Not ever, ma'am. We know better."

Mrs. Brereton nodded her head. She had not turned to look at Tickenor; perhaps that bothered him as much as the accusations being leveled. "It's not like you to be jealous, Thea. None of it meant—"

"Jealousy? Is that what you think? 'Tis business, Gerard. You should recognize it as a businessman. It is…pilferage, as much as a milliner's clerk who takes home a packet of pins."

"I am no clerk, madam." Tickenor seemed more incensed at this than at the accusations that had come before.

"You are right. You are no clerk, who might have been underfed or underpaid and thus convinced himself that it was only right to take a little of what his employer has so much of. You stole from my house, and it appears that you have bullied my staff into breaking my rule."

"Rule?"

Mrs. Brereton turned to the boy, Harry, who was white-faced and fidgeting, his gaze going back and forth between his employer and Mr. Tickenor. She said encouragingly, "You can tell me what rule Mr. Tickenor asked you to thwart, cannot you?"

The boy swallowed and looked sideways at the other man.

Mrs. Brereton smiled. "You may tell us, Harry. No harm will come to you."

"We're not to give away what people will pay for, ma'am." Harry was still young enough that his voice cracked at the end of the sentence.

"Thank you, my dear. You have been very brave. Go on, now. I believe Lord Holyfield has promised to call tonight? And Lisette, you have a caller as well. Go along, both of you." Mrs. Brereton watched them leave the room before she turned back to Tickenor. "You not only sought to steal from me, but you attacked the discipline of my house. And for what, Gerard? To claim your power like a hound pissing on the doorstep?"

285

Mr. Tickenor returned to her side, his face an unconvincing mask of conciliation. "For the love of God, Dorothea, in another week we're to be wed. How am I to maintain discipline if you permit—"

"I have no problem maintaining discipline, Gerard, in part because of the very rules you broke. I may have told you I hoped for your help; I never said you were to have the whip hand here."

Miss Tolerance had a fleeting sense of pity for Mr. Tickenor, for it seemed to her that her aunt had said almost exactly that, and now he found his license revoked.

Tickenor came back from the window to Mrs. Brereton's side. "Is it the sex that troubles you? I did not mean to wound your pride, and I did not perfectly understand the rules of the house. I may think you are over nice—"

Mrs. Brereton's expression was so cold that Miss Tolerance was unnerved. She wondered that Tickenor, his arm around the madam's waist, did not seem at all troubled.

"This is not jealousy, Gerard. It is commonsense. Once the staff start in to playing among themselves they develop little loyalties and factions, and the house is divided against itself, and there is trouble. But you have done more than that. Even the scullery boy knows better than to steal from my table or *put his fingers in my pies.*"

Tickenor stiffened at her tone, but made one more attempt to make amends. He offered his hand to Mrs. Brereton, palm up as if to emphasize his vulnerability. "If we have mistaken each other, Dorothea, I am heartily sorry for it. If you like it better, when we are wed I will take no part in the business at all. I have business of my own to attend to, after all, and —"

Mrs. Brereton pushed the hand aside. "Gerard, you do not think that, after you have fucked half my staff including a green boy, I still plan to marry you?" A pitying smile played on her lips.

Tickenor withdrew his hand and looked at Mrs. Brereton as if the sheer force of his gaze would win her capitulation. It did not. After a long and plangent silence Tickenor threw his shoulders back, a man affronted. Red as a grape, he pushed between Marianne and Miss Tolerance without a word and left the room.

Mrs. Brereton spoke into the silence. "It seems I had misjudged Mr. Tickenor and caused some anxiety among the staff. Marianne, will you tell them all I am sorry for it? Sarah, my dear, will you take some tea? And tell me what on earth happened to your arm?"

As easily as that Mrs. Brereton dismissed the matter of her engagement. Marianne and Miss Tolerance exchanged a glance of mutual perplexion, as much disconcerted by this *volte face* as they had been by Mrs. Brereton's engagement. The madam herself appeared untroubled by the dismissal of her former betrothed. She sat again at the table, rang for another cup, and looked at her niece with the expectation that she would join her.

Which, after a moment, she did.

Chapter Nineteen

Miss Tolerance slept deeply. The combined effect within a se'ennight of a blow to the head and a shot to the arm had worn upon her. The considerable emotion of the day did no less so, and it was a relief to wake in the morning knowing that Evadne Thorpe was safe, reunited with her sister, and that her own task was completed. She rose, called for hot water from Mrs. Brereton's, and bathed and dressed leisurely. The swelling of her arm had subsided enough that she was able to attend to the repair of her Gunnard coat; the coat had required several repairs of a like nature over the years, although this was the first time that shot had been the culprit.

She was writing letters, her little desk on her lap and her left arm secured in the sling, when Keefe knocked.

"Miss Sarah, a message for you, urgent."

She bade the porter enter. Instead he opened her door to admit a liveried servant—Wheeler, the man from Lord Lyne's house whom she had interviewed. Unease stung her.

"I'm sorry to disturb you, miss," he began. "Miss Clarissa—Lady Brereton—she sent me to beg you come to the house. Lord Lyne's house. Miss Evie's come home and Lady Brereton fears there'll be a ruckus."

Miss Tolerance's first thought was to refuse the summons. *What more do they expect of me?* She was hurt, she was tired, she had completed the assignment for which she had been hired. Further, she barely knew Miss Thorpe. What influence could she be presumed to have with her? What reason to guard the peace of Lord Lyne's household?

Except that Lady Brereton was her brother's wife and Evadne Thorpe was therefore, in some wise, her sister. Though the connection was unknown to the other women, Miss Tolerance knew it. They were family, and of all Evadne Thorpe's family, Miss Tolerance was the only one who had experience that approached in any way Evadne's own. *Not raped, but ruined. I have gone before her to that brutal country; must I not assist her to find her way?*

Perhaps that was sentimental twaddle. Still, a confrontation between Evadne Thorpe and her father was likely to be explosive and unlikely to benefit anyone. Miss Tolerance put aside her writing desk and took up her bonnet.

In the carriage returning to Duke of York Street she learned a little more from Wheeler. Lord Lyne had gone out that morning and Miss Thorpe arrived only a little time after. Her return had caused an immediate sensation in the servants' hall, with much joy by which Miss Evie had seemed curiously unmoved. The two Mr. Thorpes and Lady Brereton (whose husband had removed them to Claridge's Hotel only the night before, a fact which clearly troubled Wheeler) had been summoned with great excitement, and an emotional scene of reunion confidently predicted.

"Only it's all wrong, miss. I cannot tell you how or why, but—when Lady Brereton arrived she didn't seem happy but worried-like, and Sir Adam behind her had the same face on. They went flying up to Miss Evie's sitting room and never come down, and then Mr. John arrived and went up, but come back long enough to send me to fetch you."

Wheeler looked at Miss Tolerance as if she might explain all even if she could not mend it.

"When do you expect that Lord Lyne will return?"

"He told his valet before he left that he would take dinner at home. Said he didn't want to see mutton on his table."

Already it was after noon. The baron might return in an hour or at sunset. It was to be hoped that Miss Thorpe could be removed from the house and returned to the Godwins or to Claridge's or somewhere before that happened. What did the girl think to do? Upbraid her father? Make a public accusation of his crimes? Miss Tolerance had seen Evadne's vengeful wish to see her father reduced; she understood it. But she did not believe that seeing her father exposed as a speculator and traitor in time of war, as complicit in her own rape and imprisonment, would be as satisfying as the girl believed.

When the door was opened in Duke of York Street the footman wore the same expression of bewildered concern as Wheeler did. In a moment of inspiration, Miss Tolerance turned to Wheeler, behind her on the step.

"You see the boy on the corner there? The crossing-sweep? Will you give him a message, please?"

Wheeler looked at her blankly. "Give a message to a crossing-boy?"

"Tell him Miss T asks him to give a sign if he sees Lord Lyne approaching the house. What sign? If he can whistle loudly, tell him to whistle for all he's worth. I'll make certain to listen for it."

Satisfied that she had done what little she could to provide warning against Lyne's early return, Miss Tolerance allowed herself to be escorted upstairs.

She found a curious tableau. The room in which the Thorpe children had gathered was a girl's sitting room with cheery yellow paper, books, lacy pillows on the two flowered sofas, an embroidery frame. Evadne Thorpe sat on one sofa, a crow in a spring garden. She was flanked by Lady Brereton on her right and her brother John on her left, each watching the girl with a mix of solicitousness and anxiety, as if she were a petard which might explode.

Henry Thorpe stood by the fireplace with one arm draped along the mantel, which casual pose was at odds with his glowering countenance. Behind the sofa at Lady Brereton's shoulder Sir Adam stood, red-faced, ill at ease, but clearly prepared to support his wife. He was the first to notice Miss Tolerance's arrival.

"What the Devil are you doing here?" His tone was fraternal in the extreme. It seemed Sir Adam realized it; he looked anxiously to see if anyone had noticed.

Lady Brereton raised her head. "I asked Miss Tolerance to come, Adam. I thought she might be helpful—might help persuade Evie—"

"Persuade her to what?" Mr. Thorpe asked in the manner of a much-tried man.

"That Evie should permit me to take her back to the place where she has been staying," John Thorpe said.

"Or to the hotel, with me," Lady Brereton added. Sir Adam's eyes widened. Was he dismayed at the thought of escorting his Fallen sister-at-law through the foyer of London's most fashionable hotel? Wisely, he made no protest.

"You'd best persuade me first, then." Henry Thorpe drew his hand over his face. "I don't know why you're in such a damned hurry to remove her from the house. There's little love lost between me and the old man, but you can't tell me he won't want to see Evie."

John Thorpe glared at his brother. "Such a meeting would be ill-advised, Henry. Please take my word for it."

"Ill-advised? You're talking as if Evie'd broken a teacup and wanted to escape a scolding. Good Christ, the girl's been missing for weeks, it ain't like Father don't know it."

His words brought a small, bitter smile to Miss Thorpe's face.

Miss Tolerance spoke from the doorway. "Mr. Thorpe, perhaps you do not remember your father's very firm statement that he did not wish your sister returned to him. Have you any reason to think his feeling is different now?"

"He never changed his tune, if that's what you mean. But with Evie standing before him?" Henry Thorpe abandoned his pose against the mantel and seated himself on the sofa opposite his sister. He leaned forward. "Evie, you know well that Father and I have had our quarrels. To be honest," he smiled a rueful, winning smile that gave Miss Tolerance her first glimpse of his charm, "I've given the old man cause to toss me out on my ear. I've drunk and gamed and piled up debt. In the end the old man has always forgiven me. At least give him the chance."

A flush rose in Evadne Thorpe's pale cheeks. She pressed her lips together, damming words that made her tremble. "To forgive me?" Her voice was flat.

"In the end he will, you know." Mr. Thorpe was earnest. "It won't do for you to stay here, but you know the old man will want to assist you. He's bound to cut up stiff at first, but he'll come round in the end."

Miss Thorpe raised her chin. "Then by all means, I must stay."

Lady Brereton shook her head. *"No, Evie."* She looked to her younger brother, then to her husband, and at last to Miss Tolerance.

Miss Tolerance advanced into the room and, ignoring Henry Thorpe, knelt before Evadne to meet her eyes levelly. "I have some idea of what is in your mind," she said very quietly. "And I have a very good idea of what you face from this day forward. Your road will be a difficult one, even with the assistance and love I see for you here. A moment's reflection: need you make your own path harder? At least, I beg you, come away now with your brother, or your sister and my—" she broke off, aware of Sir Adam's eyes on her. "And myself. They will not say so, but such a meeting will very likely affect your sister and brothers as well as yourself. For their sake, take a little thought before you undertake an interview which will be at the very least…volatile."

A little of the rigidity eased from Miss Thorpe's posture. She looked into Miss Tolerance's face as if to read something there; Miss Tolerance returned the regard unflinching. The girl nodded.

"I will go. Johnny, will you take me back to the Godwins' house?" She smiled apologetically at Lady Brereton. "I am not quite up to the bustle of Claridge's, I think."

Sir Adam nodded and, after a moment, Lady Brereton echoed him. Each looked relieved. Immediately Evadne's spencer and bonnet were produced and Lady Brereton, fussing over her sister as if she had been a child of six, tied her ribbons and buttoned her buttons, solicitous as a nursery maid.

Evadne left the room with Lady Brereton at her side and John Thorpe just to the fore; Sir Adam followed close after his wife, and Miss Tolerance was left to walk out beside Henry Thorpe, who still could not fathom a reason for her presence. In the front hall Lady Brereton sent for her own pelisse.

At which moment Lord Lyne returned.

The baron stopped in his doorway, half-turned to give his stick and hat to Wheeler. Evadne Thorpe and her siblings were ranged at the bottom of the staircase, as dumbstruck as their father. In the silence that followed Miss Tolerance heard a sharp, shrill whistle emanating from the street. Too little, too late.

Lord Lyne spoke first. "So, girl. So you've come back." Miss Tolerance thought she heard a quaver in the baron's voice. He cleared his throat. "Do you expect a welcome?"

"Father—" Henry Thorpe and John Thorpe said at once.

"A welcome? No, sir." Evadne's voice was steadier than her father's, low and without inflection.

"Evie, dearest," Lady Brereton murmured. She put a restraining hand on her sister's shoulder. The two exchanged an eloquent look.

Evadne turned back to her father. "I beg your pardon. I should not have come."

Lyne dismissed Wheeler with an irritable wave. "Well, you're here now. We will not make a gift of our business to the servants' hall. Come." He pushed through his children and strode up the stairs and into to his office, clearly expecting them to follow. Mr. Henry Thorpe took his sister's arm and pulled her after their father, with Lady Brereton and John Thorpe following after apprehensively.

Sir Adam and Miss Tolerance were left in their wake.

"Come along, Sally," Sir Adam muttered. "I won't go in there alone."

Miss Tolerance did not argue. She followed him into the same room where she had first met Lyne. The curtains were drawn and the room was bright and cool.

The older Thorpe children clustered around Evadne, either for support or to contain a possible tirade. Lord Lyne had stationed himself before the window so that he was a stocky shadow framed by sunlight, his hands clasped behind his back. Light glinted off the frame of his spectacles and obscured his eyes.

Lyne began. "As you've come home, we must discuss what is to be done—how to save the family from the worst of it. I don't want to hear where you were or with whom," he began.

"No, sir. Why would you?" The girl spoke in a flat, hard voice.

Lord Lyne shrugged off the interruption. "To preserve the family—save your brothers and sister from disgrace, that must be our goal. As for you—I'll think of something for you, girl."

"Shall you, sir?"

Lyne scowled at his daughter.

Mr. Henry Thorpe regarded his sister anxiously: this was not the conciliatory tone he had counseled her to use. "For God's sake, Evie," he said, *sotto voce*. "Be a little—at least attempt an apology."

Evadne smiled at her brother, an expression with an unsettling taint of ferocity. "Apologize, Henry?" She turned back to her father, raised her chin. "Should I apologize? I beg your pardon, Father, but I think I will be safer if I do not permit *you* to make further plans for me."

Lyne took a step forward, one hand fisted and raised. "You take that tone with me, miss? After you leave your home and whore yourself out to God knows who—"

"But *you* know, Father. You knew from the day I was taken who had me and what he was doing to me." Lyne was driven back a step by the venom in his daughter's voice. "When I tried to escape Him you sent me back. I was beaten and...used. It wasn't I who made a whore of me, Father. It was you."

Miss Tolerance could not tell, from the baron's face, whether his horror was for his daughter's ill-use or because she knew his part in it. Henry Thorpe stood with his mouth frankly open, staring at his sister.

"The man who stole me from this house was your partner, Father. You and—" the girl had difficulty getting the name out. "You and Abner Huwe made a profit together out of *death*. What a disgrace if it were known, Baron Lyne of Wandfield speculating against the Army with a Welsh merchant."

Lyne had taken a further step backward, staring at his daughter, transfixed. It was Henry Thorpe, galvanized by his sister's words, who demanded an explanation. She turned to him blindly and shook her head.

"Will someone explain to me what she is saying? Who is this Huwe? How could my father be involved in Evie's— Evie's—" he shook his head. "Someone explain it to me."

No one spoke. At last, "I can tell you the burden of it, Mr. Thorpe," Miss Tolerance offered. "Your sister or your father will correct me when I err. Several years ago your father found himself in financial difficulties. With his knowledge of the Navy's plans and of naval history, he came up with a scheme, involving Mr. Huwe, to recoup his fortune. When he had repaired his finances your father wished to distance himself from an endeavor which, had it become publicly known, would have caused trouble for them both. Mr. Huwe was displeased; there was still money to be made, and he wanted to continue. I suppose he might have threatened to lay information and expose what your father had done, but that would mean exposing himself, which he did not like to do. He chose another lever."

Henry Thorpe's gaze went to his sister.

"Exactly so. I am not certain if your father was coerced by threats to your sister's life or by the threat that her ruin would become public. Which ever it was, he did nothing to regain her; you will remember that he forbade anyone in the family to seek her. And Mr. Huwe attempted to avenge himself on the daughter for slights at the father's hand. He *raped* her nightly—" Henry Thorpe recoiled at Miss Tolerance's merciless emphasis on the word. "He used her so vilely that once he had to call a—a nurse—of his acquaintance to minister to her."

"That was after I had tried to escape him. After you had returned me to him, Father. I wrote to beg you for help and *you returned me to him.*" Evadne bit hard upon each word. Tears ran unstopped down her cheeks.

At her side Miss Tolerance felt her brother, rigid with shock. Had his wife told him nothing when she insisted they leave Lyne's house?

"In God's name, Father, do you say nothing to all this?" Henry Thorpe had begun to pace, weaving back and forth behind a straight-backed chair.

Lyne, as marble-cold as his daughter, stared at his son, then at Evadne, then took in the whole room. "What should I say? What choice had I? He'd already got the girl, blackened her name." His voice was sullen. "Your name too, boy, if you'd take the moment to think of it."

"And the business that brought all this to our door, that ruined my sister?"

"I did what I had to do!" Lyne was no longer cold; he was spitting with anger. *He feels ill-used,* Miss Tolerance marveled. "What was I to do with you damned near bankrupting me, and dowries and fripperies to be paid for, and the damned Spanish threatening to steal my property in

Venezuela? I was done up! Should I have let you default on debts of honor? Shame the family? What was I to do? I didn't mean to go on once my finances were recouped."

It is all perfectly reasonable, Miss Tolerance thought. *In his mind the wrong would have been in being caught.*

"Where did the money come from? What could be so dreadful that it could not be known?"

Lyne pressed his lips together.

"I believe they were trading in cinchona bark," Miss Tolerance said. "When the force at Walcheren fell sick, Huwe's ships, full of your father's bark, would arrive providentially and charge whatever price they set."

Henry Thorpe shook his head. "Sharp dealing, perhaps, but—"

"Except that your father knew of earlier attempts on the lowlands that had failed for the same cause. He suspected the dangers; did no one listen to you at the War Office, sir? He began to amass quantities of bark well before the invasion, so that he and Huwe should control scarcity and mete it out as might make the most profit."

Lyne shrugged the matter off. "I saw an opportunity."

Both of his sons looked at him as at stranger.

"When the commission investigating the failure at Walcheren first met, Father, did you not feel the least—" John Thorpe groped for the word. "The least remorse? So many dead or sickened beyond recovery, when you might have been a hero to them, to the nation—"

"And who would have paid your brother's debts?" Lyne barked. "Who would have laid by a dowry for your sister?"

"I congratulate you on your excellent economy," Evadne Thorpe said quietly. "I shall never need a dowry now." Lady Brereton moved to put an arm around her sister. "Does it comfort you, Papa, to know that you traded not only my virtue but the lives of thousands of English soldiers?"

"I made it possible for thousands to have the bark that saved their lives!" Lyne countered.

"Once the price was high enough. I read your letters—I took them with me when I ran from Huwe. When the world knows how you handed me to a villain to hide—"

Lyne's outrage was explosive. "You'd let that be known? I did it to save this family! By God, you liked your pretty clothes well enough. Where do you think money comes from, girl? For your brother's charities and Henry's horses and gambling? To keep this house running? We were close to losing it all, do you understand? My mistake was putting myself in the hands of that Welsh bastard—"

"You bought his silence with my sister's honor." That was John Thorpe. His voice was thick.

Lyne smiled mirthlessly. "You know Genesis, boy. That must be my model." All four Thorpe children stared at him uncomprehending. His voice became more insistent. "The Bible—"

Miss Tolerance felt sick. "You cannot claim authority from the Bible, sir."

"Can I not? Lot gave his daughters to the town—"

John Thorpe shook his head. "He offered them as hostages for the lives of strangers—of angels of the Lord, Father. Not to hide a crime or save his name."

"Lot was a righteous man! God took him from Sodom, although he gave his daughters to the mob." Lord Lyne stood with his hands at his sides, fisted, his head jutted forward. His voice was querulous, the pitch rising.

Miss Tolerance said coolly, "We are taught that Lot was a holy man, but for my part I have never thought that was holy behavior."

"*Your* part. Shut your mouth, whore. I can destroy you—"

"And me, Father? I have Huwe's ledger, your letters." Evadne Thorpe's tears had dried.

"My letters?" Lyne stepped forward. "Where are they?"

"They are safe from you." Evadne was quiet, as though a storm had passed through her and gone again. "You will not find them. Perhaps my brothers would like to read them? Your secret lies with all of us now. I know Miss Tolerance will divulge nothing without our authorization—"

Lyne's glance at Miss Tolerance was hot with rage. "You'd trust this slut?"

"She is no more slut than I am," Evadne said. A step to the right brought her to Miss Tolerance's side.

"Or I, Father." Lady Brereton came to stand with them.

Lyne looked from one to the other.

"Most sluts do not share their clients' secrets, and nor do I. It is your children you must treat with." Miss Tolerance kept her tone as level as Evadne's own.

"Should we be kind to you, Father?" Miss Thorpe asked. "Kinder than you were to me?"

"The name, the family. I could not let it be—"

"*I am Fallen by your design, Father.* How if it became known that you gave your daughter to buy a man's silence? How would your honor fare if it was known you hid behind my skirts?" Evadne bit her lip, closed her eyes, and appeared to regain her composure. "Shall I use the letters? I do not know what to do. I suppose Henry and John and Clary and I will discuss it." Something that might have been a smile played on her lips. "If you wish to beg my forgiveness, Father, now would be the time for it, for I swear by God I shall never speak to you again in this life."

Lyne regarded his daughter as if she spoke a language with which he was not acquainted. Miss Tolerance's admiration was all for Evadne Thorpe.

"I will *not* be spoken to so—I will not."

"Very well." Evadne said nothing more. She turned and left the room. One by one her sister, her brothers, Sir Adam and Miss Tolerance followed her.

In the hall, Evadne's strength deserted her. She tottered, her knees buckled; Miss Tolerance caught her and guided her to a chair. Lady Brereton called out for water and smelling salts.

"You are a good, brave girl," she murmured as she might have to a child. "You are a brave girl."

Evadne sipped at the glass of water Lady Brereton held

for her, and waved away the salts. "I—I hoped at least he would be sorry."

Miss Tolerance shook her head. "I do not think he can be now. I think he told himself that you did not know his part. Perhaps with time?" She did not much believe it, but if the girl could, the better for her.

Henry Thorpe and his brother helped their sister to her feet, and together they guided her up the stairs to the little sitting room. Henry settled her in a chair. John Thorpe pressed a glass of wine on her. Then he and his brother stood back with Sir Adam, all of them watching Evadne helplessly. Tears slipped down her cheeks and watered the wine she sipped. Lady Brereton knelt by her sister's chair, stroking her hand. As they sat so, Lord Lyne's voice carried to them from the hallway, demanding that his daughter come down, come back, speak with him, listen to him. After a moment of this Mr. Henry Thorpe left the room. When he returned his face was grim but resolved; the rake subsumed in the elder brother.

"I told the old man not to waste his breath; he gave up all claim to authority when he let Evie answer for his cowardice. Let him sulk in his office."

"I will take you back to Godwin's house, Evie," John Thorpe said.

"Or anywhere else you like," Henry Thorpe added.

Sir Adam, who had said nothing downstairs, stood just as silent now, watching his wife anxiously. Miss Tolerance had done what she could; it was time she left.

"May I call on you tomorrow, Lady Brereton? Thank you. In the meantime, if there is any way I can—" She was not able to finish the sentence.

A noise, a sound unmistakable to Miss Tolerance's ears, echoed in the hallway. Without thought she ran for the stairs, with John and Henry Thorpe just behind her. The door to Lord Lyne's office was closed; Wheeler and the other footman, Pinney, stood before it indecisively. Henry Thorpe pushed past them, dismissing them with a nod, and opened the door.

Miss Tolerance smelled black powder even before she walked in, and saw curls of smoke against the sunny window.

Lord Lyne sat behind his desk, his head thrown back, a part of his head disfigured with blood and gunpowder, half of his spectacles dangling from one ear. Blood spattered the curtain behind him. The pistol in his hand fell to the floor as his sons approached him. Miss Tolerance waited in the doorway, trembling, although she had been certain what they would find.

"Almighty ever-living God," John Thorpe murmured. He leaned forward to close his father's eyes. His hand came back bloodied. "Maker of mankind, who dost correct those whom Thou dost love, and chastise every one whom Thou dost receive: We beseech Thee to have mercy upon this Thy servant visited with Thine hand—"

Henry Thorpe stood before the desk, looking about him blankly as if the horrid revelations of the past hour had at last overwhelmed him. He picked up a piece of paper that lay centered on the desk. One word was written there, which Miss Tolerance could not read from where she stood.

Thorpe returned the paper to the desk, turned away from his father and pushed past Miss Tolerance to leave the room. She heard him in the hall issuing instructions to the servants.

His prayer finished, John Thorpe wiped absently at the blood on his hand with a pocket kerchief. When his hand was clean he took up the paper, read it, then offered it to Miss Tolerance

Centered, in a hand she recognized to be Lord Lyne's, was the word *Thankless*.

She looked at John Thorpe. "Burn this," she suggested. "Do not permit your father the last word."

He took the paper back, crumpled it into a tight ball, and pocketed it.

Miss Tolerance turned her back on Lyne's corpse and returned upstairs to tell his daughters what he had done.

Evadne had dropped her glass and sat, wine soaking into the pale muslin of her dress, as if the shot her father had fired had slain her too.

Miss Tolerance told them, in a few words, what had happened. Clarissa Brereton, standing by her sister, began to weave where she stood. Sir Adam caught his wife, seated her beside him on the sofa, and without regard for the others in the room put his arms around her. Lady Brereton lay on her husband's breast, ashen, her mouth trembling.

"I don't know what to do," she whispered.

Sir Adam murmured shushing sounds. "You need do nothing, Clary. You've had a great shock. Just sit still; I'm here." He stroked his wife's fair hair, dropped a kiss on her brow. "You need do nothing, my love. Leave it all to me."

Miss Tolerance was amazed and touched by a side to her brother which was entirely new to her.

Evadne Thorpe spoke. "I did not want this."

The words emerged almost as a growl. The girl was not weeping; her eyes glittered. She was furious.

"I did not want this," Evadne said again. "It is too easy. I did not want Father dead."

"Too easy?" Even as she echoed the girl's words Miss Tolerance apprehended their meaning.

"I wanted him to admit what he did to me. I wanted him punished." Evadne's hands curled in her lap. "I did not want him dead."

It was useless, in this moment, to deny the girl her rage. "It may be better for you all this way," she said gently. "Whatever hurt you hoped for him, it would have hurt your sister and your brothers as well."

She could see Evadne consider it, see the moment when her hands relaxed. She did not answer by word or gesture, but the tension seeped slowly from her.

Miss Tolerance could think of nothing more to do. The family must find a way to heal itself. She took her leave, offering as she did that if Evadne wished to speak to someone... The girl nodded unseeingly. Over his wife's head Adam nodded as well.

At the front door Henry Thorpe stopped her. "I sent for the Watch. I suppose that is the thing to do?"

"I have never encountered such a circumstance," Miss Tolerance said. "I think your father must have been of disturbed mind—"

Thorpe bridled. "You would add madness to my father's...crimes?"

"My lord," Miss Tolerance said gently, "under law, a man who takes his life with cold calculation forfeits his property to the crown. I do not know if your father intended such a thing."

Henry Thorpe, the new Lord Lyne, met Miss Tolerance's eyes. "*Thankless,*" he murmured.

"Precisely so," Miss Tolerance said. "A man who takes his life while deranged is not responsible for the suicide, and his family is not punished. I think your family has been punished enough for your father's sins, my lord."

"My lord," he repeated. "God, I am head of the family now."

"Exactly so, sir."

Chapter Twenty

Young Harry was sitting by Miss Tolerance's cottage door when she returned to Manchester Square. His knees were drawn up almost to his chin; he was weaving young branches from a birch tree into a rustic mat, working to square one corner, his brows drawn down and his mouth pinched in concentration.

"That's clever," she told him. She hoped there was not further trouble at Mrs. Brereton's—she had had enough strife today, and more than enough.

"My sisters used to make baskets and such." He smiled and got to his feet, unfolding like a spyglass until he towered over her. "I came to say thank you. For all of us at Mrs. B's, I suppose, but for myself in special."

"All I did was stand and lend you my countenance; you and the others faced down Mr. Tickenor. I am very glad to see the last of him."

"A bad man," Harry agreed. "He'd have hurt Mrs. B." With no fear hanging over him he was more confident; the suggestion of a stammer was gone and his eyes no longer shifted warily as he looked at her. "Your aunt had me in this morning and rang a rare peal over me for not coming to her direct with what he was doing. Then she told me I needn't ever feel anxiety for myself here so long as the gentlemen continue to give good reports of me. I'd no idea they'd done. Even Lord Holyfield who talks so much about the last boy—"

"Matt," Miss Tolerance supplied. "Matt Etan."

"Even Holyfield—good reports, even though I'm not Matt."

Miss Tolerance unlocked her door. "Matt had one way about him—a little rough around the edges—and you have another. But my aunt has an instinct for such things, and she chose to hire you. That should give you some ease. Now, is there anything more you need from me, Harry?"

The boy shook his head. "Only to say thanks." He held the mat out to her. "Would you like this? It's handy for putting a hot kettle on." He looked, in his way, as appealingly boyish as Matt had done. Miss Tolerance took the mat.

"Thank you, Harry. Perhaps another time you'll come take a cup of tea with me as Matt used to do." The boy ducked his head, acknowledging the invitation, and long-legged it back to the house.

For four-and-twenty hours Miss Tolerance attempted to banish Lord Lyne from her mind. The last image she had of the baron, head thrown back unnaturally and face disfigured with black powder and blood, was grisly. The man's mad, self-serving justification for giving his daughter into the hands of a villain was, if anything, worse. To erase these thoughts she distracted herself with gossip and cards with her aunt. Mrs. Brereton appeared to have erased her engagement with Gerard Tickenor from her memory, as well as the anxiety and unhappiness it had caused among her staff. The most she said of the matter was, "When you reach a certain age, Sarah, the idea of a

305

partner with whom to face old age becomes... appealing. I should be careful not to let such feelings render me pathetic."

"That is a word I should never have thought to apply to you, ma'am."

Mrs. Brereton was unwavering. "What else would you call a woman of my years who behaves like a chit with a first beau? Sad. Pathetic."

"Is it not possible that a man of similar years—a man not Mr. Tickenor—might find the same attraction in the idea of a partner?"

"But it *was* Mr. Tickenor. I should have known better."

"How should you have, aunt?" Miss Tolerance had thought very similarly before, but now found herself disposed to pardon her aunt.

"Because I knew Gerard of old, and would not have married him when I was thirty. He is what he is. Men don't change, my dear."

"Women do?"

"Only to become more foolish, it seems. I believe that is my trick, Sarah."

"Indeed, ma'am, it is."

When she returned to her house in the afternoon Miss Tolerance found a note from Sir Walter Mandif. Abner Huwe, arrested for murder and attempted murder, had been making strange statements. "Indeed, I find it difficult to credit his accusations." Still, the statements required investigation into matters with which Sir Walter thought Miss Tolerance might be acquainted. Might Miss Tolerance call upon him to discuss the matter? He added that he would be at home in the evening if Miss Tolerance could see her way to join him for a glass of wine. In that way the matter could remain unofficial.

Had she been foolish to assume that Abner Huwe would refrain from dragging Evadne Thorpe and her father through the mud, merely to save himself from further charges? The last service she could do for her client was to explain to Sir Walter the desirability of suppressing Lord Lyne's involvement, or at least Miss Thorpe's. At dusk Miss Tolerance dressed for a visit and asked Cole to procure her a carriage for Gracechurch Street.

Abner Huwe had confessed to a parade of crimes in the hope, Sir Walter told her, of dragging his associates down with him. "He is one of those men who tars everything he touches," the magistrate said. "I don't think he cares for his own fate, as long as he can ruin another man."

Or woman.

They sat again in Sir Walter's parlor, ranged as they had been on her other visits. Michael had greeted Miss Tolerance as an old acquaintance and fetched in glasses and claret. Miss Tolerance was conscious of a pleasant domestic feeling to the setting and the conversation which was both satisfying and disturbing. Sir Walter poured wine for her and sat with his own glass.

"What has Huwe said? In his accusations."

"He paints with a broad brush, and the burden of his song appears to be that other parties were the instigators of his crimes. Indeed, he insists he would not have attacked you had he not found you standing over his employee's bloodied body."

"Doubtless not." Miss Tolerance tasted her wine. "Had I been gone two minutes sooner he'd not have known who had been in his office, and thus would not have felt it necessary to kill me—until Mr. Worke came to his senses and told him of my visit. Who are the other parties he accuses?"

Sir Walter raised an eyebrow. "You will make me tell you my tale before you tell yours?"

"My tale does not belong to me. When I know what you know, Sir Walter, I can decide what will not be a breach of discretion."

"Huwe accuses you of provoking the attack upon yourself. He says, both that John Worke killed Tom Proctor without his authority, and that Tom Proctor invited his own death by betraying him. He says—" Sir Walter tilted his head. "He claims that a very well connected man, a peer in fact, was his partner in a shady business, and that this man *forced* him—forced Huwe, that is—to take his daughter—the baron's daughter—captive in order to put a stop to the business."

"Does he say so?" Miss Tolerance felt reluctant admiration at Huwe's wholehearted twisting of the truth. "Does he name the peer? Or the daughter?"

"He does. What I was hoping was that, if indeed this is a matter about which you know something, you might help me teaze out the truth from Huwe's statement—if there is any truth at all. If I must lay charges at his partner's door—"

"That is no longer possible. The man is dead."

"Dead? From his manner I do not think Huwe knows it."

"It happened only yesterday, after Huwe's arrest. The peer took his own life. I believe he feared that everything would be known."

"So Huwe's story is true?" From Sir Walter's expression he had not suspected it.

"He is telling a version of the truth, a very self-serving one, and one likely to do a great deal of damage to the family the baron left behind. A family already suffering much."

Without giving the peer a name Miss Tolerance related the whole: Lyne's speculation in cinchona bark and Huwe's part in its distribution; Huwe's desire to continue the project and Lyne's refusal; the kidnapping of Evadne Thorpe—unnamed by Miss Tolerance and Sir Walter both.

"If Huwe is able to tar the girl's name with his story it will be the last cruelty in a string of cruelties. He used her worse than a tuppenny whore. That, he cannot say she instigated—"

"Can he not?" Sir Walter smacked his lips as if he tasted something foul. "I will not trouble you with the sort of libel he has attached to that young woman. And you are quite right: if the peer is dead and beyond the reach of law, I see no reason for this unfortunate girl should be connected with Huwe in any way. The charge upon which he will be tried will be Proctor's murder—and that beefy, ugly fellow Worke is singing a song of his employer's involvement in that which will preclude the need for you to testify."

"Thank God. I've had enough of courts for a time."

Sir Walter pushed a plate of biscuits toward Miss Tolerance. A breeze from the hallway made the fire whicker softly. Miss Tolerance was conscious of her own relief in having shared the whole, almost, of Evadne Thorpe's sad story with Sir Walter.

"What of Miss Thorpe?" Sir Walter asked.

Miss Tolerance looked at him, a little shocked to hear the girl's name from Sir Walter's lips.

"Huwe named her to me, and her father. As she brings no charge against him I can keep her unnamed. But I cannot help my concern."

"She escaped from Huwe—did he tell you that? She is a clever girl, and a brave one. How she will fare now..." Miss Tolerance frowned. "She is safe with friends. Her physical hurts will heal. I fear more for her heart, her mind. What kind of damage captivity and—ill-use caused her. She is very angry, as she has every right to be, and the object of her rage has been taken from her."

"She may see him hung, if that is any comfort to her."

Miss Tolerance nodded. She would let Sir Walter believe it was Huwe she meant. The thought of explaining Lyne's betrayal of his daughter sickened her.

"Will you take a little more wine?" Sir Walter asked after a little silence had passed. "I confess I am enjoying the sight of you within my walls without bandages."

"I admit I do not miss the bandages at all. Thank you, Sir Walter, for taking me in that day."

"I was flattered that you came to me. I wonder—" Sir Walter paused.

Miss Tolerance had finished her wine. "How can I be of help?"

"*Why* did you?"

This was not a question for which Miss Tolerance had a ready answer. She ran her finger around the rim of her empty glass. "You were nearby, and I could not face a carriage ride back to Manchester Square. I know it was a great imposition."

"There was no other reason?"

Miss Tolerance was suddenly uneasy. She kept her tone light. "Other reason? Only that I know you to be a sensible man who would not be overcome by a woman arriving bloodied on his doorstep."

"I see." Sir Walter pressed his lips together. "I had hoped—"

"Hoped?"

"I had hoped it was because you believed I had some sympathy, some feeling for you which would have made it my pleasure to help you."

"I did rely on your friendship, and trespass horridly upon it" She tilted her glass a little to see a line of ruby wine paint the side of it.

Sir Walter put his own glass down with the air of a man resolved. "I have too great a regard for your perceptiveness—I thought perhaps you were aware of my regard for you. That perhaps it was that regard, or reciprocal feeling, which made you come here."

It was out in the open, then. Miss Tolerance found that her breath was short; there was an electric sensation in her stomach. Panic. This friendship, upon which she relied, which was safe and neat, a harmless pleasure, was suddenly and without warning in jeopardy.

"Sir Walter, I—"

"Please do not feel obligated to reply. It was an idle question." His expression gave the lie to that. "You are a clever woman, I suspect you divined my feelings for you. With those feelings I have gained a fairly comprehensive notion of your character. I understand why such a declaration must be difficult for you to hear."

I am Fallen, what character have I? Miss Tolerance pressed

310

her lips together, waiting for a blow. But Sir Walter's answer to that unspoken question was not what she expected.

"I do not believe you would be lastingly happy now in anything less than a sanctioned connection. I have not spoken because I believed you would find many objections to marriage—particularly to marriage with me."

"*Particularly* with you? Do you believe me to be so...so insensible of your worth?"

"There have been moments recently when I did not think so. But I do not think you would permit mere love to rule you."

"*Mere* love?" she echoed. "What does rule me, then?"

"Work. 'Tis what would make me an inapt suitor in your eyes. You would feel—with a little justice, I suppose—that a person in the business of inquiry should not be closely allied to a magistrate; that such an alliance would undermine your ability to do your work, and might cast a shadow of impropriety over my own."

Miss Tolerance regarded her friend with astonishment. "I cannot dispute that." *This is a very strange wooing.* Was it a wooing? It appeared to be something else, but she could not say just what. The lightheadedness which she had felt minutes before was ebbing; she was aware of a sense of disappointment.

"You have told me you devised your career as a way of avoiding the most obvious pitfall of your situation: dependence upon a man, or men, for your livelihood. But can you tell me frankly that that is all it is to you now?"

"I beg your pardon?"

"You like the work that you do. It might have seemed a poor substitute for your marriage to Charles Connell—"

Miss Tolerance closed her eyes. "There was no marriage."

"Only in the most finicking legal sense—"

"Finicking!" Now it was her turn to laugh, but it was not a happy laugh.

"Cleaving to him only, until death parted you. It was not

the sort of marriage you were raised to expect, but I doubt that any man so fortunate as to gain your affection would refine upon that."

"This is enlightening. Pray continue, Sir Walter." Miss Tolerance had set her glass aside. Her hands were clenched; she could feel the arcs of her fingernails pressing into her palms.

"You created an employment for yourself that not only affords you a livelihood but gives you scope to exercise your talents in a way that the mere running of a household—unless it were, perhaps, a ducal property with a small city of servants and dependents—would not. You do it very well, and that competence gives you pleasure, as it should. And you think marriage would require that you cease this work that gives you pleasure."

"Would it not? So I am trapped, then. Unable to give up my work, and unable to marry."

"I do not believe so, but it is of your feelings I am speaking, not my own."

The lightheadedness returned. "Perhaps we should not speak of this, Sir Walter. I do not wish to cause you hurt or disappointment—"

"Your honor has always been one of your most striking characteristics, but perhaps you are less concerned with my feelings than your own."

"*My own?*"

"You do not wish to be guilty of hurting me."

Miss Tolerance glared at Sir Walter.

At last he drawled, "You see why I would not make you an offer, despite my feelings."

Miss Tolerance gaped at him. She was breathing fast, almost panting, and felt close to tears. And then, startlingly, she began to laugh. "Yes. Yes, I understand your restraint."

Mandif watched her sympathetically.

"Forgive me," she said at last. "Please. The last thing I mean to do is to cast any doubt upon your feelings or the honor you—the honor it appears you are *not* doing me—"

Mandif smiled slightly.

"But Sir Walter, if you believe me so unlikely to respond to a discussion of this sort, may I ask why you raised the subject at all?"

Sir Walter leaned forward and carefully took Miss Tolerance's hand in his own, waiting to see if she would withdraw it. His expression was politely direct. Only in the closeness of his gaze did she see vulnerability. *I must be careful,* Miss Tolerance thought.

"I wished to make you understand my sentiments. Perhaps you share them in some degree, perhaps you do not. In either case, I do not want to spend the rest of my life wondering what might have been had I spoken."

Miss Tolerance closed her eyes. She sought words, but sought as well to know her own feelings. He had been candid with her; she could in honor offer him no less candor.

"Sir Walter, your kindness—"

"Not kindness," he snapped. "Anything but that. You may regard yourself as an object of pity or scorn but I do not. I am not King Cophetua seeking to elevate a beggar maid, and I will thank you not to speak in those terms."

"I am sorry. I am honored beyond saying by your feelings and their thoughtful expression. As to my own feelings—" she opened her eyes to meet his gaze. "I do not know. Were I different—were I not Fallen—I could be ruled entirely by my heart. But I am what I am, and the subject is...muddied. All that I can tell you now is that I do not fully know my heart or my mind. I am sorry."

"It is better than I had hoped for." The magistrate released her hand, but he smiled.

"May we continue as friends?" she asked.

"So long as you do not feel yourself oppressed by the sentiments I—yes, I hope always to be your friend. And who knows, perhaps some day you will sort out what is in your heart and your mind, to our mutual benefit. Until that time, there is always the theatre. Comedy, I think, would be restorative. Mrs. Jordan is playing—"

As easily as that, Sir Walter turned the topic to other

things. They chatted inconsequentially for a few minutes longer. Miss Tolerance was conscious of a loose, dizzy sense of relief and excitement, and yet nothing seemed to have changed between them.

When she left, Miss Tolerance sat in the carriage Michael had secured for her, her thoughts as disordered as her mood.

The next day, Sunday, Miss Tolerance took herself to church with various of Mrs. Brereton's whores and the maid who provided them consequence, and prayed for her sins, for understanding, and for friendship. Returned home, she made herself as busy as possible with accounts, a book, some mending. It would have been a relief to do fencing drills, but neither her head nor her arm were sufficiently recovered to permit it. When at last she took herself to her bed, that usually commodious berth felt, tonight, both cold and narrow.

Monday morning bought a note from Lady Brereton.

May I ask you to call today when it is convenient? I do not wish to be behind hand in settling with you for your help, and there are some matters I would like to discuss with you. Sir Adam and I have returned to my brother's house, and you may find me there.

CB

Miss Tolerance noted the friendly tone of the letter— most of her clients did not concern themselves with her convenience or with punctuality of payment—and took a little pleasure in the fact that this woman was, all unknowing, related to her. Adam had done well for himself. She returned a message offering to call on Lady Brereton at one that afternoon, and began to dress.

Except for the hatchment over the door and mourning bands on the sleeves of the servants, there was nothing in the Lyne house to suggest the upheaval the household had

314

undergone. Wheeler greeted her and brought her upstairs to the same sitting room where Evadne Thorpe had sat a few days earlier. He announced her and left.

Lady Brereton wore mourning; the black gave her an unflattering pallor. She rose from one of the flowered sofas, embroidery forgotten at her side, exchanged a curtsy with Miss Tolerance, and offered her a seat.

"I think we should start again," Lady Brereton said. While Miss Tolerance watched her, bewildered, she rose and closed the door. When she returned she stopped directly before Miss Tolerance, offered her hand, and said, "How do you do. I am Clarissa Brereton. I believe you are my sister-at-law?"

A little numbly, Miss Tolerance took Lady Brereton's offered hand in her own. She had given her word she would not unveil herself, but certainly neither she nor Sir Adam had envisioned this. "How?" she asked. "How did you know?"

Lady Brereton smiled. "There's not much of a look between you, is there? You take after your grandmother, though. There's a very good portrait of her at Briarton. And there are certain mannerisms—you share an expression with Adam when you're impatient." She sat beside Miss Tolerance.

"Do I?" What was she to say? "Did you know of our relation before you hired me?"

"No. I learned of you from a friend. I confess I thought that your history might give you particular sympathy for my sister. It was not until a few days ago that I began to suspect the relation. Adam and your father never mentioned you, you see. But there was your room, full of a girl's things. Your father never thought to throw them away, and Mrs. Cropsey—well, Mrs. Cropsey is very fond of you and would not part with anything without direct orders. It was she who explained what had happened to you, after considerable persuasion. You father had insisted your name not be mentioned—so very Gothick!"

Miss Tolerance smiled. "You must have ingratiated

315

yourself with Mrs. Cropsey indeed, if she would go against my father."

"By then your father was dead, and I don't think Mrs. Cropsey takes Adam's orders so seriously. As she has said several times, always in a mutter when she thinks I cannot hear her, she knew him when he was in skirts and curls." Lady Brereton's imitation of the Briarton housekeeper delighted Miss Tolerance.

"So you knew the Breretons' dreadful secret before you came to London? Your family does not know, I take it."

"No. I would never have told them; it was enough that they knew about your aunt. How could they not, when she kept her name?" Lady Brereton's voice was cooler: a sister-at-law who had given up the world for love was one thing; a relative who had not only given up the world but had embraced venery to the extent of brothel-keeping was clearly another.

"I am surprised they let you know of her. I neither approve nor disapprove of my aunt's profession, as she has made it plain it is not my business to do either. But she gave me a home, and affection, when I needed both sorely."

"She did not ask you to—never encouraged you to—"

"To follow in her gilded footsteps? To become a whore?" Miss Tolerance was amused. "She has, in fact, often. It puzzles her that I will not; I suppose she really is deficient in some moral sense—but she has never let my refusal come between us."

Lady Brereton appeared to consider. "She is broad-minded?" she suggested.

Miss Tolerance laughed. "By her lights, I believe she is."

The subject of their relation having been exhausted for the moment, there were only two other topics Miss Tolerance could think of, and only one which did not involve the presentation of her bill.

"How does your sister do?"

Lady Brereton's eyes filled with unhappiness. "She returned to the Godwins; she seems comfortable there, and they say they are happy to have her there. Miss Tolerance, I tell you frankly, I cannot understand how to help her. She is fearful one moment, enraged the next, not at that man Huwe but at our father. Not that she has not cause, but—I wish I understood how to help her."

Miss Tolerance shook her own head. "*I* wish I had some comfort to give her, or you. My experience is similar to hers in only a few details: elopement and disinheritance are nothing to what she has suffered, and the only balm I can suggest is time."

A cloud swept across the sun, leaving the room suddenly dim. "That man ruined her. Unfit her to be a wife, unfit her to—" She stopped and stared at Miss Tolerance. "You are Fallen, but you are not ruined. Not that way. How is that?"

"I had love," Miss Tolerance said simply. "However irregular it was. Connell was a good man and I loved him. Even so, had I anticipated how hard our life would be, how much I gave up with that impetuous choice, I do not know what I would have done." She gave a thought to Sir Walter. "But I had love, and your sister did not."

Half an hour later Miss Tolerance took her leave. Her reticule was heavy: Lady Brereton had paid in full the reckoning for her work and expenses. She made her way down the stairs, was shown out by Pinney, and on the steps found herself face to face with her brother.

Sir Adam's face reddened. "Why are you here?"

"Your wife invited me, Adam."

He took her elbow and all but dragged her down the street, muttering "*Sir* Adam. Someone might hear. *Clary* might hear."

"She knows, Adam." Miss Tolerance regarded her brother with a look mingling sympathy and exasperation. "Apparently we share expressions. And she says I look very much like Grandmother Anna's portrait."

Astonishment appeared to make her brother unsteady on his feet. Now it was Miss Tolerance who took his elbow and urged him forward. "Let us take a little air before you faint." She waited until they had settled into a leisurely stroll of the perimeter of St. James's Square before she said, "I like your wife very much. She is neither as fragile as you believe, nor as easily shocked. She has a good deal of strength—how else could she have stood up to her father when all you men—yes, her brothers as well—cowered before him?"

Mention of Lyne took away Sir Adam's pleasure in hearing his wife praised. "My God, Sally. None of us imagined he was—how could Lyne—" Sir Adam broke off as if no word to describe his father-at-law's doing was sufficient.

"How *should* you have imagined it?" Miss Tolerance was sympathetic, to a point. "Your father-at-law seemed a prime example of a man of his age and station. Who would have guessed he would make our father seem like a paragon of compassion? No, no, I do not mean to pick a fight, Adam. Truly, I do not. I still have a wicked tongue after all these years, and far too little excuse to mend it."

Sir Adam looked sidewise at his sister. "Sally? Sally, I hope you don't think to make this reunion an excuse to—"

"To settle myself upon you? No, Adam. Emphatically, I do not. I am happy to have had a chance to mend fences with you, a little, but I am under no illusions about returning to the family. I would ask a favor, though."

"A favor?" Caution warred with relief in Sir Adam's voice.

"Will you tell Mrs. Cropsey, and Nurse, and the people in Briarton, that they will not be turned out if I come to visit? Nurse must be quite stricken in years; I should like to go pay my respects to her some day."

"Is that all? Good God, Sally, of course. I never thought of it. But is there nothing else? Your things from Briarton? I could send them; that place you live is so barren."

"My books and dolls from the schoolroom? No, thank you."

"But that place. You are comfortable there? You have friends?"

Miss Tolerance thought of Marianne, of her aunt, of Harry and Cook and the other denizens of Mrs. Brereton's house. She thought of Sir Walter. "I have friends. I want for nothing, Adam. Truly. And you have my word: I will not force my way into your family. It is enough that you and I can speak together civilly; I never expected such a thing. Of course, "Miss Tolerance's mouth quirked in a smile. "I *could* introduce you to our aunt."

A look of horror passed briefly over her brother's face, followed at once by a crooked, sheepish smile. "You're funning me."

"I am." A grin played on Miss Tolerance's lips. "You make it very easy. And you are still my brother, and still require taking down a peg."

They had reached the corner of King Street. Miss Tolerance extended her hand as if to shake his, but Sir Adam only stood, looking at her bemusedly. At last, Miss Tolerance reached out to pat him lightly on the shoulder. "I do like your wife very much, Sir Adam. I wish you both very happy."

She curtseyed and, while her brother stared after her, walked briskly down King Street.

ॐ ॐ

A Note on History, Faux and Real

This is not only a mystery but an alternate history: George III was succeeded by his son George, first as Regent (in 1811) and then as King (in 1820) and at no time did Queen Charlotte reign as Regent. Within that greater alternaty (to coin a term) I have tried to keep things as accurate to history and the period as possible. The plot to destroy Napoleon's newly-rebuilt fleet is historical, and made sense on paper, but the Navy consistently disregarded the advice of doctors (and military men with a familiarity with England's history—a hundred years earlier there had been a similar attempt at invasion, with a similar ending) who counseled against the expedition. To make matters worse, the invading fleet sailed with barely a day's worth of cinchona bark for its forces. Eight thousand men died from a mixed bag of malaria, dysentery and typhoid, and another twenty thousand survived, but were invalided out of the armed forces. Afterward it was said you could recognize a veteran of the campaign by the red waistcoats they wore—with a small pocket to carry a personal supply of Peruvian bark.

I first read of the Walcheren invasion in a review of Fiametta Rocco's wonderful book *The Miraculous Fever Tree*, a history of malaria and quinine. While I've found no evidence of war-profiteering such as Lord Lyne and Abner Huwe indulge in, it's not outside the range of possibility. The Walcheren invasion remains a startling example of what happens when politics and hubris intersect.

In creating John Thorpe's Squale House I anticipated the beginning of the Settlement Movement by about fifty years. In 1811 there were poorhouses and almshouses (the former were often used as reformatories or homes for indigent women and children; the latter often housed the elderly) but nothing quite like the settlement house, where life-skills and education were offered to the poor. Still, I suspect that William Godwin, had he known of such a place, would have been delighted to volunteer there. Mary Wollstonecraft, essayist and novelist, died 1797 after the birth of her daughter Mary (who went on to elope with Percy Bysshe Shelley and to write *Frankenstein*). Somehow the notion of Miss Tolerance meeting both Mrs. Godwin and the young Mary Shelley would not leave me alone.

I am delighted to have found a new home for Miss Tolerance at Plus One Press, thanks to my editor, Jacqueline Smay, Nic Grabien (publisher) and Deborah Grabien (resident Goddess and fellow Plus One author) for their help, encouragement, and enthusiasm. I send my thanks to Patrick Nielsen Hayden, Anna Genoese, and Melissa Anne Singer for their encouragement in the initial phase of Miss Tolerance's career at Forge Books; even though we parted ways, I don't forget. My thanks also to my agent, Shawna McCarthy.

As always, Miss Tolerance and I are indebted to M. Lucie Chin, Richard Rizk, J. David Brimmer, and TJ Glenn for teaching me what I know of the art of the short sword (and the fisticuff). Any trouble Miss Tolerance gets into is her fault and mine; my teachers are all deadly grace and pointed wit. I owe a similar debt to my writers' work-shops, and to Ben Yalow, Sara Mueller, Ellen Klages, and Eve Sweetser, all of whom wrestled with the manuscript like the angels they are, and helped me make the story a book.

Writing is an isolated business, and there aren't enough Thank Yous in the world for my friends in real life and online, for help, support, enthusiasm, and reeling things back into focus when I got distracted. I owe a huge debt of gratitude to Miss Tolerance's own friends, who have waited patiently to see what happened next.

Finally: my love and love again to Danny, Julie, and Becca, because family, wherever you find it, is where the heart is.

Writing gives Madeleine Robins the chance to focus on many of her ruling passions: cities, history, swordplay, the history of disease, and the future of mankind—with a side order of historical costuming and infrastructure (urban plumbing is far more interesting than you'd think).

Born in New York City, the Author has been, in no particular order, a nanny, a teacher, an actor and stage-combatant, an administrator, a comic book editor, a baker, typist-clerk for Thos. Cook's Houses of Parliament office, a repairer-of-hurt-books, an editorial consultant, and a writer. She holds a degree in Theatre Studies from Connecticut College, and attended the Clarion Science Fiction Workshop in 1981. She is a founding member of the Book-ViewCafe, where most of her short fiction is available for free!

A lifelong and passionate fan of cities and all things urban, Madeleine Robins now lives in San Francisco with her family, dog, and one hegemonic lemon tree.

Visit her website at www.madeleinerobins.com

CPSIA information can be obtained at www.ICGtesting.com
Printed in the USA
LVOW041646181011

251053LV00002B/16/P